A COLLECTION OF SHORT STORIES

little
BACK
ROOM

A COLLECTION OF SHORT STORIES

little
BACK
ROOM

PEARL
Rance-Reardon

Cover Picture: http://www.freedigitalphotos.net

Published by LMH Publishing Limited
Suite 10-11
LOJ Industrial Complex
7 Norman Road
Kingston C.S.O., Jamaica
Tel.: (876) 938-0005; 938-0712
Fax: (876) 759-8752
Email: lmhbookpublishing@cwjamaica.com
Website: www.lmhpublishing.com

Printed in the U.S.A.   ISBN: 978-976-8202-67-3

To my husband for his love, and unflinching support.
My granddaughter, Allessandra, who helped me find young Elah's voice.
Ed Kessler, Prof. Emiritus, American University.
Barbara Rosing.
Christy Huddle.

My mother, my muse.
1925–2000

Memberships
The Authors Guild, Inc.
The Dramatist Guild of America, Inc.

CONTENTS

▼

TEACHER GREEN

She introduced herself as Teacher Green. Cinderella Marvelous Green lost her father, Wesley German Green, in the war. He was a blacksmith by training and heeded the public call to duty. He joined the ranks of the British West Indies Regiment, BWIR. His group comprised the second contingent of island men to leave to fight in the war. Wesley, as did many of the others, saw his recruitment as a way to advance himself. He hoped, once the war was over, to send for his wife and daughter so that Cinderella could get an education in Britain. His adventure into war was to open a new world of opportunities, not to put nails in his coffin. This colored man's life was so cheap, they never bothered shipping his body back to his bereaved wife. Cinderella's mother, Marcella, thought the notice from the governor's office was official confirmation that her husband had arrived safely, but the news was tragic. He died bravely on the battlefield, not in England, but somewhere in the Mediterranean where he had been transshipped.

As she got older, Cinderella realized she was not the only one to lose a loved one in the war. There were many families left destitute because their chief bread-winner had lost his life on the front line, where many of these inexperienced war-riors were sent. Her mother succumbed to the heartbreak and to the tuberculosis that had already robbed her of one lung. Cindy, an orphan at 10, was left in the care of two primary school teachers who molded the girl in their image. Cinder-ella Green was determined not only to become a teacher like her mentors, but also to be a liberator of young minds. She felt that the blind faith, which led many uneducated men to volunteer for a war in a foreign land, should not be repeated. In taking the job as a primary school teacher, she knew the pay would not be the best, but she was committed to her chosen profession.

Teacher looked forward to her shopping trips into town when she got her monthly government wages. She used Lottie's home as a base from arrival to departure. She traveled on the only transportation that regularly plied the country roads. She had a list of items she could not get in the country where she lived. In some cases, she saved money by purchasing certain items in the town. Doors were never locked and there wasn't any formality in entering a friend's home. Teacher Green, who was a woman of proper etiquette, knocked and waited for someone to ask her to come in. Once inside, she'd announce herself: "Teacher Green has arrived in one piece, praise God and God Save the Queen." She arranged herself in the cane back chair near the window and began to remove the garter belts—stiff pieces of elastic tied below her knees. "Whew! Thank the Lord and God Save the Queen."

She traveled with a large sisal basket, a small handgrip with a change of clothes and a brown plastic handbag that made a jarring sound when she fastened the clasps. Her handkerchief, a Chinese-style folding fan, and her little "pittance" from the government were inside that purse.

There was always something to report about the transport, the driver or incidents that occurred during the voyage. Teacher dabbed lightly at her face and finished cooling off with the fan. Teacher made light conversation about the trip. "You notice I got here earlier than usual?" Lottie nodded. "In the name of the Queen of England, my entire life flashed before my eyes today."

Lottie's granddaughter Elah would fetch Teacher's slippers, take her shoes back to the bedroom and bring her a glass of lemonade with chipped ice. Teacher paused to watch her toes spread out in the slippers, took a sip and wrinkled her mouth. "Thank you, lovie. Next time use less lime. My teeth get on a bit of an edge. And please try your best to wash the sawdust off the ice before putting it into the glass. Your granny tells me you volunteer to make Teacher's lemonade. That is sweet of you. Thanks, lovie."

Elah took her seat in the drawing room next to the two friends; she also loved to hear Teacher's tales. "Where was I a-gain? Yes, talking about the drivers. The dunces who pilot these buses have no home training on the finer points. And believe you me, not a day on the school bench. Only God is to tell how they obtain driving 'dipluma' when, surely as I sit here, the scamps can neither read nor write. All right, listen to me. The lad this morning decided in his wee brain that it was best to press the throttle around Devil's Race Course. You know that hill with the hairpin curve? My God, it is taking your life in your hands to travel with these careless people. As I was saying, the laddie wanted to pass another dunce like himself. They had been locked in a wicked race going up the hill. I thought surely the rickety bus would fall apart in the process. It was only God Almighty and the Queen of England that saved us from a plummet over the precipice. As a member of the literate community, I realize my responsibilities extend beyond the hard benches of the classroom, but I tell you Lottie, I had to dip into this lunatic's language. Take my word, if that bus had rolled down the gully, it would have been sure and certain death to all on board."

Lottie interrupted to add to the consternation about these buses and drivers. "I do not take that transport anymore. On the few occasions when I need to travel, I pay a bit extra and go on the Greyhound. I remember being on a bus going up that same hill. The driver seemed to be having difficulties, because he said he was using the clutch and gas to keep the vehicle from rolling backwards into oncoming traffic. The conductor was angry. She said he should not have attempted the hill if he knew the bus had no brakes. The driver asked her, 'How many times had he driven without brakes and gotten over that same hill?' The woman asked him to open the door so she could step outside, but miraculously, he made it. I agree with you, it is a perilous journey." Teacher picked up her story.

"As the devil would have it, these kill-dead bus operators would survive to repeat this maneuver while everyone else would perish. I had to throw some patios on him. 'Bwoy,' I said, 'yu tink me is a puss? Is only one deggeh life me gat an me no wahn fe lose eh, yu hear me?' He turned to look at me and rolled his little red ganja beans and laughed as if I had given him a good joke. I told him to be careful; lives don't cost quattie or gill. Everyone on the bus applauded."

Next, Teacher addressed her feet as if they were detached from her person. "You've been locked away for many hours on a frightful journey. Anyway, never mind. Come, we have to take care of our little business in town." That was the cue that she was about to move into the bedroom to have a light wash up and change of clothes. Elah picked up the half empty lemonade glass and turned to leave. Believing that the girl was on her way out, her grandmother started to share a private joke. "She asked me the other day if Pringle was my friend and I said, 'No, but he is a nice and quiet gentleman.'" Elah rested the glass on the dining table and returned to sit. Her grandmother chased her, saying she should go outside and play. She continued when she thought the child had left the house.

"Well," Teacher Green added, "you let him that little room behind yours, and after all, you are both unattached at the moment. That black woman divorced him, didn't she?"

"I don't know his business. She brings his food and takes care of his clothes. I'm only making the point that we have to be careful around her. She listens and wants to find out everything."

"The curiosity of a 6-year-old. Anyway Lottie, I am only joking about Pringle. He is quite dashing, though. Half Indian? He looks it. I've seen him dressed in cricket whites, bowling like the devil in the street. The first time, I was looking to see who was batting, but my God, I realized the man had no ball and there was no one in front of him. I walked fast, said hello and hurried inside this house. Mark you, I was not afraid, but I didn't want to burst out laughing."

"His wife said he once played professional cricket. Something must have happened. I don't know what. He talks to himself, but doesn't bother anyone. Elah asked if I go into his room while she is sleeping."

"You have a little force-ripe banana on your hands, Lottie. Kids who grow up around adults tend to mature a bit earlier." Teacher moved to the bedroom, and Elah ran from behind the dining room curtain to share with her cousin Nell the conversation she'd heard. Elah had told many stories to Nell's mother, and Nell was not in the mood to hear the conversation. She was still mad at the girl.

"Get away from me. Take the broom and sweep up the rubbish in the yard. You mischief-maker."

"Rodney was kissing you on the lips. I saw him do it." Nell grabbed the broom as if to hit her with the stick. Elah ran into the bedroom as Teacher was wiping her private parts with a washcloth. The woman made a hasty cover up.

"Manners, child! You ought to knock."

"But there is no door, Teacher Green." She was right. There was a door curtain that had been pulled together.

"God save the Queen! Please go out and allow me to complete my hygiene. For heaven's sake, child!" Fearing Nell, Elah ran to the pantry and stayed close to her grandmother until she heard Teacher call out. "Elah, lovie, come here a moment." The woman always brought her something special. She was about to have lunch. A bully beef sandwich, and a bottle of aerated water to wash it down. She had a bunch of ginneps for Elah, but would share a bit of her sandwich and a sip of drink with the girl. Elah told Teacher that she was sorry, but that she ran into the room because Nell wanted to hit her with the broomstick. "She ought to be ashamed of herself. She is an older girl and should know better." Elah's grandmother had started cooking, as it was customary to offer her friend dinner before she left to go back home.

At the table, Teacher Green went over her list of items to be purchased at the pharmacy, the dry goods store, the meat and fish market. She purchased fresh fish, beef and pork, and salted meats, salted cod fish and mackerel. At the end of shopping, Teacher hired a handcart vendor to take her purchases to the house. She spread everything out and checked to make sure she had gotten all the items. She then packed the items in an orderly way for travel. Teacher Green knew to gauge the minutes she needed to change clothes, eat dinner, visit some more and begin the trip to the bus stop. She sat in her usual chair, seemingly relaxed, and mentally prepared for the trip home. "In the Queen's English," she looked down on her blouse, "you see this spot right here? How do you think I got it?" Lottie hadn't time to answer. "Well, yes, you guessed right. A woman with armpits full of dusting powder threw her arm over the ring in front of me. Perspiration was running off her like water from a drain. I don't know what kind of chemical these people have in their systems so that when mixed with sweat produces a lasting stain. I was trying to shift my legs, but you know how they pack the buses as if they are taking animals to the Pound? I was unable to move out of her way." She looked down at her blouse self-consciously. "My goodness, I am gaining a bit of weight in the wrong places. I'll have to reinforce these buttons and lose a bit of the bustline."

Teacher glanced at her wristwatch. It was time to go. She called out to Lottie's nephew. "Where are you, my little lad? Teacher cannot tarry any longer. Come my dear, Teacher is ready to go." Dudley was 10 and small for his age. He crept into the drawing room and eyed Teacher's basket. He gave it a try and almost lost his balance. It seemed his young body told him it was much heavier than the last time. Vera's Sabbath had not yet ended, but when she heard Teacher calling her son, she interrupted her tranquility to assess what he was being asked to carry this time. Using her hand as a scale, she seemed uncertain whether she should allow the boy to carry the basket. Turning to her sister's guest, who stood erect and waiting, Vera issued a notice.

"Teacher, if this basket gets any heavier, I will not allow Dudley to carry it. You'll have to hire a pushcart man; they don't charge much." Teacher knew the amount from the market to the house and back to the bus stop, and it was steeper than the few pennies she pushed into the boy's hand. She thought of it as giving him a chance to earn pocket change, but she had to deal with his mother's seeming angst. Vera stood waiting, as if to hear her say, "I will send for a pushcart man," but that was not in Teacher's plan.

"In the Queen's English, Miss Vera, you have made a very substantial point. Thank you. I will refuse to buy things for others. It's getting a bit out-of-hand." With that, she dismissed the concern to her own satisfaction. As soon as Vera left the room, she urged the boy to make haste. "Come on, my laddie." Dudley had been standing by the curtain looking with dismay and half-wanting and half-not. He may have enough money to buy a couple of marbles or a set of jacks. Veins popped up in his forearm like cords of a tightly strung tennis racket. There was not enough space under his skin to hide his distress. Teacher Green began her farewell.

"Elah, my dear, stay sweet. One of these days you know, Lottie, I'll steal her away to the country with me. Well, dear Lottie, thank you tremendously again and again for your hospitality. I will never be able to repay you." Checking her watch, she exclaimed, "In the name of the Queen of England, I think if we don't hurry, the bus is going to leave me. Lottie dear, thank you again for everything. See you next month, if the dunces don't drive me to hell. It's late! I mustn't tarry. Step up, laddie, or we will miss the bus."

"Thanks for the ginneps, Miss Green. Next time I would like some custard apples." Lottie slapped the girl.

"Teacher Green to you. Facety."

"She is not my teacher."

"Full of blinking cheek."

Dudley had to wait for his money until everything had been loaded on the bus. Teacher pushed the few coins into the boy's hand, saying thanks, and bade him farewell. "See you next month. Be a good boy now." She went into the bus and took a seat. People were screaming at the driver, who was standing atop the bus as his assistant threw bags up to him. They were besieging the two men to be careful with their packages. Everyone knew those bus tickets carried an unwritten warning: Not responsible for any damage to goods or persons. The driver hopped in, revved up the engine, sounded the horn and made a U-turn on the busy street. Teacher's perilous journey home began.

"In the Queen's English!" she exclaimed, as people tumbled this way and that. "Lady, kindly remove your basket off my feet. It really belongs on top on the bus." After the clamor of jerking and pitching subsided, the woman asked Teacher Green to repeat what she had said. Raising her voice an octave and slowing her speech, Teacher repeated, patois-style. "Me sey, yu fe tek de basket offa me foot." The woman found her tone offensive.

"Why yu'a ride bus? Yu should'a have yur own transport." Teacher Green did not dignify the comment with a reply, but she was annoyed at the nerve of this woman whose basket had caused a run in her stockings. She looked at the woman, whose head was wrapped in floral cloth, as if she smelled rotten fish. This unspoken insult did not go unnoticed. At about the midpoint, the driver stopped in front of a bar on a main street. He hopped out to join his friends in a few rum drinks and to allow passengers an opportunity to relieve themselves at a public facility. He wore no watch, but announced that everyone must be back on the bus in 15 minutes.

"Everybody be back here, pranto, pranto."

As passengers pushed their way back to get into the bus, a quarrel broke out between two women and a fight erupted. The driver could not move the bus. The horn made no difference to clearing a path. He hopped out and shouted, "Break it up. Those who is nat on the bus is gwineto to get leff. Woman. Yu wid de shews inna yu hand, put it on and come. Yu looks like de winnah. Yu, woman wid de big coco inna yu head and blood running fram it, clean aff yuself before yu come pon me bus." The disheveled woman held her blouse together as the driver ordered that her seat be given back. "Give the winnah har seat." The lady sat and stared glumly ahead. A woman sitting at the back of the bus stood to see the combatants and exclaimed, "Me Gad, noh, Teacher Green that?"

BREAKFAST TIME

There is a brown gal in the ring, tra la la la lah
There is a brown gal in the ring, tra la la la lah
There is a brown gal in the ring, tra la la la lah
for she likes sugar and I like plum.
Let me show you me motion, tra la la lah.

"Didn't you hear Aunt Lottie calling?"

"Just one more turn, Nell."

"You have to eat dinner and get yourself ready."

"I am not going until tomorrow."

"We do not want the bus to leave you," Nell said, as if she was happy to see the girl go visit her mother in the country. Elah wanted to take Betsy, her life-size American doll, but she wasn't allowed to. "Aunt Lottie says you can't take it, because they will mash it up." Elah ran down the list of things she was going to take and started to put them on the bed.

"You are not carrying a trunk, Elah; all those things will not fit into that small grip."

Since she couldn't take her doll, Elah was determined to take the blue and white China play set her father sent from America. It was marked "Made in Occupied Japan" and was very special to Elah. She did not tell anyone she was taking this fragile set. Wrapping each piece and arranging them carefully between her clothes, she'd ensure they wouldn't get broken. She'd take the new set of jacks and six marbles Ranny gave her. Leave the skipping rope behind; there was no flat land on which to skip. Elah thought about all the games she and her friends played, like Moonshine Baby. They'd lay on the ground on full moon nights and outline each other's bodies with stones, then get up and look at their forms in the moonlight.

Elah would miss her town friends, but she was looking forward to seeing her cousins and other friends in the country. Elah was so excited she couldn't sleep. It had been a whole year since she last saw her mother. In that year, her father had come home for two weeks and then returned to America. He brought pictures of his new wife. Elah asked if he could still marry her mother and he said, "No, it would not be legal."

"You don't have to tell your mother every little thing that goes on here," her grandmother warned. Elah blamed the old woman for keeping her parents apart, and now it was too late.

She shook Elah, then pulled up and twisted the net and made a knot in the center. For anyone still lying down, the mosquitoes would do the rest to get them up. She sat on the edge of the bed, stretched, yawned, then knelt down to pray. Elah had been watching her grandmother through half-open eyes. She waved mosquitoes off, but several were circling and one landed on her grandmother's bare shoulder. The insect was drunk with blood and didn't even move while Elah's hand hovered, angling for a good hit. Blood splattered all over the woman's white nightgown and her small handprint showed all five fingers. "You wretched child. I've told you over and over never to interrupt me when I am praying. Lord, give me the strength, O Lord. Don't forget to say prayers when you get up. I know for the next weeks you'll most likely to be praying to the devil." Elah was looking forward to a real holiday from school, church, Sunday school and prayers.

As she did every year, Elah surveyed the room she shared with her grandmother. Somehow she felt it may be the last time she would see that room. Her doll was safely wrapped in a sheet and hidden under the bed. Alvin may break the head in a fit of rage. He had those often when something bothered him or if he didn't get his way. If she wasn't there, he may very well take it out on Betsy. The evening before, Nell had used water and a fine-tooth comb to twist Elah's hair into long curls. Her cousins in the country loved to play with her hair, saying, "Yu have nice hair, mum."

Her grandmother was in the kitchen making breakfast as Elah slowly awoke. Sunlight filtered through the windows, and the morning breezes played gently with the curtains. Elah smelled coconut oil. Her favorite johnnycakes were frying. In another pot, scallions, thyme and Scotch bonnet peppers combined, in preparation for the ackee and saltfish that would accompany the johnnycakes.

Maybe this time her mother wouldn't send her back. The two sides—maternal and paternal—had an uneasy relationship. Elah heard some hurtful things said about her mother. A towel and washcloth lay ready for the cold bath Elah would have to take. "This is probably the only bath until you come back." It wasn't true.

The two sisters, Lottie and Vera, shared the home with their children. Elah joined the family when she was 3 years old. As soon as Vera entered the kitchen, the sister's voices became hushed as if they were saying things that they didn't want anyone else to hear. Lottie would take a pause to call out to Elah. "We only purchased one seat and Trevor will not wait past seven." Elah put on her duster and slippers, and started for the bathroom. "I don't hear any water running." Elah always dreaded taking a bath early in the morning because the water was freezing cold. She allowed the water to run and splash against her body. She soaped up her washrag and rubbed it all over. She washed the chimney and turned it down. By the time she immersed herself under the running pipe, she was covered in goose bumps and her body shivered from the cold.

Quickly and vigorously, Elah toweled off the water, put on her floral cotton duster and raced back into the bedroom. The talcum powder was gone from the bureau where she left it. She knew it was the trick of Alvin, her father's younger brother. He did mean things like that. He'd hit Elah, and when she cried, he'd deny that he did it. Elah found the watch her father sent in Alvin's room. When she told her grandmother, he waited to catch her alone and punched her in the stomach. She found the powder hidden under the bed. She was glad to be going, to be rid of Alvin, and not to be around when another little cousin came for worm medicine.

The crying could be heard inside the house. The child pleaded with her mother not to leave her. The woman pushed the child in, closed the gate and disappeared. Vera was the child's paternal grandmother. It was a yearly ritual for the child to come and spend two weeks to be "cleaned out." They punched holes in the outer layer of a vermifuge pill so that the foul-tasting liquid would leak out. It took two adults to hold this screaming child so the medicine could be forced down her throat inside a piece of ripe banana. Once, she accidentally bit her grandmother's finger as the woman tried to get the vermifuge down her throat. Elah herself would have to take medicine as soon as she returned from the country, but it had gotten easier. They no longer stood over her as they did Lana. She could throw away some of the castor oil and ash water.

Most children were familiar with the yearly purgative and knew the reason for it. Yet every child feared it. The vermifuge pill was sickening, the castor oil was like poison followed by ash water—water poured over ashes and allowed to sit for several days. The child was given broth for at least three days after taking the medicine. Elah did not care to see the long worms that Lana expelled, curled up in the chamber pot. Sometimes the worms tried to slither out while she was taking the pot to the toilet. Elah was glad she would not be there this time.

They called the girl's mother "the careless woman." She had been Vera's eldest son's girlfriend until they broke up. The woman used to come to the house and shout that she was there for money for the child. The sisters were engaged in conversation, and Elah was getting ready for her trip. She was singing loudly, "God of the morning at whose voice the cheerful sun makes haste to rise, and like a giant doth rejoice." She switched to a song that was popular on the Rediffusion. "Slack songs," her grandmother called some of those tunes. No one could switch off Matthew and his Almighty Dancers nearby or the scratchy music blazing from his record box.

> *Please mister, don't you touch my tomato*
> *Touch me yam, me pumpkin, potato,*
> *But please don't you touch me tomato.*

It was sexually suggestive, and singing along involved moving the hands to the different locations mentioned in the song. Elah was naked and had just touched her tomato, when her grandmother's head pushed through the door curtain. "Do not defile this house, you child of the devil. Where did you pick that up? Put on your clothes and knock that slackness out of your head right away. Outta order," she grumbled to underline her disapproval. "Your breakfast is on the table." She saw that Elah had splurged on the dusting powder. This was inadvertent because she was more focused on the song. "Do you have to cover yourself with talcum powder? It costs money."

Matthew and his Almighty Dancers knew all the songs. When he wasn't rehearsing for a show, he ran a small grocery shop. Matthew Hall laid claim to the title of cultural ambassador, stage play director and dance trainer. He never really molested children—to Elah and her friends' knowledge—but he would ask young girls who entered his shop, "Do you have any hairs down there yet? How about a little sprout? You have little sprouts?" Every girl could tell about Matthew with the full gold tooth surrounded by rot, and Gladys, his jealous girlfriend, who modeled the cheap fashion eyeglasses she sold. She would miss them. Elah remembered the time she and her friends sneaked out to go and get a glimpse of the Matthew and his Almighty Dancers.

Matthew put on shows at the local theater and got people to pay money to see them. That name, when sprawled across the movie theater marquee, drew angry cries of blasphemy, but it also drew crowds. Matthew and his Almighty Dancers rehearsed nights at a hall two doors down from Elah's house. The building was hoisted high to avoid flooding during hurricanes. It sat on stilts at least one story high; children often played running games underneath. There were concrete steps leading to the front entrance. A little porch hung off the back with a staircase missing every other thread. Elah's grandmother was having a few drinks with a neighbor, as she did occasionally after Elah was gone to bed. The arrangement was for the girls to meet in the back of the building.

"You go first." The girl stood in the darkness, watching Elah struggle to get to the landing. She listened to the rotten wood creaking and wasn't so sure she wanted to go. "You look and tell me what is going on, because I am afraid." Elah was beginning to climb back down. Elah had already planned how she would return to her room without being caught. "Ahrite. Ahrite. Me coming," her friend said, to stop Elah from scuttling the operation. They were taking turns peeping through the hole; the music was raucous enough to silence the squeaking boards. Matthew and Toots, his most voluptuous partner, were dancing in a most vulgar fashion. The friends couldn't believe what they were seeing; they were mesmerized. Matt was reclining in a horizontal position—like a limbo dancer—with one hand clicking to the beat and the other planted on the floor to support his body. Toots jumped on top, crouching over him. She whined down as Matt gyrated upward to meet his dance partner in a simulated sexual encounter.

"Jesus Christ!" Elah whispered to her friend. As her friend was about to take a turn, she fell through broken wood in the porch. It sounded like a breadfruit had fallen from a high tree branch. She thought it was funny until the girl cried out, "Me foot bruk. Lawd Gad Almighty! Rasclate, Bombohole."

"Quiet." Elah cautiously came down as the girl was slowly getting on her feet, cursing as she tried to balance. "Police could arrest you for saying bad words." As she started to limp away, Babsie had words for her friend.

"You dutty stinking dawg, I should never have listened to you. Me foot bruk, all because of you. Bomboclate. Rasclate. Pussy hole." Elah didn't feel responsible, because they had planned it together. It was easier for her to get out, with her grandmother visiting next door, but it took some doing for Babsie to sneak out of the bed she shared with her grandmother. She was not only very clever to have pulled that off, but she was foul mouth as well. It was a miracle the grandmothers hadn't heard about the mishap; one couldn't take a breath without someone reporting they had heard them exhale. Elah was in her room when Babsie's grandmother stopped to visit and inform. "Yes Lottie, that's what she told me. She and Elah were jumping off your back step."

"Elah didn't say a word."

As their conversation was coming to an end, Elah moved away from the window feeling very sure she would be asked about the incident. "You didn't tell me Babsie sprained her ankle jumping off the back step."

"She said she twisted it. I didn't know it was serious."

"Hmm. Hmm. She is one of your best friends and you didn't know? It's trouble when the two of you get together. Now she has to stay home from school." She left the room, mumbling "spraining an ankle jumping off a step a few inches from the ground." Elah sent messages to her friend and they were returned with foul language responses that the messengers refused to repeat. Elah was the planner among the group of girls. Her mind was always occupied. Trevor said she was a daydreamer. She was thinking about some of the things she would do when she got to the country. Her grandmother pushed aside the curtains and tied them to the side. Elah was startled as if caught doing something wrong, even though she had merely been thinking. "Don't bother telling your mother that I didn't wake you up in time or that I had anything at all to do with the bus leaving you." Elah wanted to ask how she would tell her mother it was her grandmother's fault, if the bus had already left her. "Come and have your breakfast." Elah was ready. She had a pretty new dress with shoulder straps and a bolero.

"Would you kindly close your eyes." Elah was more anxious to eat while the food was hot. "Heavenly Father, bless this food we are about to partake. Make it the nourishment for our bodies as well as our minds."

"Amen."

"I'm not finished. Father, bless our travels as we go on the dusty paths of life."

"Amen."

"Give us sustenance and strength this day, O Lord." There was silence. Elah half opened her eyes and quickly realized it was another pause. "Guide this child as she goes on a lonely journey." Elah was thinking for sure she wasn't coming back, or maybe her Grandmother had some visions about something bad happening. The woman owned a dream book and the pages were well worn. If she dreamed it, it would come true. Elah could point to at least one dream that came true. It was about Ralston aka Putus, the son of a well-known teacher. She dreamt she saw the boy naked, running all over town. She predicted a scandal in that family. It wasn't long after that fateful dream, rumors began that Ralston had gone "silent mad." This intelligent young man was sitting under a tree on the logwood wharf property smoking ganja and reading a D.H. Lawrence book on mysticism. Almost every day he could be found there, surrounded by puffs of smoke. Elah forgot her grandmother was still praying. She heard, "In thy Holy and Most Precious Name we pray. Amen."

"Amen." Elah dived into the plate of salt fish and ackees and fried johnnycakes like it was her last meal. The fact that Elah was not a participant in the prayer was not lost on her grandmother. "You know this is why I get so many complaints about you not remembering your Sunday School poems. Poor Mrs. Salmon had to put you to stand before the black board to get you to concentrate."

By the time they got to the bus stop, Trevor was revving the engine. He jumped out, took Elah's belongings and put them under the bus. He shook her grandmother's hand, put something in his pocket and jumped back in the driver's seat.

The front seat next to the window had been reserved for his little passenger. He tooted his horn to say, "So long," and Elah waved goodbye to her grandmother. Elah's adventure began with a U-turn on the main street. Only a child could find excitement in watching people scatter, as the bus parted leisurely strollers and pushcart vendors who thought they had a right to use the roadway. Elah gripped her seat so as not to slide off. The lady in the seat next to her had both feet planted on the floor and her legs were securely clamped together. Her fixed smile appeared to be more an affectation than genuine. She reminded Elah of Teacher Green.

Elah, please do not stare at people. It is impolite and rude. Elah gave sideways glances at her seatmate to sum up what the woman was wearing. The bodice of her blue short-sleeve dress was fitted like a corset. It was too tight. It had covered buttons running down the front and a white rounded collar edged with blue piping. A narrow fabric-covered belt and buckle banded the woman's small waistline to the white pleated skirt that reached slightly below her knees. She held a white plastic purse on her lap like a paperweight to keep her dress from riding up.

Trevor slammed on the brakes. The woman's eyelids fluttered, and her mouth opened as if she were about to say, "O." The woman looked at Elah and hinted that she, too, should hold on. She cleared her throat and pulled the skirt further over her knees. Elah turned toward the window, so as not to let the woman see how much she was enjoying the ride. She had looked forward to this trip for months. Although Trevor was charged in delivering her safely to her mother, the 8-year-old felt as if she were making this trip on her own. The woman took out her handkerchief, wiped her face and returned it to her purse. She folded her arms, as if resigned to having made a mistake in not taking the country bus. It was Saturday, and the street was busy as usual. Trevor pressed on the horn, making a path through a labyrinth of pedestrians, cyclists, trucks, tractors, cars, donkey carts and pushcarts.

There was a very popular pushcart vendor who earned his living through negotiations. Most of the other vendors wanted cash; he was flexible and would barter in exchange for his services. For a piece of fresh meat, he would take your groceries so far. For a couple of breadfruits and some cash, he would haul loads to the market. His services were always in demand and people liked the man. He had hired a local talent to paint a replica of the British flag on one side of his pushcart and his name on the other. The boy said that he wrote the name the way the man spelled it: Salahman. Trevor tooted his horn and shouted a friendly greeting to the man: "Hi there Salah-man." The fact that his name was mispronounced and misspelled made no difference to a man who was illiterate. It was a colorful town where there was always cause for excitement, fun or laughter at someone's expense.

Salahman wasn't the only one to be the butt of a joke. The owner of a fabric store was angry at the same artist. By the time he realized what had happened, it was too late. People had started to line up in front of his store to buy bath towels that were on sale. The white sheet with red lettering advertised. "Bathtowels Big Sale." The Syrian man was livid when he realized what had happened. "Ah don't sell bath towels. Never have, never will. We sell clath, an sheets an…" he trailed off into local curse words. The banner should have read, "Bardowell's Big Sale."

Ranny had already spent the cash. The boy's father rebuffed the storeowner's attempt to collect from him the money paid to his son. "There are laws about this sort of thing, sir." He was talking about the boy's age. Mr. Bardowell was on the choir that marched up the center behind Canon Cope, giving him a chance to scan the pews for the culprit. He ruined a good white sheet and damaged the store's reputation. Scanning the church pews for the incompetent artist as he marched up in the procession, the man tripped and almost fell with the cross. Ranny wasn't talking, and many people wondered how much he had paid this fellow. There was talk about what he planned to do to the boy once caught. It was only talk. The artist wasn't taking any chances. He made himself very scarce.

He was one of Elah's neighbors and a good friend. The only boy who would play dolly house with the girls, Ranny was in charge of the money and made the purchase of items for the events. The girls commemorated real life cycle events, and at the end, there would be a party. When a doll was born, there would be a christening and everyone would put money together to buy sugar for lemonade—limes were free—and bullah cake for the celebration. After the sickness and death of a doll, they would have a function. After the marriage of two dolls, there would again be celebration with bullah cake and lemonade. He participated in the eating of food and drinks, but did not contribute money because he claimed bankers were supposed to be paid. Elah had fun with her friends in town and she'd miss them.

As the Greyhound sped on its way, Elah checked her little hand basket to make sure that everything she had put in was still there. One of the Cadbury chocolates was missing; two peppermint candies her aunt gave her were also gone. The pack of cream biscuits had been opened and several were gone. She knew immediately it was the work of her young uncle Alvin. If wishes could come true, Alvin wouldn't be alive when she returned. She begged God to make something bad happen to him. Elah thought of all the horrible things that could happen and wished it on her relative. *Hope your guts get ripped out by that wild boar when next you go to collect sea grapes. You swine. I hope you drown at the wharf. I hope the sharks bite your head off first.*

Her anger gave voice to the secret bad wishes she had for her father's younger brother. "I hate you, you dirty brute." It was from embarrassment that Elah glanced at her seatmate, then across the aisle at the fat woman who seemed to take what she said as a personal insult. The eyelids of the lady next to her fluttered as she anticipated trouble. The woman across the aisle tried in vain to get Trevor's attention. She looked across at Elah.

"Hi deer, who you calling dutty brute?"

"I wasn't speaking to you, lady."

Elah's seatmate crawled into the cocoon she had built for the journey. "Oh! No? Yu too good to be speaking to de likes of me? Yu too nice, little backra gal? Ah so? Facety! Dat is what yu is, dress up inna shews an sacks, but no have no manners. Yu betta wash out yu mouth wid brown soap. Ah oh!" Elah would have expected this from a passenger of the country bus, not the Greyhound that catered to a more sophisticated clientele. This woman apparently was the exception. Trevor realized that his charge was under attack and jumped to her defense.

"Leff her alone; she wasn't talking to you. A big woman like you should noh bettah. Leff her alone."

"Den Trevor, a mad, she mad?" The woman's expression changed, as if to confirm the possibility of loose brain bolts. A bit frightened, Elah pulled herself closer to the window in time to see Trevor overtaking two long flatbed trucks. One of the Madras Indians sitting on top of the bundles of cane jumped out of his lotus position and screamed.

"Hey! Hold it. Yu Bongo man (black and ugly). A try you'a try fe kill me?" It was a near catastrophe, but it didn't stop Trevor from shouting back. "Put on clothes, coolie babu." Maybe her grandmother had a premonition, because she had prayed longer than usual at breakfast. The woman next to her tapped Elah's leg and whispered, "Don't cry, my dear. I know you were not speaking to her. You fell asleep and had a terrible nightmare. Don't cry. Everything will be all right." Her voice got softer as she whispered in Elah's ear. "She is ignorant. Someone must have paid the fare that got her on this bus." Elah was relieved when the woman got off. Elah felt safe with Trevor. They had been driving for at least two hours when Trevor stopped to allow some passengers to get off. "Bye-bye. Be a good girl," the woman said, as she left the bus amidst people gathered to solicit buyers or beg money from passengers. There were men trying to keep their legs from folding under the weight of too much liquor. Elah was startled when an old toothless man pressed his puckered lips up against the window to give her a kiss. "Boonoonoonos," he said, winking at her. She smiled and he waved affectionately, as a grandfather who had just told a girl she was very pretty.

It had gotten hotter, and Trevor pulled out his off-black handkerchief, blew his nose hard, wiped the sweat from his face and the froth from around the corners of his mouth. He winked to Elah, saying, "We soon reach, little one." They were close to her stop, where her cousin would be waiting to take her to her mother's home. Elah thought she'd tell her mother about Alvin, but she would say what she always did, "The longest day has an end." *What does that mean? One day I will die and that will be the end of the longest day?* As young as she was, she could see the futility in that response. Why did she call her mother Sister, and her grandmother, Mama? Sometime she'd try to call her mother Mama, but it seemed so confusing to call two women Mama.

She never called her father at all. He had no name in her book. It wasn't that she did not love him, but she felt that a father should be someone who a child saw on a regular basis. She saw hers only once a year. He was a good father and she believed that he loved her, but she could never call him daddy. He was hurt because he would ask her, "Who am I?" Elah never answered. Her mother said that one day she would understand why it was better for her to live with her paternal grandparent.

The windows clouded up as Trevor pulled up at Miss Mac's little shop. It was time for her to get off. Trevor took out her grip and handed it to her cousin. Leroy had a big grin on his face and hugged her. "Well, red gal, yu come. Me glad fe see yu." After a brief stop at the little shop where the proprietor had a mug of lemonade and a bullah cake waiting for Elah, she and Leroy were off. Their walk would be long and arduous—through thickets and up and over hills and a steep mountain—to get to their destination. The countryside was a contrast to her flat, dusty town where nothing besides seafood and sugar cane grew. Everything in the countryside was lush and green. Wild orchids hung from giant pimento trees like anemones. The aroma of ripe guavas perfumed the air. Elah was immersed in the smell of fresh cow dung, the sound of birds, braying donkeys and green fields of corn close to harvesting. It was the pure smell of nature that she had come to love and which made her really feel that she was in a different place in a different time.

No development or civilization had come to this favorite place. There was no running water. Everyone depended on rain for their supply. A pond was a half hour's walk, but this brown water was shared with the animals that also bathed and drank from it. Not even a pit toilet. Like the animals, people went to the bush to ease themselves. There was a co-existence and an accommodation with nature. An easy spirit that Elah relished with childhood wonder. It was a place she loved to be, but knew that her time was limited because she had to get back to school, church and her other friends.

The walk always seemed longer every year, and Leroy had the same sarcastic reply when Elah would say she was tired and needed to rest. He'd point to a clump of bushes saying, "That's the easy chair," and tell her to sit there. When he wasn't calling her red gal, he referred to her as Princiss Mawgrit. He was her favorite cousin. Her holidays were always happy and fun filled. It was really an indescribable feeling when a child felt that her presence made a difference to an entire village. Elah was welcomed by everyone. The love affair between her and the people in the village was mutual. She had enough blood family to absorb the entire three weeks visiting and having a meal or spending a night huddled with five children in one single bed. Everyone wanted to be next to Elah, so they slept crossways with their feet hanging off. Everyone having something they wanted to share.

"I'm so happy to see you Elah." The old frame house on the hill lit up with sunshine pouring through the jalousie windows. Her old granduncle, who also called her red gal, leaned from his chair on the verandah for a hug. People passing on the street called up to see if Miss Louise's daughter had arrived, some leaving their loads at the bottom of the hill to bring something from their fields for Elah. This child who had suffered physical abuse at the hands of a violent uncle could forget it all in this place. She could sustain herself on the love of a village for a whole year until it was time to once again return. There was no mosquito net over her bed. She heard the rooster crow and smelled food cooking as she was coming out of sleep. As she opened her eyes, her mother was standing by the bed. "Wake up my love, it's breakfast time." The three weeks seemed to have gone by so quickly.

*   *   *   *

Elah appreciated the comforts of the Greyhound. It was the only luxury transport in the entire parish with a clientele dictated by the restrictions or rules imposed by the company. The interior had clean cushioned seats; everyone who bought a ticket was guaranteed a seat. Travel arrangements had to be made and prepaid weeks in advance. No refunds, no standing or hanging off the doors, no open baskets or livestock. All luggage must be placed in the compartment on the side of the bus. Her grandmother insisted they get to the bus stop early to guarantee a seat close to the driver. By special arrangement, Trevor acted as her guardian; he had been doing so for years. The satisfied smile on his face as he pushed something into his pocket was a clue to the little extra he was used to getting from Elah's grandmother.

"You is in my charge now; anyting you want, juss ask me, ahrite?" In her usual seat, it was off for another summer holiday in the country. Elah was growing up and beginning to see life in a different way. For the first time, she really appreciated the difference between the country bus and the Greyhound. She had taken it all for granted; this was the way she traveled. Many of her friends, if they had to go to the country, would have taken the country bus. Her bags were always packed with cookies, chocolate, aerated water, candies—all the treats that she could share with her cousins in the country. Elah noticed everything and everyone in her surroundings. It was odd that in all the years she had been traveling, she had never seen a man on the bus. There were only ladies.

The woman next to her was dressed in a cream-color outfit. The blouse had buttons down the back, and from the waist a flounce cut on the bias flared to cover her hips. Her nails were clean and natural looking. Her hair was in an upswept style with a fancy turtle pin that held her French roll in place. She wore a black pointed-toe shoe, nylon stockings and held a fancy straw purse. She took out a little book and buried her eyes in it. After they had traveled for some minutes, she nudged Elah and held out a candy. Elah thanked her and turned to look out the window. She wanted to talk and leaned forward to get Elah's attention.

"Where to?"

"Leamington to visit my mother."

"Oh! How old are you?"

"Eleven."

"And traveling by yourself?"

"Me is in charge of her, ma'am." The woman looked askance at the wiry man with a knot on his forehead, then back at Elah.

"I see."

The woman took off her shoes and straightened the rib of her nylon stockings. Elah turned her attention back to the window. She wanted to see everything. She was excited and thinking about all the things she'd do when she got to the country. Her cousin, Leroy, showed her how to follow the myriad sweet potato vines and identify where to find those ready for harvesting. Following the root, Elah found one beneath a large rock. It must have weighed three or four pounds. She would be there for the corn shelling competition. Laborers plucked the dried corns, chopped down the plants, removed the husks, made bonfires in the field to prepare for another planting. Family and friends gathered in one house to shell and bag the corn, which was carried to meet the truck that took the bags to a factory that turned it into cornmeal. This was one of the ways that country folks helped each other and had fun at the same time. They not only shared work, but everything else. Those who had cows shared milk with those who didn't.

Elah fell asleep. She saw a man with a machete about to strike. She screamed, but there was no sound. There were people around, but no one was coming to her aid. "Little Miss. Dis is de half way pint, you can go over deer where it is private." Trevor was standing next to Elah, pointing to a large field across from where the bus stopped. It was a common practice, and no one seemed self conscious about stooping on the edge of a public road to relieve themselves. Elah didn't, now that she was seeing her period. For the few minutes the people took, Trevor felt as if he had to make up time. He had traveled this road many times, but apparently he forgot that just around the corner the road took off at an angle. He stopped short of ramming into a fragile concrete abutment that separated the road from a precipice. Elah was frightened. It was the first time she felt as if she had come close to death. The incident brought back memories of the stories Teacher Green used to tell.

The woman next to Elah asked if she were all right, sighed, and said, "Lucky you, your stop is near. I have to go all the way to Middle Quarters. I thought the quality of drivers on these buses were of a higher caliber because it costs much more to gain a seat." Trevor looked in his mirror, perhaps wondering why the woman was whispering to his charge. To assert his authority, he asked, "Are you ahrite, little miss?" Elah was happy to see her grinning cousin. The long walk on foot didn't seem as daunting. Trevor jumped off and handed her grip to Leroy. Her seatmate wished her happy holidays and Leroy sent greetings to her mother. "See yu in tree week time." Elah felt fearful of going back on the bus. Trevor was off, stirring up a cloud of white dust and leaving tire tracks on the marl road. Leroy's shirt was opened all the way and soaked with perspiration, but he was cheerful as usual.

"Prinsis Mawgrit, you come. Wha you bring fe me?"

"Nothing."

"Well, me want some of it."

Leroy was a second cousin on her mother's side. He was 14 and of medium height and of a muscular build. He had a dense clump of hair that curled tight to his skull. His lips bled in places where he had used his teeth to peel off the outer layers. The sides and heels of his feet were dry, split, and calloused. Elah knew he had at least one pair of shoes, but those were reserved for special occasions. He warned Elah as they approached the little shop where the woman always had a drink and cake waiting for her. "Whatever you get, me is to get some of it."

"Little Elah, what a way you are growing nicely. You looking as sweet as ever. What a pretty dress. The daisy flowers dem pink like you." Leroy felt slighted and reminded Miss Mac that he was also present.

"Good mawning, Miss Mac?"

"Good morning, Leroy, but me noh see you already? You juss pass here." She turned back to Elah. "So how is everything in town?" She went in back and brought out a mug of lemonade and reached into her case for a bullah cake. Elah took a sip and handed the mug to Leroy. He drank until the woman told him she had given it to Elah. He pushed the entire piece of cake Elah gave him in his mouth. The only news Elah thought she could share was the extension Crooks was putting onto his building. Everyone knew, or knew of, the man whose bar catered to prostitutes and sailors. Besides the rum bar, he had a bakery, and now was adding a fabric shop. "That Syrian man should love to hear that him is gwineto get some competition now. Anyway de government should use the money to pave this road." The ruling party used his premises to hold political meetings and rallies, so it was not surprising if they provided some of the funds for his expansion. Leroy drained the mug as if he suspected the one-quart oil tin was holding back some of the lemonade. They bade Miss Mas so long and started on their way. Leroy was not finished with what he thought was a slight from the woman who knew him and family since he was born.

"Yu tink she would say, 'Leroy, here is a drink'? No, she doesn't even say, 'Dawg, good morning.' Me is nat mulatta and me nat pretty. Look all de years me pass har shop fe come meet yu and she nevah say, 'Leroy, here is a bullah cake,' or 'Here is some bebridge.' All she want fe do is fass inna other people business. 'Wha happen a Negril? Wha happen ah Black River? Wha happen a

Mobay? Wha happen a Ochie? Wha happen a town?' She fe get bullhorn ahn announce news. Dat is all leff fe her fe do for as soon as you tell her someting, she tell somebady else. She fe fine husban and use up de time she'a noisy 'roun' fe news."

The little shop, the only one for miles, was a meeting place for people coming and going to different parts of the island. It was the bus stop, the landmark used by people when describing where they lived. It was Miss Mac's social club. To get the 5 o'clock bus, some people spent the night before sleeping on the floor. Most carried their own food and refreshments and did not buy so much as a bullah cake from Miss Mac. The little back room is where she lived. The shop barely contained the narrow showcase for biscuits, candies and cakes. Behind the counter were a few bags with flour, sugar and a barrel with salt meats.

Big mountain was the halfway point between the bus stop and the house. It looked like a dot on the horizon, an unattainable goal. Elah was always amazed how Leroy could walk such a long way to meet her, take her back, then return to accompany her as she was leaving. It took hours and it seemed as if every year the path was more obstructed by underbrush and pointed stones that pierced through the soles of Elah's shoes.

"I bet you didn't know that there is sinking sand somewhere around here?" When that comment didn't stir any interest, he said there was a deep pond and it was covered over with grass. He told Elah he had to jump in and save a girl from drowning. She knew he couldn't swim, but they kept each other busy with chit-chat. Elah was beginning to feel uncomfortable. She felt the warm blood oozing and soaking through the two napkins she had put on for the journey. She had extras in her grip, but there was no private place to change. Elah had thought of asking Miss Mac to use her back room, but it would entail too much. The woman had no running water and she would need to wash herself.

"How much further we have to go, Leroy?" He bit at his bottom lip as though trying to strip away the outer layer of irritation.

"How lang we walk las ear, ahn de year before dat, ahn de year before dat? Well eh'a goh tek de same time dis ear." The difference in age between them was only three years, yet Leroy acted as if he were a grown man. "Yu ole enough fe carry yu own grip. Wha yu have inn it dat mek eh so heavy?" He had dropped the grip several times, and Elah remembered that she had put her china set in there.

"Jesus God, me crockery in it."

"Yu wha?"

"Me china set me Fada sent for me."

"Se yah, gal." Leroy looked at Elah in an odd way. China, as far as he knew, was a country far away. "Yu noh wha? Mek we galang so we cahn reach before nite." Elah was comfortable with Leroy. They had an understanding that even when they were not talking, they were present to each other.

Elah had three sets of family: paternal grandmother; grandaunt and cousins; maternal grandparents, uncles, aunts and cousins. They all lived in town. In the country, she had many granduncles, two grandaunts and more cousins than she could readily count. As she and Leroy walked along in a desired silence enveloped only by sounds and smells, Elah felt at peace. Her mind was free to roam and wander like the many birds that chirped and lifted themselves out of the way of slingshots. There was something quite beautiful about this rugged, undeveloped place and its similar inhabitants. It defied a structure, a phrase, a definition that could adequately encompass all the emotions and sensibilities. All Elah could think is how the people and the environment seemed a good fit, and how comfortably she had fit into it as well. If Leroy were thinking deeply, Elah was curious about his thoughts.

It was close to midday. Trees and underbrush sliced the sun into small slivers of light that at once streaked across Elah's face and lit up the shrubs. Some young girls passing with large oil tins of water on their heads called out, "Good afternoon, Miss Elah." Leroy paused and looked at them as if to remind them that Elah wasn't alone. They walked on and continued to giggle. "Den me is not somebady?" He shouted after them. "Mawning Leroy." They continued laughing and Leroy believed he had been the object of their derision.

"Look pon yu, dem a call yu Miss, ahn me is oldah. Lissen yu, how lang yu been coming to dis place? Well mek me tell yu," he was about to drop the grip, but Elah reminded him about the breakables. He put it down gently and began counting on his fingers. "Yu is 9 o' 10 now; so is six ear, rite?" He didn't wait for an answer. "Is a lang time me carrying yu grip."

"I am 11."

"Ahrite, all me noh is dat a lang time since me coming fe meet you." He wiped away the sweat with his forearm. Elah thought she ought to share some of what she had in the basket with him, but was afraid that once she dipped into it, he would try to finish everything. He looked tired, but determined to press on. His feet were dry and dusty. Something about them reminded her of a man in town. Boys had painted his feet while he was asleep in his pushcart. Two of them were caught and confessed that they were just trying to give him a pair of sneakers. It was a big joke around town for a long time. Elah laughed aloud at the mischief of trying to draw and paint a shoe with laces on this man's bare feet. Leroy's eyes flashed angrily. He had seen her look at his feet. Elah told him that she remembered something that happened in town. Elah wasn't so sure she wanted to share this joke with Leroy. He put down the grip.

"Dem backra (meaning white or light skin) people yu live wid noh teach yu manners? Is nat like yu is walking an talking to yuself like a mad s'mady. Me is rite here and you buss laugh and noh tell me wha sweet yu? Anyway, yu could be mad. Wha me noh? Whole heap a mad people live a town. Anyway, me is hungry. Gimmie some of what you have in that basket weh yu holding like sey it have gold." Elah walked a little ahead, she did not want him to see everything in the basket. The chocolate was soft, so she took off a piece and handed it to him. "Ah dis you'a geh me? One deggeh piece a melt-up chacolet? Well, you red skin people really mean. Yu granny didn't give you something ahn say, 'Dis is for Leroy the one who been coming to meet yu a bus stap fe years upon years?'"

"She told me to let my mother share it."

Most islanders could easily shift from proper English to patois, some with more acuity than others. Leroy was no exception. "All right. I am thirsty and would like to have a drink. De lilly piece a chacolet stick up inna me teeth." Elah unscrewed the bottle of aerated water, took a couple sips and passed it to him. Leroy finished it and threw away the bottle. They were once again on their journey. "So Prinsis, yu bring crockery? Yu is gwineto have porty?" He let out a laugh of ridicule. "Koo yah! Pappyshow! U nat gwineto use Aunty tin mug? Den me is invited?" This provided fuel for a few miles because he continued to laugh intermittently. He didn't understand that they were tiny little dishes.

Elah was looking forward to seeing everyone, especially her mother. Louise was the first of eight children for her parents. She went to live with her paternal Aunt Missy and her husband Daniel in the village where her father was born and grew up. He was the only one who left this village to live in town. The family's name blanketed the village like Cerrassee, a bush that grew wild along stone fences. Ten brothers and two sisters, and all except one, had many children. They practically owned the village because their properties most often connected. People said that Elah looked like her mother. Louise was a slender, light-skinned woman with long, black hair. Some said that her slanted eyes made her look part Chinese. "Did I ever tell you that my neighbor in town has a Ping-Pong table in his yard? Sometimes when we play, the balls roll into crab holes and we have to fill the holes with water to get them out."

Leroy kept walking. He seemed to finally remember what he wanted to say. "Come to tink of it, me used to noh a China man wid a name like dat: Ping Pang. Him have a grocery store a tap side. Dolores did love one of him bwoys.

Mebbe him is fambily to yu." Elah wasn't surprised to hear him say that. She had been told many times that she looked Chinese. She told him she had a one-piece bathing suit. He shrugged and kept going. She told him about a play that was going on in town. It was a true story about a Pentecostal preacher who encouraged his followers to jump off a rooftop, telling them that the faithful would fly like birds. Many of his flock died from injuries they received in the fall, and the minister was arrested and sent to the asylum. That stopped Leroy. "Hear ya me Gad! What a wey town people idle. Dem go pon stage a pretend dem is somebady else." Elah said if it was still playing when she went back, he could come to town and she would take him to see it. "I want to see real thing like a cowboy picture show."

"Let's stop and rest a little, Leroy."

"Ress? Fe wha? Juss come, dem waiting for us and we soon reach."

Country folks were used to walking long distances. "Dem is suppose to build a road closer, den yu won't have to walk so far." That would make life easier for everyone. As they walked past fields with new crops of corn, Elah imagined they were coming into puberty like her. The grains were just firming up and taking their space on the stalk. She was coming into womanhood. Too old to play with dolls and too young to make decisions. Old enough to take care of her clothes, too young to go out with boys. Each plant in the field seemed to be trying to grow taller than the other. Some plants bore two ears, some had many more. They were like her family. On her father's side there were few, on her mother's side there were many. Elah had taken off her shoes and had slowed. Leroy looked back and warned that he would leave her unless she walked faster.

Elah thought that perhaps her cousin didn't have time to realize he was still a young boy. In a dog's life, Leroy may have been around 80 or 90, but he was only three years older and seemed to have so much more responsibilities. Leroy had business sense, despite the limited time he spent in a classroom. He maintained a large plot of land where he planted sweet potatoes for his own account. He ran errands for the two blind and mute sisters, Ena and Weena. "Dem two dummies is de biggest gossips inna dis village. God noh why him mek dem bawn bline an cut out dem tongue. Noh everybady business and never set foot outta dem yard." He took care of his uncle's patch of corn and milked the cows, and every year he walked for miles to meet Elah.

Leroy looked back and saw Elah walking in her socks. "See here, Prinsis Mawgrit, who is gwineto wash dem sacks? You noh what? I want a drink. Yu have more in dat basket." He sat, and they finished another bottle of soda and another Cadbury bar. Elah gazed off, preoccupied with the thought of reaching womanhood. She had taken off her bolero and noticed that her dress straps made a line over her shoulders. Leroy was resting on a tree stump, absentmindedly chewing on blades of grass and spitting them out. He was pulling on the brush to pass time, clear his head or to rest. Elah had something she wanted to share, but was reluctant. They had gotten to a tamarind tree that was lying on its side, having been struck down by the last hurricane. Leroy jumped over. Elah stopped.

"Hello, my friend. I'm back again, and guess what? I am seeing my menses." Leroy had gone some distance when he realized Elah wasn't behind him. She shouted and asked him not to drop the grip as he seemed about ready to do.

"Ah wha yu ah do? Pray? Look yah gal, yu tun obeah woman?" Elah had immersed herself as part of this natural landscape, listening to sounds of animals and birds, inhaling the fresh air, smelling the guava fruits—all the things he took for granted. Without further notice, Leroy picked up the suitcase and began to trot. Elah jumped up and ran after him, but he switched the path, making it difficult to find him. After a few seconds, he jumped out and warned her that the next time he would leave her. Elah did not think he'd do it, but her faith was a little shaken by the mischief she saw in his eyes.

"Leroy, guess what?" There were only grunts coming from her fellow traveler. "I'm seeing my period."

"What is dat to me? You'a see yu period! Juss walk fass so we can ketch de house before nite." Elah was being purposely indelicate by town standards. She called out to him again and pushed up the spot where her breasts were beginning to sprout. "Leroy, I'm going to get a brassiere." He looked at her as if to ask why are you bothering me, then he sneered, "Breezair fe wha? Yu ha breasts?" The nauseating smell of blood and perspiration made Elah's stomach sick. She asked Leroy if he smelled any odor. "Wha me fe smell?" Elah was concerned about how she would take care of the bloodied napkins. This would be the first time she would have to deal with a problem such as this. She didn't know how she'd tell her mother.

"Leroy." His face showed disgust. "How will I wash them?"

"Wash wha?"

"My private things."

"Didn't yu see de gal dem a carry wata pon dem head? Or, yu can kip dem til yu go'a town ahn wash dem deer unda pipe wata. Or, yu could wash dem inna the pond. Buck yu drink fram deer, yu drink milk fram Buck Yu; ahn see me here," he slapped his chest, "de wata no do me nutten all deese years me been drinking it." Elah wasn't so sure about his last comment. "Lissen Princess Mawgrit, me don't wahn fe hear no more 'bout yur ladies business. Me is a man. As a matter of fack, no badda wid no more tinking we soon reach. Yu can tell yu mada."

From the bottom, the sun looked like an orange ball balanced on Big Mountain. Leroy broke a piece of stick and began to use it to propel himself upward. Elah held onto limbs, or whatever support she could find, to help her up the steepest inclines. At times, Leroy extended a helping hand. He was breathing in short, staccato gusts. It was such a fearsome and arduous climb. Elah felt she was about to run out of air, and several times she had to stop and take deep breaths. They were going through a thicket and Leroy was breaking branches to clear the way. He called her name as if he were expecting to hear an echo from the gully below. When Elah didn't answer, he asked if she had lock jaw. "I was thinking about…"

"Ah tell yu, I do not want fe hear no more women's trouble. Ah gwineto leave yu if you don't walk up. If yu tinking me is so stewpid fe leff yu where yu can see de house, yu wrang. Remembah, we haffe come back and may not take dis wey." Elah wanted to ask Leroy what marked a boy's ascension into manhood and to ask if he had ever done it with a girl. Perhaps she'd ask him when she was leaving to go back home. "My God, it is half past one." They had been walking for almost two hours.

"Yu can read sun?"

"No, but I can tell the time by my watch."

"Look yah me Gad! A clack yu have awn?"

"I have a boyfriend, too."

"What is dat to me?"

"We may get married one day."

"Shet yu mout ef yu no have someting sensible fe say." He kept walking and mumbled, "Yu is gwineto get married? A have a good mine fe tell yu gramma a town." They were close enough to see small images on Aunty's veranda. The three-room frame house sat on a hill, still another climb to get to the top. The veranda ended at the door of her mother's small bedroom. This room along with the veranda was hoisted on stilts and perched precariously over a steep incline. The large front room had a small bed in one corner, a table and chairs in another, and a desk on the opposite wall. It adjoined Aunty and Uncle's bedroom, which rested on a gigantic rock in the back. As they got closer to the house, Elah saw the usual greeters: her mother, Louise, and her friend Madge, Auntie Missy, Uncle Dan and Evelyn. They were smiling and waving. "See dem up deer a wave lakka royalty coming."

Elah heard that Mass B, Miss Madge's husband, had been ill and asked Leroy how he was doing. "Him bettah now. Him is a big ole fool." Many people shared Leroy's opinion that she didn't love the man who adored her and that he would do anything to please her. "Spen all him money pon woman who no love him, no cook food fe him, no wash him one ole khaki trousers, or do nothen else womens do for man. Him sleep by himself pon patch up sheet, and Gad bless de nite shirt wha him wear. Deer is more holes inna it dan stars in de sky." Leroy waved to Miss Madge and smiled. "She is yu Mada fren, but she'a hypocrite. No like one bone inna my bady, but look how she'a grin de false teeth." Elah was happy to once again see her mother, the young woman she called Sister Lou. Leroy whispered, "Evelyn soon go'a town fe get plate." It didn't seem as if they had enough money to feed their children, much less to pay for dentures. Maybe there were people in town who knew how to mix plaster and do false teeth just as there were those who knew how to do illegal abortions, but Elah didn't know of anyone. "De bald head man bax out five a har teeth, three a tap, ahn two a battam or two a tap an three a battam. Wha me noh?" Elah thought her cousin Evelyn's husband was a nice man. "How could he be so wicked?"

"All de mans dem wicked. Me, too." Leroy sounded as if he were boasting to cast himself with misogynists who abused women. A new image of him flashed across her mind. Elah wondered if this was how boys learned to define manhood? He whispered, "Remember to tell yu mada dat me is to get some of what is in dat basket." He handed Elah's grip to someone on the veranda and helped her to balance on the stone that replaced the missing steps. Elah held onto her mother and felt as if she wouldn't let go. Evelyn's greeting was muffled behind the handkerchief she used to cover her mouth. Elah was relieved in many ways: The long walk was over and she would at last have a chance to wash herself. Her mother had always prepared a zinc tub with water for her to clean up after the long walk. It was near the rock behind the house. She would have to tell her mother. When she did, Elah was surprised how natural and normal her reaction was. There was no shame. Sister Lou gave her soap, wash rag and a paper bag in which to put her bloodied napkins. Elah had a totally different experience in town.

Her grandmother said that if the pain didn't go away by Monday, she'd have to take Elah to the doctor. At the mention of his name, Elah made out her Last Will and slipped it under her pillow. *"Please, dear Lord, I don't want to die. If it is your will, I want little Jeanie to get Betsy. And please, dear Lord, forgive me for every unkind thing that I have done. I said it wasn't me, but you know that one-eye Kettie was telling the truth. I was just angry because she found my dirty panty under the bed and told everyone about it. The Rooster shouldn't be bathing naked on a public beach where he knew girls gathered to swim. It wasn't me who buried his clothes. I did throw the stone that made a big splash near his head. Cacka Pilot lied when he said I threw the stone that hit him. I threw it, but it didn't hit the drunk. We did not go to the hospital to visit Nicca's mother. We went to the morgue to see Miss Una, the woman Ivan chopped to death. In the eyes of God I have committed many sins. I beg forgiveness."* Elah signed her name and put the note under her pillow. The Baptist neighbor across the street used to talk about retribution, saying it was written in the Bible.

Elah heard a, "sssp, sssp" at the window. The calling signal was coming from one of her friends. Elah was sick and could not meet them as had been planned. The friend was there to find out what had happened. Whatever excursions the girls wanted to take had to be done when all the adults were gone to do weekly shopping in the market and grocery store. Her friend was angry because precious time had been spent waiting for Elah and now she found her lying in bed. "We have been waiting at the bridge to bomboclate. Battiehole. Leesie has to take lunch for her uncle at the hospital. You laying down in bed after you promise. Backside. Now we cahnt go again. Backside." Elah began to cry because she didn't know how to tell her friend that she may die and never see any of them again. She was bleeding to death. Her friend hurried inside and saw the blood spreading on the white sheet. "My God, you seeing your menses. Then you never know? It is normal, so don't worry. Mine came last year. Get up and wash up yourself, I will be back. I have to go and tell them that you seeing your menses." Elah tore up the note. She was relieved that it was so easy to talk to her mother about menstruation, a topic she was embarrassed to talk about with her grandmother. Her mother was in the back of the house washing her bloody napkins. The shame was gone, and she was looking forward to visiting with her uncles, aunts and cousins, and to the end of her period.

For the next three weeks, Elah would sleep on the single bed and eat at the dining table, and share this room with her uncle whose desk held all his legal papers, and have visits with family and friends. The sound of avocados crashing down on the zinc room used to frighten her, especially during the night, but she had gotten used to that.

Aunty Missy was one of the two girls in a family of 10 boys and two girls. She inherited the home from her parents. They had built a home close by for the other girl and the boys had to fend for themselves. The history of the house and the village was inextricably tied to the history of the Maroons.

Aunty Missy was a tall, wiry woman with a kind face and ropy veins in her arms and legs. She walked for days with her donkey, Ruth, carrying the load of ground provisions that she'd sell in the market in town. She returned to the village with fresh fish and items she couldn't readily purchase at home. Aunty said the walk was made easier because of the many friends she had made on the route. There were places she could stop to rest and enjoy a meal and a cool drink. She had Leroy-type stamina and could push through exhaustion to get to her destination. She was the encyclopedia of the history of this village that had become Elah's second home. She told Elah that most, if not all, of the residents in the village descended from Africans brought to the island during the early 15th century. They were settled in this place that came to be called the cockpit karst. During the Spanish occupation, they were free to live as they pleased as long as they hunted and killed wild hogs for the Spanish hog butter trade. They remained there during and after the British invaded and captured the island. These Africans had a long history of combat with the British who tried to enslave them, but never succeeded. The terrain was so inhospitable with rocks, cliffs and ravines that only those who knew its treachery could survive. The Africans who made this their home were hardy stock, self-driven and self-sustaining. They had a sense of community and sharing that continued to the present time. The family's graveyard was in a ravine close to the house, and although years and flooding had obliterated most of the headstone markings, Aunty could point to the exact spot where her parents, grandparents and other relatives were buried. She often said that she wished to rest her bones next to her family when the good Lord called her home.

Her husband Daniel was frail-looking man with a goatee and sprinkling of grey hair. Whiskers defined the bony edges of a thin face that had little exposure to the sun. His height was shortened by stooped shoulders. He said he was born to do brain work, and those who knew his father said that he was a carbon copy. "De two of dem cut outta one cloth." Uncle sat in his rocking chair, gave orders and collected money. He was beyond frugal. Getting by spending as little money as he could, hauling in as much as he could and depending on others to offer him as much as they would. When he wasn't sitting on the veranda or doing business, he'd be in his bedroom re-counting the silver coins he kept in used oil cans on a shelf high above his bed. If the mattress could talk, it would reveal that Daniel had stuffed thousands of pounds of paper money between the Coya straws. Money that would be lost if ever there was a fire.

He had fields that were planted and harvested without him setting a foot on the soil. No one saw the cash he collected. He had been lending money for years. People would walk for miles to see Mister Daniel. If he loaned two shillings, he expected to get four back. He had many cows that provided enough milk for family, and for sale to others. These cows were the largess of his foreclosures. Her mother was making dinner in the kitchen and uncle had gone down the hill to meet one of his customers. Elah was curious to see the papers he filed in the desk drawer. She heard him legitimize his transactions by telling people the agreement was drawn up by a lawyer. Contracting with the lawyer's secretary was close enough to having a solicitor's stamp without the cost of fees. Uncle kept a number of carbon copies in the drawer. As Elah looked at the documents, many signed with an "X," she wondered why he would even bother to do such an elaborate contract when the people were unable to read it. He undoubtedly saw the error, but what difference did it make to people who couldn't read? The point of his contract was to secure repayment with the threat of the law.

The sign and seal of deliverance of said sum proscribed above, by Danuel Ezeekel Morris to (name of the borrower) in the day of the Lord 9th July One Thousand Nine Hundred and Fifty-two.

After a meal of corn dumplings, slices of roasted breadfruit, a large avocado and a full mug of hot milk, they were ready for rounds of visiting. Elah and her mother were going to see Miss Madge and her husband, and an uncle and his family who lived on top of a very steep hill. It was the yearly routine, a visit to all the uncles and aunt. Mass B peeped out of the shop when he heard them coming up the stairs. "Miss Madge gone up a tap road, she soon come back. "Well, you come to see us again. Good to see you, me dear." Remnants remained of a handsome man with an angular face, high bridged nose and bushy eyebrows. Bernard Jackson used an old necktie strung through every other loop to keep his trousers from falling off. He smelled as if he had soaked himself in the brine of salted beef and mackerel he kept in wooden barrels. Mass B went back into his shop, telling Louise to wait for Miss Madge, but to call out to him before she leaves.

The Jackson's home was situated exactly in a reverse fashion from Aunty's home. Two bedrooms rested on the edge of the road, and the veranda and a small back room rested on high pillars in the back. One of the front rooms was being used as his grocery shop and the other was his wife's bedroom. He slept in a small room that was attached at the end of the veranda. Elah had been into his wife's room, but had never seen his. Leroy had awakened her curiosity. A slantwise piece of wood kept the door closed. It swung open and almost banged against the railing. His nightshirt hung like a scarecrow on rusted nails, a dented enamel chamber pot peeped from under the bed. Leroy was telling the truth. The misalignment of the door required them to lift and push to turn the latch to close it.

They were tiptoeing back when Louise spied her friend who was partially hidden by the foliage. The woman had started walking up to the veranda. "Let's go, Elah. We can come back later."

"I am on my way up, Lou." At the sound of his wife's voice, Mass B hurried out of his shop and went near the staircase to help her. It didn't matter what gossip was being tossed about, there was no fertile ground to plant any seeds of suspicion against his wife. "Lovely." His lazy eyes lit up. He could have been referring to his wife or the fruits or both. She had walked a long way to pick up some fruits especially for Elah. Miss Madge was a pretty, dark-skinned woman in her mid-30s; when she smiled, the dimples in her cheeks made her at once child-like and seductive. Miss Madge was fastidious. Everything she had or bought was of the best quality. She had a maid who took care of her clothes and linens. Lace canopy, mosquito nets, the white chenille bedspread, fresh hand towels embroidered at the edges, mahogany washstand and ceramic basin and goblet made the room look as if it were a museum. A pink, starched, crocheted doily in the form of a princess was in the center and reflected in the round mirror. Her wardrobe had one full-length mirror.

They were in the room visiting when Elah saw Mass B standing at the door waiting. She alerted Miss Madge and the woman stepped out to talk with her husband. After a couple of minutes, she returned, saying, "He is getting something ready for you, Elah." There were muffled sounds coming from the street outside, and Elah wondered what was happening. Miss Madge said that a dentist in her side yard was pulling teeth. A long line had formed from the shop door past Miss Madge's bedroom, and people were coming out and going through a space in the hedge. They had towels wrapped around their heads, drawn under the chin and knotted on the top. Louise whispered that the dentist was from Elah's town. Elah peeped to see if it was someone she knew and was surprised to see Dexter Philpots holding a pair of rusted pliers clamped onto a man's tooth. The man braced himself against the tree as Philpots yanked the teeth out. Blood gushed like a river, and the man shoved a wet rag into his mouth and clamped his mouth shut.

"Well, tell her to keep her wardrobe and bureau locked, and to hide all her valuables and lock up her money; he is a thief."

"Listen to me, Elah, it is not good to spread rumors."

"He stole and borrowed money from a lot of people in St. Mary. He put on an American accent and a cowboy hat and told people he was from Texas and was prospecting for oil. He was in jail. He must have just gotten out. She is your friend, you should tell her." Louise seemed weighed down by the sudden burden of new information, knowing that he had been sleeping in Miss Madge's canopy bed.

"Mind your own business and keep your mouth shut. If he is such a crook, the law will find him as they did before." Their whispering was pierced by a scream as if it were coming from the gully, followed by the words, "Me dead, me dead, me dead, oh." Elah imagined it was the cry of someone whose tooth had been difficult to pull out.

"Please for God's sakes, Elah, do not say anything to Leroy." *Say anything to Leroy? That's why Leroy said Miss Madge doesn't do anything for her husband. It was the closest he could come to spilling the woman's infidelities; a fact Elah felt Miss Madge's best friend, Louise, knew.* "And beg you not to tell anybody in town about this; we don't want any scandal. Jesus Christ."

Elah knew how to keep a secret. If her mother heard some of the things her grandmother said, she'd probably not send her back to live in town. Elah would tell her friends because they all knew Dexter. He was a very pleasant and comical guy, and used to say how he loved one of Elah's friends and would ask for her hand when she was older. The girls laughed about it, as if say, "Who would want Dexter?" He boasted about his sojourn to St. Mary, saying how he "lamps" (fools) them and how mothers invited the "Texan oil man" to meet their daughters and made such fuss over him. Dexter said he would not be going back in those parts for a while, because he wasn't ready to be called pappa. Elah couldn't believe he had made his way to the village passing himself off as a dentist.

They continued walking. As they passed the post office, Elah understood why people often did not write letters. Evelyn's husband swung wide at a bend in the gravel road almost hitting Louise. After he righted the bicycle, the man waved. "One of these days you are going to kill somebody," Louise exclaimed at the near disaster. "He rides like a mad man and don't have any brakes." The uphill climb to Uncle James and Aunt Etta was arduous, but it was pleasant when they got to the top. Everything was luscious and green. Chocos hung from an orchard near the house. A tree in the back was laden with yellow heart breadfruits. Elah smelled one roasting. It was dark by the time they returned home.

Elah had gotten used to the night sounds of frogs, crickets and other night creatures, and the sound of ripe avocados falling on the tin roof. When she heard her name whispered outside the window, Elah was terrified, and ran into Aunty and Uncle's bed. The following day Leroy revealed himself. "Did you pee-pee dem bed?" Uncle was not happy. He hauled the mattress outside, refusing any help. He stayed close to his bedroom until it dried.

Elah had many more relatives to visit, but she wanted to see her Uncle Zacky. He had a sugar cane mill and a large cast iron vat in the middle of a cane field. There, Zacky turned cane juice into wet sugar. Elah watched and studied the process that he made look so easy. The sugar cane was cut, the leaves shaved and the stalk cleaned of loose dirt. The stalks were cut into about three-foot pieces and fed into a mill that was manually operated. The juice was then poured into the sunken vat and a fire underneath boiled and reduced the juice to dark sugar syrup. Uncle Zacky scooped this out and filled covered containers that he sold. It was a one-man business, the only one of its kind in the village. It got to the point that only customers of long standing could get their order for wet sugar refilled. While the cane juice bubbled, and before the alcohol burned off, people would stop by to purchase a mug of the hot liquor, a highly intoxicating substance. Elah had seen people asleep on the benches and grass nearby. She wasn't sure what she'd do when she grew up, but she was inclined toward starting a business of her own.

In a few more years, Elah knew she would no longer be spending three to four weeks in the country. The three weeks had gone by quickly, and it was time to return home. Elah wished she could have stayed longer, but it had been a great holiday. Relatives stopped by to wish Elah safe travel and brought crocus bags with gifts of corn, yam, potatoes, chocos, coconuts and breadfruits. It was much more than it was possible to take, so she left a lot behind. Uncle told her to come back soon because it was the only time he received charity. Elah bent down and kissed him goodbye. "Me gwineto miss you reddibo." She'd miss him, too; he was part of the landscape she accepted and had come to love with all its imperfections. Elah held onto her mother for a long time without saying anything, but still they were saying everything to each other. Elah kept looking back and waving goodbye. Dolores accompanied them to help carry some of the bags. Leroy seemed more reserved with his other cousin present and didn't seem to like the idea.

"Next time, Prinsis Mawgrit, yu bring cart fe haul all yu bangarang ah town. Me nat gwineto be yu donkey no more."

"Me will come wid you Elah; me and Solomon."

"Yu ahn Salaman? You mean piss-a-bed? Dat Bwoy cahnt even carry two bullah cakes unless him eat dem first."

"He can beat you, Leroy. Him is strong."

"Not one ah Uncle James pickney can beat me, dem don't get ennuf fe eat." Dolores wasn't pleased and silence followed, with each trying to walk next to Elah on the narrow path. Eventually, Dolores took herself out of the competition by going ahead, and turning her head to speak to Elah. The trip back seemed much shorter, perhaps Dolores had taken a better route. As they approached Miss Mac's shop, Elah heard the three toots. Trevor had arrived. He scattered dust on those close. Elah barely had enough time for a quick hug and goodbye to her cousins. She pushed up the window, waved, and shouted, "Tell Mama I love her." Leroy shouted back, "How about me? Yu noh love me?"

THE SHAPE OF A STONE

Bits of paper, bits of paper
laying on the ground, laying on the ground
make the place tidy, make the place tidy
pick them up, pick them up

It was an Infant School song. Elah was learning all the things little girls needed to know: Wash your dirty panties, and hang them on the line outside. Make up the bed. Shake out the mosquitos before you tie up the net. Empty the chamber, and wash it out. Do your homework, unless you are aspiring to be a dunce like your cousins in the country. Practice your recitation for Easter Sunday, so that Miss Salmon won't have to make you stand on one foot. As she got older, there were other rules. Clear yourself from that window, and knock boys out of your head. Mark O, if you don't behave in church, I will get the news and things won't be pretty when you come home. There were stages to everything, as if her whole life was being inched up one step at a time. Put coal into the iron and press your uniform; you are old enough to do that. Walk like you are a proper young lady, and do not speak to every bongo you meet on the street. Close your legs, and don't sit like a market woman. Put a handle to big people's names; you are too equalizing and facety. Why should she refer to the prostitute as Miss? Rules, rules, rules for such a lawless place. Elah wanted to become an adult so she could move away from this town and the foolish rules.

Everyone knew the ineffectiveness of the constabulary force. The officers did not have guns, no vehicles except bicycles and no protective devices to prevent personal injury. By the time the sole constable got to the scene, the young woman was dead. A man who intervened to try to stop the murder was slashed. He used his shirt as a tourniquet to stem the flow of blood. "What happen here?" the officer asked, poised on his bicycle with one foot on the ground as a brake. He looked at the lifeless woman lying on the ground. Spectators shouted and pointed in the direction where the murderer was hiding. Standing nonchalantly next to the bike, the officer issued orders. "One of you, go to the station and tell them we need transport to take the woman to hospital. I mean to the morgue." The Good Samaritan who was bleeding profusely started to walk away. "Where you going?" The man answered that he was off to the hospital for stitches. "Go to the station. We will need a witness report." The officer rode away, leaving the murderer in hiding and the crowd gawking over Mary's fatal wound—a deep gash that cut through her blouse and just about severed her left breast.

No one seemed to think it was a form of child abuse to have toddlers holding onto the skirts of their mothers who were racing to meet the incoming ships of foreign sailors. No penalty was imposed for public indecency as drunken sailors engaged in blatant foreplay on the main street. Abortionists were not held responsible for the loss of young lives whose abortions they botched. Known pedophiles were free to prey on children without being accountable the authorities. Adolescents were not taught about their bodies or human sexuality. There was a high rate of illegitimate births. Very few men took responsibility for children they fathered. Men were not taught to control their impulses because their aggression toward women was considered manly. Women were accused of being loose and wearing dresses that tempted men. The girl who was raped is kept from school, afraid and ashamed to show herself in public, and the rapist goes free to lure other children into his net. People called him Pa Grampa because his daughter bore two of his children. The younger girl was turned out of her home because she refused her father's sexual advances. His wife continued to live with the man who molested their daughters. Pa Grampa was husband, father and grandfather in the same household. Elah was angry when she thought of the girls who died at the hands of a known abortionist. The absence of objection and abhorrence was unbelievable. The silence of the community was deafening.

Elah stood across from the police station contemplating her next move. She was thinking about lessons she learned at home and school. A child should speak only when spoken to, and must be obedient and well behaved. Learning to be tidy was first among the very important life lessons. *"Bits of paper, bits of paper, scattered on the ground, make the place look tidy, pick them up."* The song had a catchy tune and children enjoyed singing it, but Elah didn't understand why she was being asked to tear up paper, scatter the pieces on the floor, then pick them up. At 4, that bit of life learning did not make sense, and at 16 it seemed ludicrous that she would be prohibited from seeing a movie about the life of Martin

Luther. Catholic schoolgirls were forbidden to see this movie. The religious aspect of the film was enough to gain her grandmother's approval. After all, the family was Anglican, not Catholic.

It was agreed that the four friends would go to the matinee. There was not enough time to go home and change out of their school uniforms. If the nuns weren't going to see the film, who would tell them some of their students went? They pooled money for treats and one was charged with making the purchase before the movie started. She stood up, turned, froze and then slid way down in the seat, calling her co-conspirators' attention to the back row. There sat Sister Superior and Sister Magdalene. A decision had to be made at this point and Elah was called on to make it. Leave now or later? If their situation could be described as anything but trouble, Elah made the choice. "We may as well see the movie, we've already paid."

"It was free, Elah," one angry girl reminded her, "and the ticket collector said your uncle doesn't own the theater. He is only the projectionist."

"I never said my uncle owned the theater, but I know I won't be giving away any more free tickets." The girl, who scarcely lifted her head high enough to see the screen, passed the money back to the others, saying she didn't want anything. "Whoever want to get something had better get it themselves." It was a long movie, and the girls stayed back to allow everyone to leave. The nuns remained, sitting upright in indignation of school rules broken. As they passed, Sister Magdalene had a word for them.

"After devotion, please present yourselves to the office." Sister Superior looked straight ahead in glum silence. Here Elah stood, looking at the forbidden building, a place the school would not approve of a student entering in uniform. A place that would have been forbidden, had she bothered telling her grandmother. The two-story stucco structure was the seat of government and the highest point in the flat town. A venue for airing disputes and resolving legal matters, it was the judge's chamber, the clerks' office, and had a large courtroom that doubled as a dance hall and for special event functions. Some people went there for the entertainment offered during court sessions. Many of the stories were passed on to others as comedy.

Elah heard one story of a man who appeared in court with a mother and a child to deny paternity. He asked the judge to examine the features of the child and concluded there was no resemblance and therefore, the child was not his. "Dis yah pickney no fe me yu Honor, a jacket."

An alleged cow thief who had eaten or sold the evidence begged the court for mercy, saying he was not the one who killed the neighbor's cow, but he did partake of some of the meat. Major cases were tried in the city where there were more lawyers, judges and jail cells. In this town there were two lawyers and, counting the clerks who regularly gave legal advice, there were four, total. Directly below the court's office was a single-story wing that housed the police station. At the back of the station, forming an L, was the five-cell jail. The front yard was directly in Elah's view and deliberations as she pondered the possible outcome of what she intended to do. This government property, marked by an old tree with ashen leaves, was a witness to the decrepit condition of the building and constabulary force. Elah made up her mind. She was going to visit her cousin who was locked up in one of the cells. As she stepped into the yard, one officer asked why she was there. "I am here to visit my cousin."

"Where him work?"

"She is in jail and I want to see her." They whispered, then one broke out of the group and asked Elah to follow him. She hoped that Dolores was not put in the same cell as Ivan the murderer. She asked about the man and the policeman replied, "Him gaane to hell lang time. Dem heng him a Spanish town." Elah hoped Dolores had not heard the officer say this, because the girl was being held on a murder charge. The constable's voice sounded as if he were speaking through a bullhorn. He was dressed in blue and white gingham short sleeves, and black wool pants with a red stripe running down the sides. "So yu here fe see baby killah?" Dolores had to have heard his crude reference to her as a baby killer. He stood looking from Dolores to Elah. "She doesn't have any resemblance to you." Elah insisted that the girl was her granduncle's youngest daughter. "Ahrite, cousen or no cousen, you have 15 minute, which wherein time, ah will come back fe eskart you out."

Elah felt contemptuous and wanted to ask, "Escort me out of where?" He hadn't opened any doors to lead her in, so why would he have to escort her out? Judging by the hungry look he wore of a readiness and ability to exercise extreme power, prudence told Elah to hold her tongue and not tempt fate. The constable stood there awhile as if to confirm for himself a familial relationship. Dolores eyes were cast on the concrete floor.

"Me glad yu come look fe me." She wiped away tears with the sleeve of her dress. The constable left, seemingly satisfied that at least they knew each other. It seemed so unfair. Dolores was such a quiet and nice girl. Elah looked inside the cell. In one corner was a single iron bed with a thin mattress covered by a dirty-looking sheet. Dolores was too young to be locked up like some common criminal. She was 15 in chronological age, but perhaps 8 or 9 in understanding the size of her troubles. The afternoon sun cast a light and dark shadow that striped Dolores's face against the grey iron bars. Elah couldn't bear the thought that her cousin could be transferred to the city to be tried for murder, and if found guilty, hanged.

Elah was sure word would reach home and school that she was visiting some-one at the jail, but she didn't care. Dolores lifted her head; it may have grown tired of hanging down. She stared beyond Elah toward the low concrete fence with barbed wire wrapped over decorative cinder blocks. A world at a crossroad defined by life forms of varying types: A rum bar, a wholesale grocery shop, two stop signs and a constant flow of tractors pulling trailers piled high with sugar-cane. The coolies reclining on top covered their eyes to shade the sun, but left spying room to look for Constable Grover Gordon, GG for short. Rain or shine, this corner was his beat.

A cut above the regular policeman, the constable wore a red cummerbund at the waist, a matching wool cap with a red band around the crown and a short-sleeved striped shirt. His whistles, keys and emblems of service were scat-tered about his person. In a town where the constabulary force did not have handcuffs, the officers used words instead. "Walk wid me." The lawbreaker may argue, but knows better than to disobey. No one was exactly sure of his rank, but the constable proved that he had authority and plenty of it. He showed every bit of his love of arrest in his square-set jaws, clenched to notify the lawbreaker that he was serious.

At the rum bar across the street there were sometimes loose ladies sipping free drinks and making carnal promises. Several workers at the wholesale store stood in front to be entertained by the arresting tactics. Constable Gordon was resolute in his power of deterrence and ready to execute Her Majesty's service. One blow on his whistle meant "stop;" two whistles signified a serious breach had occurred. Three was a call for back up to "walk wid" the lawbreaker around the corner to the station. The cyclist was just giving someone "a drop as a favor," and ended up hurting himself and getting arrested for breaking a stop sign. "Stap means stap." Constable Gordon recited the law in those three words. His whistle, the argu-ments and corresponding laughter combined to form a musical theater of the absurd. Drunks fell over in hysterics. The wholesalers clapped when they heard some new or exciting excuse. They hollered, "Leave it to the Coolie man, a bigger liar can never be found." Unable to leave his post unless relieved, the constable whistled for back up to haul people off to jail or watch over the crossroads while he took them back to write the summons.

Dolores cast her eyes back to the floor. She covered her ears as if the loud chat-ter, whistle blowing and laughter would drive her crazy. Elah wanted to laugh at the dark comedy happening outside, but she couldn't. The juxtaposition of a jail cell, the low wall, the sights, sounds and smells from the streets added a cruel dimension to the girl's incarceration. It would be better not to see people coming and going, not to hear peals of laughter, not to hear the constable's whistle. At first, Elah couldn't believe it. Dolores would be the last person she would expect to find in prison. She didn't know the details beyond the rumor that Dolores had a baby and the infant died. She hoped Dolores would say something to give her an opening to console, comfort or just empathize, but Dolores didn't seem to want to talk. She began to wiggle her toes nervously in the slippers. Her feet were dry and dusty. Dolores seemed to have forgotten, but not really, that Elah had been standing there. It wasn't so long ago that she had accompanied Elah to the bus stop and helped carry her bags.

Elah tried to think of a way she could free Dolores. Maybe she could ask a cousin to get one of his friends to unlock the cell door so she could escape. He could offer to give them the gun he brought back from America. He didn't need it anyway and his police friends didn't have any. She knew that her cousin regularly smoked ganja and gambled with many of the men in uniform. Perhaps somebody owed him money or a favor. But if they were to let her out, where could she go? Elah couldn't take her in and it seemed as if her parents' doors were permanently closed. Dolores was alone on that wing in that shallow concrete box secured by rusted iron bars clamped shut with a huge padlock. If there was blowing rain, she'd get wet. "Me glad you come look fe me. Mama and Papa vex wid me."

"How long will you stay here?"

"Me doesn't know."

Elah stood there, the sunlight bouncing off her back and casting her shadow on the wall inside the cell. It was evening and she had been there for almost two hours. She felt that by not talking, Dolores wanted to prolong the visit. Elah was already late getting home, so a few more minutes wouldn't matter. She heard the policemen under the tree talking and laughing. When it grew silent, Elah figured the constable was on his way to escort her out. Whatever kept him from coming and kept Elah from leaving was fine. She didn't want to leave. The thought had just escaped Elah's mind and was floating among the atoms of good and bad karma when she heard the jiggling of keys. According to his stopwatch, 15 minutes were up.

"Come," he said to Elah. "Me have tings fe do." Elah heard herself asking, "What things?" But again, good sense stepped in and turned her utterance into a plea for five more minutes. He promptly denied this request, asking Elah if she thought this was a dolly house. Dolores looked up when she realized that Elah had to leave.

"Ah glad you come fe look fe me." She brushed away tears with the back of her hand. Elah tried to be brave and to show some optimism. She couldn't let Dolores see the swelling of tears in her own eyes.

"I'll come back to see you."

"That is ef she deh yah," the constable said callously.

"I love you Dolores."

Elah saw her face. Tears rolled down as if on an automatic overflow, because her eyes were vacant without a trace of connectedness. She had already escaped from the body, died, leaving the shameful husk of a scorned woman. Elah became angry when she thought about the hypocrisy and double standards that drove young girls to risk death and jail so their families could avoid the shame. Elah didn't feel it was safe to leave. She was afraid of what may happen to Dolores when no one was watching. She lingered as his keys made ominous noise, reminding her that 15 minutes were up. She was slow to take the hint.

"You want to join her?" The constable shook the keys attached to his wide leather belt with a seriousness displayed by his clenched jaw. Elah assured Dolores that she was not alone, that she had a friend who would stick by her, and most importantly, assured the girl that whatever happened was not her fault. The constable entered the private conversation. "So whose fault it is? Is bad advice you giving your cousin. Anyway, me have tings fe do so come on." By her presence, Elah wanted to give Dolores hope.

It seemed to Elah, who was growing up in the church, that there was no meaning in all its teachings. They were as hollow as giving hope to a girl who would certainly be hanged or imprisoned for life. Elah knew many girls who had died as a result of botched abortions. In one case, embalmers had washed the body and arranged her small hands as if she were about to say Our Father. None of the pain she must have endured showed in her face. Melted ice dripped into the two buckets placed at either end of the curled zinc on which she lay. The sheet covering her body formed a tent with her belly as the pivotal point. Her family said it was obeah that took their daughter's life; some pointed to the married gas station owner as the one who made the payment. Elah thought about the song without which a burial could not be a burial. It was mournfully sung to wring all the tears and sadness and lay them in the open to show extreme collective sorrow and grief.

"There is a green hill far away beside a city wall where the dear Lord was crucified He died to save us all."

The mournful refrain seemed as if it were immortalized in the memory of the entire population of townspeople. Many people joined the funeral procession only to lend their high octaves and discordant voices to "Green Hill." They sang it for the American sailor that only three people had seen, a local diver who was paid to retrieve the body and who almost lost his life in the process, and the two embalmers who remarked that the man had the prettiest blue eyes and a cross around his neck with Marie inscribed on it. His wife did not come to claim the body or attend the funeral, but the entire town turned out and marched the mile-long procession to the graveyard. Many of the prostitutes had talked to fellow crew mates and said they heard the boson had pushed the young sailor overboard. The police inspector was still gathering evidence when the ship left with its cargo of brown sugar and the murder suspect. The justice system at least treated the abortionists, the pedophiles, rapists and murderers equally.

The passing of a loved one was observed in three different events. First, the wake. Friends and neighbors dropped in and often brought soft drinks or food to share on the night after burial. The spirit was believed to leave the body on the third night. Family and acquaintances sat around and reminisced. The family provided food and drinks for friends on the ninth night. This ended the formal period of the passing. On this night a group of men—unrelated to the family—walked around the neighborhood dragging tin cans on strings and banging spoons on small zinc tubs and sang farewell. "Woman pussy sweet but eh kill man dead. O. O. Eh kill man dead." The repetition of those two lines comprised the song. It seemed as if it were gender neutral, because it didn't matter whether the deceased was male or female. It boiled down to blaming the woman for all the woes. They called this lewd and lascivious display of bad taste Gerray. Her parents probably won't even have a funeral for Dolores. There wouldn't be any singing.

Elah had broken the rules and there was going to be a price at home and at school, but as long as Dolores was locked up in that cell, Elah would return to visit. The lyrics of a calypso came closest to dramatizing the ignorance of young women. The girl in labor begs her mother to send for a doctor to cure her ailment. She believes an injection would do the job.

Mama me belly ah hurt me send fe de dacta fe cure eh. Him geh me one spinal injection eh run right up in me section.

The following week, Elah took some treats to give to Dolores and was shocked when the constable told her that her cousin had been taken to the city to be tried for murder. "Baby killer gaane ah town. Check back and ah will let you know if ah find out anyting, which jail dem have her in." Dolores was now out of reach to Elah. Her fate rested in the scales of a judge who will base his decision on the facts without attendant factors: her age, her state of mind, her environment. He will pass a judgment to perhaps take her life, not knowing that this was a frightened child who was afraid to bring shame on her family. Perhaps Dolores won't feel the noose tightening around her neck; it's impossible to kill a woman who is already dead. "Ah glad you come fe look fe me."

When no one else would talk about what happened that landed Dolores in jail, charged with murder, Elah asked her mother. Louise was 15 when she found herself expecting. She, too, had to make a decision whether to carry the fetus to full term or do as many had done: Have an abortion. Louise said if Dolores had confided in her, the outcome may have been different, but she didn't even know the girl was expecting. Dolores didn't want to disgrace her family, especially her mother, who was an official in the Salvation. It was early in the morning when the labor pains started. She sneaked out of the house and went to the latrine but was unable to eject the baby into the pit as she had hoped. Wracked with pain, she moved to lie down on the grassy area nearby and the child came. Her sister found Dolores lying unconscious and hemorrhaging. Next to her, the tiny infant lay crushed beneath a large stone. "It was the prettiest Chiney Royal boy baby I have ever seen. Such a pity."

Elah was glad her mother had not made the same decision.

Roommates for Life

"Go off your head? You off it already. Your cousin Nell has a profession. What do you have?" *Elah wanted to say brains, but she loved her cousin and wouldn't want to infer that she wasn't as smart.* Elah planned to learn clerical office skills and, after all, she was not without credentials. She had excellent recommendations. The owner of the store where she worked for several summers said Elah was conscientious, a quick learner, honest and dependable. The proprietor of an exclusive day school where she worked as a teacher's assistant was not as effusive. "You need to learn to spell and to be effective in controlling the children's behavior. Otherwise, you are a cheerful, enthusiastic and a dependable young lady." Before Elah realized the letters had been transposed, the children were yelling "trian" and spelling what was written on the board. Elah was the new summer intern referred by her school. The children were unruly and unaccustomed to dealing with anyone other than Mrs. Bremmer, the authoritarian. As soon as she left the room, all hell broke loose. Three-year-old Christine began to jump, and when Elah told her to return to her seat, the child refused. "I won't stop. I won't stop." She sat quietly as soon as the headmistress entered the room. She was sure the store would take her back, but she wasn't so sure she would have a job with Mrs. Brimmer another summer.

Elah's sights were set on the big city, following in the footsteps of her cousin Nell who was proficient in embroidering, smocking and tatting. She had found work using those skills in the tourist industry. Nell was making small, Irish linen handbags for a local craft shop. Elah planned to get a government job that had all the perks, including long leave, morning and afternoon tea, and a towel on the arm of her swivel chair. She had her sights set on traveling, and civil service employment would give her that opportunity. Used to hearing Elah's grandiose plans, her grandmother dismissed them as rubbish and reminded Elah that Nell had marketable skills. The woman wrinkled her mouth as if savoring the after-taste of sour orange. "Most girls your age look forward to marriage and settling down with a family. You," she waved her hand in the air, "want to go gallivant-ing, wasting up your life. Chups." She made the familiar sound denoting non-sense. "You want to travel? On what? Air?" Elah brushed off the negative comments as a dog would shake off water. "Not right away, Grandmother. After I save enough money." Her grandmother replied, "Ha, ha, ha. Hahahaha," and doubled over in pain from laughing. When the woman straightened up, she gave Elah another shot of ridicule.

"You couldn't even keep the one penny I gave you long enough to put it in the collection plate at Sunday school. You ran to Monteeth's shop and spent it on sweeties. Save money to travel? You still owe the man money for all the candies you trust."

"Well, should he be trusting candies to someone he knew was not working?"

"You've started early, haven't you? Hanging your basket higher than you can reach it. All I can say is, pity poor Nell if she takes up your responsibility."

In a place where the opinions of children or young adults were ignored or repressed, Elah did not fit the mold. Almost four years had gone by since Nell rolled up a few pieces of clothing, stuck them in a small grip and left on a five o'clock bus for the big city. It was now Elah's turn. Elah was looking forward to joining Nell, as was agreed, but it seemed as if Nell was having second thoughts. Nell wrote to her mother, Elah's grandaunt, knowing the letter would be read at the dining table.

"*Dear Mama,*" Vera read the first several lines to herself saying, "and so on and so on." Lottie appeared anxious for her sister to continue. "*I don't think Elah should come up here because it is very dangerous. Mrs. B. would like to move from this place, but they've paid off the home and it will be hard for them to sell it now and so and so on. Elah should try to get an apprenticeship in Lawyer Mattimore's office where she could learn clerical office work. Jobs are hard to find here if you don't have experience or skill.* And so on. *Say hello to Dudley, Alton, Milda and the children.* And so on and so on. *Your loving daughter, Nell.*"

Vera folded the letter and stuck it into her dress pocket. Elah excused herself from the table, went outside and vomited all the mackerel and bananas she had just eaten. *She made me a promise.* Elah and her grandmother argued well into the night over Nell's letter. The last words were, "You are not going anywhere. Your cousin thinks it is dangerous and she wouldn't say that if it were not true." Elah had been thinking about this subject for a long time. She had never included Nell's cold feet in the equation, but her mind was flexible and capable of using the lemons to make lemonade. She may have misspelled train, but she knew how to read her Aunt Vera. She was the smarter, more liberal and practical of the two sisters, and Elah knew she would be prepared to listen to reason. The Brodricks were stuck but she and Nell could easily live together in a nicer neighborhood. With two salaries, they'd be able to do better and look out for each other. Elah had shifted the argument to the sisters, putting her bet on her Aunt Vera. Next, Elah wrote to Nell without mentioning the family had received her letter.

"*Dear Cousin Nell: Please pick up some government application forms for me, as I plan to find a government servant position.*" Elah added the usual family banter about Milda's baby. "*I held Jarret so he could see over the fence and the boy pee-pee on my head.*" Nell did not write that often. It would be several weeks to a month before Elah expected to get a response, if she replied at all. Much to her surprise, Nell's letter came back within 10 days. "*Pick up applications?*" She didn't even say hello. "*You must take a test if you want to work for the government, Elah. I know many bright people who take the test and fail it. Everything is not as easy as you think. You could do an apprenticeship at the court's office to get some experience in government requirements and procedures. Didn't Mama tell you what I said in my letter?*" Realizing that Nell was well worked up in cold feet and not wanting her to make any desperate attempts to enforce her advice, Elah decided she ought to acknowledge Nell's letter right away.

"*My dear beloved cousin: Yours of the sixth instance was received. I will be going to see Miss Hamilton at the court office and Miss Mazie at the solicitor's office on Tuesday coming. I will let you know how it goes.*" Elah did exactly what she said she would do and the news got back to her grandmother, as she knew it would, before the end of the day.

"Nell was right. It would be better for you to get some experience here before you go to the city. Miss Hamilton said that you presented yourself so nicely, that if something comes up, you'll be the first to be notified. I don't think Mazie is going to teach anybody anything to put her job in jeopardy, so I wouldn't be surprised if you don't hear from her." Elah wasn't going to hold her breath. Miss Hamilton had been working decades even before Elah was born. She had arthritis, joint pain, stomach troubles, shingles, and whitlow in several of her fingers. Elah knew this because her Aunt Vera had treated the woman with all sorts of herbal medicines and poultices. She and Miss Mazie provided legal advice to people who came to see the lawyer.

Elah began to buy up little personal items like lipstick, rouge, a pair of high-heeled shoes for interviews, stockings, a few chemises and panties. She hid everything so that no one would know the level of her preparation. Elah left a few shillings in her savings account so as not to alert the manager who would surely share the news with her grandmother. A few weeks after graduation, Elah was ready. She said, "No thank you," to the woman who wanted her to come back and work in the store. She dispatched another letter to Nell. *"Dear Cousin Nell: No luck so far at either place. I am coming up to take the government test. Don't bother, I will pick up the application forms myself. The bus will get in around 4 o'clock in the evening next Friday at South Parade. I will wait for you there, but in case you don't receive this letter in time, I will try to get a lift to the house."*

Nell didn't have time to reply. It was a rough three-hour ride for Elah. Nell was there as the bus pulled up, wearing a simple floral dress with tatted collars. Her fine, curly black hair was rolled in a bun and covered by a hairnet. They hugged as Elah stepped off the bus, but it was obvious Nell was annoyed. Nell appeared to be thinner than when she left home. Perhaps Elah was looking at her cousin through more matured eyes. Standing next to Elah, she seemed diminutive in flats compared to Elah at 5'7" in high heels.

"I thought you were going to try and get some experience at home first? I broke the news to Mrs. B. when I got your letter yesterday. They don't mind, but the room is small for two people."

The ramshackle bus driver unloaded Elah's suitcase. Nell's already big eyes seemed to shoot out like a camera's telephoto lens. It was a gift from the store owner where Elah had worked; her grandmother believed it was because Elah was always telling people she intended to travel. As Nell looked at the grip, wrinkles began to form on her forehead and tiny beads popped up on her nose. Nell was such a timid person. People were rushing here and there bouncing into each other. The sidewalk was littered with piles of fabric pieces. There were glass cases filled with coconut drops, brown and white shamshucku and peppermint candy canes. Women sat in front of open baskets with mangoes, tangerines, sweetsop and naseberries. They were calling, "Stop 'ere pretty lady, buy someting fram me." Nell's patience seemed to be waning.

"The bus stop is over on the other side, Elah. Please look where you are going, for God sake." In every direction as far as the eye could see, there were stores and vendors. In a narrow side lane, women sat on tubs with fresh fish spread out on newspaper. Nell was growing a bit impatient. "We have a bus to catch." She tested the large black grip with belts across. "Why you bring such a big grip? You are going to have to carry it. We don't have any pushcart pliers here and we'll have to transfer at Up Park Camp."

Nell pulled on the cord, signaling the driver that the next stop was theirs. When Elah saw the slanted street going uphill, she understood why Nell had been so concerned about the size and weight of her suitcase and her high-heeled shoes. The Brodricks' house looked like a tiny room sitting on the top of a pyramid. At least on Big Mountain there were ways of walking around to get up and over. Not here on this paved pyramid of a hilltop. It was difficult for cars, let alone someone in high heels. Elah was witnessing one such catastrophe in the making. "We have to walk all the way up there, Nell?"

"Unless you know of a way that we can fly with this everlasting grip. I came up for good and brought a small suitcase, and you come for two weeks and bring this big trunk." *Two weeks! That's what you think, Nell Campbell.* They took turns with the suitcase. "What makes it so heavy?"

"Auntie sent stewed mango roast, breadfruit, bammie, plum cake, ackee and a whole lot of other things for you."

"So I was the last person to find out you were coming? You may pop your ankle and have to go back home faster than you think."

Mrs. Brodrick was sitting on the veranda. After brief introductions, Elah joined the couple for a dinner of rice and peas and brown-stewed chicken. Mrs. B was effusive in extolling Nell's virtues. "Miss Campbell doesn't stay out late at nights or keep bad company. That is why me and my husband love her so much. She is like a daughter to us." Elah wasn't so sure it was as much a welcome as it was a warning. She wondered what Nell had told them about her. When they turned in to bed, Nell whispered, "So you are going to take the government exam?"

"Yes, but I am also going to look for a job while waiting for the result."

"So, you had it all planned; what did Aunt Lottie say about your coming?"

"Auntie told her it was better for the two of us to be together."

"I hope you have other shoes or you will have to find a shoemaker to glue on the heel. That hobble skirt is too tight. I don't know why Aunt Lottie allowed you to wear it."

"You should have told me you live on a mountaintop."

"Tell you? I have to go to work in the morning." With that, Nell rolled onto her side, sighed, and went to sleep.

The two-bedroom brick home had one bath, a maid's room with a toilet and shower, a living/dining room combination, a small kitchen and one bathroom in the hall. The Brodericks' furnishings were old fashioned. A sofa with circular wooden arms and a matching chair covered with plastic, a center table with a vase filled with multicolored artificial flowers, a dining table and four chairs, and a china glass case with a storage cabinet below. It was amazing how clean and shiny the terrazzo tiles appeared for a house that was so close to the road. Elah would come to find out that Mrs. B. took her housekeeping duties seriously. Mrs. B. was short and plump. Mrs. B was a meticulous homemaker; it had been her only occupation since she married. She wore a round, black-rimmed vanity spectacle. Mr. B. was tall and slender, soft-spoken and pleasant. He was hard of hearing. He was retired from the Department of Lands where he worked for many years. The couple had been married for more than 40 years and had no children.

"Nell, do you remember the last thing you said to me before you left home?"

"It is better for you to stay at home and get some experience."

"Before that."

"That's what I remember."

"You said, 'Elah, as soon as you finish high school, I am going to send for you. You won't have any problem getting a job because red people find work easy.' You remember telling me that?"

"I have to go to work tomorrow."

"I thought you said you didn't work on Saturdays."

"Well, I am working tomorrow."

"Why did you write that letter to Auntie?"

"That's inconsequential. You are here."

"I knew you'd come to meet me. Auntie said it was good for us to be together, seeing that this place is so dangerous," Elah laughed out loud.

"Are you trying to wake up the people? And please turn off the light. Don't waste the current."

Elah got up and turned off the single bulb in the ceiling and continued to talk. "This room is smaller than any in our house. That's why only a single bed and this little table can hold in it. That place where you hang up your clothes looks like Auntie's clothesline except that this is inside the house."

"It's enough space and line for one person. You can take the test and pick up forms in less than two weeks, so you can rush back to luxury. Beggars can't be choosers. I am going to sleep." Nell rolled onto her side and sighed deeply. The next sounds were the scratchy snores of someone heavily burdened with regrets. Nell's feet were constantly in her face. To Elah, a sheet on the tile floor would have been more comfortable. Within the first two weeks, Elah had taken the test, filled out application forms and had a promise of a job if she passed the civil service exam. The third week, Elah found a job at a fabric store—one she considered temporary. She had gotten accustomed to sleeping on her side. This, too, would not be for long.

Elah's education about life in the city began at Paradise Fabrics, where she worked alongside a raunchy clique of women. Every day was like being in a pornographic workshop for sluts. Elah found this exciting. It was like the U-turn that Trevor made on the main street. The women talked unabashedly about their sex lives: How they did it, with whom, where, when, and other pertinent tidbits that they'd whisper so Elah couldn't hear. Elah was still a virgin, a fact she would have been ashamed to admit, although she suspected they had already guessed. Sometimes the ladies would be joined by their supervisor, a floorwalker they called by her surname, "Sterling." She was a pretty woman in her mid-30s with smooth charcoal skin, short hair and a shapely figure. She was Sterling, or Miss Sterling, depending on whether the manager was close or there were customers in the store. They'd motion for her to come close when juicy gossip was being shared. Sterling would walk over and scribble in a notebook as if she were working out a price on yardage. Saed Webber, the store manager, knew and would shout, "Cut it out, you ladies, and get back to your posts." When he'd get word that the store owner was on her way, he'd walk by and say, "Keep voice down. Mrs. Stoner will be here shortly."

Saed Webber came with his parents from Syria when he was a young boy. He was a tall and fat man with a slight paunch. He adapted well to the native laid-back spirit and had his own version of the local dialect. He was affable, easygoing, was liked and got along well with his sales team. The three women who formed the clique were his top sales lieutenants. They were able to talk people into making unwanted purchases and buying more material than the dressmaker required. He was no stranger to their trash talk. He didn't have to say much to bring his salesladies in line. "Cut it out. Customers in store. Voice down. Back to your posts. Mrs. Stoner coming." That would get them to act quickly because Webber would never fire them, but Mrs. Stoner could—and would. Behind her back, they referred to the woman as "Jell-O Battie." It was the way she walked in those wedge heel shoes and the type of silky fabric she used to make her clothes, that earned her the name.

Her parents were Syrian, but unlike Webber, Mrs. Stoner was born on the island. She was in her late 40s. Amira Stoner had the commanding walk of a headmistress used to sitting on a hard government chair. She didn't look like an entrepreneur with two flourishing business enterprises. Whenever she was in Paradise, she'd spot audit. Invariably every piece of fabric Elah cut while the owner was in the store would be subject to re-measurement. Elah understood yards and inches, but being able to cut the material between her thumb and forefinger was awkward. If she cut behind her fingers as Mrs. Stoner told her to, the customer could refuse to make the purchase. Mrs. Stoner saw Elah's continued overcut as giving away merchandise. There were many odd pieces that were wrapped in bundles and discounted to sidewalk vendors who traded in fabric ends. To Elah's way of thinking, it was better to run over a couple of inches than to shortchange a customer, and even worse to have to sell the material at a discount that the customer refused to purchase. But to Mrs. Stoner, "An inch here, two inches there, is how we lose money." Elah never had a fear of losing the job at Paradise. As much as she never considered it to be career employment, it provided income.

At the end of the day, there was always something to laugh about and to share with Nell. The floorwalker came back from lunch bruised, disheveled and with one of her shoes in her hand. She told the women that she had been in a fight with another woman who was trying to steal her boyfriend. The other woman was a supervisor, a senior staffer at the store. Nell listened and waited for all the details before rebuking her cousin.

"Character, Elah, does not show in one's dress or position or with whom one sleeps. It is shown, Elah, in the way one conducts herself. Keep away from them for God's sake. They are dirty people." Dirty or not, they livened up a dull and boring job. One of the clique invited Elah to her birthday party. She thought it would be fun. Despite what Nell thought, Elah felt they would protect her from harm. "You are invited to a party in Trench Town? Do you have a gun or a switchblade knife? Aunt Lottie should hear this! She would send for you straight away."

"You could come with me."

"Go with you? What a way you bright. I am here going on four years and never found myself anywhere near that part of town. You came yesterday and already you have a party invitation. Take my advice. Decline." Nell picked up her *Awake* magazine and went to join Mrs. B. on the veranda. If she thought Trench Town was bad, how about the brothel and rum bars at the end of Wareika Road? How about the ganja farm behind their house? Nell could separate people from where they lived, in her case, but she lumped everyone who lived in Trench Town together. Mrs. B. had been clearing the junk from the back room and made the offer again.

"When you get on your feet, I will let you have the little back room for a reasonable price." Elah considered this a push to move and began to look for a place. Nell had to be convinced that the rent would not be more than she was already paying. Elah was prepared to move alone, if that was what she had to do. Nell's life was wrapped up with Jehovah's Witness. While she studied, read and sometimes went out to proselytize, Elah daydreamed about a government job and moving to a better neighborhood. Elah was worried about being stuck at Paradise Fabrics and in Wareika Hills. Elah went out to lunch with her friends at work and sometimes a few other girls who worked for the In-Bond shops close by would join them. She wasn't accepting invitations to go out at nights and didn't feel comfortable inviting people to the Brodericks' house. Nell finally realized Elah was not happy. She was not going to accompany Nell to the Kingdom Hall, no matter what kind of entertaining games they had there. "Some of my friends at work and I plan to have a picnic in Bull Bay on Sunday. You want to join us?" Elah didn't know where Bull Bay was, but as long as it was not a Witness event or in Wareika Hills, she was happy for the outing. Elah met the man she would later find out was Nell's boyfriend. He had been to the house, but they claimed they were doing Jehovah's work. He seemed as much a friend of the Brodericks as Nell's.

On her way up the hill one evening, Elah ran into a girl from her hometown. Elah was surprised to see Pansy so scantily dressed and leaning into a car talking to a gentleman. She wondered if Nell knew that Pansy lived close to them. "I saw your friend. You remember Pansy? I just saw her." Nell put a finger across her lips, jumped up and pulled Elah into the bedroom.

"Pansy is not my friend. She is a prostitute, couldn't you tell?" In their hometown, prostitutes wore dresses. They were poor and low class. Pansy was from a respectable family. She taught Sunday school and used to lead the young people's meetings at church. Nell must have forgotten that Mrs. B. was sitting in her usual spot. Elah thought it was on purpose that the woman's chair on the veranda was near their bedroom window. Mrs. B. cleared her throat as a signal. Nell ended the conversation as abruptly as she had dragged Elah into the room to deny friendship with Pansy. For sure Mrs. B. had heard. Nell mumbled, "Simple," as she wheeled out of the room.

Elah ignored the calls and whistles from men parked along the street, believing it was nothing unusual. But it took on a different meaning now that Nell said Pansy was a prostitute. Elah started to search the newspaper under "Houses to Share." She had to change bus three times, then walk several blocks to find the house. It was ranch-style with a garage. Green scalloped canvas awnings extended over the windows and veranda. The home was set back from the street on a beautifully landscaped lot. A low stucco fence had splashes of pink Bougainvillea creeping over it. There were two wrought iron gates, one for the car and the other led to a stone walkway that went to the house. The broad flowers on the red Antirrhinum plants in pots on the veranda looked as if they had been waxed. If the inside looked anything like what she had seen so far, Elah was sure Nell would love it as well.

They were an older couple whose grown children were overseas. The husband remained on the veranda while his wife showed Elah around. Two furnished rooms on a separate wing with a bathroom in between. They'd share the living, dining and kitchen. It was spotless. All the pots were hung on a rack and were shiny, as if they had never been used. A mop was turned up near the door and looked as if it had never cleaned the terrazzo floors. Elah shook hands and promised to return the following day with her cousin and the deposit. Nell knew the area and she was skeptical that the rent could be so low. "Are you sure?"

"Yes I am sure. Two pounds, 10 shillings is what she told me. I have the money for the deposit right here." Nell made sure the gate didn't bang as she closed it. As they stepped on the veranda, the husband sprang to his feet and offered soft drinks. Nell politely refused. In retrospect, Elah thought she should have done the same, but it had been a long walk and she was hot and thirsty. The woman gave Nell the third degree, then said faintly, "Why don't you look a bit more. I'm thinking it over and I will call and let you know."

"But Emma," the husband protested, "we told the young lady she could have the place if her cousin liked it. Do you like it?" His wife interrupted, not allowing Nell to answer.

"I didn't say they couldn't have it, Edward. All I said was, 'I am thinking it over.' I don't want to stop them from making further inquiries."

"But…"

Nell interjected a quick "thank you" to cut off any discord between husband and wife, smiled, and whispered, "Let's go, Elah." As they walked toward the bus stop, Elah saw tiny beads of sweat forming on Nell's nose. "Elah Renard, you have come here to interfere with my peace and tranquility. Do you think your little job measuring cloth can afford this kind of living? The woman said that she was looking for boarders."

"Well, why did she advertise under 'Houses to Share?'"

"What you think a boarder does, perch?"

"Maybe it's something you said that made her change her mind."

"Five pounds is more than we can afford, that's what I said." The woman never called, and Nell said it was just as well. Mr. B. got paint for the little back room, a place Elah was determined she would not move into. With more urgency, she kept looking.

*　　　*　　　*　　　*

Sunrise Crescent was a middle class neighborhood at the foot of the prestigious Red Hills. It was not worth three pounds, 10 shillings, but Nell felt more comfortable with that rent. The home was built as a two-bedroom with living/dining, a kitchen, a wash area and a servant's quarters. The primary tenants turned the living room into a bedroom and rented the girls two rooms that included the tiny maid's room with one window looking out on the driveway and a chain link gate. They'd have to share the shower. They were both slender, so that wouldn't be a problem for each of them to get in and out. They'd share the kitchen with the landlords. Nell would be satisfied with the small room, and Elah could have the larger one, which could double as a place to entertain their friends. They didn't have that many friends, and Elah agreed to pay the greater portion of rent.

They'd need to buy furniture, and Elah had no established credit. Nell was hesitant to sign as a guarantor. The salesman pushed timid Nell toward the signature line and quickly took away the agreement before she had a chance to change her mind. The move to Sunrise Crescent changed the dynamics. They were roommates, and not older and younger cousins. Elah thought her purchase was minimal; she was used to sleeping in a double bed. "Why do you need a double trunk bed with spring and mattress, a big bureau and a bedside table?" Mr. Campo, the owner and salesman, answered the question, making Nell feel as though she did not wish her cousin to advance in life. "You have to think big," he said to a skeptical Nell. After the man tallied up everything, Elah felt as if she should change her mind. Ten shillings a month, for life. She would never be able to pay it off. Nell withdrew enough from the Building and Loan Society to buy a single bed and a small table, all the small room could hold. They had to buy their own kitchen things.

Their landlords, who were themselves tenants, were another childless couple. Mrs. Reid was a stocky homemaker; she and her husband were about the same height. He worked in the construction trade as a stonemason. Mr. Reid struck Elah as a man whose ambitions exceeded his short stature and means. When she told him they had looked in Norbeck, he had a rejoinder. "I have my eye on a piece of land there to build an upstairs home." Elah watched as he mounted his bicycle and rode off to work. After the furniture was delivered, Nell invited the Brodricks to see their new home. Mrs. B. cast skeptical glances at Elah, whispering, "I don't see why you have to inveigle Miss Campbell to move and get herself into this big debt. The two of you could have stayed right in our home and taken your time. Mr. B. painted the room and it looks so nice." Mr. B. was more positive.

"You have been a wonderful, bright spirit that came into our lives and I am surely going to miss you. You can come up sometimes with Miss Campbell and pay us a visit."

It had been almost six months since she took the exam and she had not gotten the result. Elah called, gave her new address, and asked when she could expect to hear whether or not she had passed. The answer was not very encouraging. The woman said it could take up to a year because there were many applicants who aspired to work for the government and there are just so many jobs available and so many people to process the paperwork. Elah's job at Paradise Fabrics was secure and if they employed thrift, the roommates would be able to eat out at least once a month. Elah's friend in Notions lived with her mother and two brothers. They had become friends because Elah thought they had a lot in common. Neither one of them was a member of the clique.

Heather was quiet and circumspect, minded her own business and did not talk too much with the others. Her brother Clive took on the father's role in their family. He checked to see where Elah lived before he allowed Heather to spend some weekends. The way Heather explained it, she would be staying with girlfriends while her boyfriend played in his band. She would go home with Elah after work on Friday. Her boyfriend would pick her up Saturday morning and drive her back Sunday afternoon. Nell didn't know anything of the arrangement, but Elah was sure she had seen Alfredo's red Cadillac convertible. After some months, Heather said Alfredo wanted to leave on Friday because he needed to have more time to rehearse with the band. Elah did not think much about it. They were both adults and she was just being a friend. Nell would have objected to the arrangement if she knew.

Elah had not heard from her friend for a few days. She hadn't come to work and someone told Elah she had called in sick. Elah planned to call, but before she did, Heather's mother phoned to say Heather was sick. Elah found Heather curled up in bed, obviously in extreme pain and very pale. Elah closed the door and asked her what was the matter, but she wouldn't say anything except, "I am so sick. I feel like I am going to die." Many of the girls who had died in her hometown first complained of terrible abdominal pain. Elah suspected Heather had an abortion. While she was there empathizing with the secret she felt Heather was keeping, Clive pushed the door open and entered.

"So Elah, what you think is wrong with your friend here?"

"I am not a doctor, how should I know?"

"I see. I didn't think it was a good idea, but the dolly house mash up now. Heather will not be coming to your place anymore. I am going to see to that." He blamed Elah.

"Get out of my room. You can't tell me where I can or cannot go. I am 24 years old." Elah was surprised that her friend was that old. Heather missed two weeks of work. She never revealed the cause of her illness. Months later, she formally introduced her boyfriend William Winkleberry a.k.a. Alfredo. He and Clive worked in the bookkeeping department at Paradise Enterprises headquarters. Webber managed that store also, but Mrs. Stoner was their immediate boss and spent most of her time there. For a long time, Heather had kept her relationship with Alfredo secret from Clive, perhaps fearing he would not approve.

Alfredo was the base player in a popular band called Sounds and Pressure. He and Heather were complete opposites in every way. She was petite and good-looking. She wore her long black hair in large clustered curls that looked like florets on top of her head. She was always nicely dressed and had several cashmere sweaters. Alfredo had given her lots of fine gold jewelry, too. He was different from any man Elah had ever known. Alfredo wasn't handsome, but he had an allure that a woman could find seductive. He had sexy eyes with long eyelashes, thick lips that were glossy and his nails were manicured. Most outrageous of all was his conked hair that had been dyed fiery red. Elah was in the bank one day and he joined the line and called out to her. A few heads turned along with hers as she acknowledged Alfredo, and the other people stared in amazement. He was wearing floral pants, a yellow silk shirt and leather loafer shoes without socks. Alfredo was soft-spoken, not at all like the bold image he projected.

Alfredo and Heather no longer had to be surreptitious, because their friendship was now in the open. Elah invited them to dinner. Heather arrived first and opened the door for her boyfriend. Nell just about swallowed her tongue when she saw him. "Nice to meet you, Alfredo." The Reids were always very discreet when the girls had company, but this time they came out to say hello and to look at what Elah had brought into their home. The two lovebirds nested in Elah's dual purpose bedroom while Nell was helping prepare the food. As she peeled the yellow yam, dropping pieces into boiling water, Nell whispered, "Battieman." Blueprints for a homosexual were being drawn to fit the man in floral pants. Elah wished he would stay in the bedroom, but being a sociable guy, he wandered into the kitchen. His nose flared as he sniffed and approved of the aroma of spices. In an American accent, he said, "Something smells mighty good in here." Nell smiled, but Elah knew she was adding to the profile she had been assembling. As soon as Alfredo went back into the bedroom, Nell whispered and asked Elah if

Alfredo had ever been to America. She said, "No." With more certainty, Nell repeated her assessment: "Battieman."

Nell borrowed two chairs from the Reids for the guests and placed them across from the bed. She brought one tray with food and handed it to Alfredo, telling him that he could sit on the chair. "It's so comfy; we'll stay if you don't mind." He squeezed Heather, and added, "OK with you, baby?" Elah and Nell sat on the chairs. Nell, eager to make conversation, asked how the two had met. "At work." She knew Heather worked at Paradise Enterprises and had heard a lot about what went on there.

"Oh, so you work at Paradise Fabrics?"

"I certainly do, and by the way, I hear we are employed in the same business." Nell raised her eyebrows, wondering what kind of business Elah had told this man she was in. He saw the question in her furrowed brow and answered it. "The tourist business, that is. Didn't Elah tell you I am an entertainer at Tower Isle? On the weekends, that is. During the week I play with money, honey, and books with debit and credit columns."

"He's a bookkeeper, Nell."

The association with the man in floral pants who billed himself as an entertainer was not taken by Nell as a compliment. Nell kept quiet because she was paying attention, like any artist, to completing her portrait of a gay man with red hair. Alfredo ate his meal in separate parcels: rice, meat and vegetables. That confirmed it. She picked up her tray, saying, "It was nice to meet you, ahm…ahm…Alfredo," and left. Elah didn't see her until the following morning when she was getting ready to go to church. "The sooner you can get out of that place, the better it will be. Have you called to see if you passed the test?"

"Several times."

"What is a nice girl like Heather doing with something like that? Alfredo? Is that his real name? He doesn't look Spanish to me. Did you see his hair? My Jehovah!"

"He told you that he is an entertainer. Many of them wear those kinds of clothes."

"Never seen anyone dressed like that. My God Jehovah!" Of course she wouldn't. Nell didn't go to nightclubs or dances and didn't mix with people who did. Most of her friends were the women who worked with her at the craft shop. They wore hairnets and frocks that covered their knees. Her other set of friends were those at her Kingdom Hall who dressed like business folk. Elah tried to explain to Nell that Alfredo was joking. The comparison had to do with his playing at a known resort hotel where foreigners stayed and her making the small, Irish linen bags that were sold to tourists.

"Alfredo with the red hair and floral pants makes more money in a weekend than we earn in a whole month. He doesn't care what anyone says or thinks."

"It's not what I am thinking or saying, Elah Renard, it's what the Reids' neighbors are thinking about this property and the new tenants."

"You should get back to your religion. We could go to the Anglican church together. You don't have to go all the way to Wareika Hills where it's so dangerous. What if I write and tell Auntie that you've joined Jehovah's Witness? What if I tell her you are selling magazines to strangers on the street? What if I tell her you are still visiting that dangerous neighborhood at nights?"

"You are bold coming here and questioning my faith. Tell Mama? You know my age?" Nell wheeled with a parting shot. "Hell is full of people with red hair, lipstick, high-heeled shoes and floral pants."

Elah liked Alfredo. In a way, he was like the clique at work who talked unabashedly about their sex lives. There was something mesmerizing about these personalities. In their own way, they were as honest as Elah and Nell. They were not timid or afraid of what people think. Alfredo introduced Elah to a couple of his friends. Although she didn't particularly like any of them as potential boyfriends, they had lots of fun together. Whenever the band played in town, Elah and Heather would go to the club and listen to them. Elah enjoyed the company of these avant-garde devil-may-care people. It was exciting. Elah wore her curly hair naturally, but she wanted a change. Heather went to a woman who pressed her hair and made those tight curls on top. Elah wanted something with more pizzaz. She wasn't sure what style would suit her best, so she needed advice.

"Mrs. Thomas is the best. She will work with your natural beauty, honey chile. She's into tomorrow." Looking at her, Elah thought the woman was way beyond tomorrow. "She will change your outlook on life. Promise. You will never be the same." Elah told Nell she was going to the hairdresser after work, but didn't tell her where. The old Spanish-style building on Hanover Street looked more like a fortress to display old munitions than a high fashion beauty studio. Wide stone steps arched and joined a landing that led to the heavy, iron-encrusted mahogany double doors. This was in a section of the city where the old met the new. Large houses had been converted to commercial uses; a few others remained occupied as residential. Inside, the salon was out of step with the idea of tomorrow. It looked more like walking into the past, starting with the sinks. They were old and of different colors like aqua, pink, blue and yellow. The stylists' stations were small and cluttered. Students and assistants wore oddly colored nail polish. Some girls had dyed their hair green, blue or purple. All had names like Pinky, Sunshine, Moosey, and a few had believable names like Lana and Monika (spelled that way). The salon was filled with "tomorrow people."

Mrs. Thomas wore a white smock. There were tons of gold jewelry on her arms and fingers. Layers of heavy gold chains weighted down her neck. She was a hairstylist, taught cosmetology and made her own brand of hair products. While the girl with long blue nails scraped her scalp clean, she engaged Elah in gossip about some of their clients. She told her about a copasetic fashion designer name Teddie. "Listen to me. Don't say I said so, him is one of the biggest Battieman around town, but his outfits are outta sight." The best tailor in her hometown was a homosexual. He worked for an exclusive few who could afford his custom prices. Elah's father had learned the trade from this man.

"How can I find Teddie?"

"I will give you one of his cards before you leave." She reeled off names of people Elah had seen only on television who wore Teddie's designs.

Mrs. Thomas spun the chair around and used her fingers to rearrange the wet hair. She lifted Elah's chin, turning her head to look at different angles. "Cut it off. Liven up the color—a reddish auburn would look good. Get a pair of round hanging earrings—not too large. Use a cream moisturizer on your face; don't wear any other makeup. We won't straighten the hair, because it's pretty the way it is. A vegetable dye will work nicely. A monthly wash and deep conditioning, a clip every two months—depending on how fast your hair grows—is all you will need." Elah felt and looked like a new modern woman and she loved it.

"I cannot understand how you are so simple to cut off your long hair so you can look like a man." Nell didn't say anything about the new color. This new look electrified the ladies at work. They wanted to know where Elah got her hair done. Webber's somber store manager's nomadic eyes jumped out of their sockets.

"What a wey you look nice, Miss Renard."

On her next visit, while she was waiting to see Mrs. Thomas, a light skin girl who stood out for her plainness sat next to Elah and introduced herself. She was quite pretty. "My name is Lana. I'm the one who answers the phone and books appointments. Someone told me that you and my boyfriend are from the same place." Elah knew that "someone" was the blue nail girl who had washed her hair.

"What's your boyfriend's name?"

"You'll meet him next time."

"Give me a hint. Where did he live? What street? Where did he go to school?"

"I will make sure you meet him next time."

She wouldn't be going to Mrs. Thomas for another month, and Elah was curious. When she called to set up the appointment, Elah reminded Lana about her promise. She was going up the steps when someone called out. Elah turned to see a well-dressed man straddling a bicycle. He looked familiar, but she could not remember his name. "You don't remember me?" She expected that Lana's boyfriend would have a car. "Shartleg mon." Elah ran across the road and hugged Harry Brown. He looked so different from how Elah remembered him. Funny how people's names submerge while comic caricature becomes the identifying mark. She heard that he and his brothers had gone overseas. When Harry Brown left, the unfinished ship was still hoisted in his parents' front yard. The brothers (about six or seven of them) started a project to build a seaworthy vessel that could engage in the merchant shipping business. It had been in the process for many years and they were unable to find anyone who had the money or who was willing to invest in the venture. As the brothers left one by one, it was rumored they had gone to America with the farm workers' program to make quick dollars in order to finish "Adventure of the Seas."

One of Harry's legs was shorter than the other. Elah remembered how kids used to make fun of the way he walked. He had a lift on his shoe that equalized his legs. Harry had such a nice smile and pleasant disposition. "So I presume that Nell must be married by now."

"No, not yet."

"She still along with dat bowsee bwoy? What him name again?"

"Arif."

"Yes. I remembah. She still have him or I should say does he still have her?"

"He got married after Nell left."

"Who marry him?" Harry said with sarcastic surprise. "If that could find somebady fe married, me should get married too." As Elah turned to leave, Harry gave her his telephone number and asked for hers. "Maybe I will call sometime. Say hello to Nell for me." Lana must have been looking out the window, because as soon as Elah entered the salon, she asked if she remembered Harry. "He was my neighbor. It was a nice surprise because I thought he had gone to America." Elah told Nell about meeting Harry. "He looked really nice. You wouldn't recognize him all dressed up like some important gentleman. His girlfriend works at my hairdresser. They have two children. He asked for you."

"Did he say anything about the ship?"

"Only that he'd love to see you."

"It is not mutual. Anyway, Mama said Nigel had come home and he seemed more interested in Crook's rum bar than bothering with the ship. That's a bad luck family. You remember what happened to the father? They caught him with the bag of brown sugar he bought from a thief and locked him up. Papa had to go and beg for him."

"Harry didn't do it. Anyway, here's his number."

"Why are you giving it to me? I hope you didn't give out the Reids' telephone number."

"I don't understand how you were friends with Harry and Pansy and all of a sudden, since you come to town, they are not your friends anymore."

"I was never friends with any of these people, Elah. We grew up together in the same town. I knew them and their families and they knew me. I choose my friends, Elah. Carefully. Very carefully. You are too rude and facety, giving me Harry Brown's number. For what?"

She had never met Mrs. Stoner, but Elah had told Nell enough about the woman who wanted her to cut the material a few inches short. Each time Elah told Nell something about Paradise, she'd ask Elah if she called again to see about the test result. Mrs. Stoner was there, again measuring the material Elah cut.

"I warned you many times. I showed you how. Yet you insist on giving over-ages in materials. We are not in business to give away fabrics, Miss Renard."

"I am honest and I will not let you turn me into a thief."

"Oh yes? That's how you look at it? Hmm. Hmm." That was all Mrs. Stoner said before calling up one of her bookkeepers, probably Clive, to make up the three days' wages that were Elah's last pay. The clique cursed at Jell-O Battie behind her back and told Elah she would find a better job. Heather didn't want to see her friend go. Laconic Webber was impassioned in his reaction to Elah's firing.

"I really hate to see you go, Miss Renard. You could apologize and save your job. As it stands, my hands are tied; she's my boss." He shook his head. "You had such a bright and glorious futcha here." Heather had a different opinion.

"If I were you, I'd apologize to the witch. Cut the blinking cloth two inches short to please her. A lot of the people who come in here probably think 34 inches equals one yard; it's what they been getting all these years."

The unfinished ship was sitting like Noah's Ark in the Browns' front yard. Harry's father had been arrested for purchasing a crocus bag of sugar that had been stolen. His brothers left town, allegedly in search of money to finish the boat. Harry's physical deformity made him the butt of many cruel jokes. Were these all omens of misfortune? Perhaps Nell was right. The family carried bad luck genes. Harry said she was too pretty and smart to be working in a store. He expected her to have a job at Barclays Bank or some government agency. In the old country, they'd call that putting "bad mouth" on someone. Elah lost her job at Paradise two weeks to the day after she met Harry in front of Mrs. Thomas' salon. She was fired on the spot by Jell-O Battie, who said she had been begging for it.

Elah didn't think about Nell until the glass door at the bottom of the steps closed behind her. Her roommate was not going to be happy with the news. There was rent, food and installments on the purchase with Campo Furniture. Elah stepped onto the busy sidewalk in the midst of an ongoing dispute. A small Chinese policewoman nicknamed "Cobra Girl" was arresting a man for "repeatedly baking da law." As she put on the handcuffs, the officer maliciously kicked his piles of fabric, scattering them all over the concrete pavement.

"Sorry, but me locken you up today."

"Fe what? Mekkin' a livin'?"

"You need a p'mit. I have said it ovah and ovah, oonu tink is joke me mekking."

"Show me wha parmit looks like, for me nevah seen one all dem five years me standing out yah so," he replied, pointing down at the pavement with both hands.

"I'm tekkenyouin. Come." She checked to make sure the cuffs were securely fastened. As he was being led away, the man asked a colleague to take care of his merchandise. It made no sense to Elah that the poor man was going to jail for selling fabric ends on the sidewalk. She believed it was the work of Jell-O Battie and some of the other storekeepers. The small vendors with low overhead were putting a dent in their business. A crowd had gathered to watch the poor man being led away from his investment. Likewise, Elah saw in her mind's eye Campo's truck loading her bedroom furniture and neighbors peering through their windows to watch. The idea of her new circumstance blurred and became one with the vendor's grief.

Elah tried to delay going home as long as she could. She knew Nell would be worried if she stayed out much longer. They always told each other if they had to do something after work that would keep them out later than usual. How was Elah to know that she was going to be fired? Although the woman called her impudent and said that she had been begging to be fired, it was not true. She was punctual, reliable and believed she did a good job. All the way home, Elah thought about the ways in which she would break the news to Nell, and decided to do so without any flourish. As she suspected, all hell broke loose. Nell stirred up a good amount of wind, thrashing her arms about on that hot September night. This was to be their second big quarrel. The first had taken place at the Brodricks.

"Yes, now Jesus. I knew it would happen. I should never have given up my room with Mrs. B. Is not a little warning she gave me about moving with you?"

"You've been talking about me with that bitch?"

"Have mercy, me God, you look on a big woman and call her a…Well, I am not going to say it."

"Bitch."

"Back to the problem you have now landed in my lap. What you intend to do with your show-off self? Inveigling me out of my afforded room into this three-bus-behind-God's-back place then leaving the one little job. Pride can pay rent? Answer me. Couldn't you wait even six months?"

"Don't worry. Tomorrow I'm going to look for a job."

"You had one, simple. It was paying for the elaborate set you trust from Campo with my signature." Nell threw her hands in the air and sweat beads began to appear on the bridge of her nose. "My good name gone to hell because of you. Look what me have? You see? (Pointing in the direction of her room.) A single bed, eh heh. When I lay down in it at night, if not for the worry about you and the rent and staying out late at nights, I could sleep to my heart's content. Now…" She trailed off, her voice trembling with hushed tears. Nell went to her room and slammed the door. Elah was worried. She was having trouble going to sleep, thinking perhaps she should have apologized to Mrs. Stoner. She peeked into Nell's room. There she was, laying motionless on her back like a dead woman. A washcloth across her forehead filled the room with the smell of Bay Rum. Elah had not thought of the effect unemployment would have on Nell, but it was too late. Not even Webber could help her get the job back. Nell left for work early the following morning without calling out to Elah as she usually did.

Elah stayed in the bed the entire day, thinking strategy. Mrs. Reid called out to see if she was all right. Elah told her, because if she had not heard the quarrel, Nell would be sure to say something to the landlord. Elah called, but there was no word on her civil service test. Perhaps Nell was right. Many people failed and now she may be among the failures. Elah looked in the mirror trying to gather up the visible fragments of her discontent for storage. She should go back home and wait for the result. Not possible. There was rent and Campo. Elah had invested in a room of furniture, a new hair style, wardrobe and found a nice man with potential. They had gone out on several dates, and Nell said he was a decent and ambitious fellow. She liked Louis. Everything was going fine. Now it ended as it began: on yards and inches. Elah was disheartened, but not discouraged. She had her plan and was determined that she would not return home without landing a job.

She started at the places she and Heather often visited to sample perfume and to look at jewelry. Elah knew some of the girls and thought they'd tell her if there was a vacancy or one expected soon. She wanted a job right now. The same day. Mrs. Thomas did more than change her hair. Alfredo was right, she had given her a new and modern outlook on life. Elah knew intelligence was a plus, but not a requirement, in these jobs. If any vacancy existed she'd qualify. She ran the comb through her hair and marked an "X" with her lipstick on the mirror. *Nell may have already called Campo and offered them a chance to get the furniture while it was still in good shape.* Carefully slipping on silk stockings, brassiere and a camisole, Elah stepped into the yellow linen dress with the sleeves Nell had embroidered, and zipped it up. Elah closed the door softly as she left the house, but saw the landlady peeking through her window curtain as she walked to get the bus. She had never thought about the Reids. They knew Nell alone could not manage the rent and neither could they. It was the reason they were subletting what they called half of the house: A maid's room, the living room and the shared kitchen.

The search for a job began at the bottom of the street near the water's edge. "Fill out a form and leave it. We will call you if something comes up." Crisscrossing on both sides of the street, she evaded the eyes of those girls who told her there were no vacancies. Elah needed a job immediately. Her hope was fading fast, because Enriques was the last In-Bond shop on the street. It was also close to Paradise Fabrics. All Mrs. Stoner had to do was cross the street to give her a bad reference. She was probably a friend of the jewelry store owner. Elah looked at the window display and the women inside looked out at her. She had been in there before, looking at gold bangles, but now she felt intimidated. The ladies had the same greeting always: "Welcome to the world of fine jewelry, Waterford crystal and Wedgewood bone china. What may we do for the lady today?" Their demeanor changed when Elah said she was looking for a job. "See that woman there?" They pointed to a long-necked girl sitting on a stool in front of the china display. It seemed as if Elah were seeing the place for the first time. Perhaps there was a different way of seeing things as a potential customer or a potential employee. Exquisite oriental rugs on the pink marble floors gave the place an aura of refinement. The women who worked together tended to form in bundles of three; it was no different at this shop. Their eyes followed Elah to the stool, then they huddled and whispered. If the young girl sitting aloft noticed someone was trying to get her attention, she made no attempt to acknowledge it.

"Excuse me," Elah said softly.

"Yes."

"I am looking for a job. Are you the manager?" When she realized that Elah wasn't a customer referred by one of them, she slid gracefully off the stool and smiled. She spoke in that slow broad English associated with one of the better private schools.

"As a matter of fact, we are looking for an assistant in this department. My name is Sonya, spelled s-o-n-y-a." *For what she needed help? The store was empty, but maybe there were busy periods.* It was as if the joy would bust her chest open. The bumping of her heart accelerated to a frightening degree. *Keep this under control, Elah.* "Just a moment, I'll see if the manager has time to see you. If he's busy, you could make an appointment to come back." They seemed as anxious to find someone as Elah was to secure a job. The man pranced out behind Sonya like a jumping jackrabbit. He exhibited the prosperous fat man's joviality. He looked at Elah as if he were selecting fresh produce.

"Good mawning." He extended his hand. "You are looking for a job? OK, come on back with me." A two-way mirror gave him a view of the door and jewelry counter, so he was keeping an eye on his business. It was more like a conversation than a job interview. Mr. Enriques asked what school she had attended and what brought her to the city and was surprised when she told him that she was fired from Paradise Enterprises for cutting fabric an inch over. He dismissed it as someone would swat a fly. He buzzed Sonya, telling Elah she would complete the interview.

Sonya asked when she could start working. It was already late in the afternoon on Friday so Elah said that she could start the following Monday. "Let me hear what he has to say." Sonya left and went back into the office. The women were looking at Elah and smiling as if to engage her to find out did she or didn't she get the job. She wouldn't move and waited for Sonya to come back. "I think he likes you. He says you are to come at 8 o'clock Monday morning." The shops with no vacancy wanted her to fill out an application and here it didn't even come up. Elah wanted to jump in the air and click her heels. Nell worked at the craft shop on Princess Street near the Myrtle Bank Hotel where tourists who could afford the little embroidered handbags made their purchases. Elah was excited. She wanted to go and give Nell the news, but she was a piece worker so Elah decided she'd wait until evening. She kept the dinner warm over a pot of boiling water, sat by the kitchen window and looked out for Nell.

Nell opened and closed the gate and began to labor up the driveway with bags of take-home work. Elah knew she was doing this to earn extra money. She ran out and took the bags from Nell and waited for her to come into the kitchen.

"I'm starting at Enriques Monday morning. They are going to pay me more than I was getting at Paradise." Nell sighed an uneasy relief.

"It's not little praying I have done, asking The Jehovah to help you find something and help you get serious about life. I called Mr. Campo *(I knew it; let's hope it's not too late to stop those recapture wheels)* "to ask if he could give us a little more time to pay."

"I am serious about life, Nell, and don't worry, I will make the payment to Campo the crook." Elah slept peacefully and in the morning Nell called out as usual.

"I'm going now, don't make the egg get cold."

Weekday breakfasts consisted of tea, two slices of bread with butter, a scaled egg and a fruit. On the weekend, breakfasts were more substantive. The cousins took turns cooking dinner. The roommates were back on good terms. Their landlords were happy.

At quarter to 8 Monday morning, Elah was admiring the beautiful items in the display window when Enriques' car pulled up. The driver stopped in front to the music of honking horns and the man made a mad dash out of the car and onto the sidewalk. He almost crashed into his glass window.

"Hold this for me," he thrust his heavy briefcase into Elah's hand. Throwing his jacket over his shoulder, he reached into his pocket for the key. "Everybody is always in some blinking hurry. They should get up earlier." The back of his white shirt was moist with sweat. None of the other employees had arrived. He talked to Elah as they walked back to his office, where she thought he would give her an application form. "I like your honesty and enthusiasm. Not many girls would have told a prospective employer that she had been sacked." He handed her a short form and Elah began to fill it out. "You can do that before you go home. I believe I heard Sonya come in. She will train you in the details."

All the ladies had arrived and he introduced Elah as the new girl who will be helping Sonya in China.

Elah had her first lesson in salesmanship. "Don't ask if you can help. Let them waste their own time and not yours. If someone wants to purchase an item, they will ask for help. Don't tell that to those women because they are always pushing people to buy. I guess jewelry is different." Sonya handed Elah the gold-trimmed, blue and white Wedgewood platter that had been on display, showing her how to take things down that people wanted to see. Elah was afraid to hold it. "It's only crockery." The platter slipped through Elah's fingers as she was attempting to return it to the display rack. Mr. Enriques must have heard the crash. The women formed a whispering ring. They looked from the owner to the long-neck girl and to the new employee.

Mr. Enriques stood with his eyes squeezed shut as if when he opened them he had better see the gold-edged platter together again. After a second or two, he looked sideways, down and up. His gaze switched from Elah to Sonya and the pieces on the floor. Sonya finally broke the silence. "Uncle," she said to Elah's surprise. "She is very nervous. She's never done this before. Please give her a chance; it was an accident. I might have gotten too close and bumped her on the shoulder. Anyway, it was not at all on purpose."

"On purpose?" He threw Sonya a stare from over the rimless glasses he wore when looking at numbers that were incorrect and sighed deeply as he walked back to his office. Elah sensed he was thinking in his round curly head that he had made too hasty a decision. The ladies snickered as soon as he left to go back to his office. Elah wished she was placed in jewelry, but there was no vacancy. While teaching Elah the basics, Sonya offered a running commentary about the three ladies in jewelry.

"You see that one?" She used her eyes to point. "The one with her hands full of gold bangles. That's Miss Delapenya. Look! She is checking if the two dozen pairs from the married men she's been sleeping with are still there." Sonya told Elah how her uncle came up with the idea to put Delapena on display as Sleeping Beauty to attract customers. Curling up in that little glass case like she's asleep, but make a man stop by and see how fast those green eyes flash open. That is how the wife found out where she worked. She's so full of shit, but that woman fixed her ass. She came in here, pulled the slut outside and gave her one backsiding. Uncle heard about it and he never put little Miss Sleeping Beauty back in that showcase. She was lucky he didn't sack her." Delapenya was glancing at them as if she suspected what was being said. It didn't matter because Sonya continued her story. "She tried to hang on, but one of her friends down there pushed her from behind the showcase, to help the wife complete the job of hauling her out-side. I felt sorry for the bitch, but she deserved it."

In three months, Elah must have broken three or four times her wages in bone China. Short Leg's bad luck had gotten hold and was determined to dog her entire life with failure. Elah was sure had it not been for Sonya, she would have been let go. Mr. Enriques seemed to be giving her a chance to resign. He didn't know that voluntary unemployment was not an option. Elah had become so nervous that it seemed by looking at china or crystal, she could will them to break. She wouldn't even take out a plate for the customer to inspect. She'd have Sonya do it or beg one of the other ladies to help. This could never be a long-term arrangement. It was a matter of shamelessly waiting for two letters: Fire and hire.

Mrs. Reid smiled as she handed her the letter with the government postmark. She waited, expecting Elah to open it. Elah took the letter into her room and closed the door. The way things were going, it could be a letter saying she had failed the test. She had passed the test and was eligible for an entry-level clerical position. Elah couldn't even be happy, because now she had to find a government department that had a vacancy. Then she had to go on an interview and wait for months for a reply. There was one agency that told her to call as soon as she got the test result. She called and they had an opening in the uptown office, which they wanted to fill right away. The interview went well and Elah was told that she would be hired for the junior clerical position. The starting pay was slightly more than she was getting at the jewelry shop. Elah had a list of agencies that she wanted to call before accepting the very first offer. She met the woman who would be her supervisor and Elah was hesitant. Nell couldn't believe what she was hearing. "Call them tomorrow morning and say you will take it. I hope they don't have anyone else in line."

"Shouldn't I just try some other agency?"

"Try, Elah Renard? Wait? Run. You are on the verge of losing that job." That was true, but Elah felt as if she could hold them off for another week while she called around. Nell, as usual, was more practical and often was right. She had become self-conscious, because every time Mr. Enriques passed the china department he scanned the floor. The ladies apparently told him Sonya was taking broken pieces outside to the trash. Nell was happy, but not as ebullient as Mr. Enriques. Elah went to his office door, saying she would like to have a word with him. Without glancing up, he told her he was busy.

"I have been offered a job in the government and have given my two weeks notice to Sonya." He shoved the headband of the loop above his eyes, pushed the tray of jewelry to the side, put his elbow on the desk and leaned forward.

"Come in. Come in. Congratulations! That's great news. We could shorten the two weeks if you wish." Realizing that he was showing too much joy, Mr. Enriques toned down his excitement. "Of course, we'll miss you. I was only thinking that I wouldn't stand in your way. I wish you all the best; sorry I don't have something suitable here." What he didn't know was that Elah needed that two weeks' pay. The government paid monthly and she had commitments. A letter came from her grandmother.

20th Instant

My Dear Elah.

The good news was greeted by one and all as words of joy. I am very glad to hear that after all this time floundering around up there you have decided to get serious. I have every confidence that you will keep this position because, short of criminal conduct, you have a job for life. Your aunt sends her love. Milda had a girl baby. Teacher Blyth went into the hospital for an operation. Teacher Green was well sick, she didn't come down last month. Cannon Cope retired and we have a new pastor, his name slips me at this moment. Alvin wrote to say that England is too cold, etc. He may be coming home. To what? My dear. To what? Alton found a new girlfriend and plans to marry soon. Dudley moved in with that careless woman who used to live in Copie's house. That is all the news for now. Behave yourself. Tell Nell thanks for the wire.

Elah was furious and pounced on Nell as soon as she got in the door. "Couldn't you let me tell them myself? You cry about paying bus fare, yet you fork out three shillings and go out of your way to Cable and Wireless to send a telegram about something that is none of your business?" Nell looked at Elah in the usual way.

"You see? You are too simple. Your business is my business and my business— I have none except the troubles you cause—is your business."

"I had not planned to say anything until after I completed the probation. Now you have advertised my name in the town Gazette for everybody to know that I got junior file clerk position with the government."

"Gazette? Oh! I see. You are thinking that your stay at this new job may not last beyond three months? Keep me on my toes. Yes. Float like a wet leaf on a pond any which way. I mustn't tell anybody. You may change your mind about a permanent position with the government. Well, Elah, my money is done. Done. Done. Done. I have no more savings at the Building Society thanks to you."

"I've paid you back every penny."

"Yes, you pay me back, then make long-distance calls and don't have the money when the bill comes, then you want money to send for Aunt Lottie, then you take a taxi from work because it's raining. I walk in the blinking rain like a wet bird because I can't afford a car taxi. I have to keep money under my blinking pillow to lend to you every time you hang your basket higher than you can reach it. The phone company doesn't have guarantors nor installment plans; they'll cut off the Reids' phone. My signature will not go on any paper near yours again in this life." She believed in the afterlife, so that wasn't as drastic as it sounded. "Mr. Campo called me at work twice."

"He's a thief adding surcharges to the bill. The springs cry like a blinking cat—meow, meow—whenever anyone sits on the bed. I have a good mind to let him come and take back everything."

"Surcharges? That is interest on the things you trust with my name over it." Nell didn't say anything about the faulty springs because she had heard the sounds and commented that it seemed as if the springs were loose. "One more piece of advice, don't make the same mistake you made at Paradise Fabrics. You may not be so lucky the next time. I am not going back with my tail between my legs to live with Mr. and Mrs. Brodrick because I was warned many times about the danger of moving with you."

"That's a joke. You can't compare this neighborhood with Wareika Hills and that dusty house on top of the hill that sits in front of ganja fields. Here we can walk freely at nights."

"Of course, you should know about walking freely at nights. Let me tell you something, Elah Renard, I am not planning to spend the rest of my life with you in any debtors' prison. Good night and get up early so you won't be late for work."

"You can stop feeling responsible for me because I'll be making more money. And right after I come back from the minerals and have my afternoon tea, I'll be looking for a job for you. Whether you like it or not, we are roommates for life." Nell wheeled off in her customary fashion, calling Elah simple. How the tables have turned. Elah reminisced about her brief encounter with a beauty agent while she was still in high school. Nell was still the family advisor on right and wrong. Her advice was sought on anything and everything that Elah did or said she wanted to do. The two had been very close prior to Nell leaving for the city. She walked Elah to Infant School on the first day and came back to walk her home. Using a comb dipped in water, Nell curled Elah's hair for special occasions. She taught Elah a lot of things, including how to make doll clothes and chocolate fudge. Elah was among few children, who at 3, knew the letters of the alphabet, could spell her name and knew many words. Although they were second cousins, Elah had come to think of herself as Nell's younger sister. Nell had taken on a mother's role and treated Elah in that way. The relationship changed once the two were in the city; it was big and little cousins. Then they moved to Sunrise Crescent and the relationship again changed. One common thread that could never be broken was the deep love they had for each other. It often did not show on the surface, but each knew it was there and that nothing or no one could ever break that bond.

It was another bright, tropical day when everyone was going about their tasks. Men driving tractors hauled flatbeds loaded with sugar cane, kids running behind and pulling off a few stalks. Female clerks and bank tellers aloft in high heels, upraised chins, slowly hurry to work. Men in pressed short-sleeve shirts and neck-ties stroll down the main street where everyone understood the irrelevance of time and haste. Elah usually walked to school with her friends, but this day she was alone and felt a surge of excitement as she thought of joining Nell in the city. It wouldn't be long before she finished high school. In the periphery, she saw a man dressed in a suit and wearing a hat. It was unusual because of the heat. Elah was wearing her sky-blue tunic uniform and a white cotton blouse, but sweat was running down her legs. The man had a slender briefcase.

"Hello there, Miss." He crossed the street and walked to meet Elah. "Hello, Miss." Elah slowed. "I know you are going to school, please spare me a small minute of your time." He began to walk alongside. Elah could tell that the news of her seen talking to a strange man would reach home before the school bell rang for dismissal. He was a city man. She could tell by his dress and the way he spoke. I 'ave been hadmiring you from a long ways." He tried to shake Elah's hand but she did not reciprocate. "H'am a beauty agent." This suggested an individual involved in selling beauty supplies and she didn't want to buy any. "My job h'is to travel aroung the hi'land and find beautiful young ladies to h'enter beauty con-tests. Young ladies who will one day represent the h'iland to become Miss World. Take my word, looking at you and seeing 'ow you walk, 'ow nice you look in your school uniform, hi can tell you could be a winnah." Elah wondered how long he had been studying her, to come up with his profile of a winner. All she said to acknowledge his greetings was, "Good morning." The faster she walked the faster he talked.

"My name h'is Carl Cooper but most people just call me 'CC' for short. So as hi were saying, there is money for scholarship endorsements and much more. The opportunities are enormous for a young lady like you." Elah pretended that she was not paying attention, but she was listening and was secretly becoming a little interested. Everyone followed the publication of beauty contestants. Elah looked at the published photos and judges comments and tried to guess which of the entrants were likely to win. She had never thought of herself as a contestant. "H'it would change your life tremendously believe you me. You h'are a bit h'underage I can tell, but for hinstance if you 'ave to travel to some foreign place to parade for Miss World, an h'older female would accompany you—a chaperone we call it. Think about it. H'i can h'ave a talk with your parents and don't worry, you wouldn't 'ave to stop school." Elah's reaction pulled some truth out of the man intent on talking her into a beauty pageant. "Honestly, a day or two, that's all, and transportation would be provided to and fro. H'i can get a local company right 'ere to sponsor you and take care of all expenses plus. H'i can line that h'up as soon as h'i 'ave a definite h'answer. By the way what is your address?"

"Twelve Queen Street."

"Is this a coincidence or fate? Queen Street! You are the winner and that is for sure. Let me 'ave a word with your guardians. Your name? H'i didn't get it."

"Elah Renard." He left her at the entrance to the school property, which was as far as he could go. Elah had an island history quiz that morning, but she was distracted by the encounter with the beauty agent. She sat in the back as usual because the girls in the front were called on first. As ill fate would have it, Sister Superior reversed the order. Elah's mind was just beginning to settle back into the scholastic realm. She couldn't believe that her name had been called to answer the first question on the quiz. "Me, Sister?" The nun looked around the room to see if there was another student by that name.

"Your name is Elah, isn't it?"

"Could you please repeat the question, Sister?"

"In what year did the British capture the island from Spain? Are you planning to answer today?"

"May 10, 1655."

"Correct. The first islands trade exhibitions?"

"1891, Sister."

"Good. Next. The Great earthquake. Where and when?"

"16...16...1692, Sister. Port Royal."

"June. Good. The island was discovered by whom and when?"

"Christopher Columbus...19...14...1914?" Elah was still trying to put the numbers in the right order when laughter erupted. "Be quiet, girls. Give her a chance to think. Order, please!" Elah was confused with the images of parading in a beauty contest, seeing her picture in the newspaper and thinking of the speech she would make in the Miss World competition. Another student blurted the answer "1494."

"There are to be no excuses. You either know the answers or you do not. You either studied or did not. Here is another question for you."

"Sister, you said only four."

"You did not answer all the questions. Now, which pirate became lieutenant governor of the island in 1673? Elah?"

"Henry Morgan, Sister."

"Good. Next test will be wider in breath and scope. Sit, please." Elah knew her quizzes at home would be different. As she imagined, the word had gotten to her grandmother that she had been seen talking with a strange man.

"Who were you talking to on your way to school?"

"A beauty agent, mama."

"A what?"

"A person who goes all over the island to recruit girls to enter beauty contests. You see't in the papers." Mr. Cooper had also been to see her grandmother. Elah did not consider herself a minor; in a couple years she would be out of high school. Nell had been consulted or told about this occurrence and her letter arrived almost two weeks later. Her grandmother read it at the dining table. All family letters were shared this way. Information not meant to be shared would be read as "so on and so on." It was addressed to her Aunt Lottie, the one who had written for advice.

"*Tell Elah to do her lessons and try to pass her examinations and don't let anyone fill her head with rubbish. They may call it pretty, but it can be an ugly business, tell her. Some of the same men who push young girls into this affair turn around and shove them into you-know-what and many end on the street with you-know-what kind of health problems. Mek him g'weh, Aunt Lottie, you are right to run him.*" Another family adviser volunteered her opinion. She talked directly to Elah. Teacher Green brought some fruits along with her advice.

"In the Queen's English, there are better things in your future, lovie. This is not at all uplifting. In the Queen's English, Lottie, you see how dangerous these people can be. Now the child is going to school and this man decides that he is going to interrupt her education to put rubbish in her head."

It was a dead subject. Elah knew that it was a battle she would not win. Several months after the photographs and results were published, the beauty agent resurfaced. Elah wasn't alone in the regrets department. He seemed more than sorry to see that after making a deposit of her beauty and talents in his bank book, it had been summarily closed by the "old woman." Elah tried to avoid him, more out of embarrassment, but CC had whipped up her anticipation of a great and wonderful future and at the same time fanned the flames of family discord. If he had such good insight, he would have remembered that she walked on the left-hand side of the street. Yet he called to her again from the opposite side.

"How-dee-do." He crossed over. "I know your mind is on your lessons right now and I will not detain you more than so." Elah slowed and looked around suspiciously while trying to be polite to CC. "Did you see't in the papers? You see who win Miss Sandalwood?" She did see the photographs. "The Indian girl what no 'alf as pretty as you. She put down one piece of dirty dancing pon stage in the talents department. That seems to mek up for the dry foot she showed the judge dem in the bath suit parade. You can still h'enter when you come of age." He gave Elah a business card telling her to call him when she was in a position to say yes or no. "Bye-bye," he said as their paths diverged.

This was all behind her now. She was going to be a civil servant and must forge her way without crown or scholarship. The city was a very different place, but with Nell to guide her, she felt as if she had carried a bit of home. At home, thieves were known for the items they stole and were sometimes jailed on the victims say so. They were stealthy and stole food items, clothes hung out to dry, small change. Nothing big or major. In the city, thieves operated during the day armed with switchblades. They'd weave in and out of a crowd, jump on top of cars or run in front of speeding automobiles. They snatched purses, gold chains, watches and gold bangles. Elah had her sunglasses stolen by a man who pushed his hand through the open bus window and pulled them off her face. They went into the stores and ran off with new shoes, bolts of fabric and ready-made clothes. People would shout, "Thief!" But they'd have to scramble to get out of the way of the glistening switchblade and often could not remember what the person looked like.

The speeding driver slammed on the brakes, but the car lurched forward and hit a woman, knocking her to the ground. The woman got up, looked around, and took off running. The driver considered himself lucky and sped away. In her hometown, a crowd would gather around the car and stay until someone got the station to get the police. Escape of the driver or bicycle rider, as the case may be, was out of the question—because the guilty party would be detained until the police arrived. She told Nell about what she had seen, and Elah felt she should have intervened. "Mind your own business and do not talk to strangers. This is not the country." Even though their hometown was the capital of the Parish, it was still considered countryside. Elah was getting into the stride of the city. She listened to Nell and most often took her advice. Nell told her which bus to take and where to come off. It would be her first day on the job, and she was unfamiliar with the area.

Junior File Clerk

"You can't miss it; there is a car dealership right across the street." Elah got off at the right place on the first bus because everyone shouted, "Crossroad." On the second bus, Nell said she should get off two or three stops from the crossroads. It was impossible to see the car dealership, because the bus was full and she was standing. To be on the safe side, Elah got off at the second stop; she could walk the rest of the way if necessary. The bus stops were far apart, so it didn't matter if she had to walk forward or go back. According to Nell, the sign was so big it was impossible to miss. Nell was sure it was at least two stops, so Elah figured she had not missed it. She decided to stop and ask directions after walking some distance and not seeing anything close to an automobile dealership. The uptown area had been commercialized. Large mansion homes had been converted into offices. The road had been widened to cut off the long and circular driveways and pedestrian paths. Traffic was heavy. Elah's skirt flared up in the breeze as cars whizzed by so close she could touch the occupants.

It was a legal and insurance office, and the receptionist was perched on a chair with her chin pointing to the ceiling. The telephone rang. She slowly and delicately picked it up, paused, then said, "Eliot and Eliot. Hold on while I transfer you." She turned to Elah. "You are hayre to see?"

"I'm kind of lost. I am looking for a car dealership."

"Gastons?"

"I'm not sure of the name, but if that is the only one on this street, yes." A second woman came out with papers in her hand; she looked at Elah and said, "Halio." The receptionist turned to the second woman and asked, "Jessica, whot is the name of that place down the road; the Hillman place. She is trying to find it."

Elah interrupted, telling the young lady that she had a job at the government office across from this dealership. "Whot? The Coop'rative Society? Oh. It's farther down on this side of the road. You cohn't miss it. You're going to work thare?" Elah thanked them and was about to leave when the receptionist added, "You ought to tell them to clean up that place, dem stringy mangoes fall off and make a big mess all over the street."

The woman was right. The driveway was littered with green and ripe mango pulp, and flies and bees buzzed around. It was an off-white or yellow stucco two-story building with a veranda. Several of the bottle-shaped concrete bars had fallen and were lying on the ground. Car tires made a path to the side steps, stopping short of a small outhouse. The very antithesis of anything like beauty and aesthetics was presented in the form of a government office. In this place, Elah sighed, she was to be a junior file clerk. She felt overdressed. A short bronze man stood next to a bicycle leaning against the veranda. His government-issued khaki pants and a short-sleeve shirt was Monday-morning fresh. A belt gathered up the excess fabric of his pants. As Elah approached, he straightened up, adjusting his posture to represent his official status.

A small boy pleaded, "Papa. Papa me wahn lunch money." The man was more taken with his appearance, pulling at his shirt and tucking it in a bit more. He tried to dismiss the boy as one would swat a mosquito, but the child wouldn't move. He pushed his hand into his pocket and handed the child some change. "Gwaane to school, boy." The minor looked disparagingly at the coins. "Gwaane to school, me sey." The child ran toward the little house and disappeared, leaving his father ready to face Elah.

"Good morning, Miss." I guess you is the new lady who is gwineto work wid Miss Clampson. Well, she soon come." He had a firm handshake, introducing himself as Nathaniel Barrett. "Everybody call me Lucky." Feeling disappointed, Elah took refuge under a large shade tree in the side yard that she would later learn was called "Watchie's spot." A place where the night watchman passed his time during the daylight hours. Is this the job she would have for life? Her grandmother said it would be a job for life, barring criminal conduct. Almost made her feel that today she ought to kill someone. She was thinking about Nell, who pushed her to take the first offer. Her standard was the upscale In-Bond shop with Persian rugs and gleaming china and jewelry. She knew it wouldn't be the same in a government office, but this place was worse than she could have imagined. If the interview had been conducted in this building, Elah was sure she would have turned down the job. She met the people in the head office, which was so much different. "I will let you inside and you can sit in the cool until dem come." *If the inside was anything like the outside Elah didn't want to go in there to sit or to work; a definite slide downhill.*

She followed the short brown man jumping from the step to the veranda landing. They entered a large room with a wooden ceiling fan and a fireplace stacked with old files. It still had a piece of the original rope that enslaved African children were required to pull to keep their masters cool. It was now connected to a motor that scattered the dust around. Someone had tried to turn this into a real office. At one end, cracks revealed the outline of a former window opening. Inside this plaster-covered window were framed photographs of three prominent people: The current British Governor, the Anglican Archbishop and George William Gordon, a historical figure. Elah read about Gordon, who had been a member of the House of Assembly in the early days. Gordon and Paul Boogle were chief among those charged with inciting the workers uprising in 1865. General Edward John Eyre was an extremely unpopular man who was eventually recalled and dismissed for the barbarous slaughter of more than 400 natives, and the hanging of George William Gordon and Paul Boogle. One of his staunchest supporters was said to have been Thomas Carlyle, the Scotsman whose translated works included Goethe and Friedrich Schiller. Charles Dickens also found a commonality with Carlyle's ideas and is said to have dedicated his novel "Hard Times" to him. Elah lingered at the photographs as she thought about some of the turbulent times in the island's history. This house had a history very likely built from money earned on the backs of Africans. It looked that old.

Lucky thought she was looking at the misalignment of the pictures, so he offered an apology. "I know dem is not straight, me not able to go on ladder to fix dem rite now." On the right of the photographs was an alcove that led to a bathroom and the kitchen. Two desks were in this large room; one with a swivel and two side chairs and a long desk opposite. The desk was placed in front of six wooden file cabinets. On this same side, a second archway led to the entrance foyer and the curved staircase.

"Mr. Dickey will soon come with his newspaper under his arm. Him read it like the Bible—cover-to-cover." Elah's eyes darted around the room like marbles on terrazzo tiles. Lucky jingled his keys to get her attention. "Mek we go to Mavis affice." He led her through the alcove into the kitchen. The linoleum floor curled in the corners and was sticky with grease. There was a two-burner stove with a gallon bottle of kerosene, turned-upside-down glasses and plates lined the narrow counter top, hitched into a sink, and a refrigerator that looked as if it was among the first models of electric refrigeration. The back door opened across from a one-room shack. "When Mavis is late for work—which wherein is to say that is every day—she slides in through this door. Dat little house is where Watchie sleep. Him is deaf as bat, but him have good eyes." The watchman's job was to protect the property. Lucky pointed to a two-room house where Elah had seen the young boy running toward. "That is my little quarters 'til me finish building me home." The two were back in the large room. Lucky pointed to the front entrance, saying it was used mainly by visitors, or when the big man came for meetings.

He preceded Elah upstairs, pointing out the manager's large front office. Miss Chin, secretary/stenographer, sat in an open area just outside Mr. Curtis' door. An adjacent front office was reserved for foreign visitors. Mr. Dennis, the supply officer, and Mr. Leatherwood, the deputy manager, occupied two adjacent rooms in the back. Lucky offered his opinion about the files stacked high on Mr. Curtis' desk, the files that lined the conference table, and the files stacked on the floor against one wall. "Him is a very busy man. Always meeting with people and directing them what to do. Poor Mr. Leatherwood don't get a lot of acting work, that is why him dess is so clean. Mr. Curtis doesn't go any further than Lucea to visit his family or to take a dip in sea water.

The bathroom was original to the house. A piece of plywood covered the top of the water tank and a cord extended the length of the flush chain, making it reachable to flush the toilet. The claw-leg bathtub was filled with old files and the pedestal sink was chipped and rusted. The tour was completed and they were preparing to return downstairs when they heard the sound of screeching tires and scattering gravel. Lucky ran down and urged Elah to follow, telling her not to say anything. He took his post next to the bicycle. Elah sat on the chair next to Dickey's desk. A woman called out from the kitchen. "Lucky, you here?" He jumped on the veranda landing, pushed his head in the doorway, and winked at Elah.

"You just coming, Miss Mavis?"

"Me been here over half-hour now." She walked out of the kitchen. "You must be Miss Clampson's new assistance. I am Mavis Grant, the office helper." They each went back to their workstation and Elah heard Lucky greeting the people who had just gotten out of the car.

"Good morning, Mr. Curtis. Good morning, Miss Clampson."

Curtis made his leap from step to landing. He was rotund and that took a lot of effort because he seemed somewhat disheveled. Why didn't they just fix the steps? Mr. Curtis wasn't in shirt and tie as she remembered during their interview in the head office. He was wearing plaid Bermuda shorts, short-sleeve shirt, knee-high socks and sandals. His old colonial-style briefcase appeared weighted with official documents. "The sun is so damn hot." He paused to acknowledge the new employee. "Welcome, Miss Renard, glad to have you with us. Miss Clampson is coming." Mr. Curtis marched upstairs, commander-style. Miss Clampson entered with a stack of files. A slantwise smile exposed the edge of a gold tooth. She was meticulously dressed, as Elah remembered, in starched white blouse, kick-pleat navy skirt and a three-inch black pump. She was still shorter than Elah in flat shoes.

"So you are here, lady? Welcome." Eunice Clampson had large breasts, a small waist, broad hips and was of a dark complexion. Short, tight curls encompassed her forehead and temples, a black pencil made eyebrow lines. Thin lips with dark red lipstick completed the moon face, as if it were a stick drawing on canvas. "You can sit there. I will be back shortly." She pointed to a straight chair in front of a small table stuck to her desk. Dickey arrived with his newspaper, smiled, and mumbled, "Morning." He scanned a few file folders, placed his feet on top of the desk, called out for tea and then disappeared behind the Gleaner. Mavis squeezed in behind Elah's chair with a tray. She brought in tea for the two officers, but asked Elah how she would like hers. Mavis put both cups of tea on Clampson's desk. When she returned from upstairs, Clampson made space and moved Elah's tea cup to the small table. Taking ladylike sips, Clampson surveyed her department. She looked at Dickey, who had his face buried in the newspaper. "My opinion is never sought, Mr. Dickey, but you are setting a bad example." The only sounds that followed were the flipping of the pages and a loud fart. Miss Chin came running, clap, clap, clap, in her backless high heels. Mr. Leatherwood entered, slow and casual like the deputy director. He licked his lips when he saw Elah. "Delicious. We want a junior assistant, too. Welcome, Miss Renard, we will be seeing a lot of you, of that I am quite positive. Eunice, I need a file. Send it up to my office right away, please." Clampson acted as if his comment did not deserve an answer and kept shuffling papers, opening and closing her drawers, and looking into the wooden file cabinets.

Elah had measured fabrics long enough to be a good judge of yards and inches. The table was about 36-inches wide by 40-inches long. The pile of files looked as if they were meant for the trash, but she learned that they were for her to sort and to file accordingly. Elah felt as if she should not go back. Why would they offer her such a job and why did she take it? The answer came back: Nell Campbell.

Nell was anxious to know how Elah's first day went. "They don't need a junior file clerk. A jackass could carry the bunch of rotten files to the dump. As you lift up the papers they crumble. And that woman!" Nell cast Elah a look of you-better-not-be-thinking-what-I-suspect-you-are. "I swear she doesn't know the first letter in the alphabet. Worst of all, Nell, you should see where I have to sit!" Nell stopped eating as if it would interrupt her hearing. "One little ole table and a straight chair. I have to pull it in so that the office maid can pass behind to serve tea. I have to pull it in when someone goes to the bathroom." Elah was preparing Nell for the blame. "If it wasn't for you..." Nell began to pick up her utensils and plate. "Now I have to play donkey to an idiot." Nell screwed up her face, contemplating the appropriate response. She put everything in the sink and started washing. She paused and turned to Elah, who was still eating.

"It's because of me you took that job? Have you so quickly forgotten that the man was about to give you the sack after you broke up so many of his products? Hear what?" She paused again, as if what followed was of great importance. Elah knew better. "Tell them you want fancy carpet on the floor. No, that you want fancy Persian scatter rugs, a big desk, a swivel chair with arms for your towel, and long leave right away because you plan to travel. Yes. Say to them six pounds a month, almost two pounds more than you were getting at the fancy shop, is not enough because you want to buy handmade shoes from Switzerland." She washed her dish, glass and utensils, dried them and prepared to retire or to read her literature. "Well, take my advice. Learn as much as you can from the idiot. Do the work, which is what I think they're paying you six pounds a month to do. You may have other ideas. Listen to me. Knock them out of your head, because I know the letters that spell trouble and I want no more of it." On her way, she turned, paused and looked at Elah. "We are having a young people's social at the Kingdom Hall on Wednesday night. The topic is 'A New World is Coming: Are You Prepared?' Winston is picking me up. Let me know if you want to join us." Nell did a pivot and went straight to her room.

Elah was beginning to believe she had sadistic tendencies. She seemed to be the lightning rod that revved Nell's engine and she enjoyed the discordant intercourse that often resulted. Unbeknownst to Nell, she always came away from the arguments with a nugget of good advice. The pay was good, the job secure and there was a possibility of transferring to another agency. Elah had to make the best of the situation. All her family and friends at home would know was that she was in a government job. Every chance Mavis got, she'd engage Lucky in gossip within an earshot of Elah. She heard Mavis talking about an affair between Curtis and Clampson and, as usual, she shared her day with Nell. "Why are you talking to the office maid and the messenger? I don't want to hear anything. If that woman was present at your interview, she can have you fired. Do not listen to Mavis or get involved with any sort of gossip. Do your work, which is what they are paying you six pounds a month to do." Nell had a point.

Elah needed supplies, and Dennis told her to write up the list and give it to him. A few days later, Clampson was waving it like a red flag. "Miss Renard, I have told you that things must be done through the proper channel. If our department needs supplies, the items must be submitted for my approval and signature." Elah thought she could bypass the route at the invitation of the supply officer, but she was wrong. She wrote the list, Clampson approved it and Dennis checked against the same items in the previous order. If he approved, the requisition was sent to headquarters. Once delivered there by Lucky, the receptionist opened the requisition, date-stamped and routed it to the respective section. Elapsed time for simple requests could be from three days to several weeks. No wonder the people in the court's office had so much time to swing around in their chairs; they were probably waiting on supplies to come from the city. Elah must be the only person in the government who wanted to get things done in a reasonable time. Government work didn't look as attractive as she imagined, but perhaps this was because she now had clearer lenses.

She returned from lunch to find more old, faded files had been added to her stack. Elah flipped through a few and decided that those without any trace of ink should be thrown away. She crushed these useless blank sheets and threw them into the wastepaper basket. Clampson looked at her in alarm. "Dear, dear, dear. Be careful what you are throwing away." Clampson dipped into the trash and began unfolding. "All right, these are no good. Miss Renard, stack the papers and let me have a look before you discard them please." This meant that these same files would again be returned to her to destroy. It seemed like doubling the work. Dickey never spoke much, but often he'd throw a dunce look at Clampson and smile.

"If anyone asks, I'm gone to a meeting with the bursar." If Clampson heard, she didn't look up to acknowledge. Dickey made his leap onto the step and took off in his car. Elah made a discovery in the files she felt was not meant for her to see. This was perhaps the reason Clampson wanted to see every paper before she discarded them. Elah held up the form and asked Clampson where she should file it. The woman acted as if she didn't know the paper had been included in Elah's work pile.

Clampson could say anything to Lucky, but she was very careful when it came to Mavis Grant. She lowered her voice, because the woman was either in the kitchen being unusually quiet or visiting with Watchie in the side yard.

"Oh! Thatt! The careless woman spilled tea on it and I tried to dry it off and in the process erased the 'A'." Clampson removed some of the files on the table, brought down the old Underwood, lined up the form and showed Elah how to hold down the shift key to make a capital letter. Just type an "A" there. I wouldn't want anyone to think I tampered with my own thing." She made it look easy, but Elah had never used a typewriter and she wondered about writing on a form that clearly had Eunice Clampson's test result. Elah was also thinking of the repercussions if she was caught. With a slanted smile showing an edge of gold, Clampson gave Elah a gentle shove. "Let me remind you, Miss Renard, you are still on probation." Elah lost the job at Paradise for refusing to follow orders. One part of her mind reflected on the principles she learned at home and at school, while the other veered toward six pounds a month, Campo installment, rent and food.

The form looked as if someone had attempted to erase parts of it, but from what little Elah could see, it was not a favorable report on "Eun Clam." Her supervisor was beginning to lose patience, thinking perhaps someone may return, see the typewriter on Elah's table and ask questions. "You don't need typing lessons, Miss Renard. It's such a simple thing." *If it was so simple, why don't you do it yourself?* She was presented with a situation similar to that at Paradise Fabrics. Nell had called her simple for refusing her employer's instruction; her employer said Elah was impudent for suggesting that she was encouraging Elah to become a thief. The typewriter keys were stiff. She had to hit it very hard to get the key to imprint on the paper. After three strikes and an equal number of erasures, Elah was able to make the "A," but it looked like an arrow pointing in the same direction she faced: north. Her supervisor was angry. "Such a damn simple thing."

Nell had perfected the art of a pause to underline and give her points the fullest meaning. Clampson pursed her lips, put the form in her drawer and slammed the drawer shut. The woman must have been deciding whether to cook goose or lamb for dinner. Elah started to work around the Underwood, which was difficult, given the size of the table. Like a heavyweight champ delivering a knock out punch, Clampson picked up the typewriter and dropped it on the shelf. Their once cordial relations came to an icy cool. She gave impersonal orders and Elah carried them out because that was what they were paying her six pounds to do. After a few weeks, Clampson surprised Elah by inviting her to have lunch in the office. Besides making tea, Mavis had a side business of cooking, selling lunches and cool drinks. "I am treating Miss Renard." Clampson made note by her slanted smile that she saw Mavis give Elah more meat. "We must try to get along, Miss Renard. Perhaps I shouldn't have expected that you'd know how to type, but after all, you attended a private academy, that is what you said. I thought that these schools had typing as a basic part of the curriculum. My mistake. However, you are doing a fine job with the files. All I ask is that you follow instructions or check with me if you are not sure about something. I am here to help you learn the procedures."

They were having a good visit when, much to Elah's surprise, Clampson offered an opinion on Curtis's attire. "You believe that man insists on wearing shorts? He doesn't even wear underpants, the slacker. He must wrap it around his leg and tie it up." Elah felt uneasy. "He needs to have his wife replace the buttons on his shirt, he eats so damn much." She was looking at Elah with a smirk and Elah was wondering why her supervisor, purported to be Curtis's lover, would engage in that sort of talk with a junior. Elah assumed he was married, but she didn't know he lived with a wife. Mavis returned and collected the plates and glasses. Elah thanked Clampson for the lunch and went to the bathroom. She stayed a few minutes to clear her head and think, "Just what did this woman have in mind when she extended the lunch invitation?"

Clampson's elbow rested on her desk and an index finger leaned against her cheek as if she were in contemplation. Elah thanked her again for the lunch and started to do her work. She swivelled around to face Elah in a disarming and friendly way. "Do you have any idea why Mr. Curtis wants to see you tomorrow morning?"

"No, and I don't feel like going anyway."

"Stay home. I will cover for you."

"Listen to me, Elah. She may be your supervisor, but do not allow anyone to give you bad advice. She can't fire you for going to work, but she could for staying home. Why would you say you didn't feel like going? He is the big boss and if he asked you to present yourself in his office, I suggest that you go." It turned out that Mr. Curtis wanted Elah to accompany foreign visitors on city tours. She would get a few extra shillings in stipends, but there weren't that many people coming to her office to discuss cooperative ventures. Clampson was anxious to know why Mr. Curtis had summoned her junior. Elah told her. She laughed out loud. "You? Accompanying foreign visitors on a city tour? Curtis can't be in his right senses. You could scarcely find your way to work on the bus. You got lost coming here the first day, remember? Well, now you get a lift, so that makes it easy."

"I won't be driving."

"You will have a chance to teach the driver to read. He just about killed that American woman taking her to Black River. She thought he needed glasses. Ask Mr. Curtis or Dickey, they'll tell you. This man insists on going out of proper channels." The working atmosphere cooled again, until the day Curtis asked for the parish reports. He was to meet with an official from Nigeria (a future stipend for Elah).

"We'll see what we can do."

"See what we can do?!" Curtis's voice rumbled with wrath, and by the sounds of the stenographer's chair sliding across the floor above, Miss Chin was listening. Clampson had succeeded in working him up. Mr. Curtis glared at her, as if he couldn't believe what he had heard. "Sometimes I think there is a covert attempt to overthrow our entire social welfare programs—a model for the developing world—into disarray. See what you can do? I'll tell you what you can do. Make sure all those reports are on my desk by 3 p.m. today. See what you can do? Four cabinets and two full-time people. See what you can do!" Clampson smiled as if she had hit a home run. She knew Elah had worked on the monthly field report files and that they were in good order. A few were missing, but that wouldn't be a problem since each report recapped the previous month's. Many remained the same except for a date change. Clampson delivered the reports before lunch.

Elah was entering the second year on the same job. A letter came from her grandmother summing up the news and congratulating her on passing the one-year mark. She was now a permanent member of this government agency. She could not be fired by Eunice Clampson. Elah did not have a car, but the men in the office did. If they were not ordering lunch from Mavis, they'd go down-town to visit friends in other agencies. Elah had a ride downtown and back if she had to do shopping or pick up an item she had put in lay-away. There were strict rules about when and where to meet for the ride back to the office. Elah had a few minutes before she'd have to be in place to meet Leatherwood. Elah had not been back to Paradise since she left and thought she would run up and say hello to the ladies. As she was hurrying down, Webber called out. "Wait a minute, Miss Renard. Yu not gwineto say hello to me?" He walked her down the stairs. "You looking as nice as usual. Ah hope the govahment treating you ahrite. Ah ask Heather about you all the time. She never tell you?"

Leatherwood was honking his horn and shouting, "We are late. You were sup-posed to be here. You know I can't park."

"We can talk bettah ovah lunch, or if you prefah, it could be dinnah. Ah want to talk to you about your futcha, how about it?"

"I'll call you." Elah almost got run over crossing to jump into the car. It was OK for Leatherwood, but Elah realized that they had been gone for almost two hours. Leatherwood was curious to know who had been talking to Elah.

"Your supervisor is going to reorganize the whole file system again. And by the way, who was that talking to you?"

"My old boss. One of my old bosses. He is the manager of Paradise Enterprises."

"Ah so it go? Me never know you worked at Paradise. Willy, a friend of mine at the department of finance, his girlfriend works there." Elah was curious which one of those slackers was his friend's girlfriend.

"It's the first time I've been back since I was sacked."

"Dem fire people up there?" Leatherwood seemed shocked to hear that Elah could be fired from Paradise Fabrics. "Anyway, what kind of ideas boss man have, mek him follow you all the way downstairs?" Elah didn't tell him that Webber had asked her on a date, but he surmised.

"People used to think island man wild and bad 'till dem Syrian land in this country. You can tell me and I will advise whether you should give him some or not."

"He is married and more than twice my age."

"That's sweeter. Old men try harder."

Miss Clampson could not say anything to the deputy manager, but she had words of caution for Elah. She looked at her wristwatch as Elah came in and Leatherwood sauntered upstairs. "Don't follow people who have worked here for many years. Everyone doesn't have the same luck. The end of probation is not the end of supervision, Miss Renard." It was the first time Elah felt so conflicted. It didn't require much to do her work, but she had difficulty focusing. She flipped through files and then put them back to the bottom of the pile, then flipped through them again. Clampson was reading a book placed in a file folder and was unaware of what her junior was doing. Was she infatuated by the unexpected attention of her former boss? He acted in a fatherly way toward her, but she believed it was because he knew she was young and new to the city. Perhaps he was really interested in her future, but somehow she got a different feeling.

The woman marked her place, closed the folder and turned to Elah to see if she had finished what she had been working on. She realized that the pile had not changed. "Miss Renard, those files should have been sorted and put back in the file cabinet. Did you see my note? It said, 'For urgent action.' Is something wrong?" Elah had thrown away the note without realizing it was an instruction from her supervisor. It is what they are paying you six pounds to do. Elah had never felt this way before. She had a boyfriend and had gone out on dates, but no man made her feel as special as Webber by just this innocuous interest in her future. Her nature told her to run toward trouble; it would be exciting. Leatherwood said old men tried harder. She would never call Webber. It would remain a fantasy in her head.

Elah was sometimes flattered by the compliments the foreigners showered on her, but she never felt so swept up in romantic emotions. She was tempted only once. Again, this was an older British gentleman. Elah may have succumbed, if not for the thought that the car lights shining in Nell's bedroom window may wake her up and make her look outside. "Just a goodnight kiss?" Elah wasn't unfamiliar with the British, but she had never kissed one. "How about it? Blimey, you're a big girl. All right, let's huggy-do." He squeezed her close and Elah realized the man was highly aroused. A kiss wasn't going to solve that problem, but would likely make it worse. She had to tear herself away. She watched him walk back to his car, deflated and perhaps painfully disappointed. It was the easy part of her job and she was glad for the extra money. Heather wasn't surprised to hear that Webber asked her out to dinner. She encouraged Elah to accept the invitation and talk to him about her future.

While her boyfriend was fun to go out with, Louis was very stingy. When they went to nightclubs he would be the last to say, "Let me pay this time," and the first to order a second free round. He didn't volunteer to drive if they were going to a nightclub that was more than an hour away. He couldn't afford the gas and he lived at home with his parents. He didn't make a lot of money surveying, but he hardly spent any of it. When he bought a present, it would be the cheapest thing he could find. Elah had not expected nor received any gold jewelry from him. Nell would have found all his good qualities, which would sum up as outweighing any faults, but it was not her decision. Elah's heart was open, not for Webber, but for a new man in her life. It had been three weeks since Webber extended the invitation, and she had all but forgotten about him.

Elah knew instinctively that he was on the other end of the line when the phone rang soon as she had arrived in the office. "It's for you, Miss Renard." If it had been Dickey or anyone else, Elah could have asked them to say she was not there, but not Clampson. Elah pulled the cord as far as it could go, and she heard his voice. "Hello, Miss Renard. You pramiss to call and it is almost four weeks. Ah been waiting. Ahrite, you cahn't talk, so listen. How about we meet for lunch at Cockles tomorrow at 12 o'clack?" Elah hesitated. He asked if she knew where the restaurant was located. She told him, "Yes." She didn't, but figured she could look up the address in the phone book. "Ahrite, then ah will pick you up."

"No, that is not necessary."

"You will meet there?"

"Yes."

Cockles was about a mile west of her office and she'd have to travel a couple of bus stops. Elah left for lunch at 11:30 a.m. and got to Cockles 10 minutes after 12. Webber looked nothing like the staid pudgy shirt and tie manager of Paradise Enterprises. The cologne splashed playboy seemed years younger in his casual floral shirt and sports slacks. His wavy hair had been trimmed and styled. He seemed full of energy and gave the impression of a kid on his first date. *Keep this away from Nell, she will see the harm and danger in going out with a married man. Well, he wants to talk about my future. What harm can there be in that?* He was standing next to a beige Hillman Minx.

"I was tinking that you may not show up, but I remembah you as a very respansable young lady." Elah felt uncomfortable and it seemed as if her life was now taking a U-turn, as Nell would likely have put it, toward hell. She hoped that there wouldn't be anyone who knew her in the restaurant. She knew her work colleagues were going downtown, because Leatherwood asked if she wanted a lift. Webber pulled out the chair and waited for her to sit. He placed a calming hand over hers. Elah quickly pulled her hands away and placed them on top of the table. "Don't worry, business people have lunch all de time." Elah didn't consider herself a businessperson. She was a junior file clerk who was on lunch break. When the waitress came over he ordered a rum and water. Elah asked for a glass of sour sop juice. The woman was ready to take their lunch order. Showing machismo, Webber told her to order anything she liked. "I am paying far it." The waitress pointed to the curried goat, the most expensive item, and raised her eyebrows in a way that urged Elah to order.

Webber leaned over and looked into her eyes. "Didn't your friend tell you I always ask about you?" Heather mentioned it a couple of times in the context of something else. "So tell me, what you doing for the govahment?" Elah told him, then added that she planned to start night school to learn secretarial science.

"That is great. I always feel you are an ambitious young lady who would get very far in life." Elah wasn't planning on a dessert, but the waitress—with a wink—told her the corn pudding was really good. Aunt Vera made the best, mouth-watering corn pudding. There was grated coconut crust and butter on the top. No one could make it any better. She wavered, but Webber told her to order it. He let out a mischievous chuckle while bouncing her legs between his knees. "I've never stopped thinking about you since the day I handed you that envelope and said, 'Goodbye.' You know I didn't want you to go? I was very sad that you refused to apologize. I remember the first day you walked into the store. I was at lunch and one of the girls came back to get me, saying there was a young lady looking for a job. You had on a pretty dress. It was yellow, wasn't it? It had some embroidery or edging around the sleeve." That was her interview dress and the one she wore her first day at her present job. "I know what you thinking. Yes, I am a married man. Oldah, much oldah, dan you and all of that, but you make me a feel like a young bwoy again." *Leatherwood was right about Syrian men.* It was time for her to get back to work and he offered to take her, but she made him promise to drop a short distance from the building. As she was about to get out of the car, he leaned over and pulled the door shut. "How about dinnah?"

"I don't know. I don't know."

"Say yes. I promise to be very discrete. Say yes. I will call you." As soon as Elah got home, Heather called. Nell was sitting at the kitchen table with some of her religious magazines and Elah didn't feel free to talk. "Tell Nell you need some privacy. You need to get your own telephone. So what Mr. Webber had to say about your future?"

"Nothing."

"Does he want to go out again?"

"Yes."

"What did he say about his wife?"

"Nothing."

"She seems like a nice woman, but she is big and hairy. No wonder he wants to flirt with young girls. You were the 'family emergency.' That is why he left early and didn't come back to the store." Nell went to her room, and Elah whispered hastily. "Says he is in love with me and wants us to go to dinner." Nell returned.

"Call me after Nell goes to bed." Nell and Winston were not the kind of company that Elah wanted. They were temperate and circumspect. They'd go to a movie, have ice cream and be home before 10. Elah stayed out until the wee hours dancing and sometimes club hopping with her boyfriend and sometimes with girlfriends. Why would she complicate her life with a married man? It didn't make any sense, but she could not get Webber off her mind. She had dreams and fantasies about them together. Nell woke her and reminded her she was going to church. Elah was tired and went back to sleep. "You can't stay out until 2 and 3 o'clock in the mornings. Decent girls are not on the streets during those hours. Louis called and was looking for you. Call him when you get a chance. I am going to Kingdom Hall and will be back around 3. Remember, it is your turn to make dinner.

Miss Chin had encouraged Elah to apply for tuition assistance if she intended to go to school part-time. As long as it would enhance her job, Miss Chin told her the government would approve her request. She filled out the form and returned it for Curtis's signature. After some months, Elah hadn't heard anything, so she asked Miss Chin to check. The woman said Mr. Curtis had approved the request for tuition reimbursement up to 50 percent of the fees. "Maybe he sent it to the head office for the bursar's signature. I will call. Anyway, don't worry because it will be effective from the day Mr. Curtis approved it." Elah and her friend had started night school three nights each week from 6 to 9:30 p.m. It wasn't easy to pay the tuition, but Nell encouraged Elah to go ahead. She agreed to increase the amount for her share of the rent to free up a few more shillings for Elah.

Clive took Heather home after school, but they lived in opposite directions, and it would be far out of his way to offer Elah a lift. She took the public bus. There were other girls from the school taking public transportation, but Elah didn't feel safe downtown at night. Webber had been offering to pick her up and take her home. He also didn't live close to her, and she felt as if it were an imposition. Nell was looking out when he dropped her at the gate. She didn't know who he was.

"So, is that your new boyfriend? I notice that Louis stopped calling, or perhaps you have stopped returning his calls. Is that the new boyfriend?"

"He's just giving me a lift."

"He must live close by."

Elah felt as if she had to hide from Nell because she was bound to find out who he was. She did not want Clive to see Webber picking her up, either. She asked to meet him around the corner, away from the school. "That is damn foolishness. If ah don't have to explain to my wife to hell with anybady else. Clive?" He was so cavalier about it. He chuckled. "Well, you tell him to come and see me if he has anything to say." Even though Clive reported to Mrs. Stoner, Webber could find a reason to have him fired. Elah told him she would not accept the ride unless he was willing to do as she asked. He wanted to help with her school fees and she refused. Miss Chin told her that once the request had been approved, as she was sure it had been, Elah would get the assistance retroactively to the time she started school. There were some expenses that she had not anticipated. She had to pay extra to sit for tests. Although it wasn't a lot for the shorthand notebooks, she was going through them very quickly. Nell told her not to worry because she would take some work home to make extra money so that she could help more with the household bills. Elah felt guilty and selfish. Why had she enrolled in school before getting the government assistance that she counted on? She asked Miss Clampson if she had heard anything about the tuition assistance. The woman opened her drawer and began to wave the form.

"This? You continue to try and erode my authority. I told them to go ahead and approve it, but next time I may not be so kind and forgiving when you go out of proper channels."

Most girls went full-time for one year, but Elah and Heather were determined to complete their courses in the same time. Heather was doing bookkeeping and she had Clive to help, but Elah had to rely on practicing shorthand and getting to class early and getting a few minutes extra on the typewriter. She was up to 35 words per minute, and Elah offered to help the secretary/stenographer who helped her to get the tuition assistance. At the same time, she would be gaining valuable practice on the typewriter. Miss Chin accepted the offer, and Elah took down the old Underwood. She made sure that everything Miss Clampson had assigned was completed. Elah could tell Clampson saw the peril in this new arrangement. Her assistant was now typing correspondence and what would come next? "Miss Renard, sorry to interrupt you, but I need to say something." She walked over and looked at what Elah was typing. "I think it is not proper for you to do government correspondence. If you made an error, it could create lots of problems and who would be blamed? Me. They wouldn't say you took it upon yourself. No. They'd say I sat right here and allowed you to do it. Please put the typewriter back where you found it, and I will explain to Miss Chin. We have a lot of work to do, don't forget."

Whatever she could do to thwart her underling's progress was fair game under the guise of a supervisor's prerogative. Little did she know that no one or nothing would stop Elah from obtaining her objective, which was to complete the course in one year. It was her ticket out of the filing department to a job that better suited her intelligence and training. Nell didn't have to work extra or pay extra rent, because Elah had gotten a salary increase and a lump sum for tuition reimbursement. She had even gone downtown and paid down on a pair of imported shoes that she planned to pick up at the end of the month. Everyone waited to see Lucky riding in with the brown envelope that contained cash wages for the staff. Clampson passed out these envelopes to everyone on staff. Elah kept her purse under Clampson's desk because it was the only place to keep it out of the way. Dickey was leaving for the afternoon and offered Elah a lift. As Elah was about to leave, Clampson announced she had a meeting with Mr. Curtis, and Elah would have to stay to answer the phone. Dickey left. She handed Elah a file, asking her to take it to Mr. Dennis. He was clearing off his desk, getting ready to leave for lunch. "I didn't request any files. Take them back to her. The woman must be mad." Elah met Clampson on the stairs and told her Dennis had not asked for the files. The woman brushed her off saying, "Talk to me when I get back."

All the people with cars had left, so Elah called a neighbor who worked at the car dealership and asked him for a lift. After he left work, he picked up his wife who worked downtown. He picked Elah up at 4:30 p.m. The stores closed at 6 p.m. and by the time he dropped her off, the shutters were half closed and the ladies were looking into compact mirrors. They powdered their faces and were touching up lipstick, getting ready to leave. Her neighbor promised to take her home if she was at the same spot after he picked up his wife. They put the shoes in a bag and Elah reached for her pay packet. It was gone. All her cash wages and the few extra shillings for two visitors were gone. Elah emptied her bag. The contents scattered all over the counter and there was no money anywhere. Grief-stricken and angry, she was thinking how she would face Nell with this news. By the time she crossed the street, hoping to get a lift from her neighbor, she realized he had gone. She had no money. Not even bus fare. Elah felt as if she could throw herself in front of the speeding cars and end it. She saw the store owner waving and trying to cross to come over to her, and for an instant she thought perhaps he had found her pay envelope. "Take the shoes. Don't worry about money. Pay me when you have it. You are a good customer. Come, take it. Pay when you can. Maybe the money dropped out in your office. I'm sure you'll find it." Elah was thinking why would she need imported shoes if she didn't have money to pay rent, Campo installments, buy food or pay the other half of her school fees? He asked if she had money and she said, "No." He pushed his hand into his pocket and gave her money, saying, "Pay your bus fare." It was like losing another job—one whole month's wages gone. It couldn't have fallen out, so it had been stolen.

Elah went into her room and just cried. When she did not go out for dinner, Nell went to find out what was wrong. "Don't worry, we'll manage. I still have a few pennies in the Building and Loan Society. The Jehovah is watching over you and he will make things right, if not in this life, in the hereafter. You think it's little hardship I've gone through since I came to this city? You'd be surprised. We will manage." Nell slept in her room that night, and they talked about who may have taken the money and why. Elah said she suspected Clampson did it to spite her. "You still wouldn't get the money back and, to accuse your supervisor, a woman who has been working for the government for umpteen years, would do more damage than losing the seven pounds odd. Also, it could put innocent people under suspicion, and no good could come from it. Do not say anything to anyone. Take my advice." Elah didn't always agree, but she trusted Nell and knew whatever she said was honest and made sense. Clampson was not bright, but she was very clever and cunning.

It was very hard not to speak out, but Elah avoided Clampson as much as possible while sitting hitched onto her desk. She did her job, which is what they were paying her seven pounds, five shillings to do. She had to try extremely hard to focus on her studies and turn down Webber's constant invitations to go out. Elah was tempted when he made the offer of assistance again. He didn't offer financial help, as much as demand that she accept. "It is my duty as a man to help. I know you need the money. I can send a check to Gail Simpson if you prefah. Her husband and I play poker." It was one of the few schools offering night courses and a one-year certificate. The man knew everyone, but she didn't know he was a friend of her shorthand teacher and the owner of the secretarial science school. He smiled, winked and blew smoke rings from his cigarette in calculated puffs. "I will send it directly and tell Gail it's for you. You are either serious about us or you are not." Nell had seen some of the presents he had given her.

"You feel you are a woman and thus can do whatever you please. What's become of Louis and Webster? You don't go out with them anymore. They are more suited to your age. Aunt Lottie would be upset to hear that you have a married Syrian boyfriend older than her. I beg you not to make his wife find out, come here and scandalize us. My advice is to tell him not to come back. I could ask Winston to come and pick you up from school. He may not be able to do it every night, but I could at least get him to pick you up on Monday nights. Let that man find a mistress closer to his age." Elah had fallen in love with the married man.

"We could go to a hotel. What you think about that?" It was difficult, but Elah felt it was not the right thing to do, even though her heart contradicted the words. Webber was angry. "You take me for a playting? You seeing sombady else? I have a pistol. If I catch him with you, he is a dead man. I'm serious." These flare-ups were becoming more frequent, as Elah insisted on ending the affair. Winston said he could not commit to picking her up on any regular basis, and it was just as well. Webber didn't have a problem, and he was so happy to see her on the three nights. He would have driven to hell to get her.

Clampson tried several times to hint to Elah that she knew something about her stolen money. They were alone in the office. Mavis was in the kitchen cooking something very spicy, and it smelled all over the office. Clampson rolled her chair closer to the table. "This is in strict confidence. Miss Renard, there is a thief around." She rolled her eyes toward the kitchen and winked. Nell told her not to say anything and, though Elah had gone for a long time keeping her thoughts to herself, she slipped.

"Mavis?"

"Shish. I saw something, and I have been trying to tell you. I think you should put it to Mr. Curtis."

"What? Put what to Mr. Curtis?" Elah corrected her tone, because it seemed as if words were about to tumble out for which she would be sorry. "I'm sorry, Miss Clampson, but what should I tell Mr. Curtis?"

"That someone stole your pay packet; I could make sure you get it back, every penny." A little voice kept asking, what if this is true? How could Clampson get her money back? If she had seen Mavis take it, she could have accosted her on the spot. Elah knew how she hated the woman. Elah figured it out; Clampson was trying to elicit Elah's help to get rid of Mavis. It took willpower to act as if it didn't matter, but Elah remembered Nell's warning.

"Miss Clampson, whoever took it can have it, because it is not going to make them any richer. They will be poorer for it."

"Well, it seems we've come into wealth. Does he have a brother?" Elah didn't respond. "I'm sorry. I didn't mean to get into your business, just trying to help."

At least their meetings were mostly confined to the two or three nights when he'd take her home. Once in a while, they'd go out on a Saturday night. Elah hoped she would not run into any of her former boyfriends while she was with Webber. They would probably feel insulted to find out that an older man had taken her away. As she and Webber sat enjoying the anonymity of a dark corner, bad luck Harry Brown entered the club. When he saw Elah, he doubled back.

"Well, well, well, I am surprised to see you here." He apologized when he saw that she was with someone. "I am sorry, sir, but we are from the same place and I haven't seen Miss Renard for a long while now." She was glad Harry added "long while" because she could tell Webber was beginning to think the meeting had been planned. "You don't go to Miss Thomas to do your hair anymore? Lana says she hasn't seen you in a while. Well, well." He removed his hat. "I beg your pardon," he said to Webber, who offered to buy him a drink. "Yes, thank you." (What island man would refuse a free drink?) Harry took that as an invitation. He pulled up a chair and introduced himself. Elah saw a spark of recognition as the two men shook hands. Webber was a fixture downtown, and she wouldn't have been surprised if Harry knew him. He settled in as a member of the party but still seemed to be trying to figure out where he had seen Webber before. He had come to the club to dance and, when the music struck up, Harry looked around at the ladies lining a wall and started to head over in that direction.

"Say hello to Lana."

"I'll be right back, just going to get a little dance over there." Webber ordered him another drink, which in Elah's opinion, was a mistake. Harry poured the balance of the rum he was nursing into the new glass and asked Webber if he could dance with Elah. The jealous man nodded an uneasy OK. He made sure his eyes could follow them over the dance floor. Harry danced out of his sight on purpose, then began to whisper to Elah.

"Well, does all your family like Syrian men?" Elah said Webber was only a friend, prompting Harry to inform her that he was available. "Me and Lana break up. Maybe when you not so busy with old man there, we could go out sometime." Webber was sipping rum, and his eyes were searching for them. "So, where you working now? You still have the same number?" Elah said yes, but she knew that Nell didn't want him calling. "What is it again?" Harry was about to reach into his pocket for a pen, but Elah stopped him, saying he could call her at work. As soon as they returned to the table, Webber was ready to leave. Harry moved over closer to the dance floor and the single girls waiting for a partner. Webber had in mind a more private place where they could be together. They had been there before.

"Are you listening?"

"You are married, Mr. Webber."

"Why can't you call me Saed?"

"It seems disrespectful."

"Well, call me whatever you want. I will get a divorce if you say yes."

"This goes against my upbringing and religion. It really does, Saed. It makes me feel guilty."

"What religion? You haven't been going to any church lately that I know of. I am not asking to marry your family; it's you I want to spend the rest of my life with. Ahrite, it is a bit unexpected, but believe me, I have given this a lot of thought. You don't have to tell me now; we can go on like we are for the present if that suits you better."

"Suits me better?"

"You tell me you don't want to hide as if you are a criminal. I am not afraid to tell anyone who wants to know that I am madly in love with you and will marry you the minute you say yes."

"I won't be responsible for breaking up your marriage. No, Saed. My answer is no."

They were sitting on a sand mound outside the car. Webber's words flashed in her mind like meteorites across an uncertain sky. A spatial and extraordinary feeling overcame Elah, and she felt as if she was on a magic carpet that would fall to the ground any minute. "Will you marry me?" She watched the waves creep in and dissolve softly into foam ruffles. The moon was full and, for the first time, Elah saw all the stars in the big dipper. "What is your answer?" The sky looked like a deep purple blanket with eyes peeping out. Occupants nearby were making fog in their car windows. Elah wanted to go home. She was coming to the end of her course and had a heavy schedule. The moon removed all shadows, giving Elah a glimpse of the agony in his face; she knew he was genuine. They sat silently for some minutes. "I cannot live without you, Elah." She didn't tell him how she felt, but he guessed that there was some reciprocity between them. He admired her spunk and she his bold, yet quiet power.

Mavis started cooking early. Watchie was sitting under the tree in the side yard where he could observe the comings and goings of the office personnel. Clampson was reading a new romance novel tucked inside a file folder. Elah was making notes in shorthand of things she had to do, when they heard a scrambling on the stairs. Mavis ran out to see who was running down. Lucky scampered through the office, hopped on his bicycle and took off. Mr. Curtis followed, asking, "Where is he? Back pain?" Curtis looked outside. "I'll give him back pain. I should start charging him rent. We'll see who is going to give him free lodging with those unruly boys. Mavis, don't you have anything to do?"

"Yes, Mr. Curtis." She went back to the kitchen.

"Clampson, did you send that fool up to my office?"

"I didn't even know he was up there. He didn't use the proper channel, that's for sure. You've never turned them away, so they all think they can bypass me and come to you directly." Her reply covered Elah with the same blanket of insubordination. After Mr. Curtis went back to his office, Clampson flashed a slanted smile and mumbled, "Stewpid." Mavis returned to find out what happened. Clampson remained silent.

"I hope he finishes his home soon because, whatever he did, he made Mr. Curtis mad."

"Wha house? Miss Renard, Lucky tell you him a build house?" Clampson put on a half smile in ridicule. Miss Chin came down to give her version of the events leading to Lucky's exodus. Clampson was curious to hear what Miss Chin had to say.

"The doctor told Lucky that he has back pain and must stay off the bicycle for at least four weeks. Mr. Curtis was laughing until Lucky whispered something. I couldn't hear, but he got angry and chased him out of the office. I have to go before he thinks I'm down here gossiping. If Lucky knows what's good for him, he will make himself scarce for the time being." Mavis laughed outrageously. Clampson flashed her a sideways reprimand, and the woman went back to the kitchen. Elah thought about her vacation. It would be the first for them since they moved to the city. Elah had put in her leave request through the proper channel months in advance and would be paid for the time.

Nell had no paid leave, so she had been saving for months and took home work to earn extra money. It would be six years for Nell and almost three since Elah left home. Nell would not take any money from Elah, so Elah merely paid more for rent and bought enough food so that Nell wouldn't have to worry about that. Webber offered to drive them on the four-hour journey. Nell was alarmed at Elah's brazen attempt to show off a married man. "Not on God's earth. If Winston cannot take us, we'll take the bus. You came here on a bus and so did I. By the way, your boyfriend, who is not really your boyfriend, called and wants you to call him as soon as you get home. Beware! Do your work and stop begging people for money."

"I'm not begging anyone for money. As a civil servant, I'm entitled to paid leave and the tuition assistance that I get."

"That's not what I am talking about Elah." Life was never dull. Between Nell, Webber and Clampson, Elah had a full load of situations to deal with, some serious and others not. Webber wanted to keep the relationship with her at any level. Clampson told her that new duties were going to be added and that she had recommended Elah for a pay raise. Elah knew that, unless it was an extraordinary amount for outstanding performance, government employees got step increases every year.

"Miss Renard, starting next Monday, you'll be handling all the mail. I know it's a big responsibility, but I think you are ready to do bigger things." Leatherwood had told Elah that there was news at head office that someone had been tampering with confidential mail, and Elah was suspicious and wondered if this sudden upgrade was a trap. Elah was not in the habit of revealing secrets but, according to what she heard, it was no secret. She started to tell Clampson, if only to put her on notice that this new job had better not be something else in disguise.

"Did you hear that there was a problem at head office with the mail? Mr. Leatherwood said." Clampson cut her off. It appeared that she was on the outs with the man and may have known what Elah was about to say.

"Don't mention his name to me."

"Sorry."

"Let's get on with it. Now, all envelopes are to be thrown away; we really don't need them clogging up the files. Confidential correspondence should be opened, date-stamped and placed in this file; I will take them upstairs. Everything else is to be sorted and handled by you." The training had scarcely gotten a chance to sink in when Clampson announced she had a meeting at the head office and would be late. "While I am out, Miss Renard, if anything confidential comes, don't open it until I return. Put it in my drawer." Elah had learned to go along and found it was better to acquiesce, but she'd correct the instruction if necessary. Clampson would later congratulate her for the fine job without remembering what she had initially told Elah to do.

One confidential envelope was in the stack of mail Lucky brought. It was addressed to Mr. Curtis from the chief personnel officer. "'Subject: Eunice Clampson's Performance Review.'" It wasn't very complimentary of 20 years of government service. Elah put it back into the envelope and took it to Miss Chin. Whatever way it turned out, she'd be in trouble. As the weeks ticked by, Elah became less worried.

Clampson had been upstairs longer than usual; the secretary came down to say Mr. Curtis also wanted to see Elah. She pulled the chair next to her supervisor; the woman shifted so Elah realized that her protection lay in her own wits. Mr. Curtis seemed preoccupied searching for something in his desk drawer. He found the paper with a hole in it; Elah knew this was not a good thing. Was this in the category of "criminal conduct"?

"Poor Nell, Elah thought, this will be too much for her; maybe I will have to go back and wait for Miss Hamilton to die. In addition to all her ailments, Elah heard that she had lumbago."

"Now, Miss Renard."

"Yes, sir."

"We have a very serious matter here," he said, while glancing at her supervisor. "Wouldn't you say so, Miss Clampson?"

"Certainly, sir." He picked up the piece of paper and waved it in front of Elah.

"Is this your doing, Miss Renard?" Elah didn't answer right away. "Miss Renard, I am asking if this is your doing?"

"Well, sir," Elah thought about her future.

"Well sir, what? Yes or no?"

Miss Clampson whispered to Elah. "We have to be confidential and trustworthy." Then, she said aloud, "I don't know why you would do such a thing; it baffles me." Mr. Curtis looked at Clampson in a peculiar way, then shifted his glare to Elah, still waiting for an answer.

"Yes, sir." Miss Clampson seemed relieved. She shifted slightly, crossed and uncrossed her short legs.

"Well?" He wanted an explanation.

"She told the truth sir." Clampson smiled proudly.

"Miss Clampson instructed me to do it."

"Stop. Stop right there. You are a liar."

"Miss Clampson, you are out of order. So Miss Renard, Miss Clampson had you erase and change a government form?"

"Well, sir she said that Mavis…"

"Mavis? You see sir, she wants to start trouble; Mavis can't even type."

"I have asked Miss Renard for an explanation of her actions, and I am waiting for an answer. So, you were saying Miss Clampson instructed you to tamper with an official government document?"

"She instructed me to retype the grade."

"I reprimanded her for doing it, but it was too late."

"You brought down the typewriter."

"We'll ask Mr. Dickey; he was there."

Mr. Curtis went back into his desk and looked at a paper. He asked Miss Clampson what grade she had made on the filing course. She seemed embarrassed and began to offer reasons why she had not done better.

"Tell me what grade you got on the course."

"I believe it was a 'C' sir."

"You're sure it wasn't an 'F'?"

"Fairly certain."

"The personnel people have suggested that I may have something to do with this changing of your grade in order to give you a promotion." Mr. Curtis pulled out a photocopy from his desk and thrust it before a startled Miss Clampson. "Eunice, this looks like an 'F' to me. What do you make of it? This is a true copy signed and certified by the registrar of the university. Is he a forger, too?" He wheeled his chair, turning his back to the women. "You can go, Miss Renard, but I will make a note in your file. That will be all," he said without turning around.

Clampson got up and closed the door behind Elah. Mr. Dickey asked if she was up there telling lies again. Elah didn't speak because she was in enough trouble as it was, but she wished Dickey knew his name had been called to bear false witness. He hadn't even been in the office at that time. Clampson returned to her desk smiling.

"He is full of wind; you wouldn't believe what he said after you left." Dickey pretended to be working, but he was eyeing Clampson. "He apologized to me, can you believe that?" Dickey answered.

"No. Not for one minute."

"Excuse me, Dickey, I am speaking to Miss Renard." She asked Elah to step out to the veranda and began to whisper.

"He looked again at the grade and noticed that what he thought was an 'F' was actually a 'B.' Universities never have good typewriters; you put me up a little," she said, with a sly smile. "It's all forgotten and forgiven. But, I will tell you this: Thank God I won't have to retake that test. By the way, did you see the envelope with my review?"

"I saw an envelope addressed to Mr. Curtis; it was marked 'confidential,' and I gave it to Miss Chin."

"I only wish you had followed my instructions. Anyway, we won't say anything more about that; it's all settled."

Elah would need a recommendation to get another government job and wondered what Mr. Curtis was going to write in her file. Mavis was singing in the kitchen, and Clampson told Elah to tell her that this was an office. Mavis did not have kind words in her return message, at least none that Elah would care to repeat. Mavis stopped out of pity for Elah, and it was a relief. Elah had made up her mind; she was going to leave.

"Can't you wait until you graduate to start hunting for another job? Please don't have any nervous breakdown on me." Dickie, Dennis and Leatherwood all promised to give her glowing recommendations. Elah hoped those would overshadow the negative information that Mr. Curtis promised to put in her file.

The official she had the interview with did not show up, and his secretary said it was unusual that she had not heard from him. When she got back to the office, Elah was hot, hungry, tired and in a foul mood. As soon as she sat, Clampson began to reel off the messages.

"While you were lunching for almost two hours, your cousin called and wants you to pick up a loaf of sliced bread. Your neighbor says he can give you a lift home. The same man who has been ringing here nonstop for the past months called and said you'd know who. Oh, and by the way, a Mr. McNair from Lands called. He said something came up unexpectedly; you have his number. One other thing Miss Renard, only senior staff members are allowed to use the telephone; try and let your friends and colleagues know that."

The last time Elah could remember feeling the same level of anger was when a boy in elementary school punched her in the stomach. She thought she'd never get her breath back. Dickey kept wiping his eye glasses as if he could tell something was coming. Elah waited to make sure Clampson had finished speaking.

"Listen you, if you must know, I am looking for a job. I don't want to continue filing rotten papers. This may be your career, but it's not mine. Before coming to this place, I had never done anything dishonest. If Mr. Curtis does what he says, there will be negative information in my file because you had me change your failing grade report. Another thing, Clampson, while it doesn't bother me to run up and down the stairs with files, it is not my job and I will not do it any longer."

Clampson looked across at Dickey to confirm that, in her opinion, he was the cause of all of this insubordination. To show his agreement or contempt, Dickey went to the bathroom, slammed the door and pulled the flush chain. Appearing hurt, Clampson took out a crisp handkerchief and dabbed at her eyes. Elah felt as if she had just jumped off a cliff and heard the echo of Nell's voice hollering from the brink. "I make handbags, not parachutes, simple." It would take at least three months for the list of infractions to be presented through the channels and dismissal papers signed. When Elah got home, Nell had a message. "Mr. Webber said you should leave the damn job and to call him as soon as you get here."

"Why are you discussing my business with him?"

"He is worried about you. Make sure you do not follow any advice to leave your job."

Elah called her on again, off again friend, Webster. He seemed happy to tell her he had a date and would not be available to go out with her. She knew that Heather and Alfredo were going out of town; it seems everyone had something else to do. Harry Brown was delighted; he thanked Elah for thinking of him. She told Nell that she was going dancing with Harry Brown. "The last time you saw him, he was wearing bicycle clips. He's driving a motor car now? How about his girlfriend and the two children?"

"We are just going dancing."

Harry was wearing a dark-brown gabardine suit and a white hat with a matching band around the crown; his shoes were spit-shined. Elah was impressed. She wore her plastic sling-back shoes with flowers in the heels and an A-line polka dot dress with a form-fitted bodice and boat neck. Harry warmed up with a few slow numbers. While they were still on the floor, the DJ switched to swing. *Chantilly Lace*. It apparently was one of his favorites; Harry was singing along. "Hello baaa-by, this is the Big Bopper speaking." He spun Elah around with such suddenness, she slipped off her shoe and twisted her ankle. Harry let go of his partner and began to dance the words, "a wiggle in the walk." When the music stopped, he looked around and was surprised to see his partner sitting on the sidelines. Girls lining the wall seemed anxious to take his challenge, and Elah encouraged him to choose one of them. It was 2 o'clock in the morning; the club was dimming its lights. Elah enjoyed the outing and had a good time watching the floorshow. They walked outside, where many ladies and a few men were lined up, begging a ride.

"Wait right here," Harry said. "Let me go and get my cycle."

Elah felt a catastrophe coming on; it was a half hour by a fast driving taxi car. Elah felt like begging a ride, but the way the men sized up the woman asking for a lift, she figured Harry's bicycle bar was safer. He was a very optimistic person even though his family had the bad luck genes. It was a fun night, and Elah enjoyed it a lot. "I have sound tires, and I am a good rider." She wasn't happy when she climbed down from his bike; her legs were numb and one of her shoes had fallen off. Her skirt was greasy and torn where it had been caught in the bicycle spokes. "Don't worry, all the thieves have gone to bed. I'll find your shoe and bring it here tomorrow."

"Bring it to my workplace on Monday morning; I am there until 4:30 in the afternoon." He had a silly grin and winked.

"I could take it to your friend at Paradise. I work very close by."

"If you can't bring it to my workplace, how about I come to your house and get it." His response clearly showed he had been lying about breaking up with Lana—not that Elah cared.

"I will get it to you on Monday."

As soon as she got into the office on Monday, Webber called. "So, where were you Saturday night? At 10 o'clock, Nell said you stepped out." The man seemed more jealous than when they were in the heat of an affair. "Where did you go?"

"I was at Heather's house."

"She's here; I could ask her." Elah waited a couple minutes before calling the store. Heather answered, "Notions."

"I was at your house on Saturday night."

"Hold on a minute, lady. Let me check if we have yellow." Heather put the phone back to her ear and whispered, "He's looking straight at me, I have to go." She said loud enough for Webber to hear, "Yes ma'am, you can come in at any time."

Elah resented that she had to lie when she was trying to break free from this relationship; emotions aside, she was a kept woman. He was paying half her school fee, buying her expensive gifts, picking her up three nights each week and insisting that they continue the relationship.

"Good morning." Clampson moved her lips in reply, and Elah acknowledged with, "Good morning, Mr. Curtis." The man stopped in the middle of the room, turned to Elah and said, "I would like to see you in my office tomorrow at 10 o'clock." Clampson looked up as if unsure to whom he was speaking. "You, Miss Renard, 10 o'clock." He went to his office. *What is it now? Elah wondered.* Clampson was caught between being insulted and disturbed, bringing her eyebrow pencil lines as close to center as they could get, to show her annoyance.

"I put in a raise request for you, Miss Renard; perhaps that is what he wants to see you about. I hope he approves it, because you are doing such a fine job." At the same time, Elah could see from the corner of her eyes, Clampson looking askance and wondering why Mr. Curtis had summoned her again without going through proper channels. Clampson issued a handwritten memo advising the uptown office staff that, "Effective immediately, files from the department must be signed for and returned to Miss Renard." Elah went over all the rules she had broken. Opening a confidential envelope, changing a grade, taking more than an hour for lunch, using the telephone for personal reasons, being insubordinate and making lewd remarks about Mr. Curtis's Bermuda shorts. Elah was sure the comment Clampson made would be attributed to her. This time, Nell would have the nervous breakdown she told Elah was the only option left if Elah continued her reckless behavior.

Elah was meek when she entered Curtis's office smiling and saying, "Good morning," as politely as she could manage under the siege of pent-up rage. Fortunately, Curtis tended to be abrupt and to-the-point. "Come in. Come in. Sit. Sit." He may have sensed she was nervous; he paused for a couple minutes. "You are wondering why I called you in here today?" Elah nodded yes. *Nell, she was thinking, you are in for a surprise!* "I understand you are planning to leave us." This was a time for truth and consequences, lying would be to Elah's detriment; everyone in the office knew or suspected that she was looking for another job.

"I have been going out on interviews, but I do not have anything positive as yet, sir."

"How is your course coming?"

"I'll pay all the money back; you have my word."

"Pay what money back?"

"The assistance, sir." Judging from the way he looked, she had not answered his question. Elah figured he really wanted to know how her secretarial course was going. "Excuse me, sir, I am almost finished."

"Glad to hear it. The training office will be operational shortly, and we will be needing to staff it. I recommended you for one of the openings. J.W. and his associate will be conducting interviews. I think they will get in touch with you. While I cannot guarantee what post you will be offered, I am sure that you are under consideration for a position there, provided they accept my recommendation." They reported to him, so Elah felt positive. The pent-up venom went puff, and Elah felt like hugging the rotund man.

"You've been up there for at least half an hour, which is going out of channels. I am still your supervisor unless he has offered you my position." She paused and waited to see if Elah would take the bait.

"You can ask Mr. Curtis; he said it was confidential."

"They all take this department for granted after all the hard work we've done. And, to think you, of all people, want to conspire against me; that's life." The training office would be operational within two to three months, so Elah felt that she could wait. It was as if a weight had been lifted from her shoulders. Nell hugged her upon hearing the news.

"Your plan to get sacked hasn't worked, Elah. All thanks to Jehovah." They were like sisters; Elah never said it, but she worried as much about Nell as Nell worried about her. She loved her cousin and believed the feeling was mutual. She hoped that Winston would take good care of Nell.

The family would meet the man and measure him up to the husband they believed Nell deserved. Elah was sure he would fit their bill. Winston Pearson was at least five years older than Nell, clean-shaven, soft-spoken and of medium height. His hair was coarse and compacted, but neat. In every way, he appeared to be a decent fellow behind the thick eyeglasses and a painted expression of astonishment. When he said, "Yes," it wasn't clear if the word carried a question mark, an exclamation point or if he was saying "of course." Other than that, Winston was dull as dirt; the family would approve.

They were ready for the long-planned visit home. The night before they were to travel, Elah stayed out late with Webber. Nell was furious, especially because of the number of times Elah had said it was over between them.

"You make yourself busy the night before we are to leave, and you haven't done any packing. Well, Winston will be here bright and early tomorrow morning, and you better be ready. I don't want him to have to come here and wait on you."

Winston was there promptly at 6 a.m. He carried all the bags to the car and, within a half hour, they were on the road. He kept looking at Elah in the rearview mirror and, when he caught her attention, he asked, "Do you have a boyfriend?" Elah smiled but didn't answer, sure Nell told him everything. In addition, he had seen Webber that night. "Nell, you should bring her around to the Kingdom Hall; we have many eligible young men there."

"It's not for want of an invitation, Winston. I have asked her many times." Elah closed her eyes, and the tension and stress seemed to evaporate in the cool, misty morning air. It was a bumpy ride in the old Austin, but it was better than having to take the bus. She fell asleep and woke when Nell sighed and said, "Finally."

Milda's children and some of their friends gathered around as if celebrities had come to town. While Elah searched for her shoes, some of the cousins peered into the car and exclaimed, "Look, Elah's wearing lipstick and shorts." Another one said, "She'a wear high-heel shews."

"And she cut off her hair." Elah opened the door and pulled out her handbag. "What you bring for me? Remember, I ask you for a kite and six pairs of school socks?"

"Elah, you bring the crayons?"

"Elah, you promise me dolly baby."

"Elah, you bring the penknife?"

They were certain that Nell would bring more substantive things like shoes and clothes; she sent packages home every Christmas. As far as they knew, Aunty Nell was making lots of money; Elah wouldn't make them any wiser. It was a nonstop whirl of visits with Elah leaving to see some of her friends, and Nell and Winston driving around town like tourists. He had to get back to work, so the day before he was to leave, the family had a dinner in his honor. The table was spread with Nell's embroidered Irish linen tablecloth—the first article she had made after six months of expensive lessons from Mrs. Pinnock. Elah remembered Nell's brother's comment when he first saw the tablecloth and was told the splashes in the center were hibiscus. "It doesn't look like any flower that grows on this tropical island; it looks like a waste of money. Nell can get a good husband some other way, Mama." Nell was hurt; if she had her way, Alton would never eat off her table linen again. Here it is, being used again to show off her talents.

Elah took it for granted that someday Nell and Winston would marry; they had been going together for several years. It surprised her that the wedding would be within a year; maybe they made that decision on the way, because Nell had not revealed that to her. Nell knew the order of things. "Winston is an auditor for the tax office." Elah was thinking that maybe she and Heather could become roommates.

"How about you, Elah?"

"I am not planning to get married until I have had an opportunity to travel overseas." Nell rolled her eyes. Her grandmother repeated, "Travel overseas?" in form of a question that sounded ridiculous on its face. They returned to the serious business of Nell and Winston's pending nuptial. Nell's credentials were reeled off by her brothers and her older sister, who spoke as if they were already at the wedding. She did well in her studies and is a very good cook and housekeeper. Milda showed off her lacy dress collar Nell tatted. "She can bake, too," Nell's mother added. *All Nell could bake was chocolate fudge and sometimes it didn't come out perfect.* Later, in the privacy of the bedroom, Elah's grandmother had advice. "Pick carefully like your cousin. He is not a fancy man, but it seems to me he will make Nell a good husband." The two weeks went by much too quickly; Winston had come to take them back to the city. Everyone at the office was still in the holiday mood and looking forward to the general manager's yearly party/meeting. Thinking of socializing with Clampson made the party unattractive. Nell encouraged Elah to go, saying it wouldn't look good to be absent, especially since she is under consideration for a better position. This would be the first general meeting Elah would be attending.

Dickey came dressed and ready to go directly from the office. Leatherwood planned to "change off" at a friend's house nearby; he'd pick up Miss Chin at her home. Dennis offered to take Elah. Watchie would not be able to attend, but Lucky, Mavis and Miss Clampson would travel in Mr. Curtis's Studebaker. Traveling with the underlings was clearly not to her liking, but it was not her car. Clampson left to pick her new dress. Elah was already dressed in one of her modest Teddie-designed floral V-neck dresses, medium rounded earrings and flat shoes. She wore no make-up.

Elah had not seen Webber since she returned, but they had spoken on the phone several times. He knew that she was going to the office party. "Call me the minute you get home; I have your Christmas present." Elah did not promise because she was not driving, and sometimes these parties can go on longer than the time listed on the invitation. She did not want any more presents from Webber and had told him so.

Mavis was at the party in a fancy ballerina-style dress that could double as an off-the-shoulder number. She was talking to the other office helper, Delphena. The two had their own small businesses operated within their respective offices: Mavis cooked lunches on order from staff; Delphena made ginger beer outdoors behind the head office. Lucky struck up conversation with the general manager's wife, which caused the woman to glance in Clampson's direction and laugh. In the bustle of simultaneous talk, only Elah seemed to notice how Lucky was hob-nobbing with the big boss's wife.

Staff from the field offices, headquarters, and the two uptown offices over-flowed onto the partially enclosed patio near creeping bougainvilleas. Elah had never met most of these people, including the new training office contingent and AID representative. Clampson placed herself between the bosses: the general manager and Mr. Curtis. Silver threads on her Chinese dragon dress shimmered under the chandelier as she took ladylike sips from her glass of rum punch.

A long table in the dining room was replete with every island dish and desert imaginable; helpers in uniforms replenished empty dishes in minutes. Had this not been her first time attending, Elah would have asked to take Nell some of the food. Red rum, white rum, brandy, whiskey, rum punch and fruit punch, and sodas were in plentiful supply. Although the notice said 4 o'clock to 8 o'clock, there was little chance that anyone would leave before the liquor ran out. It appeared to have been catered, but Mavis said she cooked the rice and peas.

Hush fell over the room as the general manager stood to signal the start of the official portion of the evening. "My dear friends and colleagues, our family is growing by leaps and bounds. I am pleased to say that we are now in every village, teaching young girls how to be productive." He paused until the laughter stopped. "Allow me a correction, I meant to say to teach young women how to produce handicrafts, making themselves useful in an occupation that can earn them an honest living." There was still muffled laughter as he chose the right words to correct the faux pas. His wife did not make any attempt to hold her amusement and the statesman-like gentleman was forced to smile, something he did not, according to those who knew him, do very often. "We have more money in our budget, thanks to a grant from America." He introduced the official whom he said would be assigned to the office as a full-time consultant.

"The quality of our handicrafts has gone up and so have sales. He introduced the manager of the training office. Many of you probably know J.W., who has been in the government service for many years. J.W. comes to us from the minis-try of education." A scrawny man with skeletal features and sunken cheeks raised himself slightly, bowed, and sat. "And, of course, the second-in-command, Mr. Paul, who I might add is a recent graduate of Princeton University in America." A 30-something half-Indian stood up and looked around, as if to ask himself, "Why am I here?" Elah thought Paul may have been thinking he made a mistake in accepting the job. She felt that she should also have been introduced. Perhaps her junior status made that a non sequitur. Common island practice allowed guests who were not on the program "to say a few words" at meetings, parties, weddings and funerals. When Elah heard this request, she tuned out, switching her thoughts to the predicament with Webber.

In her mind, the affair had ended, but he was giving her time to think over his marriage proposal. The more she tried to distance herself, the more jealous and suspicious he became. Elah suspected that he sometimes drove around her house to check on her, but he swore he didn't. Webber had never met Winston, who had been sitting on her bed that night. Nell sat on the chair across from them. A knock on the glass door startled them. Nell opened the door, and Webber beckoned Elah to join him outside, saying he had an urgent message. They walked to the side where there were no windows. He slapped her across the face, saying that was the message. She slapped him back. When she said the man was Nell's boyfriend, he apologized and tried to embrace her, but Elah rebuffed his attempts and warned him never to come back to her house. Winston asked what happened, and Elah replied it was a private matter. Nell rolled her eyes in all possible directions. "So, as we were saying, Mama treated this woman for a whitlow, and she came back crying that her fingernail had fallen out."

"She blamed losing her nail on the hot cornmeal plaster Auntie wrapped around her finger. It was the objective of the treatment. Auntie said the woman was ungrateful."

"Nell told me many stories about her mother, including how she caught live scorpions and dropped them in a bottle with white rum to use as an anti venom serum to treat scorpion stings. Nell, you should write down some of these remedies."

"She boiled breadfruit leaf tea to bring down her pressure after she and McPherson quarreled about the pear tree hanging over our pantry."

"Mama has such a temper. Many times, I had to hold her and walk her away from the fence."

Elah had a rich life. Nell's mother taught her poetry, how to memorize poems and told her ghost stories and legends. Elah learned to knit and crochet from her mother. Her grandmother ingrained in her the necessity of having a good character. Her various cousins injected her with humor and humorous situations from which she learned that all life is not grim. Nell was more focused, but the only print she seemed to read was her Jehovah Witness magazines. Elah never saw barriers, only opportunities. Some people believed luck came to those with lighter skin. Elah was persistent, hardworking and possessed a good self-image. Elah changed her future by going to night school.

Elah had switched from the present and was thinking about past events. It seemed as if she were dreaming, because Mr. Curtis was speaking, and the place had become very hot. He was loosening his collar, taking off his necktie and unbuttoning his shirt. The general manager's wife was laughing and cranking the windows open. Someone turned the electric fans on full blast. Curtis began to remove his belt. Remembering what Clampson had said, she thought, fortunately, the slacker was wearing long pants. He has gone mad. She saw several of the male staff standing, ready to grab him. A little voice whispered, "Wake up Elah." Leatherwood nudged her. "Now that your boss is going up the ladder, you will have your chance to read everybody's personal correspondence and gossip about it; keep me abreast." Elah was angry. She shouldn't have come to the party; it was all because of Nell. She took her disappointment out on Leatherwood. "Your grade change request was turned down." He appeared incredulous and asked if she knew that for a fact.

"Yes; the memo came two days ago and it's sitting on Mr. Curtis's desk."

Elah had instant regret; it was foolish and unprofessional. Leatherwood's mood seemed to change from jocular to mean. He clenched his jaw and looked at Curtis as if he'd like to give him a sucker punch. Curtis pulled out a large handkerchief and wiped sweat from his face. Clampson was all smiles. Elah thought this announcement would push her out of the agency sooner, because Leatherwood may not give the recommendation he promised and may talk the others out of it. Curtis had misled her. Elah took a long sip at the glass of rum punch that had been on the table since the meeting started. Someone came and refilled the glass. Curtis was rambling on as usual, and people seemed bored.

"In my opinion, this recognition is long overdue."

Clampson covered her face bashfully. Elah thought this woman was telling the truth about moving up for once; she felt betrayed.

"Thanks to her, our files are in good order."

I did it; she didn't do it. "I know that Miss Clampson would agree, as modest as she is, to take credit that Miss Renard has worked tirelessly to help get our system in shape. We cannot stand in the way of her advancement. Miss Clampson joins me in wishing Miss Renard every success." Elah thought that perhaps she had gone mad. There was no meeting; she was dreaming and making things up. Elah went limp. She did not look like someone who had been promoted. She was burdened with wrong thoughts about Mr. Curtis, and her betrayal of confidential matters. Clampson's smile hardened. Her complexion darkened and her countenance changed. She began to loosen the little top buttons of her Chinese silk dress and asked to use the telephone. Dickey started clapping. Leatherwood gave a toast, and everyone shouted "Here. Here," to congratulate Elah.

The chair between Curtis and the general manager remained empty for the rest of the evening. Mavis whispered, "See if you can bring me over there." Elah, not used to drinking alcohol, finished the glass of rum punch. In a short time, everything was blurred. She felt as if her body had become lighter. Dickey drove Elah home. "We are going to take you up the road to Cockles for a farewell luncheon; they have very good food. You can bring your cousin." He squeezed her waist and kissed her on the lips.

"Cockles, Cockles? I've heard that name. Cockles."

Nell and Winston were playing dominoes with the landlords. "Virginia Campbell," Elah twirled her swing skirt. "An announcement: I have an announcement. I am going to Cockles."

"You are drunk, Elah. Aunt Lottie says you should come home." Elah tried to make herself steady by leaning against the kitchen sink. The players returned to their game, with Winston keeping his look of surprise on his future cousin-in-law. "Come on, whose play?" Nell was trying to ignore Elah.

"I got a promotion: more money, private office and swivel chair, plus, plus, plus." Nell looked at Elah as if she had popped a cork.

"You should lay down, Elah; I have never seen you like this. Go to your room and lay down."

"You don't believe? Believe this, Eunice Clampson started as an office maid. Everyone knew it except me. An office maid! You hear that? Like Mavis, an office maid."

"If you were this drunk at the manager's party, you did not get any promotion. As to your supervisor, keep your mouth shut. Don't let anything get in the way of our rent."

"I got a promotion, Nell."

"Your play, Winston."

"To what?"

"To what? To what?"

"Yes, Elah, a promotion to what?"

"Secretary/stenographer in the new training office. As soon as I get there, I will be putting in a word or two or three for you. We will be looking for reliable help, etcetera." Nell stared at Elah as if she were wondering whether it was liquor or a mental breakdown. "I'm breaking up with Webber for good, and I mean it. God witness. God be a witness. God be." Nell sat silent, as if dumbstruck. Mrs. Reid was trying to play down her shock and shouted.

"Key. I got both ends." Nell and, partner Winston, had lost the game. Elah straightened up and hugged the wall on the way to her bedroom.

"I really, really got a promotion. I am so happy, I could shit right now. Shit. Cockles. You can come to Cockles, Nell. They are taking me to lunch at Cockles. You should taste the corn pudding. Nell, honest to God, it is better than your mother ever made. I know. I finished the glass of rum punch. It was good. Winston, you should take Nell to a bar and…"

"You should come with us to youth meetings. Elah, there are eligible bachelors. Nell, you should encourage her to come." Helping her cousin to bed, Nell replied.

"Winston, Elah is a grown woman. She can make her own decisions. Come, Elah."

A Lizard in the Teapot

Flour scattered all over the kitchen table as Mammy rolled the dough in preparation to make pastries for Tata's tea shop. In a corner sat a pail with parboiled corn, drained and ready to be grated. Mauva Grant was hired by Elizabeth Crawford as a young girl. She leaned over a large bowl, with the grate pressed against her stomach. A familiar symphony began with the sounds of corn on the tin grate and the rolling pin flattening dough. "Miss Liz," the servant said to Mammy, "shouldn't de person who make the pone grater de corn?" Mammy didn't answer. She had heard this complaint many times. Miss Witherspoon was a mature woman who had been hired to tend the tea shop. She volunteered to make corn pudding; it had become one of the favorite delicacies offered at Tata's. Mauva sifted the corn flour with a vigor of someone wrongly designated to perform the task of another. She shook out the cloth, covered the bowl and pushed it to one corner. Her hands were free to gesticulate.

"Miss Liz, do you noh that Busha Johnson has the nerve fe demand rent Saturday morning? Ah tell him that I don't get my half penny in the morning. He sey everybady gets paid in the morning. I tell him that I don't get pay Saturday morning." Mammy had completed the cutouts and was laying the cookies on baking sheets. She occasionally cast a look of annoyance at the maid who sat on the upturned mortar. "Busha sey that you acting like me Mauva Grant is a slave, and slavery done long time."

"Stop chatting, and start washing the plates and forks. Miss Witherspoon needs them."

"Me was just getting a little ress, Miss Liz. Anyway, me will go an ketch the water fe wash up the tings. Busha said you was a slave because him hear sey dat you work pon estate. You believe him would sey a ting like dat?"

"It's always something with you and Busha Johnson. You ought to find yourself another room where you get along better with the landlord. Miss Witherspoon is waiting on the plates." Mauva had interrupted a conversation that Mammy and I were having about the drowning death of Mr. Meekle, a close neighbor. Mammy didn't seem concerned about what Mauva said, but I was. My sister Emily was at the dining table going over orders that had been dropped off at the shop. I mentioned what Mauva said and asked if she believed it.

"Who gives a damn?"

"I do, Emily Anne. It is my family's name that they are dragging on some blasted plantation." That got her to stop what she was doing.

"Kay, working for a family who happened to own an estate does not make one a slave. I am surprised you would take anything Mauva said seriously. Mammy doesn't. What would it matter if our mother had been a slave? She and Pappi have given us a privileged life. What more could we ask from a former slave and her master?" Emily laughed, as she usually did when she thought a snide comment had hit a mark.

"You can make a joke of it, Emily, but Pappi was a paymaster. He did not work in the kitchen. What if our customers heard these malicious rumors? You are being groomed to take over the tea shop, but what if there were no customers? Not many in this town have money or would spend it to sip tea and chat or gossip, as the case may be. Not many have money to send their helpers to pick up orders for your fancy delicacies. Don't you see that talk of this nature would hurt, rather than help, the business?" Emily called out to Mammy. I thought she was about to tell her what we had been talking about.

"Mammy," she said, "we have an order from the Nesbeths for a dozen gizadas. Kay," she turns to me smiling, "I am not in the least worried about what anyone around here thinks. I have to go," she said in a hurried voice, "and see Miss Witherspoon." Tata's adjoined our living quarters, so it was just opening a door, though Emily made it seem as if she had a long way to go. I went over what Mammy had told us about her past and wondered if she had held back something that we had a right to know. Emily and I were sitting on the back steps—we were about 12 and 10 at the time—and Mammy was telling us how she got the job on the estate as a pastry chef. Emily was thrilled, drawing closer to Mammy. I was shocked, believing that she had been a maid. She explained that it was not so. She was doing something she wanted to do but would not have been permitted by her parents. She ran away from home.

"I told them I was 20 and my parents were dead. Just think, Papa sent Douglas overseas to study and sent me to learn domestic science. They thought I would use the skill to take care of them or to take care of my family when I got married. My brother Douglas was 17 when they sent him off to college. I was 14 when I took the job. The last they heard, Douglas had married a Panamanian woman and left America to live in her country. Every week, I sent part of my small wages to my parents. They told friends that I was working in an office on an estate."

Pappi's story was similar, but his had more of a ring of truth to it. He started working in his father's shoemaking business at age 11 but wasn't very happy doing this kind of work. His father wrote to a friend in Leeds who agreed to take the young boy on as an apprentice. He was given a small back room that had no heat and very little food. "Mr. Wolf said I was lucky he didn't charge me for learning me his trade." According to Pappi, many of the people who used Mr. Wolf's bookkeeping services owned plantations in the Caribbean. Pappi had been with Mr. Wolf for almost four years when a young man came in to pick up some papers for his father. He mentioned that they were looking to hire a paymaster to work on their plantation. His preference would be for a British citizen because he did not trust the natives. Mr. Wolf said he'd keep his ears open. "He forgot his briefcase, and I ran to give it to him. I said that I was Scottish but would love to apply for the job if he would consider me. He asked if I'd travel, and I said would be glad to. Anything he'd offer had to be better than the small sum Mr. Wolf was giving me. He'd have to discuss this with my boss, because of their long standing business association. Mr. Wolf wasn't thrilled to let me go because he had heaped most of his work on my young shoulders. However, he agreed, when offered a percentage of my first year's wages, to let me leave debt-free. It took almost a month on a ship to get to my place of work. A man picked me up from dockside and drove me over some rough terrain for what seemed like an entire day. I had left a cold room in Leeds and arrived on a hot island in the Caribbean. It was some trip for a boy who had just turned 17."

"Charlie boy, do you know how to ride a horse?" I told my new boss that the closest I had ever come to horses was when I stole away from Mr. Wolf and went to the race tracks. 'My Busha will teach you. See that house over yonder, set yourself up there. A gal will come to see to your needs.'" I asked Pappi what life like on the estate. "For your mother, it was good. She stayed indoors, baked and made sweet smells all over the house, and she had a nice room there. It was a challenge for me to handle the horse, but that was the only way to get through the swamps to the paymaster's shack."

There was a lot of information Mammy didn't share with us; small bits would come out here and there. She said the African man, whom we never met, and a woman who came to our home every month were good friends. Pappi said the couple lived together in a small house on the estate where they had worked for many years. He said that they acted as surrogate parents to Mammy when she first went to work as a baker for the family. It was obvious that Mammy felt that she owed them a lot because, each time Miss Sarah came, there was a package for her to take back home. Flour, rice, sugar, salted fish, and sometimes a piece of beef or pork was put aside for her. At Christmastime, Mammy gave Miss Sarah material, shoes, a couple shirts, and other items for Tata, her common-law husband. We heard she had a daughter but had never met the girl.

Our family was doing fine, so we didn't worry about Mammy's many philanthropic activities. There were many. She gave sheets and pillowcases for the public wards at the local hospital. If there were left over pastries, she would ask Miss Witherspoon to take them to people in the poor house. Emily was right, we were fortunate. I took private lessons every day after school, and she took organ lessons. She was interested in pastry making and helped Mammy. Our parents were very strict, so we did not have the latitude to do much without their approval. Emily sometimes would sneak and give excuses, but I always sought their approval. Our parents were church going people, and there were religious activities we had to do. We went to Sunday School and were involved in all the activities. When we were older, we had to go to regular church services, youth meetings, and we had to take confirmation lessons. At every stage of our lives, there were different obligatory things that we had to do. There were several boys who were interested in taking us out, but Mammy insisted that they come to the home. When we were finally able to go out, Emily and I had to go together.

My first serious relationship was with a boy I met while riding to take extra lessons. His father was a lawyer, and his mother, a former history teacher, was a full-time housewife. They owned a small sugar cane farm that employed a staff and laborers. They had a hog pen that was managed by a man who lived on the property with his wife and young daughter. I rode a bicycle; he was driven to school. Our house was in the center of town and close to the road. He lived in a suburb and had a circular driveway that led to his house. He introduced me to his sister who went to a boarding school and was home on holiday. Emily said he was conceited; I thought we had a lot in common. Emily said she knew what that was—we both thought we were above the ordinary. He could be obnoxious, but we got along fine and were beginning to fall in love. I got tired of hearing about Emily's broken romances. It seemed to me as if my sister wanted to test how many hearts she could break. As soon as she finished high school, she plunged full time into the family's business. I went to a teacher's college for two more years to perfect my tutoring skills.

Mammy had built a solid business, and it was paying off. Pappi continued to work at his profession in a confectionary shop uptown. He did the bookkeeping, payroll and banking for Tata's. Emily had a knack for creativity and was willing to put her stamp on new offerings. Mammy was delighted that one of her daughters would be joining the business. It was Emily's idea to add catering for weddings and social events and to offer plum puddings at Christmas. Orders for this special item had to be made at least six months in advance. It took that long to soak and prepare the ingredients.

Once the word got out, orders began to pour in for Tata's catering services. After the first event, which was a garden party, they realized that a few details had been left out of the planning. The waiters had no prior training except for the hour Miss Witherspoon spent telling them what they'd have to do. They were to serve, not to engage guests in conversation, and not to be seen eating any of the items. To prevent a fiasco, Mammy and Emily had to jump in, but I refused. I did not plan to serve in any such capacity. They couldn't even think of asking Pappi. It wasn't as if I was not doing anything to help the family business. I did all the ordering of supplies and counted the cash receipts every day, but Emily was still angry because I would not agree to serve at this party. "I know why you didn't want to come and help us. You were afraid that your friends would see you carrying around a tray with lemonade and cake."

"Mammy didn't want to do it either, Emily. You chose to expand the business with your big ideas and lack of experience and planning. I made it clear what my contribution would be, and I have kept my promise in that regard."

"Lindsay. It was all about Lindsay Bronson. You knew he was going to be there. He told you, I'm sure."

"Lindsay asked me to join him, and I said no, because I suspected that there was going to be trouble. I heard you asking Miss Witherspoon how many helpers she had been able to secure, and she said only one so far. I asked you how many people were expected, and you said around 50. I knew then it may not be as smooth as should be expected." I told Emily that people don't become servers by rote; they had to be trained.

The sudden surge in business seemed to have caught Mammy by surprise. Mammy set the rules for all future reservations. Mauva didn't see why she could mix lemonade and wash the glasses but not be one of the servers. It was months before Tata accepted another order for a catered function. The fiasco was soon forgotten, and things returned to normal. Then, Miss Sarah showed up.

*   *   *   *

Tata died in his sleep, and she buried him next to the house. It seemed as if Mammy was sorry that she was not told in time to go to the funeral, but Miss Sarah said there wasn't time. The new property owners did not want her to keep the body and did not want people trudging over their estate to come to a funeral. Although the previous owners had deeded them the house and small surrounding lot, the only access was by way of a main entrance to the big house. We had never seen Mammy weep, but I believed she went into the little back room after Miss Sarah left, and cried. Several months later, Miss Sarah brought her daughter and asked Mammy to give her something to do. She assured Mammy that arrangements for housing could be arranged with friends. It would be a long walk to our house, but the girl was willing.

"She is a good girl and very obedient and has good manners. She can wash good and iron. She can cook, too, Miss Liz." We knew Mauva was listening and that this new woman would seem like a challenge to her continued employment. She was the general household helper, and her duties included those tasks. Mammy told Miss Sarah that she would talk it over with the family and let her know something the next time she came. Miss Sarah's daughter held her head down until Miss Sarah said goodbye. There was something in her looks that made me think of my sister Emily. Mauva sat on the steps while we discussed the prospect of hiring this new woman. We talked about bringing her on for three days. With the catering, we had more laundry to do. What we did not say, in Mauva's presence, was how terrible she was with our clothes and how many of the fine shop doilies, and tablecloths she ruined. At first, I thought like Mauva that we didn't need anymore household help. When Pappi added his complaint about the color of his once-white shirts, we agreed that there was no harm in trying this woman. Mammy respected Miss Sarah and said she would not say the girl was good if she wasn't. Mauva still was not satisfied that we would hire someone for three days to do washing and ironing. She complained about grating the corn, which she thought Miss Witherspoon should do but couldn't see that, with the new woman, she would no longer have to wash and iron.

"Me been doing everyting in this household for years. Me clean, wash plate, wash, iron, run a shop when anyting fe, buy tings, scrub floor, dust furniture, and buy firewood fe cook and bring it back pon me head. All dem tings me been doing for these years, and she is gwineto juss wash and iron?"

Anne was older than Mauva by at least a few years. She was of a medium height, dark complexion and had a round face. Her shoulder length hair had a part down the center. Two coarse plaits shot off to each side of her head like a cow's horns. Mammy thought that, if Anne could find work for another three days, the girl would be able to make enough money to rent a room. Miss Sarah's friend and the woman's husband would have to share one room and bed with Anne. "Mammy ought to let her have the little back room. We could lock it so that she wouldn't have access to the rest of the house. She looks quiet and clean, and Miss Sarah is not a stranger to us." I looked at Emily with contempt.

"What a silly idea. We have already partitioned off the largest room in the house, which is being used for the shop. If you recall, it required a lot of adjustments so that we could maintain our privacy. Now, you want to move the washer woman in and have us reconfigure the back room to suit her occupancy." Emily wheeled off, saying I had a problem. I was not the only one with a problem. Mauva would be livid. Mammy was concerned that three days a week was not enough to keep a roof over her head and buy food. She found someone to take Anne for another three days and, fortunately, the family allowed her to move into their unoccupied maid's room. That solved one of the problems. Next, Mammy started on a program to teach Anne to read. She took at least a half hour and sat with the woman under the almond tree. It didn't bother me that Mammy taught Mauva a lot about doing domestic chores, and Pappi helped people who couldn't read take care of their correspondence. It occurred to me that feeling that Mammy was going overboard in Anne's case was incorrect. Objectively, this was in keeping with our faith as a Christian family. Mauva did not profess to be a Christian. She was a strong believer in voodoo magic, and she objected.

"Learn the alphabet? Me cahnt learn her to liff up a mortar pestle and bring it down on coffee beans. What a way she lucky! Nobady nevah do dat for me. Anyway, me can read and write. If she can spend time unda tree, Miss Liz should make her help me wid de housework or come two days instead." Anne didn't have much to say, but the words she occasionally uttered to Mauva were caustic. She referred to our loyal helper as, "Dat natty head gal." Mauva kept her complaints around the edges knowing that it was not a good idea to upset Mammy. Although she had a lot of patience and no better employer could be found, Mammy had her limit. Emily was like her; they knew how to deal with the helpers. The business was going well, and Emily seemed to be enjoying the good-daughter compliments. She was helping her mother, supervising wedding receptions and parties and going out with her boyfriends.

Mammy could not accept that all I wanted to do was tutor high school children. "Kay, you've seen and heard what happened to Antoinette Tate. One day she was flying high being driven in a Bentley, had two servants and yard boys and what have you. She was living the life of the spouse of a wealthy man and where is she now? He's gone. Took off with their servant girl."

"Mammy, you don't have to go through that again."

"Let's say she had learned to type or to do bookkeeping, dressmaking or baking, she could have found a job to employ her skill. How many people in this town can afford to pay a tutor? It wasn't cheap to tutor you and Emily in French, but what are you to do with elementary French? That is how a lot of people look at this extra expense. Yes, you have a couple students but, remember that you have no financial responsibilities. You live rent free and never have to worry about food."

"I will be tutoring English, Mammy, and there is a demand. You had to run away from home in order to follow your dream. At my age, it wouldn't be considered running away." Emily laughed, saying age had nothing to do with it; there was still time if I were so inclined. She left the table, and I heard her reminding Anne to press the sash for her choir robe. I didn't see myself looking over the top of bifocals and carrying around an eraser pencil clipped to my shirt like my Pappi. Mauva used to complain that it was difficult to get the lead stains out his shirts. Anne has found a way to do it. I never thought bookkeeping skills would be of any benefit to me. However Pappi was willing, and I knew it would make my mother happy that I was learning a skill that I could fall back on, if necessary. I enjoyed sitting with Pappi. He made debits and credits fun. I practiced on the shop's accounts the same way Emily practiced icing cakes. Only, I had an eraser to correct my mistakes. Her ruined products became the dessert. She had many before she perfected the art of mixing up the white sugar and egg whites for the icing. Anne was well entrenched in the family. She and Mauva had their share of run-ins, but she was conscientious and did an excellent job.

I noticed a seeming familiarity had developed between her and Emily, and it concerned me. It was bothersome to see them whispering like friends. I warned Emily of the dangers of becoming too familiar with servants. "We are all God's children. Going to church every Sunday hasn't done much for you it seems." Emily was not too religious, even though we had the same amount of a religious upbringing and continued to be involved with church. "You are just jealous because Anne has shown a preference for me and that is your fault. You act too impersonal and aloof. They are people just like us, Kay." Anne called Emily, Miss Em, Mammy was Miss Liz, and I was simply Miss. "Yes, miss. No, miss." My clothes had to be done in the course of the three days, otherwise they'd have to wait for the following week. Anne would come back on a Saturday evening after she left her other job to iron something for Emily. When I asked her to try and press a dress I wanted for the weekend, she said, "Ef you cahnt wait, then mek Mauva dweet." I knew she was speaking to me because she was standing in front of me and looking down at her feet. I was so angry. As soon as Pappi came home, I went to complain.

"Kay, my lassie, don't be so sensitive. That is just the way she is. She wasn't brought up right. Those people didn't know how. She may not know the right way to speak, but she knows her worth to this family. Since she came here, I once again have shirts that are white." I thought, that clock-face woman may not be as dumb as everyone seemed to think. She had Mammy teaching her to read, Emily as a confidante, and Pappi singing the praises of his white shirts. As long as I could remember, Pappi had never been robust, and he didn't want to use his small amount of energy on household matters. So, talking to him about Anne was a useless exercise that I should have known would not have any desired result. If I complained about anything, he'd always remind me that, as a family, we have done well. He'd add, "Today the only things I fear are the clutter in my office, my failing health, and your mother's wrath." Mammy got after him to wear a merino, a suit jacket to take his lunch to work, and to drink a glass of the tonic she made for him every night. Mauva and I were alone in our dislike of this washer woman, but there was nothing we could do.

Pappi was given to bouts of illness that kept him in bed, sometimes for a few days and, sometimes, a couple weeks. When he couldn't go to the office, his boss would have someone bring the orders and receipts to our house. He did the work, and they'd come back to pick it up. I'd read to him, and we'd discuss books until he got tired, slid down from the pillow and closed his eyes. I thought it would be a good thing for him to see flowers growing outside his window. I know he loved flowers and often brought home a bunch of roses or pansies for Mammy, and I wanted to make a garden in front of his window.

The fishermen who caught conches unloaded them on the sandy beach, where they cracked the bottom, pulled out the mollusk and discarded these beautiful pink and white fluted shells. It was a short walk from our home to the seaside, and I could carry only two shells each time. It would go faster if I had help. Anne hung the wash on the line and sat under the tree as if waiting for the sun to dry the clothes. "Anne," I called to her. "Yes, Miss," she replied without looking up.

"Anne, could you please follow me to the seaside. I want to pick up some conk shells to make a garden for Pappi."

"A fe yu Fada so a you fe dweet wid yu own-na hands."

"What she means, Kay, is that you should do it yourself out of love for your father." I looked at my mother the same way I sometimes looked at Emily when she'd make comments I thought were out of place. "Some day you will understand that these helpers are not always compliant. The essential traits are honesty, loyalty, and a sincere effort to satisfactorily perform the work. We may not like the way they talk, but sometimes we have to overlook some of the things they say. Take Mauva."

Of course, Mauva volunteered, and together we made a border around a small spot in front of Pappi's window. He had gone back to work by the time the garden was planted, but I was sure that the flowers would soon bloom. While I hoped his health kept up, realistically, I knew sooner or later he would be back in his bed. Pappi had given up serving on the Board of Trustees of our church. He couldn't squander his limited reserves on anything other than work. I never thought that I'd use the skills I learned until a trustee died, creating a shortage of people with financial background. The vicar asked me, and Pappi urged me to accept, if only to fill his slot. I was up to four students, helped with the work he brought home, and did most of the bookkeeping for the shop. It kept me busy.

Lindsay complained that I didn't have time for him anymore. He'd have to borrow his father's car, a loan the man was reluctant to make, to come and visit me. We met at church when he attended; if his parents had something to do, we'd go for ice cream. They'd wait to take him back home.

"He could ride a damn bicycle if he loved you so much."

"Lindsay does not have a bicycle, Emily."

"As rich as his parents are, they could buy him one. What is happening, Kay, as far as I heard, he is fooling around with the pen keeper's daughter. She is much younger than him, but I guess she can't refuse." I knew the layout of their property, and it wouldn't be a far walk to lure the girl and be sheltered from sight by the foliage of sugarcane plants. Perhaps that would satisfy his physical urges in a way that our relationship did not. Emily had broken up with many boyfriends, while Lindsay and I were still going together. I never told him what Emily said for fear he may admit to it, and I would be hurt. We had talked about our future. I knew he had postponed college for a few years to help his father with the property. It was time; he told me one evening. It was time that we made the commitment. He didn't want to marry until after he finished college, but he didn't want to lose me to anyone else.

*   *   *   *

Lindsay asked for my hand, and Pappi told him an engagement is a far cry from marriage and only then should he ask for my hand. Mammy wanted to make the announcement that Lindsay and I were engaged. She invited his family to dinner. The families knew each other but were not close friends. Mammy was happy. She was humming as she instructed Mauva to take time to rub the silverware before setting the table. It was a dream come true; she would finally have a doctor in the family. It was Lindsay's stated plan to become a medical doctor.

The Model T pulled up in front of our house with Lindsay at the wheel, his sister Molly next to him and his parents in the backseat. Pappi was in his chair by the window and saw them hop out of the car. Mammy rushed to the door to greet the Bronsons. She hugged Catherine Bronson and Molly. Emily stuck her head from behind the dining room curtain and said, "Hello." Pappi, as if he were watching a spectacle, half-rose from the chair to greet Mr. Bronson. "Hullo and good afternoon, Edward. Have a seat. Have a seat." Mr. Bronson had gone home and changed from his conservative church suit into formal attire, a waistcoat and cravat. He sat upright, as someone would if he were sitting on a bed of hot coals.

"Hullo, Caroline. Couldn't tell the last time I heard all the words of the reading of the scriptures so clearly." Her husband had read the previous week. "The vicar should have you do it more often."

Lindsay and Molly went off to visit with Emily and Mammy, leaving me in the drawing room with his parents and Pappi. Edward Bronson was a very pompous man, a trait Pappi detested and had detected in his son. Everybody in the town who was anybody worked for WESCO, one of the biggest employers in the entire parish. They owned hundreds of acres of sugarcane, refined sugar and had an interest in the making of rum. Mr. Bronson was one of their high-paid lawyers. There were two leading attorneys in the town. He was corporate, and young Albert Tidings was a criminal lawyer. Mr. Bronson pulled up his chin and cleared his throat, as if his cravat was too tight. "So, Charlie, Lindsay told me you are originally from Scotland. I thought I heard England, but people in this town are noted to produce misinformation in great quantities. I have filed against many. Well, England, Scotland—close enough."

"Born in Dumphries, home of one of our famous bards. Correct myself. He was born in Alloway but adopted Dumphries and rests there in St. Michael's churchyard." Mr. Bronson looked perplexed. How could a mere bookkeeper stump him, a learned man? Pappi did nothing to clear up the matter, so I laughed, a bit embarrassed, hoping that Emily would hurry and call us to dinner. I liked Mr. Bronson. He had always been nice to me, and I never minded his stuffiness. I believed that was a genuine part of his nature.

"Pappi was referring to Robert Burns, the poet, Mr. Bronson." He nodded to acknowledge my clarification, not in a way that suggested he did not know, but to infer it was a childish ploy of no significance. Mrs. Bronson worked for a short time as a history teacher and wanted to join the conversation.

"Oh, yes." She knew Pappi was referring to Robert Burns and added that Thomas Carlyle was also Scottish. "He took sides with Governor Eyre, who ordered his men to fire on unarmed natives, slaughtering hundreds in the process." I was glad that Mammy was not there to add her opinion, this being one of her pet subjects. She would have liked to rewrite the history of the 1865 rebellion and reverse the outcome. Mr. Bronson said the governor was punished under the law and anything more would have presented a case of double jeopardy. Mammy did not believe the punishment fit the crime; suspension and recall were not enough for what Edward John Eyre did. I could tell the way Pappi looked at Mr. Stuffed-shirt Bronson that he was thinking, here sat the architect and molder of that boy, Lindsay, in his own drawing room. Lawyer Bronson took charge of the conversation again, speaking as if I were not present.

"I see where Karolyn got her love of literature, Charlie. Lindsay told me you sit together and read. He was never able to pull Karolyn away in mid-sentence. That is so admirable. I have a love for the classics myself. A necessary part of my legal training included the study of drama. You know, being a litigator, a bit of flourish is needed some times." Pappi was looking at him with unspoken words that I could tell were not complimentary. "My Molly wants to study law like her Daddy, and I tell her she ought to take piano and voice lessons. She has such a vocal range; she'd be a great opera singer. They've asked her to join the choir, but she doesn't have time." Emily called us to the dinner, and it was a great relief. Pappi went to his room to wash his hands and returned after everyone was seated. It was a pleasant afternoon. Mammy and I walked the Bronsons to the gate and watched Lindsay crank up the car. The automobile pushed off to a jerky start, with Mr. Bronson bouncing like a mannequin and his wife holding onto the edge of the seat. I sat feeling all excited and in love, but Pappi was somber.

"Lassie, being engaged to a man who is going off to pursue medicine is a useless exercise and only for show. You are both old enough to get married. Do you know how long it takes to graduate from medical school? He will only be able to get a first degree from the university, then he will have to go abroad for the medical degree. You've tied yourself to this boy who can't make up his mind whether he loves you enough to marry or not." I hadn't thought of it in that way. I had only been thinking of four years and hoping that it may be shorter if he studied hard. Mammy heard Pappi and came into the room.

"They are in love, and they are young. Lindsay is a gentleman, because he could have left without saying a word. He asked for her hand, and you rebuked him. He has given a ring of engagement, and you are not happy. What more do you expect?" Pappi got up and went to his bedroom. Emily joined us.

"In a way, Pappi is right. What if Lindsay changed his mind? Molly told me that her brother was not the most faithful fellow in the world. She said so in the kitchen, and she said 'He must really love your sister.' He was standing next to me when she said it. He laughed, telling me I shouldn't listen to Molly because he would always be faithful to you. I didn't believe him."

"Emily Anne, leave it to you to say something negative."

"I don't think that was necessary. Lindsay and Karolyn are officially engaged with our blessing."

"With your blessings, Mammy."

"We plan to make the official announcement next Sunday. Please ask Mr. McHale to have his soloist sing an appropriate song for the occasion." Emily said she would ask the choir director. Mauva, never one to be left out, wanted a compliment on the delicious meal she prepared.

"You see how me fix that pork? Miss Caroline did love it. The pigeons come out nice an brown. Miss Emily mek the stuffing. Miss Liz so happy that you is gwineto marry solicitor Bronson son. Him look good, but him don't have no manners. Him never say, hello, Mauva. But him look pon me and smile, so I guess that was to say how-de-do. Me noh you will teach him manners, Miss Kay because you is a very high class and mannersable lady. Dem Bronson people have 'bout," she counted on her fingers, "three o four servants in dat big house. Is nuff land dem have an him is de onlgiest boy in de fambily. Mean to sey, him is gwineto get most of it. When yu marry, ask Miss Liz if me can come and work for you. Me love it here, but me noh how fe take care of you." Mauva had a way of mixing disparate comments. "Miss Kay speaking of dat, me hear Manleng a holler God Save De King 'bout lantern slide a parish church Saturday night coming. Me would like fe see it, but six pence is almost all de pay me get." I offered to get her the ticket. "Wherein me wasn't asking you, but I will accept it since you volunteer." Despite all her rambling, there was something about Mauva that endeared her to me. I was very happy. Lindsay and I saw each other every day before he left for the university.

Pappi had several bouts with pneumonia, colds and fever. With every bout of illness, he seemed to lose more of his strength and stamina upon recovery. The walk to his office was a struggle. Mammy begged him to give it up, saying that the business was making enough money to take care of everything. He could no longer stay after work to help with letter writing for those people who had been coming to him for years. Some Sundays, he was not able to attend church services. When he shortened his work week, I knew it was the beginning of a downward slide. "What does he know? Dr. Harper was good, but he died; this fellow just graduated from medical school. He is too young and inexperienced." I told Mammy, if she did not have any confidence in Dr. James, to take Pappi to the hospital, where he would be tended by a medical staff. "He is getting the best care right here." Sometimes, it is better not to say what you are thinking." Mammy made me feel, as if by making these suggestions, I was splashing bad karma over any possible recovery.

Miss Witherspoon was running the tea shop, and Emily and she were doing the catering. There was enough experience between them to staff and choreograph events so that they ran smoothly. This freed Mammy to spend more time taking care of her husband. There was a request for me to take on a couple more students but, due to Pappi's worsening condition, I turned that down. After reading with Pappi, I'd slip in my room, reread Lindsay's letters, and reply to them. The postmistress, seeing me standing in line every afternoon, would give me a thumbs up—meaning there was a letter or thumbs down—none. Lindsay practically lived at my house when he was down for a weekend or holidays. We'd go out and have a great time. He'd tell me all about his courses, and we'd share silly stories. I worried about Pappi's declining health. I wanted him to walk me down the aisle and every day that seemed to look more like a pipe dream. When Whitmore Chapley asked for Emily's hand in marriage, I thought he would see at least one of his daughters married.

Whitmore and Emily had an on-again, off-again relationship. In between the breakups, Emily went out with other men. Theirs was a tumultuous affair that I had come to believe was destined to fail. He often accused Emily of flirting with his friends, which was true. She accused him of playing with fire—romancing married women. I never said it, but I wondered how a marriage between those two would work. The engagement was for one year, and I was praying that it would happen, despite my misgivings. Emily said the year would allow them to plan and prepare for the wedding. She said she might split off the catering and form her own business, doing only that after she got married. I know Mammy would not have objected. I hoped Pappi would live long enough to see them married, but not long enough to see them divorced.

Months after their engagement, I was riding to a student's home when I ran into Joan Marsh. She was one of Emily's best friends. She waved me down. Emily was catering a garden party Monday afternoon and was busy preparing for it. She had asked her friend Joan to take the Sunday school class. "I can't get to your house, but I heard that Whitmore has left town or is leaving town shortly. Does Emily know?" I didn't think so. I was surprised myself. When I got to my student's home, his mother called me aside and whispered that she heard Whitmore Chapley got himself in trouble. He was caught in bed with a man's wife. She said that he had to leave through a side door dressed as a woman because the man took his clothes as evidence. I could scarcely focus on the lesson plan for this boy. This news would send Pappi hurtling into his grave. I could barely wait to get home. Emily was calm when I told her what I heard.

"We are still planning on getting married, but he decided to start school earlier because he was accepted." I knew she was lying. "We are not talking years, Karolyn. He is not studying to become a doctor. He wants to get an executive position. What about the woman? He is a wild man, and everybody knows it. If she is married, she shouldn't be entertaining another man in her house, let alone in her bedroom. How stupid. I am not worried in the least. A lot of men do the same thing, but he gets himself caught." I didn't let on that I was hurt when she told me that Lindsay was seeing the pen keeper's daughter, but I was upset. Here, she seemed to believe it was OK because everyone knew Whitmore was wild.

"Keep the news away from our parents, Emily. They would be concerned about the character of the man who intends to marry their daughter."

I kept busy with my students, helping Pappi with the bookkeeping work and taking care of the tea shop accounts. I wouldn't mind if Emily opened her own catering business. That way, she could employ someone to do all the extra work that I was doing. "What a shame," I thought, "my Pappi may die before seeing any of his two girls married." Mrs. Tate once told me that it doesn't matter how close you are to another person; it is impossible to know the depth of any of their feelings. I had come to think that she was right. Perhaps Pappi was more resilient than I thought. Perhaps he, too, believed that the nature of man was to carouse with many women. Maybe it was something he did when he was younger. I couldn't protect him from getting news of the antics of his soon-to-be son-in-law.

It was funny that he would accept Emily's faults, and I knew he would. But, he expected me to be perfect. I told Pappi that I would be going to the city for a weekend with Lindsay's parents. He shrugged and said I should pick up where we left off the evening before when we were discussing the soul. Pappi argued that the soul is life and breath, and that the mind relates to intelligence and is physically located in the brain. I believed that the soul and the mind were inseparable because they could not be physically identified within the human body. I was not fully invested in our discussion, because all my thoughts were on seeing Lindsay. Pappi fell asleep, and I left the room feeling sorry for his condition, and the disappointment he must feel. They didn't have a boy, and it looked as if the two girls would remain single.

Emily and Mammy were going over some upcoming catering events. It seemed it was all the two ever talked about. Emily said that if they needed more help at these social events, she may have to use Mauva. "It would be a fiasco to place Mauva in a situation where she would have an opportunity to talk and spread gossip about the most private aspects of our lives, especially yours, Emily. Let Miss Witherspoon take charge of that. She is responsible, and she knows a lot of people." Mammy said Mauva didn't have to be one of the servers, but she could help set up. In essence, she was agreeing with Emily to use Mauva in some capacity. "One thing I will do in my own household is hire experienced and intelligent helpers. People who can read recipes or who have gone to school in the domestic arts." Emily laughed. She said I should never put my eggs into one basket and that I ought to go out with other men. "Emily Anne, I am saving myself for Lindsay." As soon as Mammy left, she whispered.

"You are not a virgin. I know it. Saving yourself, ha! If I were you, Karolyn Elizabeth, I'd accept some of those invitations floating around. What did he say when you went to see him the other day? He asked you to have patience? No man could put me on such a leash." Two years had gone by, and I was beginning to feel like a rag doll on the shelf, gathering dust. Although I was angry at Emily's bluntness, I began to think that she may have a point. Going out with other people was easy for a woman who didn't care what others thought; I was different. Several weeks had gone by, including one long holiday weekend, and I had not seen nor heard from Lindsay. I began to suspect that Emily may have intercepted my mail.

I worried about losing the only man, next to my Pappi, whom I truly loved. I wrote to Lindsay. I'd be willing to sacrifice, even if it meant that we couldn't afford a servant and even if we'd have to live in one room. I would be prepared to stay at my parents home after we were married so as not to burden him. I wanted Pappi to give me away even if we had to get married at his bedside. I told him Pappi was gravely ill. I felt that I lost a bit of myself in that letter and regretted mailing it. I was being absorbed into Pappi's illness and feeling desperate about my situation.

Emily was happy as a lark. She seemed more involved with choir practice, staying out later and later and entertaining the choir director at home. I wished I was like her. "What about Whitmore?" She acted as if she had not heard the name before. "Whitmore, who?"

"The man you had go to Pappi's bedside and beg for your hand," I replied. "That one, Emily," I said." She told me they weren't engaged anymore. "He was here only a week ago, Emily, and you seemed quite loving then. Have you told Mammy?" She said that she was over 18 and didn't have to tell every detail of her life. "Have you told Pappi that he may not live to see you and Whitmore tie the knot?" Just then, the choir director arrived for another of their business meetings.

I heard from Lindsay. He was very apologetic, saying he had a series of examinations. He said he'd come to see me the first chance he got. It had become more difficult to act cheerful around Pappi, given his declining health and my despondency. I suggested to Emily that, since she had so much time to spend with the choir director, she could use some of it to sit at her father's bedside some evening and try to cheer him. "You are telling me what to do? You appointed yourself the philosopher and literary critic in this household. It is your choice to wear poor Pappi out. Haven't you noticed that he is asleep half the time you are reading and telling stories? I am doing the tasks that you do not want to do, freeing Mammy so that she can tend to her husband. What do you do? You tell Pappi jokes to make him laugh when you know it is bad for him, because it sets off a coughing fit. It weakens him to sit up to look at that crooked conch shell garden under the window. You ought to get Mauva to help you dismantle it; she helped to set it up. I can't blame Anne for not getting involved with that project. There aren't even any flowers for him to look at. How long does it take for plants to grow and bloom?"

"Mauva put too much cow manure. It burned the plants, but new ones are springing up and will soon flower. I know it doesn't take years to grow plants, Emily, but the soil is not the best; we have had a slew of insects that ate the leaves." Emily looked at me, as if to pity my ineptitude at growing things. "Pappi loves it when I read to him. He enjoys it and, even if his eyes are closed, his mind is alert. Everyone doesn't have to be so glum around him. It makes him depressed." I was surprised Emily stayed around to listen, but the more I talked, the more compassionate she became. She must have seen the sadness in my eyes.

"I'm sorry, Kay. I know that you are not in the best of moods, and I should not criticize your garden. We are all saddened by Pappi's condition. You shouldn't think I don't care because I don't sit at his bedside. I love him just as much as you do. I do what I can. I make him special custards that we don't sell in the shop. I make them because Pappi has a difficult time swallowing, and they contain eggs and milk and are nutritious. I am the one who gets the stout that Mammy uses to make him eggnog. Some of the stuff he vomits stains his shirts and is difficult to get out, but I see to it that Anne bleaches them because I know how particular he is about his clothes. Pappi knows that I love him. And no, I have not told him that Whitmore and I broke up, but I told Mammy. She said to keep it away from him. If he dies soon," she made the sign of the cross, "at least he would have died believing he had given my hand in marriage. So let's leave it that way. You never take my advice, but I will give it anyway: Throw that ring Lindsay gave you in the trash and get on with your life." I was no match for my sister, but I saw more clearly that I was not the only one who was carrying the burden of care for the man dying in our front room. I saw one student for two hours; one each week. I worked from Monday to Thursday leaving myself time to set coursework, review assignments, prepare and administer tests. When combined with all the other things I had to do, it was burdensome. It was a relief when Pappi told the confectioner he could no longer take work at home. That was one less responsibility for me.

When we were alone, I mentioned to Mammy that, if we got married before Lindsay graduated, I would be willing to help to pay his school fees. In her mind, men were supposed to support women not the other way around. She couldn't see that her business was the mainstay of our family support. "School fees? What kind of work could you do to pay full-time university fees, to carry someone onto a medical degree? I hope to God you have not mentioned that foolish idea to Lindsay. His parents, I am sure, are taking care of that, but even if they weren't, it would be his responsibility, not yours." Emily said I should give him an ultimatum just as she had given Whitmore. We know what happened; she returned his ring. I figured in one more year he would be through with his first degree, then he'd have to make the decision. I told Lindsay that I was not prepared to wait any longer than that. Although apprehensive, I anxiously awaited his reply.

Dear Karolyn,

I hope you are well. It's been a long time and true I have been weighed down with studies and in a way with guilt. Dad said your mother stopped by. As you know my parents are very fond of you and want to see us as a couple. This is what I wanted with all my heart."

Emily came in because I was sobbing loudly. She reminded me that Mauva was in the kitchen and that my cries will disturb Pappi. She hugged me and said it was the best thing that could happen. I felt as if everyone had been conspiring against us. I read the rest of the letter aloud. Emily said Lindsay may be weighed down with a guilty conscience, but I was free and should take some solace in that. *"I know perhaps this is one of the biggest mistakes of my life, but please believe me, it was not planned. She helped me with chemistry, one of my worse subjects. I resisted, but these things happen, unfortunately."* Emily said he was using that woman the same way he had used me. *"We plan to marry, please find it in your heart to forgive me."*

Lindsay Bronson wanted me to wait for him to complete his medical studies, but he proposed to another woman and planned to marry before he graduated with his first degree. I was sick with grief and took to bed for three days, venturing out only to read to Pappi. Now, Mammy had an ailing husband and a heart-broken daughter. I could tell she was distraught, perhaps blaming herself for going to his parents' home. "Kay, you cannot allow anyone to injure your soul." Funny, that Pappi and I talked about this very subject. If it wasn't physical, the injury had to be emotional and that could heal. "There is something good in what has happened; you'll see it after the tears are gone. It is better to break an engagement than a marriage. Lindsay surprised me, but he obviously would not have made you a good husband. Judging from his deception, he would probably have made your life unhappy." I didn't want to tell Pappi. His eyes were closed, and I asked if he wanted me to read.

"I never liked that bastard. He was too full of himself. No damn good just like his bloody father. A pompous ass. Blast them to hell. Don't worry, me lassie."

✳   ✳   ✳   ✳

Pappi died shortly afterwards, and Mammy followed one year later. We laid off Miss Witherspoon and Anne and shuttered the shop for several months to mourn the loss. Mauva was once more queen, and she delighted in her boast that she could do as well as the others combined. After a while, our lives gradually began to move toward a sort of normalcy. We reopened Tata's and brought back Miss Witherspoon and Anne. When my mind was not focused on some task, I would think about Lindsay. It became a distraction and was the reason I fell off my bicycle, and the reason I met Aaron. He was on-duty and confirmed a broken wrist. He offered to drive me home, but I was able to ride without putting pressure on my left hand. He said he would come by and check on me so that I wouldn't have to ride all the way back to the hospital.

Since Pappi died, I had never found any man who would admit to being interested in poetry or literature. He'd sometimes come to pick me up and take me to my student's home and come back for me. He didn't want me falling and further injuring my hand. Aaron was sitting under our almond tree in the back yard, reciting his favorite parts of Julius Caesar. Caesius' advice to Brutus: "*This it is:— Tis better that the enemy seek us: So shall he waste his means, weary his soldiers, Doing himself offence; whilst we, lying still, Are full of rest, defence, and nimbleness. Brutus. …There is a tide in the affairs of men Which, taken at the flood, leads on to fortune; Omitted, all the voyage of their life Is bound in shallows and in miseries. On such a full sea are we now afloat; and we must take the current when it serves, Or lose our ventures.*"

"After your experience with that son-of-a-bitch, you should stay clear of anyone who wears a white coat or says he is a doctor."

"It's time you call me Aaron, and I hope you don't mind if I call you Karolyn." Somehow, poetry served his passion because we stopped being platonic that night. There in the dark, we become lovers. He and another young intern lived in a rented house. He'd pick me up, and we'd go there for our trysts. We kissed and had light romantic touches, but Aaron was surprisingly not sexually aggressive. He waited for me to make the first move. Aaron was in our town to do his internship. He told me that he would be returning to the city at the end of two years, where he had a job waiting for him at the public hospital. The subject of marriage came up. I brought it up. I told Aaron how disappointed I was that my parents did not live to see either of their two daughters married. "That's a shame, but marriage is such a huge commitment. I've thought about it and have come close to proposing a few times, but medicine is so demanding. There are the patients, the paperwork, the professional conferences and seminars, and the politics. It is unbelievable what doctors have to endure. You would think doctors are supposed to be healing people, but so much time is spent on getting the right connections, the right slot, the right…It gets easier over time I suppose, but in the first few years, it requires almost 100 percent, not much time for a wife and kids."

I didn't realize that a doctor's life was so complicated and full of work and intrigue. Dr. James seemed to have time to go to all the parties around town and flirted with all the women. He didn't seem burdened by all those responsibilities. For my own sake, I had kept an emotional space even though I had fallen in love with Aaron. "You are trying to replace Pappi and that is impossible. Be practical, there are many men who would love to be with you. You could encourage them to develop an interest in the arts. Men are like dogs; they can be trained. Ordinary people like Donald don't interest you but, take my advice, they will treat you better."

"We have different requirements, Emily. Yes, Donald has a good government job that will provide a pension in case he leaves you a young widow. I still have time to choose a suitable mate. It may not be Aaron, but for the time being we enjoy each other's company. It's not like I have not gone out with anyone else. Aaron may change his mind and pop the question, who knows?" That was just to tease Emily.

"Don't hold your breath, because he clearly said that he will be returning to the city where he has a job waiting. Another thing, Kay, do you think that perhaps he may be so? He could be." My sister was suggesting that Aaron may be a homosexual. All the months we had been going out and holding long philosophical discussions, Aaron never mentioned that he knew Lindsay Bronson. Emily had recently catered the wedding reception for a nurse at the hospital. Aaron had been one of the guests, and he was telling me how lovely the affair was. He said it reminded him of Lindsay's wedding. Realizing that he had hit a raw nerve, Aaron apologized. I wondered what else he knew about me and Lindsay Bronson. His comment was either thoughtless, disingenuous or an unintended careless remark.

The hospital staff had a going-away party for him at one of the doctor's homes. We promised to stay in touch, but I did not want him even as a friend anymore. He told me there was a woman he had been going with since they were both in medical school. She wanted to get married, but he was not ready. He gave me reasons to believe that his interest in me was serious and that something would come of our romance. But, since the night he mentioned being a guest at Lindsay's wedding, I felt differently about him. He wrote, and I wrote back. Aaron came down to visit, and I went to the city to visit him. I could tell there was no future in our relationship and, after a while, we were just friends who corresponded now and again.

*   *   *   *

"It's a shame we've never met any of Pappi's family." We heard from his sister occasionally and wrote to them when Pappi died, and later Mammy, but none came. They sent sympathy cards and money. They continually invited us to visit them in Scotland, and Emily decided she'd go. I wouldn't have traveled that distance to visit people whom I had never met, but Emily didn't seem worried or afraid. She was excited to finally have an opportunity to see where our father was born and meet some of his relatives. I wondered if Miss Witherspoon alone with one assistant could handle the shop and the baking. Mauva was not good. Emily assured me she would arrange everything, so I needn't worry. She said she would bring Anne back to do the linens. "She will not be coming back to this home, Emily Anne. That is final." Emily was incensed.

"I did not ask your permission, Kay."

"You ought to before you go headlong into making arbitrary decisions that impact this household."

"You don't cook; you don't bake; you don't do housework; you want maids who are literate. Who the hell do you think you are?

"One of the owners of this home and the business establishment. That is who I am, Emily."

"Well, I have told the woman to come back here on Monday morning. It's done, Kay."

"You had better untell her."

"You damn well think your blue eyes and yellow skin gives you some imperial right over this household. It does not, Karolyn Elizabeth." She lowered her voice. "Probably, that is why Lindsay and now Aaron didn't." I slapped her, and it turned physical. She pushed me. I fell, and she sat on me and began to pull at my hair. I bit her hand. She scratched my face and neck. We were oblivious to the presence of Mauva Grant, who stood looking at us with one hand resting on her cheek, as if she were in shock. Mauva seemed to be always around, sometimes being so quiet it was only when the door curtains moved that one could detect a presence. It was embarrassing. Mauva had witnessed the most bizarre behavior ever exhibited in our household. Emily didn't seem to care, because she brushed herself off and went to her bedroom. I sent Mauva away with a warning that she had better not relay what happens in the privacy of our home to anyone.

"Shame of you to tink dat. Who me fe tell? Plus is nat my biznez, but me is well surprise for all these years me been a member of this household nutten like dis nevah happen."

"You heard what I said."

"Yes'm. I am leaving. I will be here bright and early tomorrow mawning an a hope sey oonu mek up by dat time. Good night, Miss Emily." Emily and I stopped speaking for several weeks. Mauva became the courier and more or less conveyed messages between us, sometimes adding comments of her own. "Miss Emily says that you is to pay the money to Mr. Ambrose because you always slow to pay for de tings an you is the banker for the tea shop." If we fired her, we'd be doomed. Anne came back and told me that she was sorry for any trouble she had caused, begging me to give her one more chance. I knew Emily had put her up to it, and I thought, OK, it's done. Emily said that she would leave Miss Wither-spoon in charge of the new assistant, Lorna, and Anne. Emily was all set; and her trip to Scotland planned.

Donald wanted Emily to set a date for their wedding, but she wanted to wait until she returned from her holidays. I was apprehensive about the responsibili-ties of running the shop, but the separation would be good for us. Emily could take her time to decide about Donald. Mauva repeated what she told Emily and what Emily said to her. "Ah tell Miss Emily nat to worry because you can manage by yurself. She sey dat you don't know how fe bake or sell inna shop, but me tell Miss Emily dat me is here to be of assistant and of course Miss Witherspoon know everyting an dat fool-fool girl Lorna who cahnt count money is here to help." Emily was due to leave on a Friday. Anne was not due to work, but she showed up the day before to wish Emily a safe journey. Donald drove her to the city to board the SS Brigadoon. I couldn't accompany them because I was now fully in charge of the tea shop.

We were nervous since this was her first trip abroad. Emily said she'd keep a journal and mail me the pages; this way I could share the trip vicariously. The family in Scotland was anxiously awaiting Emily's arrival. She would be away from May to mid-June. I didn't think of it before, but the timing was bad. While we were not offering wedding cakes, we were booked for several receptions. Miss Witherspoon was invaluable. I helped with the planning, and she handled the hiring of whatever extra help was needed to do the functions. Everything was going along smoothly, and I believed Emily would be proud that I was able to hold things together.

"Miss Kay, me could help if Miss Witherspoon run short. Me is not so back-ward like Anne." Fortunately, there was never a shortage of suitable help, so we did not have to press Mauva into service. Emily's letter and journal notes came midway through her vacation. I don't know what she told Donald in the letter she wrote to him, but Emily said that if it were not for me and our business, she would seriously consider making Scotland home. She loved it, and Pappi's family was wonderful. Emily said the mood was so joyful, she even took a few sips of liquor, which immediately went to her head and made her act foolish. I thought, Oh, no, she had better not get loose with any of those Scotsmen. *"Kay,"* she wrote, *"you must make the trip. They act as if they've known me all my life."* She met a lot of cousins, and she said that Pappi's sister had a son who had been a pilot in the War. *"Miss you but not too much. Will tell you everything when I return. Love, Emily."*

Anne came the three days and did what she had to do and left. She listened to Miss Witherspoon but would never take any instructions from Mauva. I wanted Anne to iron a dress for the weekend, and thought, after all, I was paying her wages, why should I have to go through Miss Witherspoon? I summoned her, and Anne was standing before me at the dining room door, staring at her ashen feet. She told me the dress would have to wait until the following Monday or Tuesday when she was ironing clothes. This was her week to take care of the shop linens. If I wanted it before next week, I could do it myself or have Mauva do it. She went further with her insolence to remind me that Mammy said, even if I got a rich husband, I still needed to know how to do housework. Mauva cleared her throat to let me know she was listening. I paid Anne and told her to finish the day and not to come back. "Miss Emily nat here fe beg fe her dis time. Ah tell you how facety the gal is but you nevah believe me. She tink dat she is the boss in this household." Mammy would say I was cutting my nose off to spite my face. I would have to find something else to wear, because I was not going to let Mauva ruin my white linen dress. Mauva, always the last one to leave, sat quietly observing me as I sat pensively in the dining room staring at the old china wagon. The piece of furniture had been in our family for generations. The platters were never used; they were always on display on the two shelves. I thought how easily one could just fall off and break, but none ever did. The silver and other valuable pieces were all locked away in a cedar chest Mammy kept in the bedroom. Why do we need these things? Mauva interrupted my thoughts.

"Miss Kay, don't fret."

"Why would you say that?"

"Because you nat eating good for the past few weeks. I noh you miss yur sistah but me is here to take care of you. Is lang time me been along wid dis family. Yu noh, Miss Kay, come to tink of it, I was talking about de hurricane but you notice how troubles come in three? Dis year we get new governor an what kind a name him have? Foot. Dis year hurricane look like it a goh come an wash wey people, an dis year yu run Anne fe good." I asked Mauva how she managed to put all those events together. "Glad yu ask me, Miss Kay. Yu remembah how dem British drag us inna fight we noh have nutten to do wid?" Now, she was talking about World War II. "Dem white people ketch up inna fight an wha happen? Eh kill a whole lat ah fe we people? Yu remembah how tings was scarce because dem was dropping fire bomb an de captain dem nevah want fe dead so dem wouldn't sail dem ships here.. So wha happen? We couldn't get kerosene. We couldn't get flour and sardines and salt fish. Now dem a push new governor pon us who juss come yah fe holiday and fe sun himself an him pickney dem. Him is gwineto boss we prime minister and mek him do wha dem a Britain want him fe do. Where is de dress you want fe iron?"

No sweeter words had ever been said or heard by me: "Kay, Kay, my darling, your sister is home." Emily hugged and kissed me as if we had been apart for longer than six weeks. Mauva would fill her in on the details but, for the time being, we talked about the trip. Emily told Donald to go home and rest, after the long drive to pick her up, and bring her back home. Emily popped open her trunk in the drawing room to show the things she brought back from Scotland. Mauva was standing near by. "What is Donald going to do with a woolen scarf?" She said it was a memento given to her by one of Pappi's relatives who knitted it. Among the souvenirs was an encrusted gold cross that belonged to Pappi's mother—that was for me. She'd also brought a broach with the Scottish flag, a wedding ring that belonged to Pappi's mother, and several other items she picked up as gifts for friends and our helpers. Emily talked into the night, telling how she learned more about Pappi and his family than he had ever told us.

Pappi had written to them, saying that the man in Leeds worked him from sun up to sun down, that he gave him a small room that had no heat, and barely enough food to keep his ribs from caving in. His father wanted him to return home and join him in the shoemaking business, but young Charlie never liked the trade. They heard from him once in a while when he had news to share. He told them there was a beautiful island woman he was aiming to marry some day if she would have him. Pappi's sister asked if he had any other children because he had mentioned something about a girl. Emily found it odd but said they were perhaps confused, because Pappi's handwriting was so terrible.

A few weeks after Emily returned, Anne showed up with a welcoming jar of stewed June plums, Emily's favorite, and a couple breadfruits and pieces of yellow yam. She complained to Emily about my letting her go, but I had already made it clear that, if she were rehired, I would wash my hands and have nothing more to do with the business. I didn't mind sharing with Miss Sarah because we had promised Mammy, but the girl had used up all credits as far as I was concerned. Emily asked Anne about Miss Sarah because we had not seen the woman for some time. "She dead and me bury her two weeks now." We looked at each other because the woman had told us before that her mother had died sometime ago. Emily gave her money and the broach with the Scottish flag. I was surprised and told Emily that it belonged in our family. She said she decided what to do with the items she brought back and that I could do the same when it was my turn. "What is Anne going to do with a gold broach?" Mauva was a mind reader because I had not verbalized my thoughts.

"Is the same ting I was tinking, Miss Kay. What she gwineto do wid gold frock pin?" Mauva still had the small change purse, as if to show comparison with the gold broach. "You see how de gal bare face? You run her way an see how she present herself as soon as Miss Emily come back?" Emily said she would like to bring Anne back for at least one day because Miss Witherspoon could not find the person she had been looking for to do the laundry. I told Emily to give me time to think it over. It was a bitter pill to swallow, but I was leaning toward it since Emily seemed so disappointed that I had let go her most prized employee.

"Okay, I will send for her. I hope you weren't thinking that I made arrangements behind your back, but since you agree."

"I did not agree, Emily. Capitulation is a far cry from agreement, but I do understand it is important for us to have the shop linens done."

It seemed that Emily was ready to set a date with Donald. She slipped into my bed and woke me up, telling me that he had given her a ring. "I should give it back. We could use this money for something more important. I am not going to wear it, because I'm afraid the diamond will fall out. He is such a stupid man. He didn't have to do this, but I guess he has his reasons. "That is a sign of his love and devotion, Emily," I told her and added that it was not a good way to enter a promise of marriage. We figured he ordered the ring when he drove her to the ship and picked it up the day she returned. Emily put the ring in her drawer, saying it was not practical for her to wear it when her hands were so often in dough. In a way, that was true, but to my mind it wasn't the whole truth. I had learned over the years that, unless she asked, I should be careful about giving my sister an opinion.

We were busy with my students, the shop and our separate activities. Donald and she were planning to be married near Christmas. Mauva broke the news that Whitmore was back in town. Emily knew, saying that he was the new hospital administrator. It was a big job. His wife and young daughter were expected to join him as soon as he found suitable housing. It wasn't long before Whitmore was dropping in to visit us. Sometimes, he'd stay for supper. Often, I had work to do and left them chatting in either the living room or they'd go to her bedroom. I considered him a family friend, so it wasn't that odd.

One evening, I left them in the drawing room visiting and went outside to sit under the almond tree. I thought about the nights I sat there with Aaron reciting from Shakespeare, and I remembered when we were young. Emily and I used to play in the branches of this tree. We had a tree house up there. Emily fell and broke her leg, and Mammy said we could never climb it again. Emily said it wasn't because she broke her foot, but that Mammy was afraid we could lose our virginity. She came into my bed and talked nonstop about Whitmore. I told her Donald may not like it if he found out that her former beau was visiting our home. What I didn't say, and what was on my mind, was that I was sure he would somehow believe that I was in collusion with her. "Well, I can have lunch with him. There is nothing wrong with talking, is there?" I didn't know she had been meeting Whitmore for lunch.

"Perhaps you ought to wait until his family gets here and have him invite you to dine with them; this would seem more appropriate." Whit told her that the woman had tricked him into marriage, saying she was pregnant. "As far as I have heard, they have a child, Emily. She was telling the truth." He told Emily that he was unhappy. I warned her again about troubles that may be in store, but Emily was not one to listen or take advice once she had made her decision. She had always been reckless that way. Some weeks after this conversation, I heard Mauva conversing with someone in the drawing room. I knew immediately it was Donald and rushed out to stop the flow of information.

"You should'a noh dat Miss Emily gone to choir practice." I scolded Mauva for not telling me that we had company. "Him nevah ask for you, Miss Kay." Mauva looked at Donald as if to confirm that she told the truth. "Him ask if Miss Emily is here and..." I shut her off. Donald paused, and I took this as a signal he had something to say to me. I asked Mauva to leave the room, and he sat.

"I heard Mauva telling you that Emily had gone to choir practice. She mentioned she was meeting Joan to look at fabric samples for the bridesmaids' dresses." I had inadvertently placed myself in the middle and become a co-conspirator. It now became necessary to delay Donald so that he wouldn't drive to Joan's house searching for Emily. He lowered his voice so much I had to pull my chair closer to hear what he was saying. He said that this conversation was to be between us. An alarm bell went up because there was no way I wanted to keep any secret with my sister's fiancé, but there I was leaning over to hear what he had to say. I wished that Mauva would reappear to give me an excuse, but she was perhaps indignant because of my reprimand.

"As a woman on the verge of marriage, you would surely agree with me that there is certain expectation. I have been a proper gentleman for all the time we have been together." I urged the man to get to the point, because Emily may soon be returning home. "Your sister, the woman who is wearing that big diamond— well, she is not wearing it—is having sex with Whitmore Chapley." I stood up, saying this was a subject more appropriately addressed in private between himself and Emily. "Beg your pardon if it sounds a bit shocking, but they were seen coming out of that rooming house. I approached the little cockroach, and he admitted it." I sat back down, because as much as I hated to be involved in this type of conversation, it was important to know what people may be saying about my family. "The boy said I am not to work myself up because he is happily married, and his wife will be joining him shortly. You must remember the scandal. When Mr. Barrett caught the little squirrel in bed with his wife, he was going to kill him. He was engaged to your sister at the time, and I am sure Emily knew about it. That is the real reason behind the break up and his quick exit. Now, he is back to make more trouble."

"I do not make a habit of reacting to dirty rumors and, Donald, I suggest that you avoid as best you can those kinds of situations. Whitmore tends to be boastful and what he says should not be relied on for accuracy. I doubt that there is much truth in the accusations. Be that as it may, what would you have me do? Emily is a grown woman."

"Have a word with her, that is all I am asking." I was still in the drawing room when Emily returned, looking very disheveled. Mauva bolted in to say that Donald had come looking for her. I left to go to my bedroom, motioning Emily to follow me for a private chat. She did after listening to all that Mauva had to say.

"Donald said you were not at choir practice."

"Mauva told me. Of course I was not. If I were there, he would have seen me. He is such a fool."

"I told him you were probably at your friend's house picking out bridesmaid designs."

"Mauva told me."

"Listen to me. Emily, you are engaged to be married to the fool. It is your own doing; no one is forcing you. If you are not in love with the man, as it seems obvious to me you are not, break it off. In Mammy's words, Emily, 'stop a quarrel before it becomes a fight.'"

"Mammy, Mammy, Mammy, Mammy this. Mammy that. She is dead and gone. You think she didn't hear about the scandal? She never said, 'Don't marry him.' Anyway, what I do with my life is my business. Donald had no right coming here, and you had no right interfering. Instead of whispering behind my back, you should have run him." I apologized to Emily, because it seemed as if she was steaming for a fight, and I was already agitated and angry that I was now ambushed in a situation not of my making. I waited for her to leave my room. She didn't make any attempt to get off my bed and seemed to be thinking of what tact she would take next. "If you want to know, I was at Joan's house looking at samples, so you guessed right." I did not believe her but was relieved that at least Donald would not hear anything to the contrary and blame me for a false-hood. "I don't have to give Donald an accounting of everything I do." I warned her again to be careful. "There are too many bad-minded people in this town. What is wrong with having ice cream in broad daylight with an old friend? God Almighty! People can't even piss in private." She swung out of my room, having had the last word, and I vowed never to broach the subject again. I hoped that Donald would not find it necessary to lodge any complaints with me in the future. I was going to make sure that I didn't put myself in a situation that he would find it convenient to do so.

*   *   *   *

They sorted out the disagreements, because Emily purchased port wine rum raisins currants and prunes, saying she was going to start soaking fruits for her wedding cake. All the arrangements had been made, and the upcoming nuptials were published in the church. We had not seen Anne in some time, but Mauva told us that she had stopped by and left something for us. Emily and I were in the dining room when we heard voices in the kitchen. Anne appeared at the back door, saying Mauva was preventing her from saying howdy-do. Mauva joined Anne at the doorway with the mortar pestle still in her hand. "She is a liar. I was beating corn an she appear up don't even say, 'Hello, dawg.' She bring someting fe Miss Em. Like me is nat somebady. I tell her I will have to announce to you dat she is here. She begin fe curse." Mauva turned to Anne. "So, you come back fe mek trouble? You betta clear off and get outta me yawd. Ah O." Anne lifted her head—a first—and stared straight at Mauva.

"Is nat yur yard, so you can't tell me fe clear off. You ole natty head bongo gal. G'wey." I thought Mauva would clobber her with the pestle, but Emily stepped in. She gave her a few shillings and some flour, sugar and rice. As she was leaving, Anne spat contemptuously on the ground close to where Mauva was standing.

"Gwaane ah you yard gal. De people up ah Frome mussey run yu becausen you is too facety." Mauva said to the back of the woman who had wheeled and dashed off, perhaps in the same manner in which she had come. We weren't sure if she still had the second job, but now Mauva was suggesting that perhaps she didn't. Anne left behind a jar of stewed plums for Miss Em. "She don't have no manners or respek. You remembah a two time Miss Liz did run her, and then Miss Emily hire her back because me cahnt wash and iron." Mauva threw in a bit of sarcasm to point out that she was now doing all the work that Anne did. "Well, she is crosses. We juss stop mourn fe King George. Don't ask me why because me nevah even noh de man but haffe go a court house go stan up in front of flag an sing Rule Britania ahn God Save De Queen. Dat gal Anne tink sey she is royalty. Mek har g'wey." She was referring to the death of King George, the coronation of Queen Elizabeth, and voicing her resentment toward Anne. She could mix things up and still make her point.

Donald joined us for supper. For dessert, Mauva prepared a dish of sliced mangos and brought in a small dish with plums for Emily. The three of us visited for a while, then I turned in to bed, leaving them in the midst of a disagreement about the soloist Donald wanted to sing at the wedding. They reduced their voices to whispers. I read for a while, and then went to sleep. Sometime before daybreak, I felt Emily's knees poking my back. She complained of abdominal cramps. She had those every month, and Mammy used to say they will go away after she had children. She asked for the chimney and began to vomit. I could tell that it was more serious than the onset of menstruation. I lit the lamp and went to the kitchen to boil water for the hot water bag. That was all I knew how to do. Mauva had readied the stove so all I had to do was pour kerosene over the wood. Smoke billowed and burned my eyes. I blew persistently until orange flames shot up. Emily told me where to find the water bag. I filled it, wrapped it in a towel, and placed it on her stomach. I wet a rag with Bay rum and put it on Emily's forehead. I forced her to sit and sip a cup of hot green tea, and we visited for a few minutes. She seemed more relaxed and said she felt better.

It seemed to happen simultaneously that I fell asleep, and Emily returned to her room. I was awakened by someone whispering. The sun had come up, giving Mauva an ash glow appearance as she stood grim-faced next to my bed. My first thought was that Emily had died during the night. I should have stayed awake and not let Emily go back to her room alone. I was relieved when Mauva said Emily was very ill, not dead. I rushed into Emily's room with Mauva chattering away.

"Ah ketch up de fire wipe aff all de soot tek out de ashes an fill up de kekkle pour more hot wata inna de bag because it was cold, stop it up, an mek cyrasee tea, empty de chimney pot weh she throw up inna till it full, an do everyting but it look like she wahn fe dead pon me, so dat is why me had was to come wake you. Dat gal Anne work obeah on dis house an eh ketch Miss Emily. Parpahs is you she did mean fe get it but." I interrupted and asked Mauva to go and call Dr. James. Emily continued to bring up a green-like mucus. It was all over the pillow and her nightgown. Mauva was still standing, looking at me cradling Emily's head in my lap.

"Dr. James have bad dawg an me 'fraid fe goh inna him yawd."

"Go on. Knock on the gate. Tell him it's life and death."

"Is de same ting I was tinking. Even if de dawg bite me, I will deliver dat message."

"After that, go ask Mr. McHale to come. We may have to take Miss Emily to the hospital. Hurry please, Mauva."

Emily had a high fever, and I kept sponging her with the Bay rum and lime juice. She was throwing up faster than I could reach for the chamber pot, and green stuff was all over her nightgown. I cleaned her up, changed her clothes, placed a towel on the pillow, and prayed that Dr. James would hurry. By the time he came, she seemed to have slipped almost into unconsciousness and was in no condition to answer his questions. Dr. James sat on the bed and took out his stethoscope and a small flashlight. He pried her eyes open and looked into them. He felt her pulse and ran his hand over her forehead. Dr. James motioned me to step out into the drawing room, where he began to whisper questions. "Did she eat anything unusual?" I told him we all had the same meal and, to my knowledge, she did not eat anything else after supper. He asked if Emily had any of the nerve tablets left. I didn't know she had been taking nerve tablets. "Do you have any reason to believe Emily may have been trying to kill herself? You can be frank with me, Kay." I reminded him that she was to be married soon and had gone to visit our relatives in Scotland and returned very happy. "Well, sometimes an impending marriage can create abnormal stress. I was at a function she catered the other day. It was beautiful. Don't be upset. I need to narrow things down. Do you think Emily may have been trying to throw away a baby?" I told him that Donald would be the happiest man if that were the case because he was anxious to get married. It was Emily who had been dragging it out. "Well, if it's poison, it had to be a very potent dose to give her such severe reaction. Keep her hydrated and send someone to the pharmacy to pick up some cocoa syrup that will help with the vomiting. Give her lots of fluids. It should work through her system in a day or two. To be on the safe side, I will take a blood sample and send it to the lab, but I expect that she will probably be better before the results come back.

Mammy never had much confidence in this doctor. She said he was young and inexperienced, but he was much older now and still didn't seem to be any better equipped. I would have to get Emily to the hospital. Mauva came back puffing, as if she had run a marathon. Donald was not home. The neighbors said they had not seen him since the day before. I wondered if he, too, may have fallen ill. He lived alone and, if he were in the same shape as Emily, he would probably not be able to answer his door. I wish I could have sent for Whitmore but that may have made matters worse. Time was running out; Emily had become delirious. She was seeing angels flying around the room and calling out for Mammy. I sent Mauva to see if any of our friends with cars could come to take Emily to the hospital. A few minutes later, she came back with Donald. He had gotten the message when he returned home and was on his way when he saw Mauva. I begged my sister to hang on, but she died in my arms. Donald broke down. Mauva wiped tears and cursed Anne. I was numb and devastated. I felt as if I were cursed. Everyone I ever loved had been taken away.

"Take my word, Miss Kay, dat gal Anne have someting to do with Miss Emily poisoning." Pappi's death was expected, Mammy's was sudden—a massive heart attack, but Emily? My young, vibrant, feisty sister died in my arms, and I was helpless. It was the cruelest fate. I knew we could not keep Emily's body surrounded by chipped ice longer than a few days. There wasn't enough time, even if I sent a cable to get in touch with Pappi's family and then wait for them to come.

I looked at Emily, and she had changed. It didn't look like her. She had turned blueish black, and it appeared as if someone blew air and inflated her body. There were complaints and rumors that perhaps I was trying to hide a secret because I ordered the casket closed. I would not allow anyone to see my sister this way. They had walked past Pappi's coffin, which was laid out in our drawing room. Mammy had wanted it that way and, when she died, Emily said her body should also be on display. Townspeople had a fascination with death. The burial was not complete unless everyone could see the dead person lying in a coffin. It was my decision to leave an image of my sister the way she had been: robust and full of life. Emily's Sunday school students joined the choir and paid tribute to their teacher and fellow choir member.

Emily had been buried for more than two months when Dr. James sent for me, saying he had the report. Emily died of poisoning. It was from the castor bean family. That did not make any sense, because Emily would not knowingly swallow castor beans. I was beginning to give credence to what Mauva had been saying, but still could not reconcile this with what I knew about Anne's reverence for Miss Em. I remembered Mammy giving us vermifuge tablets and castor oil to clean us out. Emily had to be held down so that she would swallow. The tree grew wildly all over the island, but one would have to chew the seeds to be poisoned. I regretted sending for Dr. James instead of one of my friends to take Emily to the hospital. I remembered Mammy telling us how people on the estate used a small, flat, brown cocobeh seed to test rain water collected in community drums. A couple of seeds would be thrown in and, if they sank to the bottom, the water had been poisoned, and no one would use it. It took less than a minute and no doubt saved many lives. I thought, here we are in the 20th century, and it took

no doubt saved many lives. I thought, here we are in the 20th century, and it took months to get a result back from the lab. Pappi's sister offered me an old house, saying that I wouldn't have to pay rent. I began to think that maybe I ought to take them up on the offer, but I had Mauva and my many friends to consider. I couldn't see myself starting over in another country. I was familiar with every square mile of this town and, although I despised its smallness, there was a warmth that I may never find anywhere else.

Except for Sunday service and a few important appointments, I closeted myself. I referred my students to another tutor and told my fellow committee members that I would be taking a sabbatical for a few months. A few friends visited me at home. Adelaide said it would be cathartic for me to let out some of my feelings. There was nothing more that I could share with anyone. It was a grief that I alone would have to come to terms with and that I alone had to bear. Adelaide complimented me on the funeral arrangements. "I used to think Emily was the planner in the family but, Kay, you arranged it all so beautifully. Emily would have been proud to see you so poised and graceful. Everyone was going to pieces, including yours truly. I stayed away from you because I was afraid that my sympathy would not have been helpful. You are truly one of a kind. You looked stunning. I will always remember you in that outfit. And that hat! You wore it to your mother's funeral. Oh, Kay, it made you look as if you were floating in the clouds. We miss you at church. At every committee meeting, the first thing we do is pray for your recovery.

"I am not sick, Adelaide."

"I know, Kay, but you are not an island either, and your friends know that even though you act as if you are fine, you are human like all of us. Anyway, you know we care and love you."

My friends all knew that I had dressed Emily in one of Mammy's favorite floral dresses with all the stains and that I had placed our grandmother's wedding ring—the one she brought back from Scotland—on her finger. I gave the engagement ring back to Donald and suggested that he return it to the jeweler and recoup some of his money. I shuttered the tea shop for good. I planned to incorporate the space back into our living quarters. The organ went to the Presbyterian church. I gave severance pay to Miss Witherspoon and her assistant, Lorna, and a lump sum to Mauva. She took the money but refused to leave. "Afta me cahnt leff you now. Me is the only family you got. Even though plenty people a run a England even though dem fraid like puss fe goh pon ship. Dem borrow money and geh pramise fe pay back wid nuff interest in one month afta dem land a Great Britain. Me nat going to no foreign land because me foot is on solid ground right here so. Me nat lending dem me good money fe dem go get sick and dead pon ship before dem cahn pay it back."

As British subjects, many islanders were migrating to England looking for better opportunities. Some people saw this exodus of West Indians going to Britain as colonialization in reverse. Mauva apparently had been approached for a loan to pay passage, but she refused. Sometimes, I secretly hoped she would jump on the band wagon, but that was halfhearted because I really had come to see her as more than a servant. For the next several months, I sorted the physical aspects of my life—gave away many household items I wouldn't need, began to read books I had set aside and tried to clear my mind. Dr. James had raised some thought-provoking questions, leading me to think more deeply about my sister. If he thought she was pregnant, why didn't he examine her instead of asking me if I thought so? Suppose she was carrying Whitmore's baby? I didn't even want to think that way. This would lead me down a road I didn't care to go.

I had been able to block out gossips and paid little or no attention to people passing on the street. Our news came chiefly from Mauva Grant and my friends. Now, as I lay in my bed or sat by the window, every whisper on the street was amplified. The barefoot town crier added my street to his route, and I could hear him shouting: "Er, ye. Er, ye. God save the King." Someone ought to tell him that the King George VI died. Not that this would have mattered to the paid advertiser of all news holy and unholy. "Dance at town hall Saturday nite, 8 o'clock. Come one, come all. Er, ye. Er, ye. American evangelist coming to Presbyterian church. Many souls will be save Sunday, 5 o'clock. Free." Everyone in town knew that he was illiterate, but Manleng had a good memory. He had a special style and was known to get things wrong and often mispronounced words, but he was all we had for local bulletins. There was no one else with the tenacity and enterprise to take on the tasks he performed. He could be heard for at least a mile shouting into his bullhorn and ringing the bell. "Er, ye. Er, ye. God save the King." Mauva suggested that, with my influence, we could have him move his business away from our quiet street. I didn't like it because, rather than walk fast to finish his route, he seemed to linger in front of my home. It was best to ignore, rather than try to confront the barefoot man.

Lately, I found myself thinking about this western dot on the island's map. I knew most, if not all, of the people who called this place home. The idea of moving to some other parish or to the city had never occurred to me but, gradually since the death of my sister, the thought kept creeping to the forefront of my consciousness. When Emily was alive, we'd stay up some nights and just talk about events in our lives, or gossip about some love interest either ours or others we had heard about. Emily was also my friend. I didn't know it. I had always been an introvert and was very selective in what I'd reveal to anyone outside my family, but I spoke freely to my sister. She was me, even though she was so different. Everything in our home and in this town had a place in my head and was assigned to either a good or bad memory. It was impossible to insulate oneself, but our family tried as best we could to stay above the fray. We seemed to have managed this with very little spillage; we had a happy life in this town.

Every now and again, a tourist or two would appear on the main street in shorts. We'd wonder why they had come and what they hoped to see. The sailors had a purpose because the ships brought goods, took away sugar cane and allowed them recreational time. People were generally friendly and a walk or ride in the town would elicit "howdy-do," "good afternoon," and would end with "walk good." It was a close-knit town in a funny sort of class-conscious way. Country people viewed us lacking moral authority when they saw prostitutes parading on the arm of sailors. There were a couple of people in temporary lock up; some waiting to be transferred and some waiting to get sober. The town hall doubled as a dance hall. Rum bars with regulars who went there after work and stayed all day Saturday and Sunday, while their wives were at the market or at church. Town people didn't share with neighbors the way country folks did. My family would have been thought of as the exception. We shared with the less fortunate, and we served our community in many ways.

Some young folks and particularly unruly boys often gathered around the country buses as they came into town and hurled ridicule at the people getting off these buses. They brought us food but left downtown smelling of rotted and spoiled produce. They cleaned and threw the fish guts into the gutter, creating a haven for flies and hungry dogs. These people believed in obeah and baths to wash away voodoo curses. Many traveled with protective charms to ward off evil spirits. These were people who, given the hilly terrain from whence they came, ought to be wearing shoes but often did not. Our Mauva came to us from the country and, over the years, had both maintained and refined some of her contrarian ways of looking at life. Anne, on the other hand, was unchanged. Miss Witherspoon grew up in the town and went to school. She possessed a sense of reasoning that made her different from Mauva and Anne.

"Miss Kay, ah tink yu consider too much. Maybe yu should'a do someting wid yur hands instead of yur brains an geh it some ress because yu always a read an fret 'bout yu fada an Miss Emily. Me noh you did luv yur mada but is yu fada was de favorite ahn you miss him. Me miss dem too but…"

"Mauva, do you believe that sometimes I just want to be left alone? Why is it you talk so much?"

"Sorry ef me bother yu but who else me fe talk to? Yu is de only family me gat. Me noh me is nat real family in de sense of it, but me is closer to yu than many of yu frens an me is de one fe look afta yu. So me sorry ef yu tink sey dat me is a worry. Me don't want to be a worry."

I felt bad and had to assure Mauva that she was not a bother and that I knew she had good intentions. She didn't have much to do and, no matter how I'd tell her to go home early, she wouldn't. I had her go to the post office to both mail and pick up letters. At least she could wile away hours in a line waiting for the one postal clerk to take care of registering births and deaths for the entire parish and sorting and handing out mail. Mauva brought back several letters, but she handed me the one with Bronson's name first. She waited for me to open it. I told her it was Mr. Bronson, and he sent his sympathy. She acted as she had been waiting to hear from him. "Is about time him write and say someting. Den you gwineto answer him back, Miss Kay?" I told her I would, in time. "Well, instead of him writing so long after Miss Emily dead, him should'a did bring himself to the fineral. Mister Charlie never like him an..." I stopped her, saying that I did not wish to continue talking about Mr. Bronson and that the letter was personal. I did not tell Mauva that Lindsay asked if he could stop by to see me the next time he was in town. I quickly replied and thanked him but said I would let him know when I was taking visitors. I mailed the letter myself. Whitmore Chapley had not come to Emily's funeral either, and he was in town. I understood the delicate nature of the situation with all the rumors that had been going around. As Mauva advised, it was time for me to stop brooding. I ran into Whitmore and his wife at a cocktail party. He pulled me to the side and whispered that Donald McHale was not to be trusted. I didn't know exactly what he meant by that, but I knew how Donald felt about him.

I had picked up once again my committee activities. It was my turn to visit Mrs. Lewis, a parishioner who was now disabled. After her husband died, she bequeathed all her possessions, including giving the church charge over her bank accounts and the benefit of any residual monies left after her death. She kept a life estate in the two story frame home with a provision that, while she was alive, it could not be encumbered to defray expenses. Her husband had been a past treasurer of our church, and he was astute when it came to matters of financial interest. It dawned on us that Mr. Lewis had the bequest where the chances were good that nothing would be left and the church would have to subsidize his widow.

As Christians, we were bound by our commitments, but the committee members took a dim view of the way things were going on the Lewis account. On top of it all, we were committed to visit her weekly but, since there were several volunteers, these visits were not particularly burdensome on any one of us. It was my turn and, as usual, Mrs. Lewis talked endlessly about the most trivial mundane and depressing subjects, including the frequency or infrequency of her bowel movements. She knew who was stealing food from her next door neighbor and wanted me to report the matter to the authorities. She said school children teased the old lady next door, and the woman threw urine at them.

Mrs. Lewis asked me to write a note telling her neighbor that the urine was unsanitary and that the horrible smells drifted into her drawing room. I told her to write the note herself, but she said her fingers couldn't hold a pen. I suggested that she walk next door and tell the woman, but she said the neighbor was hard of hearing and, because of her arthritis, Mrs. Lewis couldn't climb the steps. The woman showed me a crooked finger through the pocket of her skirt, saying it was time she got some new clothes. We even had to get her clothes made. Mrs. Lewis had gossip to share about some fellow male church members. It was common knowledge, but she must have only recently got the news. "By the way, Miss Crawford, have you heard?" I had to ask her what I should have heard. "That you-know-who the first and second one were caught in the act." She was referring to the man who carried the cross in our church, and the one behind him in the procession. I told Mrs. Lewis that I was expecting company and had to run. I thought that perhaps I ought to take up knitting, as Mauva suggested, to use my hands instead of my brains. This woman seemed to suck not only my energy but taxed my brain power. I always had to be thinking of the best way to put things to her and to steer conversations away from the drivel. She was an intelligent woman, veering toward dementia. Mauva had a cup of tea waiting for me.

"Mek me hat it up, Miss Kay because me noh yu well exhausted." She rushed to the kitchen to heat the tea. It was a relief to be home. I sat on the edge of my bed and slowly began to change my clothes. In my next committee meeting, I would suggest that we sell the house while there was a structure to sell and place Mrs. Lewis into a nursing facility. Not that any official home existed, but there were a few single women in our town who would welcome a little cash to board and lodge those in need. It would be less costly than the current arrangement where we were responsible for every detail of her life, including house repairs, paying a woman to clean and prepare meals, and someone to maintain the yard. Fanny would be opposed to this idea because she had been one of the chief architects of the Lewis life plan. It was one of the first acts of benevolence after her husband became the vicar. Those of us who bore the brunt of her decision were volunteers and contributors. A knock at my front door jolted me out of my thoughts on how best to introduce the subject at our next committee meeting. Mauva cleared her throat and poked her head into my room, and then I heard Alba calling out from the drawing room and Mauva explaining why I would soon be out.

"Miss Kay juss come from Miss Lewis, and she tired. She muss an bound fe visit dat woman because she geh all her earthly belongings to parish church and it noh look like sey she'a go dead anytime soon." It was fortunate Mauva couldn't read my thoughts because she would certainly have told Alba that I was thinking about turning Mrs. Lewis out of her home. To halt the flow, I asked Mauva to make a pot of tea for Mrs. Tidings. "Miss Alba don't want tea, Miss Kay. Me ask her ahready."

"I would like some, so please make it for me." Mauva came close to the bedroom doorway to whisper.

"You never have tea at this time, you feeling ahrite? Dat woman mek you so sick." It was difficult to get angry with Mauva because I know she meant well and all my friends had gotten accustomed to her. Alba was fresh and radiant in a powder blue suit a white chiffon blouse with lace collar and a simple string of pearls. She complimented me before I had a chance to tell her how nice she looked.

"You're gorgeous in that Mu Mu, Kay. The colors are so pure and vibrant. When you are through with it, hand it down to me. It's really very lovely. The way they chop up good fabrics and sew at random in this place, I know that wasn't made locally."

"You're right. Mrs. Tate ordered it from France. She has all those beautiful catalogues. If you ever need anything let me know."

"I thought she had become blind. Her husband ran off."

"Yes, he did, but she isn't blind."

"That's good to hear. You look wonderful. I don't know why you chose the single life. Anyway, here who's talking? We marrieds have our own pot of discordant stew." The dining room curtain moved. Mauva was setting up a tray with teacups. Alba stopped talking, waiting for Mauva to leave. I called out and told Mauva to go start dinner.

"I start it ahready. I am gwineto put on the kekkle."

"Well, Mrs. Tidings, what brings you to this side?"

"Had to meet Harold and Francis to work out details for the upcoming concert. I don't know why I agreed to do this again. Albert suggests that I should say no to Fanny, but you know no one says no to Fanny. I think about acoustics. To a musician's ear, it's just never right."

"When the heavy Spanish doors are closed, the sound is distributed a bit more evenly. It generally works out."

"I know, but we are expecting a far greater crowd than usual, and there may be people standing outside. Anyway, Kay, the driver has to take me home and return the car to Albert's office, so I will not tarry. By the way, did you hear that bare-foot man calling the musical instrument a vandolin?"

"Why Fanny believes she has to give him business, I will never know. He mashes up the language, reports wrong information, and I have heard him advertise past events, not realizing that they already occurred."

"Emily's garden parties used to generate some money to help, but now it is up to us to find all the funds. This started out as a treat for our members' children but, over the years, we have been seeing more children flock to the picnic. Fanny believes, that with Manleng advertising the concert, we may be able to attract people with hidden coins in their mattresses to spend a half crown to support the endeavor." Mauva had returned to clear up the tea cups and wipe off the center table, even though it didn't need cleaning. She had her own idea about the concert.

"Me don't know anybody who could come up with two shillings and six pence juss to sit down and listen to somebody draw piece a stick pon guitar. It is too expensive." Alba put a handkerchief over her mouth. Mauva knew that I was annoyed, and she backed away. "Sorry, Miss Kay, me noh it is nat my biznez me did just come in to see if you want more tea."

"Take my cup. I will have the rest before bed. Mrs. Tidings and I are having a private conversation."

"Me will stay in the kitchen until you call me." Feeling a bit more comfortable, Alba began to share the real reason for her visit.

"Kay, do you remember Walker Jones?"

"Walter Jones?"

"Yes, that's him. He was one of your suitors, I was told."

"He was not a suitor, but we grew up together. After he left for a job in the city, I lost track. The last I heard, he and his wife were residing in Canada."

"Married, divorced, and back home. Walter seems to have struck gold—a millionaire in pounds, according to Lionel. Mary invited them to dinner."

"Mary? How odd. Something happened between those two, and I remember they had a distinct dislike for each other. If he were sitting on the left, Mary would go to the right."

"Apparently, the dinner wasn't a planned thing. She passed my house on her way to the grocer and asked us to drop over if we were not too busy. I didn't know she was going to have food. Lionel was there dressed up in a suit."

"Unlike Mary to have an unplanned dinner."

"Well, that's what she said. Lionel and Walter ran into each other at an investor's seminar in the city. Things haven't been going good for WESCO—at least that is what Albert said—so they sent Lionel looking for people with good money to throw into the cistern. You know, every country, including America is growing sugarcane and making sugar out of beets; all we have left is rum. It's not enough to balance the books and make a profit. Albert said he had been approached to invest but declined. When you see Mary, you can ask for the details. Lionel pulled me aside and whispered that he was amazed how Walter, who used to run around barefoot, had pulled up himself."

"What a thing to say! Did he check his fob for the gold watch he claimed belonged to his grandfather? Probably stole it from some poor cane farmer."

"I didn't know about the grandfather watch. I was in Cotswold trying to keep earwigs from falling into my ears. You know, to this day, when I tell people that I grew up in a thatched cottage, they don't believe it. Many people still think that thatched houses are only in the tropics. And, before that, we heard that everyone on the island lived in trees. Ha. What a myth. Anyway, Kay, back to the subject. Walter asked Lionel about you and some other girl he dated."

"Connie Mabry probably. That's the one I knew about."

"Oh, and Lionel said Kay is a confirmed spinster. Single life seems to agree with her because she looks fantabulous. Those were his exact words, and he and Walter had a little chuckle. Then, he said something about his wife visiting family in the city. She wasn't at Mary's."

"Maybe his huge company home is up for sale if WESCO is in such financial straits that they have to go fishing for money."

"That's what Albert said. They ought to put those properties up for sale and use the money to bail the company out of trouble. I suppose Lionel will have to get rid of his servants, drivers and club memberships. His poor wife. Perhaps she is really in a sanatorium trying to recover from what is to come." Alba became animated talking about Mary and her guests. "There was a car and driver in front waiting to whisk them away. I got the impression Walker was staying with Lionel. Anyway Kay, you should have seen Mary. She was dressed up in a fancy dress with a crinoline. I thought I knew all her outfits, but I had never seen that one before. It was a dinner party and that dress was not at all suitable. Albert said it made her look like a peacock. I felt like a servant in my simple floral dress.

Mary was all over Walker like an infatuated school girl. It was surprising she didn't tell you about it, seeing he was more your friend than hers."

"You know, Alba, that I do not do impromptu events. I have long since stopped riding a bicycle and so must arrange transportation in advance."

"You have a point. That is probably why she didn't tell you, but why were they so dressed up? In my short conversation with Walker, he asked me to say a special hello to you and told me how he was madly in love with you, but your parents didn't approve."

"The things men say."

"That is all the news for now. I must go. I am meeting with Fanny later, and then it's off to my dressmaker. I have to keep a close eye on what that woman is doing. Everyone claims she is the best, but to be on the safe side, I usually buy a couple extra yards of material. I ought to get my clothes from a catalog, that would probably work out less costly. See you on Sunday." As soon as Alba left, Mauva informed me that she had heard about the party.

"Did Miss Alba tell you ol' man Bronson was deer wid Miss Caroline? She very sickly deese days an she fine harself a party." Perhaps in deference to me, Alba did not mention that Lindsay's parents were also at Mary's party. I told Mauva that I was not interested in knowing who was or was not at Mrs. Bunting's home. "Afta me wasn't listening. Miss Alba have a strong vice an it carry. Me was in the kitchen when me hear har talk about the party up at Mistress Bunting an me did hear before but me nevah say anyting."

If anyone were to ask, I had long since forgotten about Lindsay, but it seemed everyone was cautious about mentioning the Bronson name in my presence. I had visitors from time to time but, as soon as they showed a glimmer of romantic interest, I found excuses to cool the relationship. There had been enough rumors and innuendos concerning our family, and I wasn't anxious to add any more fuel to that simmering charcoal. Mauva was very careful about repeating any rumors concerning me or my family. She knew that I did not need a full-time helper, and she was not going to do anything that would set off that trigger. She was sometimes overbearing in her protectiveness and, at times, I found it stifling to be around the woman for so many hours of the day.

"Miss Kay, ah turn down the bed an getting ready to go home. Ah warm up the tea an set it on de table. Ah rinse out the commode an put water inna your face basin for tomorrow an ah tink de net will have to wash because you clap maskitta and blood spots is all ovah an."

"Go, you needn't stay so late. The mosquito net does not need to be washed."

"Yes it do, Miss Kay."

"You need to go home and get some rest. I appreciate what you do, but I am not so helpless."

"Ah noh you is not helpless, Miss Kay, but is me job to do deese tings an tek care of you."

I read classical literature and poetry and, by that, kept my mind intellectually engaged, or I'd go mad. I had seen people walking the streets talking and shouting to imaginary companions. One of my neighbors, Bell Meekle, cooped herself up in one room while the rest of the house was crumbling around her. She went to pieces when her husband died and would not have survived without the help of neighbors and a few friends. Mauva and I were about the same age, so I could not depend on her as a caregiver if anything happened to me. I had made all the arrangements and placed my will and papers in the hands of the vicar's wife. Mrs. Meekle had no money and no relatives to help. When she died, I brought her case before our committee, and they accused me of trying to squander the church funds on a non member. Adelaide said that, since Mrs. Meekle died as a pauper, the government should be responsible for burying her. "You were so kind sending her meals. Perhaps you should have had her sign the bequest forms since she had no known relatives. The property is not worth much, but it surely could have paid the cost of her burial."

"The woman was senile and, legally, not in a position to understand this document, Adelaide."

"Exactly."

"Her husband gambled away their savings, and then jumped off the logwood wharf and killed himself."

"That is beside the point, Kay." Mary kept unusually quiet during the deliberations but, by her demeanor, she seemed to be agreeing for the first time with Adelaide. "If he jumped off the pier, where was his body? They sent divers and nothing was found. Not a trace. Could have been foul play."

"Let's not hold that against the woman; she didn't push him. In those shark infested waters, everything that falls in is food."

We got a discount on the coffin, paid the embalming women, and Isbel made the dress free of charge. It was a short service, and the vicar reluctantly did a grave side prayer. A long procession of townspeople followed the donkey-drawn cart to the public burial ground. They sang mournful songs and cried as if they had lost a close friend. Most of them had never met the old Syrian woman. I would not be a burden to anyone, and I prayed that I did not lose my mind and come to such an end as Mrs. Bell Meekle. I was fortunate that my parents had left us well off and now, being the only remaining heir, I was well set financially. There was enough money in the bank to take care of my burial and Mauva's. The church would get the house but, if Mauva survived me, she would have a life estate. That was the least I could do for a woman who had dedicated her entire life to the service of my family.

I asked for volunteers to help me in making a proposal to the parish council and asked them to demolish the Meekle house and build a park in honor of the family. We would transfer the land to the church, and the park could be used for community events. I imagined that there would be legal requirements but, since there were no relatives, it would go fairly quickly. I wrote it up and, a week later, Alba said Albert had made the necessary changes, and his secretary would type the proposal. To my surprise, we heard that the Meekle property had been sold. It wasn't a good month since we buried the woman. I called an emergency meeting in my home. It was a contentious session, as I had expected.

"I was right about not using church funds to bury that woman. She must have known that there were relatives. As it stood, there was nothing we could do to recoup the monies spent on her burial. If we are to file an injunction against the property, it would appear unchristian." The ladies were angry at me for having suggested the burial expenditure.

"It's done, Adelaide. There is no point being bitter about it. It's not as if the church is poor. We have money in our coffers."

"Alba, do you think your husband could send a letter for reimbursement?"

"To whom, Mary?" She turned to me, "Kay, do you know the relative who sold the property?"

"I do not."

"And who is to pay Albert for his services?"

"Let's agree not to do this in the future and leave it at that. No need for Kay to put in her personal money because rightly or wrongly we all agreed. The bill can't be that much because his secretary hadn't even typed the document."

"It's his time, not his secretary's, Fanny. You all know that Albert has given freely in advice, but he has to make a living." At the end of the meeting and after everyone had left, Mauva had a few words.

"Dem rob the property. Mek her sign paper because her head used to go and come. When me go over there with dinnah me used to ask her if she don't have anybady fe look afta her. She tell me she don't neither have pot to piss in—excuse me Miss Kay—or relatives to take out the chamber." Adelaide had suggested that I should have had Mrs. Meekle sign the house over to the church. We would be able to sell it to defray the expense of her burial. Mauva was saying that someone took advantage of the senile woman, and she did not know what she was signing.

There was nothing more to be done. If someone had indeed stolen the property—which was likely—a non-relative could do nothing.

*   *   *   *

Augustus Frye, a.k.a. Shuggie, had become the new owner of the Meekle property. Mr. Frye, a stocky built man in his mid-40s, entertained boxing ambitions in his youth. He turned his aspirations towards real estate. Mr. Fry grabbed the property two blocks from the beach as his new venture. No one in town seemed to know this man or had seen him prior to this acquisition. On several occasions, I saw him pass my home, pausing as if he wanted to enter. I've heard him call out "Howdy-do, Mistress Crawford," as if speaking to the shrinking shadow at the window. From what little Mauva told, he wasn't an acquaintance I'd want to make.

Our house, like all the others of its vintage, was built close to the road. The few morning glories, hibiscus plants and a solitary mango tree were not sufficient to keep out the night sounds of people walking by. Some voices I knew; others I guessed the identity from the context of whatever gossip or rumor was being discussed. Now that I was alone, all the street sounds seemed as if they were amplified. It made me wonder how could I have lived all my life in this place and not have paid any attention to what was going on around me. Emily had said I was too aloof. My friends said that I was stoic like my father. The people who knew me saw a shy conservative woman who would rather read a good book than engage in gossip. Perhaps as one of my suitors told me, "Karolyn, you don't belong to this town. You are much too sophisticated and intelligent to keep yourself in this back street." This was not a back street. It used to be one of the better places to live. It ran directly off the main road and was in the heart of downtown. Many of my neighbors were solid, middle class people. Most have moved, some have rented to families, and some have died and their homes sold.

At the time, I found the comment arrogant and insulting to the good people and culture of this town. But lately, I've had to rethink my opinions and how I feel about living here. It seemed to me that the town veered toward a slide into the ocean of ineptitude, incorrigibility and decadence. The new neighbors did not add much. Many had small children, and we had nothing in common except some were members of our church, and I'd see them there. I had my old friends and acquaintances, but they lived uptown in the suburbs. Their lives had not changed much because it was the same people and their children and grandchildren that they all knew. I must have been sitting at the window for longer than I realized because Mauva began to whisper.

"Miss Kay, you is gwineto mek yur lunch get cold."

"I will go to the table when I am ready."

"Sorry, me tink someting happen."

"What is to happen? I am sitting here reading a book." She picked up the food to carry it back to the kitchen. "You don't have to warm it. I do not like hot food." Mauva took it the kitchen, brought it back, and sat on the doorstep while I ate.

"Shuggie is gwineto fix up Miss Bell house and let out rooms, Miss Kay." It made me shudder to think that the very character of our neighborhood was about to plunge like Mr. Meekle into the sea and be devoured by land sharks. "If him do a good job, me might let a room."

"Mrs. Meekle died from pneumonia because it leaked so much she couldn't keep dry in that room.

"Me did kip far when me go ovah deer because me never wahn fe catch T.B. Me glad to hear sey someting else kill her."

Meekle's house had been sold to a total stranger purported to be a rum bar owner from another parish. The news of what he intended to do with the place was all over town. It was necessary to take action to protect my privacy, since both my side and backyard adjoined this property. The contractor told me how many sheets of zinc, boxes of nails, and wooded posts were needed to complete the fence. After a couple months, the order came. The man ordered the wrong type of nail. We'd have to wait several weeks until the correct nails were ordered from the city. The nails came, but the lumber man delivered the wrong length posts. He had cut the posts to the length of the one post that the contractor gave him. To break the impasse, I agreed to pay for two sets of posts. In the meantime, Mr. Frye found people to patch his roof, do ad hoc repairs, and began to let rooms on a weekly and, some say, on an hourly basis.

The prostitution business had been kept on the opposite side of the main street. There were one- and two-room houses, that the women used to entertain sailors, going off into the lanes like spider webs. I was horrified at the thought of that possibility in my back yard. As if to make me feel better, Mauva informed me that the hourly business was for local married men who had lady friends. The fracas was constant, especially on Saturday nights. The hollering and cursing penetrated the walls and reverberated inside my home. As a rum bar owner, Mr. Frye was no stranger to brawls and, as a former aspiring pugilist, he was able to use his fists as weapons. I once sent Mauva the mile to get the police but, by the time the constable showed up on his bicycle, the congregants were friends again, laughing and playing card games. According to Mauva, the officer joined in the merriment after he was offered "a rum."

"Miss Kay, you don't know Nicholas Barrett. Him let the little side room over deer." I didn't recognize the name, so she gave me a further clue. "Him was along with that woman, Mazie Gunter weh throw hot water an burn him up an him had was to go inna hospital for a long time?" I remembered hearing that story. "Well, him juss get back the little job at wharf fe weigh sugarcane. Him is honest; nevah even thief a bag a brown sugar. Him was in some hards and tell Shuggie him going to the country to borrow money from a cousin to pay the rent. Shuggie tell him that his belongings will be on the street, and him can pick them up when him come back. Him call Shuggie a thief and a whorehouse kipper. Shuggie land him a right. That nice quiet man give Shuggie a left hand, send him a hospital fe get eight'o nine stitches under him eye." Mauva continued talking, but I was not listening. I felt as if I had been hoisted in the air and was floating on a cloud of bad dreams. *Emily Anne, my darling sister, dream to me and tell me what to do. Where can I go? This bar man has made my property undesirable so that no one besides him would want to buy it. I couldn't stand the thought of this property falling into such careless hands. Pappi and Mammy would rise from their graves. Do I dare meet face to face with him? How could I get to his level? You know how I hate to use patois and that is probably all that he'd understand.* My lips must have been moving because, when I opened my eyes, Mauva was looking at me in a peculiar way.

"You talking to somebody, Miss Kay?" She glanced around as if to answer her question. "Oh, you talking to yurself."

"I was silently calling on the spirit of my dead sister for help, so my lips may have been moving."

"Me nevah noh you believe in de spirit."

"It's a joke, Mauva."

"Ah O."

Her response was more of a "thank God you're not thinking that Miss Emily's duppy is in this house." I didn't want her bringing any concoction to throw in the four corners of my home to drive spirits away. Mauva was very superstitious. I went to post a letter and, on the way back, I stopped in to visit Albert Tidings. He was busy and said that we should talk another time. As I was walking home, Adelaide drove by. She seemed to be going in the direction of the market. Her driver almost hit a man who was crossing the street. I heard Adelaide scream, "Man, can't you see?" I wasn't sure if she was talking to the man who scampered out of the way or to her driver, but I kept out of sight so as not to be offered a ride. By the time I got home, her car was parked in front of my house, and the driver was picking something out of his teeth with a wood splinter. Adelaide and Mauva were in the living room talking. "Where have you been, Kay? I was just about to leave. Tell me that the news I have heard is not true." Mauva was nodding her head affirmative. "Where on God's earth are they going to put houses, Kay? It must be less than a quarter of an acre. That house takes up most of the land space. You have my sympathy." I still did not know what Adelaide was talking about, but Mauva chimed in.

"Mister Shuggie is renting out house spots, Miss Kay. Some house is deer already yu nevah notice? Manleng did announce it because somebody on main street tell me that dem hear him a call out fe house spots next to our property."

"That is what I heard, and it is what brings me here today, Kay. I had to pick up a few things, but I said, 'Adelaide, we must inform Kay what is taking place in her neighborhood.' The driver was blowing the horn, and it irritated Adelaide. She went outside the door and shouted to him, "Remove your hand from the middle of the steering wheel, Hubert. How many times I am to tell you not to lean your head there?" Adelaide returned to say I had better be prepared for what was to come. I wanted to talk to Albert about the letting of rooms, but now another problem had been brought to my attention. I made an appointment to see solicitor Albert Tidings and to ask, what, if any legal remedies could be undertaken to stop this misadventure. Those round rimmed glasses made him look like a silent movie character much older than his years. They were much too small for his plump face. Alba said that she tried to reduce his intake, but he was an insatiable eater. And, we all knew he drank heavily, also. His desk was cluttered with piles of papers. His secretary came in to remind him that he had a meeting with Judge Comfrey. I suspected it was a ploy to get me out as quickly as possible.

"Kay, it's a matter for the parochial board. Perhaps you could also write to the lands department, water works, and health ministry in the city. In a case of murder, yes, but even then, it's doubtful any of those dwellers could afford my fees." His belly shook as he chuckled. I reminded him of the seriousness of the situation.

"It's not a laughing matter, Albert, and it does not have to come to murder. There are other crimes that can be punished under our civil society laws. Even though it's not your specialty, you should know a bit about different types of legal remedies. Dr. James knows something about all the branches of medicines, even though his practice is limited to taking tests and sending them to a laboratory for results."

"Oh, him." He dismissed Dr. James as rubbish. "I do take your concerns seriously. If I were in the similar situation, I'd probably move."

"I will not allow anyone to push me out of my home." His secretary appeared again, this time with papers for him to sign.

"We could research and find the applicable laws under which someone could be cited for something. I doubt we will find anything on the books that would prohibit Mr. Frye from populating his land with shanties. There is nothing criminal in the letting of house spots, the common use of one latrine, and having several people use one open pipe. On that other matter you spoke of the other day, you will be required to bear the burden of proof. The man could sue you for slander. I'd be careful on that."

"It is what Mauva told me, Albert."

"Mauva?" He asked with reproach, as if I must be unstable to take the word of my servant.

"Why would anyone rent a room for an hour or two unless it was being used for nefarious purposes?"

"Proof, Kay. Proof. Another thing, prostitution is not a crime. The ladies who walk the main street arm in arm with sailors don't believe they are doing anything wrong or illegal. It's a useless exercise writing to the government, so I take that suggestion back. In my experience, they rarely solve any problem and sometimes can make matters worse. Let's suppose those people who paid for the house spots or hourly room found out you filed an adverse complaint." He trailed off in a seemingly exasperated tone. "Let's suppose," he paused as if to allow me time to think of possible consequences. "If you insist, draft a letter to the authorities, and let me have a look. I can try to throw in some legal jargon to bolster your case, but I wouldn't rely on any remedies coming from that end." He stood up, suggesting our meeting had to be over.

I would have to confront the situation head on. On my way home, I worked out a plan. Mauva was waiting to hear what Mister Albert had to say. I dispatched her with a stop warning to the pushcart-advertising man. "Tell Manleng I will see to it he gets no more business from the parish church. That the merchant who carries the cross in our church bans him from picking up customers in front of his store. That we could take action against him for disturbing the peace. That the police inspector will enforce the law stopping him from sleeping in his pushcart on public roads." Mauva's furrowed brow showed a level of confusion and attempts to sort through my list of grievances. How much she would remember or convey was anyone's guess but, even if it was 10 percent, Mauva would deliver a message. She was almost boastful in her assurances.

"Don't you worry, Miss Kay. When I finish wid him, he will tink it is the government talking. Trouble gwineto tumble dung pon his head, believe me."

After a couple hours, Mauva returned, looking grim and vexed. I had to prod her to tell me the outcome of her meeting. "Him sey Augustus Fry pay him and tell him what fe say." Clearly, whatever threats she conveyed had not worked. I suspected that the barefoot man said more than Mauva was telling, but sooner or later it would come out.

"Kay," I said to myself "it is up to you." I rolled my hair into a French knot, put on my plain white linen dress—it wasn't so white—cut on the bias, black flat shoes and slung a colorful scarf around my neck. The house was around the corner. Without the fence, I could have walked from my yard to his.

It had been a quiet street with homes of varying sizes but none smaller than three rooms. Many were of frame construction, but the larger ones like the Meekle home were concrete. I picked up a stone from the trash-strewn yard to use as door knocker. As I approached, it became clear that the door could easily have been pushed open because it was barely contained on the hinges. Mr. Frye gave me a start, as he lifted and flung open one of the doors.

"Howdy-do, Mistress Crawford. Would you like to step inside? We have done a wonderful job getting this house in shape. I know you were a friend of the lady," he made a sign of the cross. "Rest her soul." I pointed to the logwood tree in the side yard, on which a loose piece of rope had been tied. Mr. Frye had been removing the few trees from the property and selling the pieces as fire wood. This string signaled another tree had been earmarked for cooking fuel. A small voice kept saying: *You are too aloof, try and look friendly.*" I smiled, and this seemed to give Mr. Frye an opening. He buttoned up his shirt and began to push it into his pants. I turned my head so that I wouldn't see his pubic hairs; the pants were so loose. "You are but a vision of loveliness. An angel." He must have seen the involuntary fluttering of my eyelids. "I am sorry if I sound a bit forward, but I hear so much about your fine upstanding family and how they poison your..."

"The purpose of my visit, Mr. Frye, is to ask you as kindly as possible to desist from using my family's name in your advertisements."

"I beg you a thousand pardons, Mistress Crawford. It was that barefoot man who make the suggestion, and I only agree to do it because I didn't want any riff-raff to try to move here." Mr. Frye may not have had book smarts, but he was well able to turn his actions to suggest he used my name to protect the neighborhood from undesirables. "I will stop forthwith if it is displeasing to you; take my word as a gentleman." I thanked him and started to walk away. "Come around any time, Mistress. You are welcome to see the good job I am doing with this place." On my return, Mauva was anxious to know the outcome of my meeting. I told her that the matter had been resolved to my satisfaction.

"I ongly hope so because Manleng say that your fren the ole Battieman couldn't stop bus from parking on government street or stop him from picking up people. Him so drunk that him can hardly walk straight on Sunday fe carry the cross a parish church. And him sey ladies involve in dem kind of tings too and…"

"That's enough, Mauva. We have resolved the problem regarding the use of my family's name." Neither Mauva nor Manleng had ever been inside our church during services, yet this was the news in circulation. The man who owned the store was a known homosexual, and Manleng was suggesting that women engaged in that activity also. He showed his contempt without calling names. The announcements stopped, because it seemed Frye had more requests for spots than spaces available. While the fence afforded some privacy, there were many holes in the zinc. I'd hear Mauva shout in the direction of a hole, "Kip oonu yeye outta me yawd." I don't know what they expected to see from those small openings and told her to ignore them, but she considered herself family and wanted to assert her rights to privacy as well.

"Me noh wahn yu fe dead, Miss Kay, God noh me heart. Yu no ha no close famibily leff but me. Mauva yu good'n faithful servant." She was right about family because those relatives in Scotland were so far removed that, if anything happened to me, they'd probably never find out. Fortunately, I had friends, and we often got together for a social evening to play cards or plan some church function. I kept up with my volunteer activities and accepted a few invitations to dine out or have an ice cream at the local parlor with certain gentleman friends.

It was our game night at Alba's home. I could depend on Albert to come and pick me up. Knowing all the characters with automobiles, I was very particular from whom I'd accept a lift. "We are lucky that he makes it the two miles to church. Fanny keeps him from running into the ditches." Mary made that observation once when I said I'd ask the vicar for a lift to her home. Mary lived close, so she could walk. Fanny and Adelaide had their own transportation. Mauva kept looking out the window at me sitting calmly in the drawing room waiting for Albert. It appeared as if she had dressed a child for a party, and the adult coming to take her was late. She was annoyed, saying that I could get there by this time if I had started walking.

"You could get yur own car an hire driver like Miss Adelaide." I needed to get a lift to take me everywhere except to the post office, church, courthouse and market. Although it was quite safe, I did not go out of my home on foot at nights. Realizing that Albert was almost an hour late, I wondered what the rest would be saying about me during my absence. I knew they were all at Alba's waiting for me. When Albert came, he was effusive in apologies, saying that a business meeting ran over. He had to go home because Alba had asked him to pick up something she needed. He drove faster than usual, prompting me to remind him that it was only a social gathering to play cards. I hopped out before he turned to enter his garage, which was in the back of the house. I went to the front door, which was slightly ajar and stood in the twilight for a few minutes. Someone asked, "Where is she? She ought to arrange transport with that man. He has a car and, as far as I know, he is still single."

"I don't think they are on the best of terms because rumor has it he may have had a hand in Emily's death. He was seen leaving the home in the wee hours of the morning."

"They were engaged to be married, so what? He even approached Albert to make up a will."

"Of course, it's natural for him to think about dying and leaving such a young widow but, see how things turned out? I heard that they had supper that night, and you remember that it was in the early morning that Emily took sick. Kay said he fainted at Emily's bedside, and Mauva had to pass Bay rum over his nostrils to bring him back. Kay had to whisper something to him at the funeral. She seemed annoyed at the emotions he displayed."

"Guilt. Perhaps it was guilt."

"For what, Mary?"

"How should I know? I was just thinking if he had done something to Emily, he may have been feeling badly about it."

"Emily was the real rebel in that family. She didn't care about anything. Even when she was engaged, she was flitting all around in broad daylight with Whitmore. She was telling everyone they were family friends, but there is a limit. I don't think her parents liked that fellow. His parents are decent people, but he is a rascal back to do damage. The wedding was all set. It was announced in church. What a calamity."

"The man was on the edge of a nervous condition. The vicar had many counseling meetings with him—not to be repeated outside of this room, please."

"Not a word from me, and the same goes for what I said about Albert making up his will. But, what Mary said seems true. Guilt. I don't think a thorough investigation had been done. Everyone is pointing to that washer woman, but who knows?"

"Poor Kay. First her father, then her mother, and finally Emily and of course we will never know the whole story on that. They keep secrets—that family. Now this bar man has taken over the property next to her and opened a brothel."

"By the way, Mary, talking about dinner parties, have you heard from Walter?"

"Walter merely dropped in because of a mutual friend. Walter's son went to school with one of the Arthur Godfreys boys and of course Lionel Scrugg is his tennis buddy. Small world. He promised to keep in touch; that's it in a nutshell, Adelaide."

"I see. Kay was friendly with him at one point. That was before he became wealthy. Did he stop in to see her, I wonder?" Alba answered my knock.

"Come in. Come in. Why do you always have to be so formal, Kay? The backdoor was open. You could have entered with Albert. Anyway, let's get on; it's getting late."

"We know Albert was late leaving. Mary suggested that I have my driver pick you up, but…"

"I'm fine, Adelaide. Albert has not complained about giving me a lift once in a while. He has 20/20 and represents criminals, so we know he can read." Everyone knew that Adelaide's driver was illiterate and partially blind. The cards had been shuffled and cut. I steeled myself, so as to remain calm to help reduce the palpable tension in the room. The women apparently were not sure whether I had heard any of their conversation, but I was bothered by what I had heard. I had never known Emily to allow a man to sleep with her in our home. Not to say she never slept with anyone, but to my knowledge, not in our home. This was news.

"It's Adelaide and Kay vs. Fanny and me. Since Fanny has to leave early, Alba will finish her hand. In the meantime, Alba serenade us would you, please, with a few pieces from your repertoire. It is always so nice to come to your home. You are such a wonderful hostess. We say this even behind your back."

"Thank you, Mary." It was true that Alba was an excellent hostess. She reminded me very much of the evenings we sat around and listened to Emily playing the organ to entertain the family, but it was difficult to keep my mind on the cards. Donald would have been the last person I'd suspect of harming Emily. I remembered Mauva saying, "silent rivers run deep" referring to Donald and imparting a smidgen of mistrust about him. This latest gossip seemed to add a motive, which I had never thought of before. At breakfast, Mauva took up her usual seat on the step. She was fidgeting with her fingernails and glancing in my direction. "What is it, Mauva?"

"Since you ask. Is not my biznez but ah was wondering if Miss Alba noh that her husband been having drinks with that Indian gurl who work at the building society?"

"You are right. It is none of your business, and you ought not to repeat such contentious rumors. I prefer not to hear gossip, especially of this nature. It puts me in a very awkward position because, as you know, Mr. and Mrs. Tidings are my friends."

"Me sorry, Miss Kay. I like Miss Alba and was thinking that maybe you could…"

"I do not wish to continue this conversation. Please make some mint tea. I'd rather have mint this morning."

"You not feeling good?" She waited for a reply and, when none was forthcoming, she hurried off to the kitchen. There were truths hidden in the information Mauva supplied but, each time she tried to blur the line, I reminded her that she was not a colleague. Alba had been making more than the usual midday visits to her husband's office, and I had more than the usual drop-in visits from her. I guessed that she had been using me as a decoy to snoop on Albert. If he were having an affair, I guessed it would involve his secretary. They were very close, and he often took her along on his foreign, as well as his local, trips. She was married to an executive at WESCO but had been rumored to be having affairs with other men. Alba would have to come to her own decision and sort truth from hurtful gossip the same way that my family did for years.

Donald and Emily had been sitting in the drawing room when I turned in to bed. From what the women said, he never left. I sought counsel from the vicar—not the most pious for a man of the cloth—but nonetheless one who knew all the parishioners and their little secrets. And according to his wife, he had counseled Donald McHale. His cheeks were the usual afternoon rosy. He told me to come in, but it seemed as if his office was in some disarray. The church secretary had left and whatever he was searching for he did not find, leading him to stamp on his desk and proclaim "bloody hell" in exasperation. He listened as one would when his mind was otherwise engaged. He shook his head out of tune with what I was saying but nonetheless offered advice in a hurried fashion.

"There is nothing to be gained, Karolyn. Let Emily rest in peace. You can't bring her back by irritating an old wound."

"Vicar, you know Donald. Perhaps better than any of us who have listened to his baritone drowning out every other voice."

"That he does; that he does. A loud singer."

"You see him Sunday after Sunday with that piece of stick directing the choir, and then marching in front in the flowing robe with the long purple scarf. He may speak more freely to you."

"You don't like the man. Never did. Emily said it. He was a bit older. True, but love knows no bound, Karolyn. Take me and Fanny," he added to inject humor. Everyone in church knew that he and his wife often had disagreements. "Well, now you ought to have a word with Donald. He is a decent chap, and I know he respects you." The vicar picked up his search for whatever he had been looking for. I thanked him and left. He was right, a more direct approach may answer any doubts or lingering questions. It worked with Mr. Frye.

Our committee meetings were generally held after service and ran for an hour or two. Donald lived close to the church so, on my way home, I decided to stop by and have a word with him. Funny, that for all the time that he and my sister had been friends, I had never visited his home.

The house was set in a bit from the road. The neighbors on either side who recognized me as Emily's sister waved as I walked up to his door. He answered my knock and seemed surprised to see me. Donald announced that his visitor, a young member of the choir, was about to leave. He looked a bit ruffled as he carried the glasses and a rum bottle to the kitchen. Not that he needed to offer any explanation, but he said that they had been discussing some church business. He and Emily had many such discussions in our home before they became officially engaged. Donald offered me the sofa chair. It had rounded wooded arms, and the seat and back was covered with a vinyl material. The chair was lower than I expected. When I sat, my knees came up to my chest, and it was awkward to sit in a dignified manner. He sat opposite. On the wall behind him, was a photograph of two older people he said were his parents. A vase on the round center table was filled with plastic flowers. "Where," I wondered, "had he obtained the white plastic curtains with embossed design that hung at both windows lopsided like loose sails?" I could clearly understand why I was never invited, and why my sister may have been so uncertain about him. Whitmore may have been a scoundrel, but he had class. Donald was politely silent and waited for me to speak.

"It's been a long time." He nodded. "You have gone on with your life as is expected, and I with mine in a sort of semi-recovered state. God knows I am not a superstitious person, but Emily has been appearing in my dreams." This is how I introduced the hint of my purpose for stopping in. I waited for him to speak, but he did not. "Do you believe that woman killed Emily?" He seemed startled.

"Which woman?"

"The woman who worked for us, doing laundry. The one who took care of Emily's choir robe?"

"Oh, her! The finger had been pointed in that direction and, as far as I understand, she hasn't been seen since. I don't know what to think. I didn't see any reason that she would have malice toward Emily."

"Mauva said that when she came to work the morning after you had supper with us, she found two glasses, and they smelled of alcohol." Suddenly, after all these years, I felt fearful of the man. I started to get up from that deep chair, in case it became necessary to move swiftly. I had not told anyone about this visit, but his neighbors and that girl saw me enter the house. Donald hesitated and appeared to be searching for the right words.

"I have prayed," I settled back in the chair, "and asked the dear Lord to forgive my transgressions. Of course, we are all sinners. Yes, I had a bottle of estate rum in my car and we had a couple drinks from it that night after you turned in to bed. When I left, Emily was fine. A bit intoxicated but OK."

"What do you think became of the jar with the remaining plums? Mauva said that it had disappeared from on top of the china wagon in our dining room. She swore that after she served Emily the plums, she put the jar on the shelf. It was there before she left, but was gone when she returned the following day."

"It's too late for an investigation of this sort, I suppose, but that is a new element."

"What time did you leave our home? I've heard it was in the wee hours of the morning. Someone saw you."

"Actually, we fell asleep together."

"In other words, Donald McHale, you got Emily drunk with contaminated estate rum. Why didn't we know about this and have the contents of that bottle tested?"

"I hope you are not accusing me. I drank from it myself and threw away the empty bottle." He was nervous, clasping and unclasping his hands, crossing and uncrossing his legs, and shifting his body in the chair. "You can accuse me for not being the gentleman on that night, but we were soon to be married. Is a scandal now worth it? Haven't we suffered enough, you and I? There are many in this town who would testify that Emily had been having sex with Whitmore Chapley. I could have changed my mind about the marriage, but I didn't because I loved your sister. Let me assure you that I had nothing to do with her death." It took some doing to raise myself from the chair, but this time I planned to leave. He had a motive, but he was right. There was no evidence and an investigation along those lines would cause a scandal that could affect us both.

I went to see Dr. James and asked for a sedative. He was among few people in the tow that I trusted not to repeat confidential conversation. He gave similar advice as the vicar. "Let Emily rest. No good will come out of it. No one would believe Donald McHale capable of murder. If anything, Kay, it had to be the stewed fruit. Again, I suspect it may have been accidental. As you know, country folks are not the most hygienic. It was a stroke of bad luck and coincidence. Leave it at that, Kay. Leave it at that. People will start to think that you are unstable if you continue to pursue these dark avenues." I will never again raise this topic but, in my heart, I firmly believed Donald had something to do with Emily's death. It was not Anne. And it was not accidental. I must get on with my life and try to put all those bad and negative thoughts as far as possible from my conscious mind. Now, more than ever, it seemed my survival depended upon my ability to get beyond it all.

"You are on the same committee, and I see him giving you the eye, Kay. As you know, we buried his wife, what? A year? He is a widow. Stanley enjoys classical music, loves to read and is a very dignified fellow. It doesn't hurt that he is well set. He still receives money from that coffee plantation his grandfather owned." Stanley Whitehead was the only male trustee and, being the bookkeeper, we often had to review the church's accounts. His good looks came from being the progeny of a British settler and his Indian sweetheart. Stanley was educated in Britain. He returned home and was appointed to an executive position at WESCO from which he retired. Stanley and his wife were regular church members, and I remembered Margaret complaining about what a tight wad her husband was. We were talking about a budget item, and he brought up the subject of my full time helper.

"I could see when Emily was alive and you had the shop, but to continue with that woman full time seems extravagant and wasteful."

"I would ask you kindly not to interfere into my personal affairs, Stanley. What you do in your home and what I do in mine is no one's business." He wasn't the type of man I'd have any interest in, even though he had the right intellectual qualifications. From that day onward, he was circumspect; we dealt with the church business at hand in a cordial and polite way. I was open to a relationship with a male as long as it was not Stanley. Mauva coughed to notify me of her presence. She was standing next to the curtain that separated my bedroom from the drawing room. I had heard someone walk up the steps and suspected she wanted to tell me who it was. I had been looking through some private papers. I locked the chest, put the key into my bureau drawer and asked her who was at the door.

"A gentleman. Him sey that you know from long time and him juss come into town and would like to have a few words wid you. I don't hear what him sey him name is, but him is dress like a real high class gentleman. Him look fameeliar. I can go back and ask him name."

"Invite him in and offer him a cup of tea or some lemonade." I peered through the window, but the person had already entered my drawing room. My round bureau mirror reflected a spinster with graying hair tied up in a bun and wrapped in a nylon net. I heard Mauva talking too much as usual but still could get no sense of whom the visitor was. "Kay," I said to the image in the mirror, "you would look so much younger if you let your hair down." I brushed it one hundred times. Mammy said this kept the hair healthy. It flowed in curls and covered my shoulders. I was too old to have flowing hair I thought but, again, it made me look and feel so much younger. There was an excitement rushing through my veins as I sauntered into the drawing to meet the male guest that Mauva didn't recognize. He was standing.

*   *   *   *

"Karolyn, you look swell. After all these years. How are you?" If it wasn't for the missing thumb, I would have had trouble recognizing Walter. He looked so different in casual slacks and sport shirt. There was no wedding ring on his finger, but I heard he was married. Anyway, a single man would sooner wear a band on his left finger than a married one.

"Walter, you look distinguished and, from what I've heard, you are. This is a surprise. How did the WESCO deal go?"

"Truth be told, we are working on it, and I see you got the news. How are you, Karolyn?"

"I am well. Please sit and stay a while, Walter."

"I heard about Emily after I returned from Canada. What a sad thing. She was engaged to be married."

"She was." Mauva brought in a tray with tea and biscuits.

"Ah noh dat yur face was fameeler. Mister Walter, me glad fe see you. It is a lang time since yu leff dis part of de country." He acknowledged Mauva, and then turned his attention back to me.

"Tell me what you have been up to, Walter Jones. Who would have thought after all these years, you'd come knocking on my door?" I glanced out the window, expecting to see a motor car with a driver and was surprised when I didn't see one. "Where is your driver?"

"I moored my boat down at the old Logwood wharf and walked the short distance to your house. My, how the place has changed. There are squatters all over. There are bottles tied up in trees with pink and green liquid. What happened here?"

"We are in a constant flux in these parts, and the situation is getting worse every day. Those are the obeah men and women who have moved onto the wharf's property. I never go there, but Mauva tells me that long lines sometimes form to see one man in particular called, "Me Can See Me Can Do." This place is totally different from when we were growing up; the changes have been for the worse. So, here we are, orphans you and me. You've come here in a boat, and I am still in this old frame house, weathering the storms of the past." We caught up on old times, and Walter offered to take me around the lighthouse in his yacht. Although it wasn't a far way out, I was a bit hesitant. Not that I was superstitious, but it had been rumored that ghosts inhabited the lighthouse. Many fishermen told stories of near death as their canoes got close. Walter pulled the chair closer to mine and was about to whisper something when Mauva appeared asking if we wanted anything else. I told her that we were going for a spin in Mr. Walter's boat. She seemed worried and, if anyone had asked her, she would have forbidden me from going. As we walked down the road toward the abandoned wharf, I saw Mauva shielding her eyes from the sun, looking in our direction.

Walter's boat was anchored on the dock in the deep shark-infested waters into which Mr. Meekle was said to have thrown himself. The property had been abandoned for many years because the export of logwood had stopped. The closure put many men out of work and created a shortage of firewood. Rumors had it that the place was being used as a lover's rendevous and obeah haven. It was scary walking on the rotten pier, but Walter held onto my hand and reminded me that he was an excellent swimmer. *Little comfort; tell that to the sharks.* It was a nice looking vessel with the name Sylvia emblazoned on the side. "Truth be told, the name of my soon-to-be ex-wife" he volunteered to answer the question I had not asked. "The third time is a charm they say." He was married twice!

The boat had berths to sleep four, a tiny kitchen and a bathroom with a shower. He put on his captain's cap and off we went into the open Caribbean sea. Walter told me proudly about his two children, one a medical doctor and the other a mechanical engineer. He said if I had shown the least bit of interest, he would never have married his first wife. Walter said he always thought I'd make the perfect partner. I quickly corrected that perception. "Emily, perhaps, but certainly not me. I do not cook, wash or iron, and I do not like to keep house." Walter said he admired me for my intellect and, of course, my great beauty. The things men say. I considered myself too old to be flattered, but I was. I wondered what he told Mary at that dinner party to have gotten her as excited as Alba said she had been. It was a pleasant ride, although the water got a bit choppy toward the end.

As we began the walk back home, the squatters came out of their huts to look. Walter waved in a friendly manner so as to embolden a few men to put their hands out. He dropped some coins, and we hurried out of the compound. Walter kept talking. I asked him to let go of my hand, as rumors have a way of misinterpreting everything in our small town. His first wife ran off with one of his friends but, after he met Sylvia, he thought they were better suited. They had a good marriage up until about five years ago. The separation and details of the divorce were amicable. "Truth be told, I am under contract to purchase a house in the hills, but my lawyer advised me not to consummate the deal until the divorce becomes final. I am not worried about Sylvia, but you know lawyers are cautious." We reached my house, and I invited him to sit for a few minutes. "Bring me up-to-date, Kay. I heard about Lindsay. What a bastard. Your parents passed; your mother's death was also sudden."

"She couldn't bear living without Pappi but, clinically, it was a massive heart attack."

"Then, you and Emily were running the business, and you were tutoring some children. Emily broke off with Whitmore, went to Scotland, and took up with Donald McHale. Donald McHale! Then, took up again with Whitmore and…" The way he said the name made me feel that there had been talk about my Emily and her relationships.

"I am trying my best to put all of the sadness behind me, Walter. It's very difficult but worse when I am reminded."

"You are right. We should be talking about us now—you and me. This is our best time, whether you believe it or not. We are mature and level-headed. Marrying you would be like getting back together with my high school sweetheart."

"That was Connie. Whatever happened to her?"

"She married a government official, and she works for the tax office. That was puppy love. It's an idea, Kay. Think about it. We have time. If you'll have me, I will come back to see you and, perhaps then, you will give me your answer."

"Are you proposing to me, Walter?"

"Truth be told, the thought had been running through my head for several years. It's funny how fate works. I had given up the idea of us and, lo and behold, I ran into Lionel. We started talking about the good old days, and the girls we knew." I wondered what Lionel said about me that prompted this visit and quick marriage proposal. Had he not brought up Lionel, it wouldn't have occurred to me that there may be something sinister in this surprise visit and marriage proposal. The man was still married and living in the house with his wife. So far, I had not done anything foolish except stepping on that boat. I wanted to get myself out of the compromising situation I felt I had been pushed into by Walter Jones's flattery. I hoped that Mauva hadn't been listening.

"The ink is probably still wet on your divorce papers, Walter. And, I believe Mary would be crushed if she found out you came to visit me and hadn't dropped in to say hello to her. Further, she would be shocked if the tone of our conversation were repeated."

"We are mature adults, Kay; I have put my cards on the table. I opened myself up to you. Why would I travel all the way from the city to visit if I were not serious? Truth be told, I am not Lindsay Bronson, and please do not put me into that category."

"Try and seek some counseling, Walter. It works especially for those who have a lot in common, like you and Sylvia. You have two lovely children, and it would be a shame to leave a marriage after almost 30 years. It is never too late to reconcile. As you say, the divorce is not yet final."

"If you want me to chase you, Karolyn Crawford, I am quite willing. The more you try to resist, the greater my passion. I know that is one of the traits of the Crawford girls, us fellows used to talk about it. I am dead serious." Walter kissed me on both cheeks, squeezed my hand, and left. I watched him stride toward the pier and understood why Mary acted like a school girl in his presence. Age has a way of making one more attractive or less. It had worked well in Walter's favor. We were about the same height. He looked lean, strong, and healthy. He was dressed as one would expect a person of wealth to be, and Walter had the air to carry it off. A multitude of emotions were running through my mind. I wanted to dismiss him and his flattery, but I didn't have the strength.

"Bring me a hot cup of tea please, Mauva."

"Miss Kay, the two of you match. You could move from here and go to his mansion up in the hills. She said the same thing about Lindsay; that the two of us matched. How did she know that Walter had a mansion in the hills?"

"Please Mauva, get me the tea."

"You ahrite, Miss Kay?"

"Yes, I am all right." I snapped, giving Mauva a start.

"I was juss tinking dat you don't have to put up with Shuggie Fry because him doing tings dat upset you. Me is quite willing to work for the two of you. I don't have a chick or chile to worry 'bout. Maybe him even have a maid quarters. I hear most of dem house in the city have servant room and inside bathroom."

"Are you going to put on the kettle?"

"Yes'm."

It was up to me to choose between staying here surrounded by a slum or accept Walter's sudden proposal and fly away to the city. Walter had managed to arouse a feeling I thought had died. I had never questioned Mauva's loyalty, but now I feared that, in making her plans, she may very well reveal whatever she overheard in my drawing room. We were never linked together, but he had visited our home many times. We'd see each other in church. It wouldn't be as if Mr. Frye had pushed me out. I'd be moving to the city to marry one of our most successful sons. Everyone knew Walter. He was a few years older than me. Mauva was right; we were suited as a couple. It bothered me though that he was being divorced for a second time. I was surprised that he didn't have a regular woman. I wondered whether his divorce was as a result of his unfaithfulness, a common occurrence on the island. I would probably never find out because Sylvia was not one of us. She was a city girl. Mary would dig up the facts, but I couldn't count on her being impartial or objective.

Walter sent a lovely card, saying how much he enjoyed the time we spent together. He had business and would be back in town soon. He promised that he'd stop by and perhaps we could go to a restaurant for dinner. Walter asked that I write to him at the address on the envelope. It was his place of business. If the pending divorce was amicable, why couldn't he use his current home address? Well, Kay, don't be so judgmental, I told myself. Open your mind to a new relationship. It would do you good. On my birthday, Walter drove himself to town and took me out to dinner. I wasn't sure if he expected me to invite him to stay in one of the bedrooms in my home, but I didn't. Walter invited me to visit him in the city. "I am sure Sylvia wouldn't mind if you stayed with us. I have told her about you. If you'd feel more comfortable staying in a hotel, I'll pay. I'm sure you'd like Sylvia; she's a nice person." *If she was so nice, why are you divorcing her, Walter?* The news had gotten out so that all my friends knew that Walter and I had become friends of a sort.

"Have you decided to leave us, Kay? Mary said he proposed but, according to what she heard, Walter wanted a trial marriage. We think he is a good catch, by far more interesting than any of the men in this town. If you don't want him, you can give the nod to Mary; she is interested." "Walter is married, Adelaide."

"He is? Well, someone had better tell Lionel Scruggs. Consider the matter closed unless you see fit to confide in me."

We had been seeing a lot of each other and corresponding regularly. I wrote and asked Walter to be discrete with regards to any information that contained my name. He denied saying anything about trial marriage to anyone. Despite some apprehension, Walter's proposal was becoming more attractive by the day. Women in the tenement were pushing out babies faster than Mr. Frye could collect rent. Their screams at all hours of the night and day rang like the barefoot man's bell and resonated in my home. Albert suggested that I move and I was adamant I wouldn't be shoved from my home. It would be different if I were to marry and leave. What about Mauva? Walter said I could bring her along, but he had a capable helper who may be out of a job once he moved. I would be prepared to make accommodations but nothing that required total surrender of my independence. I would like to have a car at my disposal, particularly since Walter traveled frequently.

"My driver would be available at any time you want, so there wouldn't be a need for a second car." That was a detail that we could work out later.

"Miss Kay, you look so nice. You always look nice, but you look extra special, nice today."

"Thank you, Mauva."

"Is me did wash and iron that dress. You see how the starch make the embroidery look good? It's pretty anyway because brown fit your complexion. You nevah believe me could iron like Anne, but you see? What time Mister Walter coming? Oh, you put on that nice perfume that Miss Tate did get from foreign. It smell good." This woman knew everything about me. "If any leff inna the bottle, and you don't want it, me could rub little bit 'round me neck when me go visit me frens. Den Miss Crimpson noh dat him is coming?" She answered her own question. "Ah don't tink so because she would'a fine some reason fe stop by here an say she was juss passing." I asked Mauva to excuse me and closed my door curtain. "Me will be in the kitchen if you need anyting." I brushed my hair 120 times in both directions forward and backward. My cheeks were flushed with excitement. It wasn't necessary to add rouge, but I dabbed a bit of Vaseline on my lips. I wouldn't have wanted Mauva to see me preening in the mirror like a teenager, but this was the day I would give Walter an answer. He hinted that it was time and, although I did not tell him, I was poised to say yes. Mauva didn't want to go home until Mister Walter arrived, but I insisted.

Walter drove the four hours, and I felt silly not asking him to stay at my home. He assured me that he was set for lodging. Walter was eerily subdued, not his jolly, intense self. We drove the short distance to the restaurant where we had a reserved table overlooking the water. Walter had pictures of the new house—

our home—as he called it. "Look Walter, there is a marlin! Maybe a barracuda!" He went to the railing and looked into the sea, lingering there for a minute. "Did you see it?"

"I don't know what I was looking for." Walter seemed as if he had been searching his soul, rather looking to see jumping fishes. I was apprehensive, but for a man who had been twice married, it seems to me that he ought to be more self-assured. He appeared so when he first visited me and since. I realized that I had interrupted him in the midst of his showing me the new home.

"Your home is beautiful, Walter. We'll have to see it." He returned to the table and took a sip of rum.

"You'll love the view; it's spectacular. There are a few things left to be done, but it should be ready within a few months." We talked about how we'd merge two households. We both owned pieces that had sentimental value, but he said there was space for it all. Walter wanted to keep one of his helpers, saying she was young, had worked for them for a while and understood him, and that Sylvia agreed. "I know you are attached to Mauva, but she is getting on in age. We could give her a small pension." It wasn't about money. She was as close to me as my great grandmother's bed with the pineapple design that I would refuse to leave behind. If Walter only knew how Mauva yearned to live in the maid's quarters with an inside bathroom. I felt as if I were being asked to chop off my right hand. This woman gave me little or no privacy, entered all my conversations, treated me as though I were a child, was no good at laundry, and had more grey hairs in her head than me. How could Walter even suggest that I leave her? Mauva would just fall in the reeds and die. The thought made me wonder about his honesty and sincerity. He assured me several times that there was a place for Mauva. It seemed he had changed his mind.

Here was my opportunity to be married to a very successful man. Someone I had known since childhood. Move from this godforsaken place into a beautiful home overlooking the city. Have a car and driver at my disposal. Join the country club and play cards with the wives of his colleagues, and all I could think of was my faithful servant Mauva. I was certain she'd go with me without pay. Walter realized that I was eating in a quiet and forced manner, and he must have seen a change in my facial expression. "Kay, was it something I said? It's Mauva, isn't it? I know how you feel about her. Perhaps Joyce would agree to live out and let Mauva have the room. There won't be a lot for her to do, but she can be your personal assistant. You see Kay, when we entertain, I bring in caterers. They take care of everything and clean up. I take my clothes and will take yours to the cleaners. We have a washing machine and dryer. I take most of my clients out for drinks or lunch, and of course I will be happy to have you join us. Sylvia wasn't a social bird; she wasn't interested in meeting business clients with whom she said she had nothing in common. We had a few dinner parties at home but never more than 6 to 10 people. Of course, you will have two guest rooms where friends and family can stay when they are in town. I hope this puts you at ease." Walter had it all worked out. "The divorce is final, by the way; the ink has dried, Kay." We clinked glasses. "Sylvia doesn't mind if I stay until the new place is ready."

"That's great, Walter."

"I told you there was no animosity in our break up. Sybil and I talked about our two children. They were home and took the opportunity to tag items they wanted, and I had a good chat with them also. It was healthy; for that, I am grateful. I took them up to the house. My son had seen it, but my daughter was seeing it for the first time. I told you she lives in Canada. I talked about you and me, and they were all for it. My son said he saw you once at Arthur's house and that you are such a dignified lady."

"That's nice of him. There were always boys running around in that house. I had to lock the room off for some quiet in order to tutor the younger boy, Edmund."

"My daughter said, since this would be my third marriage and your first, we ought to be sure it was what we both wanted. She suggested that we live together for a while before taking the final step. I realize my proposal took you by surprise, but I believe my Christine has a point. She said her mother could attest that I was not the easiest person in the world to live with and that's right. Truth be told, I like to be the boss. Sometimes that worked; sometimes it could be disastrous. As I told my children, I am committed to you with all my heart. We are mature people, Kay." I felt as if I were wearing the scarlet letter. *Adelaide was telling the truth, even though he denied it he must have said this to Lionel.* I felt as if I could throw up the steamed snapper fish. I had the same gut wrenching feeling when Donald told me how he had given Emily drinks and that they had relations. I felt violated.

"It's not as if we won't get married; it's to give us time to adjust to a new relationship and you to city life."

Mauva would have said, 'Your dinner is getting cold, Miss Kay'. "Please, don't speak to me anymore, Walter. I need a few minutes to digest all that you've already said, and the food that seems to be stuck in my throat. I should never have trusted anyone who was on close terms with Lionel Scruggs, but I thought you were different. I consider your proposal an insult and a violation of the trust I put in your declarations of love. You are a liar and a deceptive person, Walter. Allow me to speak. You've had your say. You are not my boss and would never be. You are difficult to live with as evidenced by two divorces to women you call wonderful. Please, do not interrupt me. Your daughter dictates what you should and shouldn't do, and you must rely on your maid Joyce to say whether she will or will not occupy the maid's room before you can give the green light to Mauva. I wouldn't want a man with these character defects as spelled out by your daughter especially one of your age, who has to rely on others to help him make personal decisions. Mammy said it is better to break a relationship than a marriage, and you have broken not one but two and counting. From your declarations, you were about to embark on a third. I ask you kindly to take me home, Walter Jones, and I never ever want to see you again." Pappi had told me never to let anger get the upper hand, but this evening it had. Like Emily, I did not care if anyone overheard or if the trumpet man repeated our quarrel word for word, marching up and down Main Street. I had come out of my self-made cocoon and opened myself for the first time to the idea of a companion, especially one I had known since childhood. Walter was stunned. He seemed confused and perplexed.

"Kay, why would you make it sound so final? It's not as if I changed my mind about us. I am merely suggesting, primarily for your benefit, a temporary arrangement. Give yourself time to think it over. We can talk it over." I believed Walter had changed his mind because he knew that I would never agree to what his daughter suggested. He no longer wanted to marry me but was too cowardly to say it.

"Talk over what, Walter? There is nothing you can say to make me feel less betrayed and violated. I'm close enough to home that I can walk. You needn't feel as if you have to drive me. I beg you not to say anything else, lest I behave in an unladylike fashion that I would come to regret." I was thinking of throwing the glass of liquid in his face. The waitress was lurking nearby. The orange liquid wouldn't look so good on his white, immaculately pressed, shirt. I had a fitful night going over the events of the evening. I was too old to be living as a sweetheart in anyone's home. "Let Mary have him." Perhaps I should have employed a more diplomatic approach and tried to compromise. Alba practiced the art of compromise. She was married to a man who, rumors had it, was as wild as the fever grass that grew along the sides of the road. Yet, she clung to him and acted as if she was his staunchest defender in all things tawdry. Adelaide once said to me that it wasn't so much Albert; it was his potential as a good wage earner that kept Alba tied to his wallet and all the things he could buy.

Mauva checked to see if I was alright and asked if I would like to have a cup of tea in bed. She could tell I was not in a good mood, but she had something to say.

I told her whatever she had to say would have to wait until I got dressed. The boiled egg spilled onto the table cloth. It was too soft and not the way I liked it, but Mauva never made anything the same way twice. She ran to the kitchen and came back to clean up the mess on the table cloth. She sat clearing her throat, hoping I'd ask what was wrong. I didn't.

"Me hear is a big house pon top of one hill that Mister Walter buy for you, Miss Kay. If him never want to marry rite away, you could live on one side and him could live on the adder. You could still kip this home or rent it out for the time being." Mauva was giving me an escape hatch. If things didn't work out with Walter, I would still have this house. "Me was even tinking that if you did decide not to tek the bed, you would'a give it to me." She probably had heard that Walter already had a maid.

"Anywhere I go, the bed goes with me. And please do not bring this subject up anymore; it disturbs me."

"Sorry. Me won't bring up Mr. Walter name again. But Miss Kay, why you crumple up the dress wey me juss iron? You could'a wear it again. Is only one time you wear it. I am sorry. I know you is nat yourself, and I won't bother you but if you want mint tea I will mek it. Hush," Mauva said, as if to a hurt child. "Hush." This woman knew me too well. In her own way, she was comforting me. How could I have thought for a minute about leaving her behind? Several days later Fanny stopped by, which was unusual because we always met in church or at someone else's home. Since Emily died, I have had few gatherings in this house. Fanny looked grim as if she had bad news.

"Kay, I agree with you. Money isn't everything. He is too conceited. Lionel was upset because he felt that he had a hand in getting you two together. He believes you are angry with him, so he asked me to come and explain his side of the situation."

"There is nothing to explain. I am not angry with Lionel, but many of the rumors you may have heard are untrue."

"So he did not propose?"

"I did not accept."

"I see. Well, Lionel thought that he had jilted you for that other woman. My husband is the vicar and, between us Kay, I have had to keep a good eye on him over the years. This is strictly confidential. According to Lionel, at the same time Walter was courting you, he had a girlfriend who was waiting for him to get the divorce. This is why he continued to live with his former wife. Then, this woman became pregnant and promised to make a scandal if he did not marry her as he had promised. Kay, it seems as if you are better off without Walter Jones. Let

Mary have him." Walter continued to write and even to visit me at my home. It was easier to allow him to enter than to have Mauva chase him away. I still carried feelings for him and, at times thought if things were different, he'd be the perfect companion for me. If there was another woman, why would he encourage me to move into the new house? My refusal would be his excuse. There was more to this than Walter was willing to let out. I asked him not to visit my home anymore. I neither trusted him nor was inclined to believe anything he had to say.

News of our conversation had trickled out, sufficient to advertise that we had a disagreement. Thankfully, my friends were very supportive and discrete. Like sports players who say they got a second wind that pushed them toward victory, this was my second wind; I would not sit wringing my hands and bemoaning the break up with Walter as I did with Lindsay. He would not push me back into seclusion, as Emily's death had. I began to accept invitations to social functions and agreed to serve on several boards. Although the nomination was by secret ballot, I thought Whitmore Chapley had a hand in my being asked to become a member of the board of trustees for the local hospital. He couldn't have known that my will included a significant sum to refurbish the public wards because only Fanny and Adelaide had that information.

*   *   *   *

Mary invited me for dinner, saying there was a gentleman visiting that she wanted me to meet. "Take him yourself Mary, because I am not interested in any introductions to the opposite sex." Mary greeted me at the door, saying, "Go on and mingle, Kay. I will be out in a few minutes." It was a beautiful, sunny day with a light breeze whispering through the Julie mango trees in her backyard. The yard was perfectly manicured. There were chairs and tables dressed in crisp, white coverings, each with a vase containing one trumpet flower. Mary had done it this time, I thought, seeing several men dressed in Royal Air Force uniforms. Now, she wanted me paired off with one of those Brits. Alba was in her element. She reverted to Cockney and was chatting it up with one of the younger military men.

"Oh, Kay!" Adelaide exclaimed as she stepped from the back veranda onto the lawn, "you have elevated this garden party to an 'elegant' affair." I looked around and hoped that Mary had not heard this comment. "Don't ask me how she got these officials to grace this godforsaken part of the country with their presence." I did not quite agree that mine or these officers' presence was so important to Mary's function or the island, but Adelaide had never been an admirer of Mary. I said hello to Lionel but otherwise did my best to avoid him. There were serving people with drinks and hors d'oeuvre walking around. A man dressed in an apron stood turning the suckling pig that was roasting on a skewer over an outdoor spit. The vicar had just arrived. He stepped onto the lawn with two drinks in his hands. Fanny stood by the pig man and was asking about the aromatic spices he used. Whitmore and his wife Merle were chatting up Martha Bellows, a woman I knew but saw only occasionally. Molly Bronson came over to say hello. She was a lawyer, as her father had predicted, working for the power company in the city. Jeanetta, Adelaide's helper, would have to have a good memory to give Mauva a list of all the attendees. She somehow placed herself strategically to supervise the servers and to have an overview of all the guests. I had moved away and was obscured by a large, spreading Ackee tree. One of the nurses at the hospital came over to say hello, and we chatted for a while. Everyone at the party seemed to head in my direction to say hello. Perhaps it was because I had been closeted for so long, or they had heard so much about me that they wanted to use their own thermometer to check on my well being.

"There you are, Kay." Mary was walking toward me, holding onto a Englishman's arm and pulling him along. "I want you to meet my friend, Karolyn, in whose honor this party is being held." She whispered to me, "He is single. Can you believe it? Wife died. Go. Go." She said, as if trying to get us to be alone. I was shocked that a party was being held in my honor. This must be the first time in the history of this town that Mary or anyone else could have carried off such a surprise. The Englishman reminded me very much of Pappi and, before long, he told me that he was from Scotland and that his mother's maiden name was Crawford. He was the son of Pappi's sister, Mary, who had been married to Bryce Macalister. Boyd Macalister and I were cousins, and we met at Mary's house. I knew from this day onward I could never leave this town no matter how disenchanted I became; this was my home and where I belonged. No house on the hill could take its place. No haggis in Scotland could entreat me to leave, but I felt better coming face to face with my cousin Boyd. In her journal from Scotland, Emily made mention of an Aunt's son who was in the RAF, but I had given little or no thought of ever meeting him.

Adelaide would want to know how come these men in uniform had come to Mary's party, so I asked Boyd. It so happened that they were on the island on Her Majesty's business, and one of the men had been friends with Mary's husband, Howard. He sent a message to Mary that he was going to be on the island and would like to pay her a visit. So, their presence at the party was sheer coincidence. Mary's husband had joined the RAF and had been in flight school. As

Mauva recalled it, "Him is one foolish man gone to jump outta airplane while it'a fly an kill himself but Miss Mary get nuff money fram England because is dem tell him fe jump." During the continuous drive to recruit West Indians, Howard had been selected to attend officers training in Britain. He died during a parachuting maneuver, leaving Mary a widow with a pension from the Crown.

Boyd stopped by for a few minutes to see where I lived. Mauva was very polite, but she watched with trepidation as I showed him around. As usual, she had comments about the encounter as soon as he left."Him really look like Mister Charlie. Same scrawny long face." I also resembled my father and didn't like her description of my cousin's face as scrawny and long. "I only hope him don't have no ideas fe tek the house from you. You noh English people luv hot sun. Dem want fe mek dem skin turn black likka fe me. Dis is a big house ahn. Miss Kay, you sleeping? Oh is you tired? Tek a ress." I felt good thinking about the party at Mary's and the willpower it must have taken to keep a lid on the affair. "Come Miss Kay, come ahn lay down. It was a big party yesterday an you still tired. Nuff people was deer. Did you see Mister Whitmore little gurl? Oh you still sleeping? Me going to turn down de sheet so you can ress. She grow big." I had not seen Whitmore's daughter, but Mauva knew the child had been at the party. "Miss Primrose nevah come down to de porty. She don't like all de tings people say about how she marry man weh don't even ha chair pon him chest yet." She was referring to the vicar's son-in-law, who was years younger than Primrose. "Dem was living together before dem marry. Remembah, she got job a town an leff? Miss Fanny, mussey nevah noh sey she was livin' a sinful life." I sat in the chair next my bed as she fluffed up the mattress and straightened out the sheets. Funnily or ironically, my best ideas always came to me while Mauva was nearby.

Mauva was talking about how pineapples were grown. She always admired the pineapple patterns on my bed head and the bed posts. Mauva began to educate me on the horticultural aspects of planting this fruit. "Yu noh Miss Kay dat if de farmer want to get him crop quick him haffe mek sure dat when him put de head in de ground him don't dig too many times. Like for an instant if him dig one time and bury de head it will tek one year fe bear pineapple. If him dig two time..." I stopped her, telling her that I understood. "Ah O," she said, feeling pleased that she had imparted knowledge. She convinced me of the necessity to keep my mind engaged and accept the fact that I was a spinster and, in all likelihood, would remain so. That she would remain the only constant companion in my life—a distressing thought fraught with recriminations, but we were bound.

Despite my social activities, home was where I spent most of my time being watched over by a woman a few years older than me. I was such a private person, yet Mauva seemed to be able to read my very thoughts. Perhaps she could get a bottle of that pink liquid the obeah man hung in the trees to ward off evil spirits. Is it me, or is there bad luck in this house? Every man who entered and every relationship that began in this house had been broken. It started with Lindsay. Pappi died soon after we broke up. Aaron left and went back to the city. McHale was suspected as having a hand in Emily's death. And now Walter, who proposed in my drawing room, wanted me to move in to live a common-law life with him in his house on the hill. It's me. It must be. Perhaps I couldn't sustain a loving relationship after Lindsay. There were other men whom I dated or flirted with over the years but pushed away as soon as I thought they were getting serious. I ought to ask Mauva's opinion. I was sure she'd be honest but honesty about my faults or failings would do nothing to boost my sagging spirits. What do I do with the rest of my life?

The idea came to me one evening while Mauva was talking about how several people in the tenement yard had taken ill and that they were poisoned by contaminated canned sardines. There was so much ignorance around; it was depressing. "Miss Kay, de government dash way the sardine an dem people go dig it up an eat it. De government tek every lass one from the shop an bury dem under ground an dem nevah believe say the government was telling the truth. Emanuel in the back deer him well sick. Him wife tink him is gwineto die from sardine poison. Him eat three can. Not one, not two." As usual, I cut her off because I got the point. Many people got sick after eating the cans of sardines that the government had ordered destroyed and buried.

Mauva embarked on some other topic. We were already doing the monthly get-together for card games and that was fun, but we needed something that would challenge our intellect. There were some of us left who understood the difference between Mr. Keiths, the hog butcher, and John Keats, the poet. Why not a group to discuss literature? This would provide me some intellectual stimulation. The Society Ladies' Committee for the Enrichment of the Arts was born as my good and faithful servant poured too much disinfectant into my commode. Jaiz is lethal if ingested, but I wasn't so sure that the fumes were benign because it made me sneeze and my eyes water. Mauva had no sense of measurement. Sometimes, it seemed as if she poured half the bottle instead of the few drops that were needed.

The title sounded a bit too lofty. It would undoubtedly leave me open for ridicule by the illiterates whose propensity to make fun of others is only upstaged by their ignorance. Mauva had a sense of the street, so I asked what she thought of the name for my literary group. She stopped and looked at me with a hesitancy that had come to mean: I really don't want to say what I'm thinking because it is none of my biznez, but since you asked. Mauva answered with a question of her own. "Miss Kay, don't sey yu is rich ahready?" It came to me that was all my helper understood. My proficiency with patois never failed to delight Mauva. "Ah O," she said after a long pause to confirm she now understood. "Den Miss Kay, me fe dress up special like Conchita, I mean Miss Witherspoon?" She asked with the broadest smile. This brought me to the next level. If I were to host this group, they'd probably expect to have tea. If I served tea, then perhaps I should have biscuits. This would give Mauva something else to do.

"You can wear that apron I gave you last Christmas. You've never worn it."

"Afta me noh wahn fe dirty it up. It too nice."

"You will have a chance to show it off now."

"Yes 'm," she ended with the glee of a child. As old as she was, Mauva never lost her sense of wonder and surprise. I thought that, while the women wouldn't have to pay, the enterprise, if it were to work, must be carried out on a shared expense basis. I mentioned this idea to Mary one day after church.

✳   ✳   ✳   ✳

"Such a splendid idea. Culture is your family's signature, and it's so refreshing to see you fully coming out of that ill-suited cocoon, my dear Kay." Mary's words always had a double-edged meaning even when she was trying to be sincere, but she had credits in my book. Anything she said, I took it to be genuine. In a couple of months, it was all set up. We had six ladies in the beginning. Mary Bunting, the former English teacher and widow of Howard Bunting; Adelaide Crimpson, a retired headmistress whose husband had died a slow and agonizing death from lung cancer; Alba Tidings, a trained concert pianist married to a solicitor, Tidings; Fanny Vanderhauffer, a social activist and wife of the vicar of the parish church; and Darcy O'Brien whose husband returned to Ireland, squandered his money, and died in a poor house. I had triple roles: hostess, moderator and discussion leader.

Fanny brought in her dressmaker, Isabel Fuller. The woman lived in a back street and, although Fanny said she was a member, none of us could recall seeing her in church. She brought her without relaying much needed social data that Adelaide in particular needed. Although the voting was secret, no one dared deny Fanny the occasion to say that she was doing something uplifting for the peasantry and the parish church. The fact that my drawing room was the venue didn't seem to matter. Mauva refreshed my memory that, "Miss Isbel was along wid

Busha Johnson," one of Mauva's former landlords. Isbel had the name Sailor Pickney fastened to her until she became too old to wear the title. Her mother had been a known prostitute who died from venereal disease. "She nevah set eye on her fada. Him is American but nobady no where him is." Isbel brought the number to seven, an unlucky number in my book, but our first covenant stated: All are entitled to the same respect and esteem without regard to lineage. At the time we did not know or remember the full story about Isbel. That amendment was subsequently voted upon and out during one of Fanny's absences. The new covenant made me the final arbitrator of approving any new member. The woman was pleasant enough and, as far as Mauva knew, lived a clean and decent life. Her membership seemed to solicit unseemly and vulgar remarks about what some of the ignoramus thought was the real purpose of the "woman's committee."

We met every third Friday at 10 o'clock in the morning—January through November, except for Easter. Mauva wore her pinafore apron with the lace around the edges and her Grumbey. Many people wore these local-made sandals fashioned from wood, with a strip of canvass nailed across the instep. It made a clacking sound that resonated throughout the house, no matter how unobtrusive Mauva tried to be. Periodically, she appeared at the edge of the room to ask if was ready for more tea or biscuits. She waited for a nod "yes" or "no." I'd sometimes see her using her tongue to clean the biscuit residues from around her mouth and off her teeth. It's a privilege she got after being with my family for so many years; we ate the same foods.

"Miss Isbel is a nice s'mady. She is quiet and don't cause any trouble. Ef Busha Johnson did married to har she would'a have de ole house weh him was charging so much money fe rent one lilly room. See wha happen when him dead? Family weh no have nutten to do wid him affairs come an tek wey de house and Miss Isbel had was to move. Good she have a profession she noh haffe depend pon nobady but dat little ole hand machine an de pair of dull scissors weh she have." Mauva knew that Isbel's scissors were dull. Isbel was a timid woman. She was fearful of being ridiculed by idlers who often gathered nearby. She waited until she was at my door before she'd slip on the glove she made from an old lace blouse. Under Fanny's guidance and tutoring, Isbel read and memorized one line of whatever poem or subject was up for discussion. She would interject this bit of hard pressed learning at the first opportunity, and then shut up for the rest of the meeting.

"My God, Kay, I think Fanny even taught the woman how to sit," Adelaide whispered. "Look, she crosses her legs at the ankles and smiles as if she were looking down from heaven on dumb angels." Adelaide had a point. Isbel had a studied way that was obviously unbecoming. Adelaide boasted that her blood line could be traced back to Robert Burns. So, to placate her and because it was traditional, we sang Auld Lang Syne at our committee's Christmas social. "He'd have died here on the island if he wasn't chasing after that woman what's her name…" she'd say to cement her relationship with Burns' memory. Your father was Scottish, wasn't he Kay?" I may have mentioned in conversation that my father enjoyed Burns' poetry, and Adelaide knew he was Scottish, so her question was rhetorical. These ladies' demeanor changed now that we were engaged in intellectual pursuits.

Mary Bunting, the encyclopedia of all things right, wanted a footnote: "Robert Burns wrote in Lowland Scottish vernacular as I recall, which was frowned upon in the early 18th century. Let me see." Mary fiddled with her glasses, and Adelaide hoisted her chin up in the air, ignoring Mary is a bigger insult. "Yes, now I remember. Adelaide, are you familiar with these few lines: 'With tupp'ny ale fear no evil with whiskey neat we'll face the devil?' This, I believe, God rests your cousin's soul, was his mantra. In your genealogical studies, have you ever come across such a poem?"

"Can't say I have, Mary, but I'll tell you this: Russia's greatest poet Alexander Pushkin used the vernacular in many of his early works, and he got plaudits for it. Kay." She stopped abruptly.

"I'm impressed, Adelaide." Mary paused as if trying to come up with an example. "I'll have to look it up. Yes, I suppose you're right." I cut short the verbal combat. Further discussion along this line would call Pappi's family origins into question; he, too, descended from the Lowlands of Scotland but that was neither here nor there.

Adelaide occupied inherited property in the form of an old frame house that was kept intact by the bushes that grew wildly around it on the five or so acres. It had been in her husband's family and passed to her along with a small government pension when he died. Her main income was derived from the operation of a hog pen; she did the book work. It was a wholesale, one hog at a time, business. The animals were dragged off at night by one of Butcher Keiths' lieutenants to be slaughtered for the meat stall in the market or sold in his side yard.

Mary seemed pained to reveal a hint of insufficiency that's been rumored for some time. She was island born and bred but, to listen to her, one may get the impression she was from another country. "The tropical climate leaves me no choice but to carry on and live out my days with the little pittance called widowers' pension. Why, if I were to employ a full time maid like you Kay, I'd have nothing left to buy food. Goodness gracious that would be tragic; wouldn't it? All the prices have skyrocketed, stretching my measly income to the breaking point. I'd have to marry rich and of course that is now out of the question. Who would want a 60-something woman with white hair?" Mary was the encyclopedia of words and historical facts and a fierce challenger on most subjects. She may not have been paying Jeanetta for full time work, but the woman, like Mauva, refused to leave her employ. Her well-manicured yard had gone into decline. It was not up to her standard, but the old man maintained the yard in exchange for meals. Mary counted R.C. Dallas, the son of early English settlers, among her very distant relatives. He did write two volumes of a book on the island's Maroon wars but, according to some historical circles—lies, lies, lies. This brings us to Alba Tidings.

Alba was the wife of solicitor, Albert Tidings, who was known for the nefarious characters he often defended. Much to Alba's chagrin, his services continued to be in great demand by friends and fellow church members who expected to receive his counsel gratis. Alba had credentials of her own; she came from a wealthy family who lived in the Cotswold. She attended a prestigious music conservatory and was trained as a concert pianist. Her social duties precluded any sort of employment outside the home. Albert's parents were British, but he was born and, except for the time spent at a university in England, he lived on the island.

"Wouldn't want it said I'm bragging, but Albert didn't get his appointment because he's such a brilliant solicitor." (Not new information to many of us familiar with his breath of knowledge.) "Not discounting that fact, however, when the word gets around who some of his royal relations are, they literally begged him to accept the appointment to the Privy Counsel." Albert earned a handsome living representing rich vagabonds, so much so, his name and the infamous defendants had become synonymous. He won most of his cases due to the extravagant amount of money the perpetrators or their families were able to pay.

Now, to introduce the social activist. We all had our reservations about Fanny, but she had a good heart and most of what she did I believe was done with good intentions. Here was my quandary: How could a Dutchman become a vicar of the Church of England? Like the mosquitoes that brought us malaria and killed my Pappi, the Dutch were agitating for the island during the early 16th century but did they succeed? No. But, here we have Fanny, who still made trouble. Now, she does it under the aegis of her husband the vicar. Fanny wanted to turn our committee into a referendum for equality. It became a big and bad mistake, voting her in. A few of us suspected that Fanny fed news to Manleng. By the way, this letting of news, if proven, contravened our fifth covenant: No part of the group discussion will be publicized unless there were votes and agreement by at least six members. Fanny and Isbel abstained, as we suspected they would.

"This contravenes my rights as a free British subject." Isbel kept nodding ever so slightly to show her agreement with her sponsor. "I may have to check with Albert if such a matter can be called to vote." Trouble. That's what she was. With that she said, "Ladies, you will have to excuse us because Isbel is working on the vicar's Easter robe." They got up and left. "Who's going to vote to throw out the vicar's wife?" Mauva would, but she was not a member.

"She always ah look pon me funny like." I've noticed a few times Fanny casting a look of poppyshow at my servant, but she did seem a little comical with that nice ironed apron and the wood Grumbey. I planned to buy her a pair of Bata soft rubber soles. Asked to say a few words, by way of introducing herself, Darcy O'Brien launched into a soliloquy as if she were alone in a room, dredging up the past. Apart from the rumors that I had heard, she was not a member of our inner circle. We'd meet at church and exchange pleasantries but that was about all. Bringing her in was Mary's idea.

"Me name is Darcy O'Brien." She began as if everyone in town didn't know about the bad talking Irish woman, who used her cooking pot to wash her privates. "Me ancestors all from Cork Ir'eland. Me Muda died when I was a wee gurl and me Fada Patti O'Brien, bless his soul, raised me to marrying age. Me Fada came to this kuntry to advise the British guv'ment on Irish potato farming. One hundred acres of Irish potato is what the guv'ment wanted me Fada to plant. Who's to buy em? Can't ship em rotten the bunch would be before they get to foreign."

"Me Fada sent for me and me husband and me two boiys to help. Eight and 9 yars old they were at de toime; strong as oxen. Blimey if the guv'ment didn't give us free lund and me Fada made a promise to plant sweet potato on't. On the occasion that he was drunk at the toime he planted sugar cane made him a rich bugger it did. When Pa went to heaven, he left the lund to me and me husband John and the boys, Terrence and McCulley. Now, Johnny was boon right here on the island. He was but two yars of age when me Fada doid. Little Johnny helped as soon as his head reached me knees. He was riding horses and givin' arders to people older than him. Too much bloody work me husband said before packing in taking his share of cash he did and left for parts unknown. But we made out all right without the bastard; we did. After guv'ment tax me three boiys went to college in Lundon from it; they did. Oiy got 50 good acres left and Oiy sublease all but the circle 'round me house to honest peasant people. They pay me fifty percent of everything they grow and sell. Oiy truss them; oiy do. Hurd the bugger went back to Cork and drank himself into the poor house. Doid there he did. Me sons work in respectable jobs and oiy never wants fe nothing. Oiy give money to the local orphanage and help vicar's wife in her ministry business."

Darcy O'Brien said it all, squandering the meeting on her private life history. The Committee for the Enrichment of the Arts was born. It was a real hit, and the ladies looked forward to the communion of kindred souls. The group was devoted to discussion of literature and the arts but, oftentimes and not surprising, trivial matters became the preamble. Members who wanted to share observations or heresy had many opportunities.

"Primrose is having another baby. Did you hear?"

"Don't you think she is too old to be having another child now, Alba?"

"Fanny couldn't understand why, after spending five years studying for a four-year certificate, Primrose returned without a mate. And what do you know, months after Fanny confided her fear in me, Primrose began to gain weight. We learned that she had found someone to blow up her tire and marry her; that was Ronnie."

"A nice lad." Alba lowered her voice, "Albert said he went to Oxford but did not graduate, but I hear they are doing very well in the city. As you all know, Albert and I met in London, so Fanny was right to have been concerned that Primrose had such difficulty and ended up marrying a lad at least 10 years her junior."

"Sorry to interrupt Alba, but we must get on with our meeting. By the way, thanks for the South African tea, the best in the world I understand."

"We ought to talk about tea one of these days, Kay. For instance, the origin of tea. Did anyone know it was quite an accidental discovery? It all began in ancient China more than five thousand years ago when some dried leaves blew into water that was being boiled for one of the early emperors. I have forgotten his name at the moment. He liked the brew so much he sent his cavalry to harvest and study the tree."

"Cavalry, Mary?" I stepped in to cut the animus between these ladies.

"It would make an interesting discussion. I'll make a note, Mary."

"What I intended to say, Kay, is that I think the best tea comes from China, but we should be grateful to Alba for sharing the South African tea. We must get on with our discussion."

"Your reading and general knowledge of French novelist, Flaubert, was most impressive and interesting. When you announced the formation of this committee, I said, 'Mary Bunting, that is something you will enjoy.' Here, I am a devotee to culture. Thank you, Kay. I am going to ask a friend to borrow Madame

Bovary from the library and send it to me. Can't find it here, but I would like to read that novel."

"He must have been a very special type of man, living with his mother until he was 50 years old, my God! I thought only women well." My mother had died long before but, if she were alive I'd probably still be single and living with her, and Mary must have thought of this. "Imagine, he had earned money and fame and ended up in relative poverty, becoming a hermit in the end."

"I've warned Albert to be more judicious with his spending because we all know what happened to Mrs. Tate."

"Your marriage has been going well, hasn't it?"

"Of course, Adelaide, but so was hers until she hired that servant who took her husband to that hut and did awful things that made him leave her. He gave up the three fireplaces, his Bentley, and acres of land." We were sliding once again into the realm of gossip. I attempted to bring the discussion back to our literary topic, but Darcy had something to add.

"He went with prostitutes. I mean gurls of the nite. Got the disease he did." Darcy could have pounced on anything else to add to the discussion, but she chose the worse. I was glad that Isbel Fuller had already left. I called the meeting to an end and reminded everyone that we would be discussing Shelley, the poet, at the next session. Their exuberance and comradery at our gatherings made me feel that I had done something worthwhile.

At our next meeting, all seven members were present. Alba was the first to speak. "Albert wouldn't want me to discuss this outside our home." She hesitated as if she were thinking, should I or shouldn't I? To loosen Alba's lips, Adelaide prompted.

"Well?"

"Well, what?

"What do you have to share?"

Alba talked faster than usual. It was more like blurting nonstop. "He was found guilty and will be going to the gallows, despite the considerable sum his father paid flying Albert, his secretary, and his associate Martin, to London. An eye witness came forward to say that Mitchell was the boy he saw walking to the wharf with the girl he heard the screams and saw Mitchell leave the lover's hideaway alone. Someone bought him clothes and shoes and paid to fly the boy to Britain. He claimed to have seen everything, and his testimony contradicted Albert's carefully laid out line of defense. We don't know who it was that did it, but Albert vows he will find out." Alba stopped speaking and seemed nervous.

"Certen-ly him is gwineto pay for killin' Miss Ulalee Grant one gurl pickney then have de nerve fe blame it pon poor Pussboot juss because de boy family poor."

"Pardon me. Whom did you say he blamed it on, Isbel?"

"Oh, sorry, Mistress Creemsen." Mary let a faint smile cross her pursed lips. This did not go unnoticed by Adelaide.

"My name is Adelaide Crimpson."

"Colvin Reed nickname is Pussboot is him I was talking Mistress Cremp-sin." I interjected that it was time to move on, but Darcy wanted to speak. She must have thought about the topic discussed at the previous meeting and wanted to put everyone on warning that she had no secrets that could be revealed in case she missed a meeting.

"Me life is an open book, and everybody knows that me husband was—excuse me—me husband and Fada were drunkards."

"Yes, Darcy you were very forthcoming, but we must carry on. It is not the purpose of this gathering to delve into the details of anyone's personal life." She looked at me as if to accuse me of hypocrisy. "This is an intellectual enterprise ladies and our topic as you know is Percy Bysshe Shelley, one of the great romantics of the 18th century. We have chosen 'Evening,' which is among the many poems Shelley wrote. Written in 1813, he dedicated this poem to his wife who had turned 18 years old."

"How apropos! By the way, Fanny how are Primrose and Ronnie doing? Their little son, so cute and precious, must be growing nicely."

"They are doing well and hoping for a girl this time. I have been going to see them every chance I get. It's such a long and tortuous drive by bus, but Ronnie comes to meet me at the depot. They have a nice home in the suburbs, and Primrose is immensely happy. Praise the Lord."

"Have you heard that Lionel Scruggs left his wife?"

"That's gossip, Adelaide. We must draw the line between high and low literature." Darcy was depending upon me to make the distinction. Although unsaid, she must not have been pleased that I allowed such a prolonged discussion to have taken place about Fanny.

"I would beg to disagree on implication that gossip is literature, Karolyn."

"It may not be now, Mary, but in years to come our very committee will come under some unscientific microscope and the magnification may not be as pleasing as Shelley's poem to his wife. Shall we move forward ladies?" I paused and searched the faces present. "Mary, would you like to start by reading the first four lines?" Mary took a long ladylike sip, turning her pinky away from the handle of the bone china teacup.

"Alba, do convey my thanks to Albert for the fine South African tea and the reassurance that the Mitchell boy will be punished for his crime."

"Mary, it means Albert lost the case, and he told me not to say anything outside our drawing room."

"Well blimey, we are in the drawing room now, we are." Darcy said with a mischievous giggle then added, "Me lips are sealed, Alba. Oiy wouldn't do nothing to drive a man away from his home."

"One thing is certain, once word gets out, the town crier will be marching down Great Georges Street singing 'Er, ye, er, ye God save de King' as a precursor of the salacious news to follow."

"Salacious is the incorrect word for an announcement about the hanging of a young man, Adelaide. Gruesome definitely, not salacious." The earmarks of discord echoed in the awkward silence that followed. These two friends seemed to delight in rearranging each other. I was forced to cut in once again to keep things on track.

"Mary, is it your intention to lead us into discussion of Shelley's love poem?" Mary put on her spectacles, setting them on the very tip of her nose, cleared her throat, and began to read.

"'O thou bright Sun! Beneath the dark blue line
Of western distance that sublime descendest
And gleaming lovelier as thy beams decline
Thy million hues to every vapor lendest.'"

"Thank you, Mary. Now ladies, what shall we make of this tribute to Shelley's young wife, Harriet Westbrook? His biographers tell us Shelley eloped to Ireland with the 16-year-old Harriet; they subsequently had two children. In 1813, he wrote 'Evening' to commemorate Harriet's 18th birthday. In 1816, he eloped again to Italy; this time with Mary Wollstonecraft Godwin. They had four children but only one survived."

"Didn't Harriet commit suicide?" Alba threw out a question to show she had done some reading.

"Indeed she did," confirmed Mary Bunting before she offered her own opinion. "She was much too young to have been married to a philanderer and an atheist. He was also a little queer, didn't believe in God and wrote about it? Scandalous! Got him kicked out of Oxford."

"Purported, Mary; purported to be an atheist. Furthermore, there is nothing wrong with an older man marrying a younger woman," Adelaide said to put a dimple in Mary Bunting's encyclopedia of personal knowledge.

"A known fact if we are to believe his friends and historians of note, Adelaide."

"We ought to discuss his second wife. I read somewhere that she was a poet and feminist."

"We are discussing this poem, ladies. Shelley was not only flirting with his young wife but with the beauty and mystery of nature it seems. 'Oh thou bright Sun!' Surely is adulation; he worships her. She brings a spark to his life."

"'Beneath the dark blue line?' What do you suppose he meant?" Alba threw out the question to the authorities, and Mary answered.

"Dark blue in this context could mean a depressive state. So young Harriet brings what's lacking in his life: the strength, energy and radiance of the sun to pull him up from the blue line that seems to delineate his state or condition."

"I don't understand how we could say he was depressed by the mere mention of blue. The sky is blue; is that depressing?" Adelaide wanted to know.

"Oiy wasn't much on poetry, but oiy have to agree that Shelley could be talking about his own condition what if he was a poof and heathen as Mary says he'd have plenty reasons to be depressed, wouldn't he?"

"It was in his biography, Darcy" Mary said to take her knowledge out of the gossip column.

"Dark blue line is what we are discussing, Darcy. The contrast all on one line of the bright sun and the dark blue line. Well, I think it's time we paused for a tea break and to cogitate on the meaning of Shelley's poem." I called out twice to Mauva, who had been leaning close to the doorway, enraptured by the discussion. My voice gave her a start. Adelaide took one sip and declared it was the best tea she had ever had.

"A bit on the strong side, but oiy agree with Adelaide."

"Exotic is how I would describe this tea; there is an edge to it." Of course Mauva sometimes poured too much water and other times too little. I'll have to wean her off her sense of the right amount by insisting that she use a measuring device. Mauva came in smiling proudly with a fresh pot of tea and biscuits.

"These biscuits are scrumptious and go nicely with our new tea. The English biscuits were much too costly. When is Albert going back to South Africa, Alba?"

"Let's not be duplicitous. Alba told us a relative in South Africa sent Albert the tea and that the Mitchell boy would be getting the rope." Alba showed her displeasure by putting on her gloves and stamping it down excessively between her fingers. Mary got up before anyone could respond. "Excuse me, Kay," she whispered, "I'd like to use your privy." When she returned, we began to wrap up the meeting.

"Next time ladies, we'll continue with the following lines:
'What the gazer now with astronomic eyes
Could coldly count the spots within thy sphere?
Such was thy lover Harriet could he fly
The thoughts of all that makes his passion dear.'"

"The following week, we'll turn our focus to John Keats. Please read the letter he wrote to George and Georgiana Keats on April, 18, 1819. And, perhaps take a look at the fifth Dante Canto. It is said to have influenced the sonnet he wrote in 1820. You will have to pass the sheet around because I do not have extra copies."

"Miss Kay."

"Yes, Miss Fuller."

"Is supposed to be my turn to seleck a tapic next time."

"Forgive me, but I thought since we had begun to discuss the Romantics for this month, it was fitting to include John Keats."

"So me nat gwineto have a turn 'til month after next?"

"Let's see, if we could move Keats to the following month, then I suppose we could satisfy Miss Fuller's request." Not one to ask for a consensus, I assured the woman that she'd be put on the calendar for the coming month. "We may have time to start discussion on Keats. We'll see."

"We ought to vote on the order of things," said Adelaide. "That way if we are to devote a whole month on the Romantics, it would be a consensus opinion." Isbel was on track; she would not be deterred. Mary moved to the edge of her chair, pretending to show keen interest.

"I would like to discuss 'Beautiful,' a poem by W.A. Bixler."

"Never heard of such a poet. Who is W.A. Bixler?" Adelaide asked and the other ladies leaned forward to hear the answer. Isbel fumbled because she wasn't quite sure; except she knew she had read the poem and liked it, committing much to memory. Fanny had left, so Alba jumped in to lend some support to the poor woman. Mary Bunting leaned forward, and her eyelids went into involuntary spasms.

"I think one of those early 19th century Romantics."

"How does this poem go? Say me a few lines, Miss Fuller."

"'Beautiful sun that giveth us light.' The title is 'Beautiful?' By…"

"Please Isbel, go ahead lest we lose continuity. Pick up the second line."

"'Beautiful moon that shineth by night
  Beautiful planets in the heaven so far

Beautiful twinkle of each lickle star.'"

"Oh hh! Sounds like a bedtime story. We don't do bedtime stories, dear."

"Pardon me, Mary, but wasn't nature a theme in all these poems by the so-called Romantics?" Adelaide asked to tickle Mary with her own hat pin.

"Ladies, we are a democratic committee and, if Miss Fuller wants to do a bedtime story because she thinks it fits in with the Romantics we are discussing, so be it. We'll discuss 'Beautiful' by W.A. Bixler. Miss Fuller, please get us some biographical on your author."

"W.A. Bixler?" Mary Bunting rolled her eyes. No familiarity flashed across the blank whites. *Futile exercise; this woman is an idiot.* Mary brought her exasperated pupils back to center. Her expression showed to those who could read it that, if Mary Bunting hadn't heard of such a poet, the poet just did not exist.

"A 19th century Romantic poet, Mary," Alba said authoritatively.

"Never heard of him."

"It's her, Mary." Isbel had prepared but not for this turn of events. Her one opportunity to add to the literary debate, and she didn't know whether W.A. Bixler was male or female. She had to rely on Alba Tidings, seeing that her mentor was absent. It seemed as if Mary, not to be the one left holding the dummy bag, wanted to continue, but Karolyn interrupted and closed the discussion.

"Miss Fuller will provide some information on the poet at the next meeting to further our intellectual enterprise of discussing great people in literature." Mary pulled out her handkerchief and pretended to be dabbing crumbs from her widening mouth; her stomach jerked, belying her motives. "Isbel, I will put you down for the last Friday. Ladies, we must call this meeting to a close."

Alba took off her gloves. "A reminder that our discussion is confidential. To be candid what I said about the Mitchell lad would create a nasty upheaval in my household if it were revealed. I mean it. Albert would be quite furious." Alba put on her hat stood up and bid them so long. She paused only to hear what Kay was about to say.

"All our discussions here relating to any other subject other than literature—high literature—must never be repeated. We must feel freely to speak and have confidences kept. After the last meeting, ladies, two of us forgot our donation. Fortunately, the tea from South Africa is free, compliments of Alba." Mary cleared her throat to call last-minute attention.

"We talked about news getting out of the meeting, but it's being passed around that the mother of some prominent socialite in this town had been an African slave, and there was some illegitimacy somewhere along the genealogical line."

"Oh my dear Lord! Who? Did you get any hints?" Alba Tidings wanted to know.

"This is not a good note to end a literary discussion. Mary, try and dig out some facts before you let foolish rumors pass your lips"

"You are the researcher. Mary, you can dredge up the facts for Kay." I began to wonder if this was the revival of rumors of years past. Was dimwit Anne back in town stirring up trouble?

"Well, Mary, if you are inferring that it is one of us, slavery was abolished in 1837. We are all about the same age. Was your mother around in 1837? I shouldn't think so. There is, apparently no truth to this vicious rumor and my advice is to put it in trash as soon as you are able." The repartee was over because to Mary's mind Adelaide had made a good point, albeit using her mother to illustrate the ridiculous. The crystal bowl on the table clinked with coins as they bade adieu. My leadership needed more command words to stop irrelevancies. While the discussions were only once a month and intellectually stimulating, I was exhausted at the end. I let the weight of my body down in Papa's old rocking chair. "Quite a lively meeting," I said to Mauva who welcomed the opening.

"Mistress Creemsin is a chatty 'oman. Yu notice how fe har mout inna everybady biznez, Miss Kay? Ongly Miss Bunting noh fe put har in har place. Did ah tell you sey that Anne sneaked inna de kitchen an try fe put some'm inna de kekkle? Ah run her wey an she sey you is har sistah. I says to har g'wey gal a push you'a push-up pon backra people. Yu noh how she facety ahn equalizing. She tun 'round tell me sey ah Miss Sarah tell her sey dat fe har fada name was Tata the African man." I felt a sense of pending doom. Why must my life take these disastrous turns? What is the purpose of living? Why am I left to bear all the burdens of misfortune?

"Mauva, please put the lid back on the teapot; I plan to have another cup."

I decided to make another trip to Dr. James. Like the rest of us, he too had aged and suffered hearing loss. His waiting room was filled with people, so I wrote my complaint and handed it to him. He read it aloud. As I left, one of his patients offered advice on a type of bush I could use to calm my nerves and help me to sleep. Mauva was waiting for the result of my visit. "What doctor say, Miss Kay? Him give you anyting? Plenty people tell me sey him give dem wrong medicine. Him did give Miss Liz dat medicine for the pain in her side and it turn out her appendix did burst and it nealy kill her an him nevah even noh. You remembah? She had was to go to the hospital for two weeks." Sometimes it was hard to tell if Mauva was being kind or cruel. It was a relief to spend some hours away from home. My friends who fired arrows at each other constantly were pious on

Sundays, laughing and visiting and sometimes staying after church for a cup of coffee.

This Sunday, I planned to slip out right after service but, before I could make my exit, Adelaide hurried to catch me. She wanted to have a private chat. This request raised my alarm level as to the matter Mauva had mentioned and of course the topic broached in our last session. We went into the small, windowless room next to the vestry, and she closed the door. "By the way, Kay, I ran into Rodney at Martha Bellows the other day. It is true; Lionel left his wife. He saw Lionel in the city having lunch downtown. Rodney asked how you were doing and told me to say hello. Walter Jones died. I was shocked, but I suppose you heard. He had a heart attack while visiting his daughter in Canada." I felt a tinge of sadness and surprise. Adelaide paused, as if to allow me to say something, but I refused to comment.

"Well?"

"Oh yes, we were talking about Busha, that man."

"You started talking about Rodney and Martha Bellows."

"Isbel Fuller used to live with Busha Johnson. They were paramours for many years. Then he died, and they pushed her out."

"Okay."

"Busha's death was sudden. He was gone in less than a week if you remember. The talk was all over town."

"I heard."

"Which brought us around to discussing Emily's death."

"Adelaide, I think we'd better unlock this door; someone may want to use the room."

"I asked to be allowed a few minutes. As I was saying, those two deaths had certain similarities." I stood up and was about to open the door to end the conversation. I was annoyed.

"Mrs. Crimpson, I do not see any connection between my sister Emily's death and that of a drunk whose liver failure was partly responsible for his death."

"Please sit, Kay, and hear me out. I consider you a friend of long standing and that is why I'm saying this to you." She made it difficult for me to walk away. "Rodney said you sent Mauva to purchase strychnine."

"What? That's ridiculous."

"Let me finish. Mauva said cats were sliding under the fence from the tenement and entering the pantry, and you wanted something to take care of the problem."

"Rodney said this?"

"He was the chemist that sold it to her. When we calculated, it was around the time Busha died of liver failure as you say. It was well known that he and your Mauva had constant altercations that resulted in him giving her notice to leave his place." If there was logic to this gossip, I wasn't following the strain or its relevance to me or Emily. I thanked Adelaide, who asked me to promise to keep an eye on Mauva and to be careful. I had never sent her to get any sort of poison from the chemist and was curious that Mauva would have used my name in that regard. As Adelaide was hinting, this could link me to the murder of a man I was not at all acquainted with except through the comments Mauva made about him and their troubles. On my walk home, I began to try to see if Mauva had exhibited any signs of unusual behavior. I detected none; she was the way she was. I had come to accept her, but I couldn't help dredging up some of her past statements.

"Me sarry sey Miss Emily haffe dead but me glad yu nevah eat none of de poison June plum." Why was she so quick to say the plums were poisoned and to point the finger at Anne? It was strange that Anne showed up for both Pappi and Mammy's funeral but not for Miss Em's. Perhaps I had not been vigorous enough in seeing that every detail surrounding Emily's death was investigated. We all said things especially Mauva that, if laced together in the wrong pattern, could point to a totally different design. When I got home, I mentioned to Mauva that it was strange Anne did not show up at Emily's funeral. "Ah nevah said it before because ah noh how upset you was but me send a message wid that woman who live up inna de bush. Me sey tell dat facety roun' face gal that if she show herself at Miss Emily fineral she is gwineto to get lock up and go straight to the gallows wid rope 'roun har neck." That explained Anne's absence from the funeral, but no one had seen her in the town since that time.

Mauva reheated my lunch because she had expected me home earlier. Looking at that innocent face, I could not bring myself to ask her about the strychnine she supposedly purchased using my name. It seemed logical that if she asked Rodney for cat poison, he may have given her that as the one to do the job. Maybe she needed it for her place to kill rats; rodents wouldn't be a surprising occurrence in a rooming house environment. Why did she tell me that Anne looked different when she brought the jar of plums? From whom did she get the information that Anne was spreading news all over town that she was my sister and that an African man named Tata was her father?

"Mauva."

"Yes'm."

"I'd like you to go home early. You needn't stay here on the weekend. Today is Sunday, and you should be home reading your bible or resting."

"You vex wid me, Miss Kay?"

"No."

"Den you noh sey me like fe mek yu cup'a tea an tun dung yu bed before me leff. Is nat you tell me fe come on Sunday, but who else is gwineto mek yur breakfast lunch an dinnah?"

"Okay, Mauva, do it this time, but please do not do this in the future. I need time alone to think about the group and make an agenda, write notes and letters to friends and so forth."

"Ahrite, Miss Kay, me will be here brite an early tomarrow mawning."

∗   ∗   ∗   ∗

"Adelaide, I cannot believe it! My God. Did Doctor James say how she died? She wasn't ill. My God. Maybe it was a heart attack. Her mother died from it. Mary, did she say anything to make you feel she had a troubling secret?"

"She would have said it to you first, Adelaide. The embalmers said she looked terrified, and they had to press coins on her eyelids to close them." The parish church bell tolled mournfully, as news spread that Karolyn Crawford died in her sleep. Her faithful servant found her in the morning when she reported for work. "Did you know she moved in and put herself in Kay's bedroom? You did say she was suspected of poisoning that man whose house she lived in, what's his name?"

"Mary, I said there was suspicion around the untimely death of Busha Johnson. Kay said he died from liver failure due to excessive drinking. All I know is that Kay was well last Sunday."

"And what you make of Emily's poisoning? That was untimely. You think that woman, the round face one who looks like Emily, had anything to do with it? Kay said she didn't believe the woman had anything to do with her sister's death. There is another rumor going around that this Anne was Mrs. Crawford's," she whispers, "out-of-wedlock child and that was why her parents sent her away."

"Mary, it is only the two of us here. You don't have to whisper."

"The trees have ears, Adelaide. I wonder what other secrets have yet to come out of this family closet? By the way, did you know that Emily's middle name was Anne?"

"Kay told me there was a mutual dislike between Mauva and this other maid, Anne. They often quarreled. So it comes as no surprise that Mauva would somehow name her as a suspect."

"Excuse me, Mrs. Crimpson."

"Oh, Mauva! Yes?"

"Ah noh people a chat sey me ha someting fe do wid wha happen to Miss Kay but is lie. When me leff, she was getting ready to go to bed because me did turn down de bed geh har one lass cup'a tea ahn tell har me we see har brite ahn early de following mawning. She was like family to me. Me no have nobady leff in dis world." Mauva wheeled and walked away, blowing her nose and using Kay's handkerchief to wipe away tears.

"Well Mary, what do you think?"

"It's all so confusing. Perhaps by the time we meet for the reading of Kay's will, we will be able to sort it out. Did you hear what the woman said? She gave Kay one last cup of tea before going home. Think about that. Perhaps we ought to hold off the reading until Kay's death has been thoroughly investigated to make sure the killer doesn't profit from her crime.

"What a dramatic display if she is the culprit! Did you see how it took three grave diggers to restrain her from jumping into the hole? She was sobbing that she wanted to be buried with her mistress."

"Kay's elegant black dress covered her ankles, and it was too tight. She had everything: the black clutch purse and the hat. I warned Kay about her. Nothing stays secret in this town for long, so we will find out. Little dribs and drabs will begin to float around. I sent a message to Boyd, the cousin Kay met at the party. He wrote back to say he couldn't make it to the funeral and had no interest in staking any claims to his cousin's estate. I will be making enquiries and speaking to the inspector of police. In the meantime, let's pray her death was from natural causes."

It was rumored that Mauva Grant and the woman Anne had been hauled in for questioning. It was beginning to look like foul play, but no motive or method of death had been determined or would probably ever be determined. The reading was arranged in solicitor Tidings law office. Those present were: The Vicar and his wife Fanny; Kay's friends, Adelaide Crimpson and Mary Bunting; Stanley Whitehead, trustee; Whitmore Chapley, administrator of the local hospital; and Mauva Grant, all beneficiaries. Albert took off his jacket to expose a fiery red waistcoat. There was no doubt who was the performer in the day's drama. He acted as if he didn't know a soul in the room of friends and acquaintances.

"Good afternoon. Ladies and gentlemen, I have been asked to read and interpret the last will and testament of Karolyn Elizabeth Crawford, deceased." Albert was interrupted by his secretary, who handed him a note. He asked to be excused, saying there was an important development. Mary drew closer to Adelaide and whispered.

"What you think that is, Adelaide?"

"An imminent arrest, maybe." Both women looked at Mauva. "Would be rather dramatic if they plucked her from this room, slapped a handcuff and hauled her off to the jail. I warned Kay." Albert returned, followed by the inspector of police. "It appears as if we guessed right." Mauva Grant sat like a leper in the back, far from her mistress's friends. She tapped at her eyes and looked apprehensively at the police inspector. The man switched his gaze from Mauva to Whitmore. Adelaide whispered. "I had counted him out. Maybe Kay found out he paid for the abortion."

"What abortion? That's a new one."

"As many of you may have heard, there has been an on-going investigation surrounding the untimely death of Miss Crawford. We interviewed several people in this regard, including Donald McHale. Someone saw him driving away from the home that night. He admitted it, but denied he had any involvement in the death. It was routine, you understand. The detectives scheduled a second interview with Mr. McHale, and he was expected in our office this morning. When he did not arrive, constables were sent to his home and found him hanging from the ceiling." Mauva was nodding her head, as if she had been vindicated. "Some of you may know that Mr. McHale and I were friends for many years. He left this letter addressed to me! I will read it."

Dear Gus,

I have betrayed your trust and that of my fellow church members, let my choir down, and disgraced this town. I couldn't live with the thought that a woman who had lived and worked all her adult life had become a suspect for a crime I committed. I didn't mean to kill or harm Emily because God knows that I loved her, but..." The inspector looked at Whitmore, who had loosened his tie and appeared as if he were uncomfortable. *"Emily told me she wanted to call off our wedding. I had supper with the family. After that, I stayed to have a few drinks with Emily. I poured myself a drink and then, when she left the room, I dropped the poison in her glass. I couldn't stand the thought that I would lose her. Kay confronted me, but I denied I had anything to do with her sister's death. I didn't tell her all that I knew, and I guess I will take that to my grave. I waited until her servant left.*

Mauva cleared her throat to remind everyone that she was the servant mentioned. Whitmore seemed to be uncomfortable but didn't want to miss out on the details. *"I knocked. Kay called out, asking who was there? I entered through the unlocked back door, and she came to the drawing room in her nightgown and robe. She was startled, but I assured her that I meant no harm. I only wanted to talk with her. She was about to scream, but I clamped my hand over her mouth and eased her into the bedroom. I told her everything that happened that night but, as I lifted my hand and prepared to leave, she started screaming. We had a struggle. She bit my hand, and I grabbed one of the pillows and held it over her face to keep her quiet. I begged her not to scream, but she jumped off the bed as I lifted the pillow. I pushed her back and held the pillow over her face. I must have passed out because when I came to we were laying crossway side by side. I shook her, but her body was limp. I checked her pulse, but there was none. I didn't know what to do, so I removed the robe, cleaned the blood that was coming from her mouth and nose, laid her lengthwise, pulled up the sheet, and covered the bed with the mosquito net. I threw the pillow with blood in my car and left. Gus, pray for my soul.*

Whitmore seemed more like a pariah than an administrator about to hear what Karolyn had left to his hospital. Mary whispered, "This time he will have to leave the town for good." Albert rang his secretary, and she brought in a glass of water and set it on his desk. Whitmore looked at his watch, beckoning to Albert that he had to leave. He followed the secretary and pulled the door behind him.

"Whew! This was a surprise, wasn't it?

"No, Mister Albert, it was nat a surprise to me."

"Thank you, Miss Grant. It was alarmingly new information to most of us. It is fitting that, on this day the true murderer of our friend and colleague Karolyn, revealed himself. It is unfortunate that he wasn't man enough to allow this town closure by trial. He took the easy way out by slinging a bed sheet around his neck and kicking away the bucket." Mauva stood up again.

"I did tell Miss Kay nat to truss him. Silent rivers run deep. Him is rite ef I was deer him couldn't do nothen to Miss Kay. We nevah lock de doors all deese years an him noh because him use to sneak in a nite time to see Miss Emily. Him is de one who tek weh de plum jar. How me fe tink sey a man who stand up in front of choir every Sunday would have blackness inna him heart?"

"Miss Grant, I would like to continue with the reading of the will."

"Sorry, Mister Albert, but you see how dem can sen innocent people to de galleons fe someting dem don't do." Mauva forgot that she tried very hard to put the blame for Emily's death on Anne. "Dem policeman was trying fe get me fe confess to something poor Mauva Grant nevah do. How me did love Miss Kay, and she did love me. Me did really tink she did dead in har sleep because she was in har nightgown an the net pull ovah de bed same way me leff it the night before. God have a wey to turn tings around."

"Miss Grant, we will have to move on with the reading of the will."

"Excuse me, Mister Tidings, me is de only me leff fe clear Miss Kay name because me noh sey people say all sart of tings about de family. As me was saying de gal Anne show up an sey dat Miss Liz was fe har mada an dat she wahn room inna har mada house. Me run har again but she ha somebody who ah put har up to trouble. Dem all believe say dat me is gwineto to get de house. Miss Kay did tell me so, but me tink say dat Shuggie Fry want fe tun it inna brothel like what him do wid Miss Bell house. Undah me dead body. Me will get the law on him. One more ting. Is nat me who did put the lizard inna the teapot. It could be de gal Anne do dat fe frighten Miss Kay." Solicitor Tidings told Mauva if she did not stop talking, he would have to ask her to leave his office.

"Well, Fanny this closes a chapter in our town's register. Perhaps Donald McHale did Kay a favor. This rumor that Anne is the illegitimate child of Elizabeth Crawford would have had the same effect as the poisoned estate rum that killed Emily and the pillow that quieted Kay's screams. So, Anne was the one who dropped the lizard in the teapot?"

CONFESSIONS OF
LEOPOLD SHADE

I turned 11 and thought of running away from home. I thought it best to tell my parents they may not see me in the morning. I was sitting outside their bedroom for nearly an hour, waiting for a chance to knock when their quarrel took on a higher than usual pitch. They were not talking about my brother, William. "Leopold, you have damaged that child."

"You brought him here that way, Clementine, and now you want to blame me for the messed up pirate genes he seems to have running up and down his narrow, little body. I have been trying to put some sense and right into him, that's all. It's not from my side of the family. If you read history Clem, you ought to remember the devil they kicked up in the early 17th century, sacking ships on the open sea. The Spanish were a bunch of thieves, Clem." Mother's blood line ran from Kentucky to Spain, where her grandparents were born and grew up. My father's ancestors were British.

"Go to sleep, Leopold; you are drunk."

William had sleep in his eyes, but he was furious and blamed me for waking him up by my absence from our bedroom. He grabbed me by the collar. "What are you doing here? Why aren't you in your bed, Leo? You want to tell them you are running away again? Why don't you just go? That is how running away works. Get in your bed. I am tired of you sneaking out, leaving the lights on. Take the top bunk. That way, when you wake me up, it will be for a good reason because you would fall off the ladder. And you could break your neck, Leo." It didn't make sense what William said, but I climbed up the ladder and soon fell asleep.

My mother would tell dad that his negative comments were damaging my self-esteem. "What self-esteem? The boy is bent on being worthless. He has proven time and time again to be a reprobate. Why would he sign your name to a letter excusing himself from school for an entire week? Do you know where he went dressed up in that uniform? No, Clementina. You knew not. On top of this subterfuge, he had the temerity to claim the reason he walked home was that he missed the school bus. This ruse did not stop until the coppers drove him here, saying he was caught stealing video games. The owner told me that the boy was caught on camera stuffing himself with sweets and chocolates. Of course, they redeemed the videos and could have pumped his stomach and brought up the cache, but they made me pay for what they estimated he swallowed. If he sets a foot in that store again, the owner told me he will be arrested and a felony charge put against his name."

"Felony charges for a few sweets, Leopold? Moreover, he wasn't the only boy the police drove home that day; there were four of them."

"Four of them? Oh, you are proud to say your son had coerced three others in his crime spree? You still believe the leather strap is cruel and unusual, Clementine? Do you?" My father said he regretted allowing me to be named after him. "Mr. Mulligan told me you stole his watch then tried to sell it back to him. He said several gold pieces were missing from his bedroom, and the only person who had access was you. He did not want you coming back to his home, and he has prohibited his daughter from having anything to do with you."

"That is the thanks for tracking down the thief, paying money to get his watch back. I did it for Sarah because she was crying, saying it meant so much to her Dad."

"You dishonest sonof…" My mother was standing next to him. "A liar and a thief, that is what you are, bud. Don't say I didn't tell you, Clem."

He promised to pay for college, even though he had misgivings that I would survive the first year. I graduated with a bachelor's degree in business administration. I applied for a job with the postal service and failed the test twice. What does abstract thinking have to with sorting mail? If dad had been a different person I would have asked him to sue the post office. It seemed unfair that I passed all the other parts, but they decked me on the abstract part. William had finished college, was accepted in the seminary, and was working on a Ph.D. in religious studies. When Dad came home from his office, it was the hardest time for me. He always pushed my bedroom door open and would light into me if I was in there. If not, he'd leave the door open so that Mom could see what a mess the room was.

William had moved right after college to a small house behind the church. His housing was free. When he wasn't busy with church affairs, he'd come home on special occasions for dinner. "Can't you draw any inspiration from your brother? Well, son, you better lift your lazy ass out of my house before I have to kick it out. Find yourself a job that can pay rent and buy food. It seems that is all you need in life." It was getting to me. Just to get out of the house, I picked up odd jobs. I worked as a short order cook, sold hot dogs on wheels, and rode around town as a bicycle messenger. I accepted anything that could burn up some hours and earn a few bucks for cigarettes and dates. I told Mom that I was looking for a place; she told me I could come back anytime for a home-cooked meal. I saved up enough money to pay four months' rent and found an efficiency close by because I did not have a car. Dad slapped me on the shoulder and said, "Well done." I put all my belongings into a couple pillowcases and moved. Dad arranged to deliver a few pieces of furniture, and I was all set.

Bryce Swindle was dad's main drinking buddy. Their law offices were close, and they got smashed to celebrate the end of the work day, the weekends and every holiday. Their wives also had a lot in common. Helen and mom belonged to the garden club, were active in church affairs, loved to bake, and had been stay-at-home moms. Bryce had two daughters: Sybil and Cindy. They were night and day different. Cindy was like a house mouse, but Sybil Swindle was hot. I remember, in high school, every boy wanted to become a man with Sybil and most did. She was voluptuous. Cindy may have had dates but not anywhere close to the attention her big sister received. Sybil was interested in boys who had money to spend. I had lust; that was about all.

I was out of his house, but Dad still was not happy with the way my life was going. I had no pots so, naturally, Mom's open invitation suited me fine. It didn't sit well with Dad. He thought that any man of 23, who had to sponge on his parents, had to be defective in some way. He put himself through law school at nights. He took care of his parents. He started to work when he was nine. Something had to be wrong with me. "You ought to seek counseling Leopold, because it seems to me that your life is headed toward a dead end. Unless you make a decision to bring your life to heel, do not come back to my home. I will pay the costs for therapy because I know you barely work enough hours to pay for the one room, but you must go and talk to a professional." Mom was so upset, she went into the bedroom and, I believe, she cried. I had been thinking that, unless I got a steady job, I may have to ask to move back into the family home.

Now, Dad was giving me an ultimatum that, either I get my head checked, or no more free meals.

"Leopold, are you coming over for dinner on Sunday?" Before I could answer, dad reminded her that I had been over three days in a row. "Well, Leopold, do you want to have dinner with us on Sunday? I need to know because I would like to invite the Swindles and their girls over." Dad raised his eyebrows, took a toothpick and started to clean food particles. He didn't object to inviting the Swindles. "Well, Leopold, don't let me down. We will be expecting you on Sunday." I got to the house early, because Mother told me she was baking my favorite rhubarb pie. Sybil came in a mini skirt and low-cut blouse. She had a small purse, and it fell. Dad wanted to get it, but Sybil had bent over, saying that she'd get it. We both looked at her red panties. She was a temptress. Dad kept his eyes peeled, except when I'd catch him, and he acted as if he were really interested in making conversation with Sybil. Cindy was dressed conservatively. She was plain and soft-spoken, but clearly the more intelligent of the two. After the Swindles left, mother was all smiles and said, "What a lovely girl."

"Oh yes, lovely. Very lovely."

"You know, Leopold, she would make a good wife for you." Dad didn't comment, except to say hmm. "She is so different from that Sybil. Helen is up to her eyeballs with her antics. Unruly, that girl." I could see the surprise on Dad's face. "It's time you start thinking about settling down and starting a family, Leopold. Cindy is a decent girl and really quite charming. I want grandchildren, Leopold." There was a way that each of us knew which one of the Leopolds was being addressed, even if the conversation was out of context. Dad picked up the newspaper and began turning the pages.

"By the way, Leopold, have you talked with that therapist? I think you need to square a few of the cobwebs before your mother pushes you into the fire."

"Leopold, how cruel. Why would you say a thing like that? Wouldn't you want to see your son married and settled with a decent young woman?" It became obvious that mother was trying to pair me off with Bryce Swindle's squirrel-face daughter. I was confused about the whole thing. Dad was going to pay for me to talk with someone who could be objective. When the therapist asked me what brought me to her office, I said my mother was pushing me to marry a woman I did not love. Then, it was my father who has never shown me any love. I only had 45 minutes to lay out my case, so I wanted to put the primaries out first.

"What do you mean? He blamed everything on your mother? Give me an example."

"He said he regretted giving me his name, and he blamed her for my birth because she was the one who brought me into his life. He said that her family had pirate genes, and I had inherited them." The counselor said my mother was the prototype of a battered woman. "I am the one who was battered. He had a belt over his bed for me, and he used it. He never hit Mom." She explained emotional abuse to me. I realized then that we were both abused; only, I had the added physical component, namely the leather belt. I had come to dislike my mother but, the more sessions I had, the more I saw her as a weak person who inadvertently became a facilitator.

Cindy invited me to her house, and sometimes we'd go out to eat. I protested, but she would always prevail in picking up the tab for the meal. "Don't feel bad, Leo. I have had so many meals at your parents' home; this is the least I can do. Furthermore, you say you do not own any pots and, even if you did, the way you describe that apartment, it would be difficult to do any cooking there." I usually called Mom ahead of time; that is how Dad wanted it. As soon as I got there, Cindy happened to be passing and stopped in to say hello. Dad wouldn't light into me when Cindy was around but, as soon as she left, he'd say that I needed to learn how to cook or take myself to a restaurant. Every time he turned around, I would be sitting at his dining table. His spit hadn't had a chance to dry, and there I was mooching. The man hated me. How was this possible?

The closer she came, the more I tried to discourage Cindy. "I understand you need space, Leo; it's just that I want to take care of you. You are such a sweet and gentle person." No one had ever said those words to me. No one except one guy in college who saw me naked in the shower and said I was sweet, gentle, sexy, and had a great tush. I told him that I may not have a black belt, but I was close to getting one. I wasn't even taking karate, but he stayed away from me. There was nothing I could say to Cindy to push her away. Anything I said, she understood. Dad had gotten in the way. He had forced me, according to his boast, to stand on my own two feet. At times, I thought perhaps Cindy was too close in temperament to my mother. The therapist said, if Cindy is as kind and caring as I say, in time I may come to love her. And if it happens, we will have a stronger bond and deeper affection toward each other.

I was still trying to find a steady job when Bernie Baumgarten called, saying that John Mulligan told him I was looking for work. Bernie slapped me so hard on the shoulder that I felt as if my joint would snap. A big, unlit cigar hung from his mouth. Bernie owned the building, and his suite was on the first floor. The place was nice, with expensive looking rugs a reception area and a conference room. Bernie's office had a clean desk, and the window had decorator drapery that could be pulled shut. There was a smaller office that looked like it was for a salesman or junior staff. Bernie took me into a small, windowless, back room. Although it was only the two of us in the place, he pulled the door shut.

"From what I've heard, you have the traits of an enterprising young fellow." *Mulligan told him about the watch caper, and he took it as a recommendation.* I told him that I had a bachelor's degree in business administration. "Good, that won't hurt but in this business you need all your wits about you at all times. You have to be straight up and honest with me, Bernie, all the time. It's not mandatory, but things could get very unpleasant if you are not. Are you with me so far?" I assured him that I understood. Bernie said if I agreed to work for him, he would provide the necessary training and, if I applied myself, I could do very well and make up to six figures. I would have an opportunity to travel. At first, it would be to the Bahamas but, as I gained more experience, he would have me represent him in distant lands. Honestly, he was afraid to get on an airplane.

Baumgarten Enterprises sold arms, new and used. Bernie dealt with government officials, local and foreign. He said they came to his office with their wish lists, and he helped to put the money and deals together. A previous employee had disappeared with a briefcase containing thousands of dollars. Bernie said he and others were searching for the guy. "I know your family. Your father is a respectable lawyer, and I am sure you wouldn't do anything to cause him anymore trouble." We shook hands. I was going to start working with Bernie Baumgarten.

"Six figures? If you trade in contraband, Leopold, I won't be able to help you. My specialization is family law. Don't say I didn't warn you of the possibilities for trouble working for an arms merchant. You seem drawn to unseemly people. So many young men find jobs in legitimate businesses. Maybe they don't make the six figures, but..." He stopped short. "Leopold, good luck. Make the best of it. Perhaps you can learn something, and then move on." He was just jealous. Dad had been practicing law for so many years and had nothing besides a modest house to show for his efforts. I was happy to be getting a chance to travel and make good money.

"Leopold, will you come over on Sunday. I will invite Cindy, and we can celebrate your new job." I decided that I may as well keep Cindy. She did everything to please me. I would never find another woman like her, and the counselor said that I may come to love her. Sarah Mulligan was beautiful, but she was spoiled. Her parents would probably add a suite to their home so that Sarah would always be in their periscope. We wouldn't have any kind of life. Mom even said that, in talking up the virtues of Cindy, Sybil was attractive and distracting. Every time I saw her, it seemed as if I got involuntary thrombosis you know where. She wasn't often at the house when I visited but, when she was, Sybil would walk into the living room in her underclothes. It was as if I was already her brother-in-law and didn't matter, but it disturbed me. "Do the right thing, Leopold. Talk with her parents, and ask for her hand."

We were exploring a formal engagement when Mom dropped in with a freshly baked rhubarb pie. Pretending to be surprised to see me, she said, "I didn't know you were having dinner here again, Leopold. See you on Thursday, Helen. Hi, Cindy." Bryce was not at home, but Helen sat in her grandmother's tufted chair, with the tacks running across the top and along the arms and stared at me as if to send me a warning that unflattering thoughts were going on in her head. Dad didn't have anything good to say about Cindy, but he didn't dislike her.

"Plain looking. Wish her luck. People tend to become more responsible when they have families. I hope Bryce won't hold it against me. They're putting together a humdinger of an affair, and he will be paying the bill; the poor lad."

"Leopold, the bride's parents usually pay for the wedding. What are they to hold against you? Can't you say one encouraging word? He is your son, and he is trying to do something positive with his life. He has a steady job now."

"Steady job?"

"Mr. Swindle said that he'd give us a few dollars to pay down on a house, Dad. Once I learn the trade from Bernie and business picks up, I will pay him back. Bernie said that I could earn upwards of $100,000 a year." Dad looked at his watch.

"What time are we going to have supper tonight, Clementina?"

The news had been circulating about our marriage. I ran into Sarah Mulligan; she shoved her sunglasses to the top of her head and looked at me. "You are going to marry Cindy? How much is Mr. Swindle paying you, Leo? Don't tell me you love her because I know you are still hot for me, and I'm available, Leo." She brought her shades down and put on a special walk for me. "See you around, Leo."

"Cindy is a better choice. Anyway, you can't stop the carriage after the horse has gone through the gate, Leopold." Mother thought I was trying to change my mind. I was 26, and Cindy wanted to be married on her twenty-fourth birthday, which was in October. Most girls wanted to marry in the spring. I found the fall depressing. "It is a beautiful time of the season, Leopold. The foliage has hues of red and gold and the mountain views are spectacular. And the sunsets are lovelier, especially after the leaves have fallen off." It was also a time when trees were getting ready to go into hibernation. It wasn't the time I would choose but that is what Cindy wanted.

The wedding was held in the Swindle's backyard. Cindy wanted it simple. Sybil was her only bridesmaid. A buddy of mine from high school was the best man. William officiated. Dad came dressed in the same grey suit he had worn to his law office every day for as long as I had known him. He alternated between the two identical suits. Mom wore a frilly, chiffon dress with a scarf she threw loosely around her neck to cover the low cut. Sybil helped her to pick out the dress. She was happy that at least one of her sons had married and may give her grandchildren. With the help of Mr. Swindle, we moved into a small two bed-room home. I wanted to wait a couple years before starting a family, but Cindy stopped taking birth control pills. Carrie was conceived on her birthday a year after we were married. Unfortunately, my mother did not live to see the birth of her grandchild. She and dad died in a nasty automobile accident a few months before Cindy delivered Carrie.

The infant looked exactly like her mother, having the same squirrel face, small forehead, tiny ears, and pointed chin, but she made up for it all in personality and spunk. She was a lively and lovable child, and I was a proud and happy dad. Three years later, Kathleen came along. She favored my mother but had Cindy's shy nature. Cindy was working full time and making twice what I was making. I wasn't making anything close to the six figures Bernie promised. I threatened to leave, but Bernie said something big was coming down that would gain me a big commission. The insurance company settled on the wrongful death suit I brought against them in the accident that took my parents' lives. William, who was not for suing, did come up with some of the legal fees. He said he would put his part of his money in the bank and name my girls the beneficiaries. When they reached 18, he would let them have it. I spent my share on mortgage and other expenses while I was waiting for my big break.

I was making a trip almost every month to the Bahamas. Sometimes, Cindy's mother would watch the children so that she could accompany me. I had become Bernie's main man. He started to pay me a regular salary plus a small percentage of commission. I still felt that he was taking advantage. I was still waiting on the big commission he promised. Bernie saw the handwriting on the wall. He called me in that back office and said that I had earned full partnership that meant a greater split of commissions. In a few months, he made good on that promise. I was get-ting a combination of cash and checks; some taxable and some not. He encour-aged me to move into a nicer home, saying one had to look successful to be successful. Cindy was thrilled. We sold the house, repaid the loan from her father, and made a small profit.

Our new place was grand, but it carried a heavy mortgage, even after making a large cash down payment. It had swimming pool and sauna. Cindy enrolled the girls in private school and cut back on her work hours to spend more time with them. She hired a full-time housekeeper and began to have lavish parties to entertain her friends from work. I was traveling more, and Bernie was causing me to worry about the cash-filled briefcases. What if I were caught? He said cash wasn't illegal; drugs were illegal. He wasn't asking me to do that. I was stressed and, having two children to take care of, worried about something happening. It was causing me to snap at Cindy and the children for small things. I remember we had stopped at the supermarket to pick up a few steaks and a gallon of milk. While I was getting ready to pay, Cindy came running with this tree on the cart saying, "Leo, it is marked down to 10 dollars. It's a bargain, and I love it. It will fit perfectly in the sun room." She pushed the cart next to me and got out of the line. I was getting my wallet when a woman behind touched my shoulder. "Young man, have you ever grown Schefflera?"

"No. This is my wife's purchase."

She walked around and examined the price tag. "Good price. They usually sell for upwards of 30 dollars." She began to give me detailed instructions on how to care for the plant. I am thinking that I'll have to put this huge plant in the back of my car and, if any of the soil spills, it would make a mess. I was becoming more agitated, as this woman continued to rattle on about it needing lots of light, and how I could train it to form a design, and that I should make sure to turn it at least once a week, and water no more than once a month. She kept going on about this plant, in which I had absolutely no interest.

"Lady, I do not want horticultural lessons. I'm just here to pick up some meat and milk." I added thanks to soften her crushed appearance. Then, I heard a male voice say, "Gertrude, he's an animal, what does he care about plants? Let him be." Suddenly, the four large T-bone steaks I had put on the counter looked like lion food. I wasn't about to argue with a man who had a cobra twined around a sword that was tattooed on his biceps. His crew cut stood straight up, as if his fingers were fastened inside an electric socket. I paid for my groceries, shoving the cart with the bushy plant to Cindy with a warning that it better not spill in my car. After Cindy took hold of the tree, I faced the man who called me an animal. Cindy pushed the cart aside and pulled me toward the exit.

"Leopold, you should be ashamed of yourself, thinking that you'd deck a man old enough to be your father." Maybe it was his tone that made me overlook the fact that the man's hair was all white and all he had left was a deep voice and a fading tattoo. This was not the only time my judgment or lack of it was brought into question, and Cindy was right because the old guy put up his fists in a challenge. He wasn't about to back down, and I thought, wham in the kisser, and he would be out like a light.

When anyone asked what I did for a living, I'd tell them what a general once told me. My job is to help spread democracy and bring peace to nations. "Nothing," I remember him saying, "heralds peace faster than looking down the barrel of a machine gun." He convinced me that the Uzi and AK47s really made people better. I remember my dad telling Mom that the leather strap he kept hung near their bed was to make me a better person. I was glad that he hadn't met any of these generals; I may not have lived to tell this tale. Cindy would make the correction. "He is an arms salesman. That is what he does. He sells guns and ammunition to governments." She'd later say to me "Don't tell me you or Bernie give a damn about democracy."

Cindy felt I was underpaid for the work that I had been doing and, even though she didn't know everything I did, she was right. I was more like a gun runner for Bernie. He was sending arms to countries through third and fourth parties, and I had to keep track of the duplicate paperwork and the mislabeling on crates. He had me meeting people with envelopes stuffed with cash and flying to the Bahamas to make deposits. If I didn't get in trouble; it was a swell life. We had lots of untaxed cash. I told Cindy that I had invited Mulligan to stop by for a drink. "Why on earth would you invite a man to our home who wanted to send you to jail? I'd be ashamed if I were you, Leo." I had my reasons. Much to Cindy's chagrin, Mulligan was stretched out on my chaise lounge next to the swimming pool, drowning his regrets in a bottle of old Bushmill.

"Got to give it to you L. Woodward Shade—or whatever you call yourself these days—you've done well." After he staggered out of my house and behind the wheel of his Ford Grand Marquis, Cindy told me that he was not welcome back to our home.

"You could have given him pictures of our three-column mansion surrounded by shrubbery and security cameras. This should be enough to taunt him and let him see what a mistake he made in breaking up your love affair with his daughter. I know why you invited him. You can't fool me, Leo." She was jealous. "I am curious. Where did you find that kind of liquor? It smelled horrible. I have never heard of Bushmill."

"He brought it with him, Cindy." She looked at me as if I was lying, but it was the truth.

"I hope he took the bottle with him." I told Cindy that's what he and my father used to drink when they got together. They had stopped meeting for a while because they were on the outs. It was a bit of nostalgia. Not that I wanted to remember my father because I did not like the man, but the Bushmill brought back memories. It felt as if I were showing them that they had me wrongly pegged. Cindy was telling me not to bring him back, but she was inviting all these people from her office that I didn't know. She saw it as helping me to develop tax write-offs for the above-board money I got from Bernie.

"We have a great stereo system. Why couldn't we play recorded background music? We don't need a live trio, Cindy." Even though I wasn't around much, Cindy and I were having frequent disagreements. She had changed. My Cindy was no longer the shy, little mouse. My job was to cultivate friendships with influential people who could help Baumgarten Enterprises. That's how I got into high-stakes poker, joined a club, and took up golf. She said I didn't have to stick around for the parties because I had more important things to do like hobnobbing with nefarious characters who gamble and play golf. I suspected her workmates wondered how someone holding a GS-07 job could live in such a palatial dwelling.

"Isn't it great to marry into money?" The depth of their thoughts could easily be read in facial expressions, and I enjoyed watching them reconcile their doubts with a revelation: *"That's it!"* The individual would look at me and say, "Cindy is a lucky girl" or ask, "Do you have any brothers." I'd say, "Yes, but he isn't into women." That sent Cindy up the wall.

"My husband's brother is a priest." She pulled me off to the side. "Go count your warped marbles, you sicko." Something was terribly wrong with our marriage. Cindy suspected that I was having an affair. It wasn't serious but, when you hang around a club with money people, there were bound to be women. Little did anyone know that our world was about to come crashing down. Bernie notified me of an urgent, secret meeting. Do not mention this to Cindy, he warned. "I thought you were going to stay home tonight. You said you weren't going to the club. Suddenly, you have to step out. We are still married, Leo. I don't know for how long but for the time being. Where are you going?"

"What did you tell Cindy?"

"I told her that your car broke down on the beltway, and I was coming to give you a jump. She didn't believe me, but I left anyway. She couldn't make a stink because there was company. Well, Bernie, what is so urgent and secret that couldn't wait until tomorrow?" He started laying it out to me in that back room. One of his Egyptian contacts accused him of cheating him out of a commission.

The man threatened to take his story to the United States government. That would implicate us along with several local and foreign officials in bribery and other crimes. Bernie was sweating, looking like a scared rabbit about to leap. The accuser would sing the song of Leopold Shade traveling to the Bahamas with cash and bribe money. My father may not have liked me, but he predicted it would come to no good working for BB Enterprises. Bernie kept everything close to his vest, but this time he locked the door to the little back room, as if he expected to see fire coming out of the barrel of a gun. Bernie put it to me, as if he was trying to protect my future, but I knew better.

"You have a lot to lose, Leo. If this guy bumps me off, you wouldn't have a job. You may even be arrested. You think Mulligan's threat was scary? I have met him, and this guy is no pushover. He will come here in broad daylight and shoot you five or ten times, wipe off the fingerprints, and hop on a plane back to Egypt or wherever. It's you or him, Leo. This is our business. You are a full partner."

"You have always reminded me that this was your business, Bernie. You promised to make me a full partner but that hasn't really happened."

"You heard me. It's happened."

"Now it's me or him? A guy I have never met? How do you figure that, Bernie?"

"Get it into your head, Leo. If anything happens to me—you lose everything. That big house with the swimming pool, the horseback lessons for your girls, the private school. Cindy will have to work two full time jobs to pay that mortgage. And you, Leo, you will go to prison. Be smart. The guy doesn't know what you look like, so it will be easier if you did it."

"You want to send me to kill a man before he kills you? Murder is not my thing, Bernie. I am sorry, but I have two young children. I have a brother who is a priest. How would he feel about a murderer in his family? For Christ sakes Bernie, I have a huge mortgage on the house you encouraged me to buy. We were quite content in our small home, but you said…"

"OK, let's not start turning on each other. It's not like the guy is one of our own. He is a bastard. He is threatening your way of life, Leo. I have a picture of the sonofabitch right here." He pulled out the picture of a short, rotund, balding man with thick hands. "He has never met you, but he and I posed for many smiling photos at the conclusion of our various deals. There is more risk to you if you don't than if you do. I have a contact that can help direct you to his place. Don't worry; I will cover all your expenses. One day go; one day in country; one day get out. He works out of an old warehouse in a bad part of town. I should say a dangerous part of town where anything could happen. My friend would take you

there. He will provide the tool. Pop, pop. No pop, pop, pop, in the head—
he's a tough sonofabitch—and our troubles would fly away." Bernie had his
hands floating like a bird. "There is money to be split. Lots." How could he ask
me to do such a thing?

"Why don't you ask your friend who has all the information and the tools,
to do this job? What if I am caught....... with murder? They torture people in
these countries, Bernie. No, my answer is no. I won't do it."

"You won't?"

"That's what I said, I won't."

"Who's to catch you... My friend will offer you all the protection you need
to get in and out. By the time they find this guy slumped over his table, you will
be home with your wife and beautiful daughters or at the Club." He winked.
"Think about it."

I was scared of a man who would resort to murder to end what I thought may
be a fixable problem. I told Bernie that I wanted to think about it overnight and
would give him an answer the following day. "Your family is at stake, Leo. Keep
that in mind. Those cute little girls who call you daddy." It sounded like Bernie
was threatening my family. I did not give him the answer the following day. I
avoided Bernie as much as I could, but he knew where I lived and dropped by for
a drink. We walked back to the swimming pool. Cindy came out offering us
drinks, but it seemed as if she knew something was amiss. She kept walking close
to the sliding glass doors and pulling them open after I had closed them. I had to
whisper because Bernie would not go away until I told him what I had decided.

"Here's what, Bernie. I'll work with the guy, throw in some of my commissions, get him off your back, and keep him happy." It sounded good to Bernie.
He was hesitant at first but, after a few minutes, he was nodding to agree with my
brilliant idea. I told him that we would discuss the details in his office, as it wasn't
a matter I wanted Cindy to be involved in or find out about. I explained just how
I was going to take the heat off, by disarming this guy and making him believe
that I was undercutting my boss. Bernie smiled, as one who had done a great job
training a junior employee. Bernie was sure he had maneuvered me into bed with
a known bad man. It was my job now to save his neck and mine.

He looked much more relaxed as I sat in front of the old cluttered wooden
desk in his back room. He stretched and breathed a long and sustained sigh.
Bernie wanted to impress upon me how unreasonable this guy was. "If his country bought one extra case of rifles, the sonofabitch wanted to renegotiate his cut
of the entire commission paid to me for my hard work. Yes, he was putting business my way but, if I did what he wanted, it would put me out of the competitive
range for these contracts. You can have him but, if anything happens to my

money in the Bahamas, something will happen to you, Leopold." Bernie shook my hands and said he knew he could count on me. He promised he'd take care of Cindy and the girls if anything happened to me, but he assured me that I would be perfectly safe. I told Cindy that I was going to sign a big deal and that all the money from future business with this client would be ours. I gave her the phone number and name of my contact in Egypt, telling her he was a friend of Bernie.

Shali met me at the airport. He spoke very little English. He drove me to the warehouse, set a specific time to pick me up, and said, if I didn't come out, he'd notify police. The place looked like a shipping depot. There were huge boxes that lined the walls of the large open space. The man sat in the middle of the room. There was a gun on his desk. I told him the shaking was from a mild case of cerebral palsy. He offered me a cigar and lit it for me. I convinced him that Bernie had lost money on the deal, but I promised to make it up to him by giving him a bigger cut of the profits if he would deal directly with me. We shook hands on his promise not to tell Bernie or the man who drove me about our arrangement. I felt like a hero. Leopold Shade was now in the arms business.

In gratitude, Bernie helped me to get all the necessary licenses, and I was on my way to big fortunes. I didn't trust Bernie, so I kept my papers at home in a locked cabinet. We met several times each week to go over mutual business, but I didn't let Bernie know that his man had put other deals my way. If that leather belt could talk, it would say: Leopold Shade, you have me to thank for the man you have become. I continued to act as Bernie's courier and continued to do some of the paperwork to keep him happy. Leo was once again flying high. "You are working from home now, Leo?"

"Yes, Cindy, that means keeping more of the commissions." I traveled to meet with new clients and had a wad of cash in the bank and some in the small safe I kept next to my side of the bed.

"Now you are trying to run rings around Bernie? He is smart, Leopold. He didn't get rich by being stupid. He will find out that with the commissions he is paying, you can't do all the things you are doing, including high stakes poker gambling. You think I don't know, but I know everything about you. My mother does too." We were sitting on the deck overlooking our beautiful kidney-shape pool and in the midst of a heated discussion. Cindy was throwing hurtful words that seem to fly out of her mouth without any thought and consideration to how they landed on my feelings. She'd stop polishing her nails for a few seconds, send unpleasant messages with her eyes, and then get back to business.

"Your mother is wrong on many counts, Cindy Consuelo. She is wrong about me; whatever it is that she"thinks she knows. Wrong that you are beautiful on the inside. Wrong, that you would make me a good wife. Wrong. Wrong. Wrong. You have too much time on your hands. You were a better person when you were working two jobs. Cindy picked up the nail polish and threw it into the pool. The red splashed on top of the water and looked like blood. She got up and pitched the chair so that it collapsed.

"I've had enough of you, Leopold. You need more intensive treatment for the worms in your head. I'm not going to take this torment anymore. I will walk out of here, change my name and cut off all communications, because you are incurably mad and crooked and getting worse."

"Walk?" I said feeling a bit mischievous. "There is no one to stop you, bitch. I have someone to step into your shoes the minute you step out."

My therapist said angry people can be cruel. She pointed out some of the things that I had told her about Cindy in confidence as examples of my cruelty. She reminded me of what constituted abuse and said that I was acting the same way my father did. That was my last visit, and I refused to pay the bill. Why should I pay someone to give me reasons why my wife is right in wanting to leave me? It was a conflict of interest, especially after Kathleen told me that her mother had a meeting with my therapist. How could she be seeing me, and then meeting behind my back with my wife? Cindy was taking clothes out of the closet, and wrapping our china set in newspaper, putting them into boxes. The girls had practically moved to their grandmother's house. Cindy had packed boxes and clothes in the guest room, which was where she had made her bed. Carrie was in her last year of high school and had been accepted to Penn State. She would be living on campus, all at my expense. It was part of the agreement I made with Cindy.

While we were cordial, there was coldness in the air, but neither one of us wanted to move first. I certainly wasn't going to leave the place I worked so hard to get. We each hired a lawyer. Cindy was pushing me to file for divorce, saying that it had been over a year since we had stopped conjugal relations. She said we should agree on property and asset division, and then go for a no fault divorce. It would be easy and less costly. My lawyer told me to refinance the house, take out a wad of cash, and hide it. I found out later that this advice was not altruistic on his part; he merely wanted to guarantee his fee. He made me rehearse what I was going to say to Cindy. "Try to sound sincere, you sonofabitch. Throw in a glass of wine if you need to; get her drunk. Make love. I will write an instruction book. Sure. Damn Leo, you are no stranger to subterfuge. I know what you do for a living." *I'm dealing with you, bastard.* "I'm a business man, and this divorce is nasty business, Leo."

"Cindy, darling, I'd rather throw myself off a pier than ask you to agree to taking a loan on the house but…"

"You go home or go to the john and talk that crap."

"Okay, okay. That may be over the top. What do you think of this: I pray for a miracle to keep our marriage together, if only for the sake of our children. I may not show it, but I am still madly in love with you."

"As an attorney at law I cannot be an accomplice, you stupid sonofabitch. Get out of my office. Remember this: if you tell anyone about our little discussion, I will deny everything." I was direct; that was the only way. Cindy looked at me, as if to ask if I were all right in the head. Of course she knew the answer.

"A loan on this house, Leo?"

"Listen, honey."

"Don't you call me honey." She stared at me with those mean, little periwinkle eyes that pierced like a laser. "A loan for what?"

"My deal went bad. You remember I had to fly to Hong Kong? I could straighten it out but…" Cindy got up and left the room, saying she'd be back in a second. I thought she was going to call her mother, but she came back with a drink. "You remember the deal I was telling you about? It fell through, Cindy. There is no other way unless I give them my half of the house. They are not people you would want to be partners with, believe me." Cindy got pen and paper.

"What are we talking about, Leopold?"

"The agent in Belarus asked me to return the deposit. He is a crazy guy, and I don't want to do anything to make him panic. None of us would be safe. He has friends in this country. Here is what I will do: give him a partial payment to sort of hold him off. Then, I'll pay off the boat, the three cars, credit cards, and other miscellaneous bills, so we don't have so much hanging over our heads. Keep some cash to make the mortgage payments. Had to use up the savings for advance on the equipment, but I'll get that back from the distributor. We have enough in the checking account to tide us over." The following day Cindy withdrew another ten thousand dollars from our account. My lawyer said that was okay because we will need her signature on the new note.

The bank appraised the home for $1.5 million, so I had no problem getting a loan of half a million. I may have been a stupid thief, but I wasn't doing badly in the liar's department because skeptical Cindy believed me. It was a mistake for me to allow my attorney to handle the settlement. He demanded half of his fees up front, in the form of an increased retainer. This man with whom I may have had four appointments was demanding $250,000 for a retainer. I'd sooner represent myself, I told him. We made a deal for a lesser amount. Cindy was all packed up to move. I reminded her that some of the things she had tagged for the movers belonged to me.

"I will be happy, Leopold Shade, to give you back what's legally yours. You don't have to wait until the divorce is final here." She wrote SHADE in big letters and handed the paper to me. "From now on, please address me by my maiden name."

I had expected Cindy to move in with her mother. Carrie had left for college, and she and Kathleen would be more than comfortable in that four-bedroom bungalow. Helen wasn't making life any easier for me. Cindy said her mother told her to "stick to her guns" and not give an inch. I remember Helen Swindle sitting in that old chair staring at me. Bryce Swindle, the instigator of the marriage arrangement would have talked sense into Cindy, but he is dead and gone. Cindy's anger seemed to far exceed my faults as a husband. My therapist kept saying, "Cindy needs time to get over the hostility; separation is difficult, even on the one who chooses it. Be patient."

"I am just tired of you, Leopold."

According to the agreement hammered out by our lawyers, Cindy will get half of the net proceeds. The other half is to be divided between myself and the girls. If I had a gun on me, I would have shot my lawyer right there in court. He said it had to do with my taking most of the money from the refinance. He wanted to tick off the amount I paid for the Porsche. "You sold the boat, Leo; you made the dealer take back your daughter's car and...."

"Stop right there. Aren't you supposed to be my lawyer? Did you tell me to refinance the house and pocket the money, except for the cash I used to bribe you?"

"Not in my office. I am not Cindy, you sonofabitch. Talking to me like some of your sleezewiz turban head crooks. You want to find somebody else? Maybe you have a hundred thousand left." I sat in his office and began to cry like a baby. My lawyer was not working for me. The thought that he may have to give money back made him more furious. Bernie didn't like him either and told me he was a shyster. He apologized that he lost his temper. He said that he could have worked out a better deal if I had maintained my calm and stopped shouting, "Swindle" while she was on the stand. Our home is on the market for $950,000, priced for quick sale. Cindy didn't want to sign on the listing, but I told her I would just as soon have this over with than hold out for a bogus bank appraisal of $1.5 million.

Our marriage lasted longer than I expected—almost 20 years. It's been a little over two years since Cindy left, taking the girls, my great grandmother's lamp, our dining room set, family pictures, and most of the furniture in the house. She wanted time away from me to think. How much time do you need, Cindy? It wasn't so much her leaving that bothered me; it was the inequity of the situation.

I believed the lawyers screwed everything up so that we would continue fighting, and their bills could keep skyrocketing. The divorce had become acrimonious, and I was consumed by the injustice. I wasn't returning important business calls. I told Bernie that I could not go to the Bahamas for at least the next two to three months. It was in my interest to try and persuade Cindy that we ought to work things out, otherwise I would be out of money and a job to fulfill her demands. "Most people get along, if only for the sake of the children."

"Get along, Leopold? We tried it for 20 years. You can't say that I didn't make every effort to make this debacle of a marriage work. I did, much to my loss of esteem and regret. Now, you want to leave me in the lurch. Children? You had to be forced by the court to pay tuition and minimum support for your children. Forced, Leopold. Had it not been for my mother, I don't know where we'd be. She has been helping us with her small pension and savings."

"You need to settle with Cindy and get this thing out of the way quickly; we are not running a charity enterprise, Leo. So she wants half; give it to her. You can make it back in no time. Remember where you are coming from, Leo. In the early days, it was Cindy who was working two jobs and, as you told me, it was her father who loaned the no interest down payment on your first house."

She hangs up as soon as I say, "Cindy." I told her I just want to keep things civil for the girls' sake.

"Civil? You try to steal the Mercedes from my mother's garage, and you want to be civil? Please stop pretending that you are normal, Leopold. Grow up." My new analyst told me to do as Cindy suggests and allow the lawyers to work things out.

"Do what she suggests? Each call I make to my lawyer is an hour, even if I talk 10 seconds. I don't know how many times she has called hers and how long she speaks. I know the judge had better not grant her wish for me to pay her attorney's fee." My analyst said that sounded like a veiled threat, and I should refrain from the words, 'better not.' I have come to hate the month of October. It is the month Cindy was born, and the month I was forced or coerced into marrying Bryce and Helen Swindle's younger daughter. Cindy moved into the Chase Apartments in October. It offered her peace of mind and security, with a guard on duty 24/7. She has a friend across the hall. She couldn't send this message through her lawyer because it would make her appear spiteful. She picked up the phone and called me. "I told you about my neighbor, Vicky. Well, she was once married to a miscreant like you, Leo, and suffered much the same way I did. Can you believe the idiot tried to get someone to kill her, so he wouldn't have to divide their assets and could cash in on her life insurance? He is in jail, Leo. Take heed, you night shade."

Her lawyer was real buddy, buddy with the judge. He was calling for bench conferences, but the one smiling at the end was not my lawyer. The judge said that I'd have to keep up the mortgage payments, pay off my wife's car as agreed, share the proceeds from the sale of the yacht, pay college tuition for both girls for four years or until they earned a bachelors degree, and pay her attorney's bills. Since my lawyer wasn't objecting, I jumped up and said that it was all a swindle. "Another outburst like that, and I will charge you with contempt. He flipped through some papers. "I see here that your wife indicates she does not want any alimony from you but would like half of your 401(k) plan." I wrote a note to my attorney, who was sitting as if he were listening to opera.

"Hey $500-a-minute man, aren't you going to say something in my defense? How about the fifty she took, and then the other ten after that? How about the furniture? My grandmother's lamp?"

"After lunch, Leo. We will talk later." The judge hammered his gavel and adjourned for lunch. "And, let me warn you, Cindy's attorney is not through. He will put her on the stand before we get a chance to put in two cents." He was right. When the court reconvened, Cindy was called to the stand. She looked straight through me, as her attorney coached her into being a believable witness. His preamble included insinuations as to my character. He announced that I was an arms merchant who dealt with nefarious characters and in that way I had to work very hard if not with my hands then my head to outmaneuver the clients. He said that I was using the same tactics on poor Cindy. No interruption by my attorney. He went on about how John Mulligan may be called about my child-hood shenanigans before my lawyer jumped up and said, "Objection. Irrelevant, your honor." I had my head down on the defense table. I had decided that this high-priced lawyer was low on litigation skills or was my enemy. Finally, he came alive. "Objection. My client paid the debt to her parents with interest, your honor. Ms. Swindle long stopped working the extra part time job. Mr. Shade used the money from his parents insurance to pay expenses. And your honor, his brother has since given half of his share to their daughter Carrie, and the rest will go to Kathleen when she turns 18. Mr. Shade provided a mansion for his family. His children had the benefit of horse back riding, piano, ballet, tennis, and swimming lessons. In the later years, Miss Swindle had given up her job. So where did the fifty, no sixty thousand come from? She has a 401k and will get a government pension when she reaches the age. What has she done with all that money, your honor? My client is paying support for the two children and college tuition for the eldest girl." I lifted my head and took my thoughts back about the incompetence of my lawyer.

"Your honor, that is but a drop in the bucket. This man was or still is making at least half a million a year. What has he done with all of that money, including the money he got from the sale of his parents' home? I will tell you; he gambled it all away. He made her loan him the fifty thousand by telling Cindy that their lives would be in danger if he did not return a deposit that been given to him by one of his clients. That is where that fifty thousand went. He promised that, as soon as he cleared up the matter, he would give the money back, but he has told her many things that have turned out to be untrue. Lies upon lies your honor. A man was caught using keys to get into her mother's garage, saying he was sent to pick up the Mercedes." He began to look over the inventory list and questioned Cindy about the boat, the BMW, the five hundred thousand borrowed on the home, about the deal that fell through, and about my trip to Hong Kong. "The story changed so many times your honor; we can't keep track. First, it was Hong Kong, and then it was Belarus."

"Where is that?" The judge asked with a sneer, as if he too, were going along with Cindy's skepticism.

"China, your honor."

"I mean that other place."

Next, they presented my attorney with depositions for me to provide receipts, even the stub of my airline tickets, the hotel I stayed in, the company I met with, and questions that covered thirty pages of legal papers. As we were walking out of the courtroom, my attorney shook the bastard's hand, saying good job. After walking a short distance, he turned to me and said, "You know how to get yourself in the sling. You didn't tell me you took the money back from your wife. So you went to Belarus? Where are the airline tickets or hotel bills? Give me names of business associates—of course that won't be a problem because you or Bernie could provide the evidence, right? You gave the tow truck driver a map and keys to your mother-in-law's garage?

"So it wasn't breaking and entry if he had the key. The police let him go and told Helen Swindle that she could take legal action against me. I warned Cindy that it would be the wrong thing to do because her mother lives alone."

"My fee has doubled as of this instant. I am going back to my office, and I'll spend the night at your expense to read this bullshit. I suggest that you keep your mouth shut until I give you permission." I couldn't fire the man. He had to file all kinds of costly motions to keep the repossession company from bringing in the tow truck driver to testify. Cindy had planned every detail of her move, yet she forgot to take her mother's house and garage key off the rack in the mud room. It crossed my mind to slip into Mrs. Swindle's house and find out what else may be hidden there that belonged to me. Perhaps I would disappear with a briefcase of Bernie's cash. My parents were dead anyway, so he couldn't hold them ransom. Bernie knew how to fix things, and he owed me.

The lamp on his desk was the only light in the windowless back room. He fixed it so that nothing on his desk could be read by anyone sitting on the other side. He straightened out a large paper clip and was cleaning dirt from under his fingernail. He nodded or said uh huh. Uh, huh. Divorce is a nasty thing, Leo. The kids will get over it. Uh, huh. Uh, huh. "Remember the Egyptian, Bernie?" Suddenly his head jerked up, and he looked at me and toward the closed door as if any minute he'd call for a straight jacket or the police. "Cindy is your wife. The mother of your two children!" He yanked the door open and screamed, "Get out. I'm going to have to think hard if I want you to continue as my partner. Get out." He took me seriously; he didn't believe I was kidding.

William said he'd meet me in the office in the back of the church the following day. The first thing he did after I told him how sorry I was about saying what I had to Bernie was to bring up the funeral. He said that I should try my best to let the demons of childhood go. I reminded him that Mother said many times that I had been damaged. "How could you stand up and say something like that in public?"

"They asked me to speak, William. Everyone wanted me to say a few words. I was truly sad; my mother was part of the deal. Dad had it coming. There is a thing called retribution. You can't deny that he was a commanding authoritarian who believed that a law degree conferred upon him the infinite wisdom of the universe. Mother could never stand up to him. When she got tired of his ranting, she'd say, 'go to sleep; you are drunk.' He was always comparing me to you. I never wanted to be a priest. 'Leopold, why can't you be like your brother? Why must you hang out with vagabonds who cause so much trouble in our neighborhood? Decent boys don't go around setting fires in people's trash cans and ringing doorbells after lighting firecrackers and leaving them on someone's front porch.' You remember him saying that, William?"

"What I know and perhaps the reason they often compared me to you was that I was not as mischievous and did not keep rowdy company. You did, Leopold. You have children, and I hear that Carrie tends to be on the rebellious side. You wouldn't want to have all that trouble on your hands. Dad wasn't all bad. You needed to be disciplined, and he applied it. I got a taste of that belt myself but deservingly so. I don't hold it against him. He was doing the best he could as a father. You must remember the good things he did for us, rather than dwell on all the negatives."

"Do you remember the names he called me, William?"

"He was drunk. Let it go. You are a married man. Well, soon to be unmarried, I suppose. You are an adult, Leo. He paid for therapy, which was supposed to help. Has it?"

"I should thank Dad for paying for the therapy? He was the reason I needed therapy." William got all his gripes out of the way, and now he seemed to be focused on my problems. He got up and closed the blinds on a window that looked out on the small graveyard with a few scattered monuments. William took off his eye glasses and stared into my eyes.

"I had to allow what you said earlier to settle. It seemed unbelievable but, after thinking back to your childhood, there was some likelihood of that sort of warped thinking. Now, Leopold, you tried to get Bernie to hire someone to kill the mother of your children? You had better hope he doesn't report you to the authorities. Pray, my dear brother that nothing happens to Cindy. People have been tried and convicted for crimes they did not commit, but it was the word of someone who heard them make a threat. Oh, Leo. I pray for your tortured soul. Dad was right about Baumgarten. He is a through and through unscrupulous man, and you have been his student. He may have made you rich, Leo, but he has indeed made you poor in the morals department. Perhaps it is time to get out of that business. Give Cindy all that she asks for. It's only money. I am sure you will survive in lesser circumstances. If you know how to, may I suggest prayer? I certainly will be praying for you, Cindy, and the girls." William made the sign of the cross and watched me leave the room. Now, there were two people who knew that I was desperate to change the way things were going with the divorce settlement.

I hinted to Cindy that I could get into her apartment if I really wanted. She laughed. "I am not worried about you, Leopold. I'd like to see you get by security." As the elevator doors closed, I saw the guard scurrying back to his station. I punched six on the button. I thought Cindy may have changed the locks after Kathleen reported her keys missing. I was visiting with Kathleen in a restaurant and something I said seemed to upset her. She got up and ran to the bathroom with her aunt Sybil in that tight form fitting jeans trailing behind. I meant to give her the keys that fell under the table but somehow left with them in my pocket. If this place is supposed to be so safe, why was everyone scrambling to park in front when there are so many empty spaces in the back next to the park? At least Cindy has a nice view of the trees from her bedroom window. She must be out on a date and had Kathleen go to her mother's house.

Carrie said her dorm room was bigger than this apartment, and she was right. "Until the house is sold, it's all I can afford, Leopold. Kathleen and I are very comfortable here." Cindy and her neighbor were standing outside the building, as I drove up to get Carrie. "Leopold, meet my friend, Victoria." The woman walked over to the car, said hello, and looked me over as though she were confirming every bad thing that Cindy told her. Before I could offer a defense to the accusatory stare, Carrie had thrown her suitcase and backpack in the back seat and jumped into the car.

"Hurry up. Dad, you are late. I don't think we have enough time to get to National. You'll have to drive through the park, and I hope we don't get lost again or worse thrown into the creek. Jesus, we can never do anything right, can we?" I didn't plan to run over Cindy, even though it would have been a good accident. Carrie was in such an upset state that I forgot the gear was still in reverse, and Cindy was standing behind the car chatting with Vicky.

"See, I told you about him," I heard Cindy say after she jumped out of the way. Carrie picked up on her complaints.

"Why can't we ever do anything right? Why would you send a stranger to grandma's garage to steal mom's car? Christ, when will this thing ever end?"

"You've been discussing me with your mother. Why didn't you ask her to take you to the airport in the Mercedes?" Carrie attempted to open the car door. I had to restrain her by pushing on the baby safety lock and holding on to her arm. "Carrie, you could get seriously injured, and walking won't get you there any faster, believe me, honey."

"Dad," she countered, "it's like you don't think we have a mind of our own, but we do. Spend the money on floozies, what do we care? So you resent paying the tuition, is that it? We are not forcing you. You can stop paying anytime you want; grandma will be happy to do it or, better yet, I could get a j-o-b," she spells it.

"That is not what the judge said, Carrie but, of course, how are you to know? You were not there. He said I had to pay college tuition for four years or as soon as my children received a bachelor's degree, whichever comes first. Whichever comes first, Carrie." Almost a replica of her mother in looks and now temperament. I hadn't had that many drinks, but it seemed that liquor affected me more since the breakup. The road looked as if someone with crazy chalk had made squiggle lines along the edges. When Carrie stormed out at the airport, it was as if my right ventricle just busted with relief. At first I thought it was a heart attack, the way the pain radiated along my left arm and crept to the middle of my chest, but I felt fine again in a few minutes.

I was 5 years old when dad bought me and William water pistols. We played cops and robbers. William would fire off his pistol, and I'd crumple fall on the ground and stay really still like I had been killed. He'd stare at the water pistol like somehow he believed that it had turned into a real gun, and he had killed his little brother. He'd walk over to look at me, and I'd jump up and say, "Psych." It happened several times before he caught onto the fact that it was only a water pistol. I guess that's why he went into the priesthood; he believed in miracles from an early age. "This is a damn fine pistol. They don't make them like this anymore, Leopold." I was 16 and remember saying to William that the show and tell was meant for me because dad realized I had become too old for the belt. William said I had a wild streak and vivid imagination and perhaps should consider acting as a career.

We were going through our parents' personal effects when we came upon dad's pistol wrapped in a towel in his night stand. Not even a scratch on the chrome handle. He should have taken care of me like he took care of this gun. It was valuable, and I told William that he could have it. He didn't want it, saying he hoped the day would never come when a priest had to keep a gun for protection. Of course, he had Jesus and Mary to keep vigil over him, but who did I have? "Maybe you ought to mount it and hang it on the wall in memory of dad." I had other memories of dad mounted in my mind. I took it and kept it in my chest of drawers. I never told Cindy about it. Perhaps I should have.

You stay right there on this end table. I am going to see if Cindy has decided to come home. It's way past her bedtime. Why is she not doing her wash? It's Wednesday. She always did the wash on Wednesdays. You stay right there, buddy; let me take another look. Nope. No sign of Cindy. I better get a drink. My God, Cindy is drinking scotch whiskey. Maybe it's for entertaining. I'll just finish it off. Thanks, Cindy. How did she get so mean and vicious? "You stink, Leopold junior. I know it's you. You are a coward." Me, a coward? "I'm home if that's any of your business, but I may be going out later, Leopold. Get off my phone and take your hot foul breath to the smut shop." On one of the chaperoned visits with Kathleen (as soon as Sybil and her overhanging breasts left to have a smoke), I asked the girl if that was her auntie's boyfriend. She said no. "Your mother's?" She confirmed with a quick nod. On the next visit, I couldn't tell for sure, but it looked like the same man. "Look me in the eye, Leopold Shade, and tell me you are innocent. Kathleen told me that you tried to feel her breasts and that, while she was sleeping, you rubbed yourself up against her. Look me in the eye and say it is a lie."

"It's a lie, Cindy."

"Coming from a known liar, I will have to let a judge decide if he believes you. I certainly don't."

"Don't do it, Cindy. You'll regret it. Don't do it."

Stay right there, my friend. This is a good scotch. Let's take another peek to see if Ms. Swindle has decided to come home. What do you know? He is parking my car. A school boy with his cap turned backwards. Nothing heralds peace like staring down the barrel of a gun. I want to make peace with Cindy. I want her to talk to me. Her boyfriend will probably run as fast as he can to get away from a crazy ex-husband. I'll cock the trigger, and she will probably faint. I'll stand over her and say, "Psych. Get up, Cindy Consuelo. Let's talk." I sat on the white overstuffed sofa and waited for them to enter. I heard the keys rattle. Cindy entered first. I didn't look up because I had the gun trained on whoever entered.

"What are you doing here?"

"Daddy, please put down the gun."

"You've called me many names, Cindy, but never daddy."

"I am going to faint. Please."

"Mr. Shade! Carrie. Carrie. She's. Carrie."

"Psych. Psych. Stop faking, Cindy. Get up. Psych."

"Mr. Shade! Oh my God. You'll mess up the couch, and I'll get in trouble. Don't do it."

"She'll wake up; ask my brother, William."

"Help. Help, please. Anybody. Help."

"Calm down, Sam. I've called the police. They'll be here soon. How did that nut get into the apartment? Did you let him in? My God! I thought Carrie was at school. Oh my God. Cindy was right about him. Calm down. Let me get you some water. You poor boy. You'll have to tell the police what happened."

"Wake up, Carrie. Wake up."

"She's dead, Sam. He killed his own daughter."

"Kathleen will never date me anymore. Carrie flew home for the surprise birthday party. I drove her here to pick up a birthday present that Kathleen left in the closet. He kept calling her Cindy. I wish he had killed me too."

"Calm down; it's not your fault. Poor Cindy when she gets this news. I didn't know it was her birthday. Oh my God. Okay, they are coming. Have a sip of the water and try to keep calm."

"D.C. Police. Homicide. What happened here? Two dead people. Back up. Double homicide. Cuff the fellow with blood on his hands. Who are you?"

"A neighbor and a friend of the woman who lives here. My name is Victoria King. I live across the hall in 614. I'm the person who called. The boy is innocent. It's that man. He killed the girl, and then killed himself."

"Did you see this happen?"

"He told me, and I know the man. Mrs. Shade recently got a divorce from him. The boy is innocent."

"And who did you say this young woman is?"

"His. Their daughter, Carrie."

"Okay, uncuff the fellow. Tell me what happened here. First, what is your name and relationship to these people?

"Samuel Baumgarten. Mr. Shade, there, worked for my father. I am Kathleen's boyfriend."

"And who is Kathleen?"

"Carrie's sister."

"Carrie?"

"She's dead. The one laying on the floor. He shot her to death, and then killed himself? That's what you say, but you didn't actually see him do it?"

"I heard the shots and looked through the keyhole. I saw the young man pacing in the hallway and calling out for help. Then he told me what happened. I recognized him as Kathleen's boyfriend. Poor Cindy."

"Who is Cindy?"

"The mother of the girl and the ex-wife of Leopold Shade, the one with the bullet in his temple. Cindy and Kathleen are at her mother's home, waiting for Carrie to get back. You see, today is Cindy's birthday."

"OK. We have your name and address, and your phone number is registered at the Station. We will certainly call you to come down and give a statement. For the time being, you will have to come with us young man. We will need to take a statement from you. Let's go."

"After he shot Carrie, I asked him to give me the gun. He said I should tell everyone that he confessed."

"The dead man said that?"

"He wasn't dead at the time."

"How old are you?"

"Twenty sir."

"Get in the car. We'll have to put your fingers in some black stuff but that'll wash off. We'll have to book you."

"I didn't do it."

"You said he confessed to the murder and to his suicide? Did I tell you that you have the right to remain silent and that anything you say may be used against you? I did. OK."

"Hello, Mr. Baumgarten. My name is Victoria King. I am a neighbor of Cindy Swindle."

THE OBLONG LIGHT

This life is a hospital in which every patient is possessed with a desire to change his bed.

—Charles Baudelaire, *Le Spleen de Paris*

Although she felt safe inside the building, Myrtle thought she should go back on the regular shift that allowed her to get home during daylight hours. She had chosen the 3 to 11 shift because it was usually quiet at nights. By seven, she had checked all her patients, given medication, and made notations on their charts. By nine, most of them were asleep. Myrtle often used this quiet time to take care of personal items, call her mother or finish a crossword puzzle. When she reported to work this day, she became aware that a number of surgical procedures had been performed, which meant keeping alert and responding immediately to call buttons. Doctors would be calling the duty station to have the nurses check on patients or requesting them to give special or additional medications.

It was close to midnight when Myrtle got home. In the hallway, the florescent tubes flickered and made light and dark designs on the grey hallway ceiling. "Why," Myrtle thought, "would they paint the hallway and ceiling grey?" Nothing she could do. It was a common area, and they didn't have to have permission to paint. She did not have time to attend the condominium association meetings. After Arnie moved out, she changed the lock and added mace and a small flashlight to her key ring after a dirty note had been placed under her windshield. The door to the building was kept locked and needed both a code and key to enter. The new security locks on her door were guaranteed burglar proof. Her key will not open the new lock, and she could hear her cockatoo flying around the room. Skimpy was another post-Arnie acquisition. The locksmith warned her to make sure that, when she left her apartment, the notch on the lock was turned to 'YES'.

When she turned in to bed, it should be set to 'NO'. That way, no one would be able to enter.

Myrtle only allowed workmen to enter her apartment and always scattered a few pieces of Arnie's clothes to give the impression that there was a man living there. "You'll never be rid of that leech, Myrt. If you followed your better judgment, you would see he is not the man for you. If your father were alive, he'd tell you so." Ules Dygaard said she could see through Arnie, and he was bad news. It was late, and Myrtle felt her efforts to unlock the door were futile. Tired and exhausted, she sat and leaned against the door. She could have gotten back in her car and driven to a friend's house, but she hated disturbing anyone at that hour. She would have to go to a phone booth to call anyone. Her tiny flashlight had faded, leaving her in the hallway in an eerie twilight-like atmosphere. In rural Pennsylvania, where Myrtle grew up, the doors were never locked. She could walk to the neighbors at any time and not feel as if she were imposing. Everyone was friendly and helpful. Here, in this building, people kept to themselves. Many of the widowed or divorced women on her floor would not want to get involved. Many still used their deceased husbands' names. Mrs. James Spriggett, Sr., her closest neighbor, was pleasant, and she'd sometimes tell Myrtle what was going on in the complex.

When Myrtle would be asked why she left such a safe place to move to the nation's capital, she said it was the perfect place for a young nurse to gain emergency room experience. Seeing the constant flow of murders, gunshot wounds, etc. was too draining so, after some months, she moved from the ER to the geriatric wing. She requested the night shift, and it had been working out to her advantage. On her days off, she'd go with friends to singles bars. That's how she met Arnie. He told her that he worked in the intelligence field, but he had retired on disability. Arnie was very charming and, according to him, as honest as he could be without revealing national secrets. They dated for almost a year. She had Arnie's address but had never been to his apartment. He often visited and sometimes stayed overnight. He told Myrtle that his landlord was selling the building, his roommate was moving out of state, and he had to find a place. He asked if he could move in with her and help with the rent. Myrtle wasn't sure whether her mother disliked Arnie because she was suspicious of him or because, if he moved in, he would take her space.

"Let him rent a place. I can't see the advantage from what you have told me to allow this fellow to move into your condo. You don't need help to pay your mortgage." Myrtle had been there three years; it was close to her job. She was in love with Arnie and hoped that their relationship would lead to marriage. He didn't have any cash in the bank, but he received a sizable disability check from social security. After he moved in, Myrtle found out that Arnie was taking medication for several mental disorders. His mood swings made him sweet and cruel but, when he threatened her life, Myrtle called the police. It was then she found out that Arnie had been out on parole. He had several major assault charges against him, including intent to commit murder.

"I warned you to do a background check before allowing him to move into your condo. He could have killed you and what? He would just go back to his friends in prison. I want you to call me every night after you are safely locked in your apartment. If you are not going straight home, please, Myrtle, call me." Myrtle hated this reporting but, in a way, she could understand why her mother may be worried. She called from the hospital to let her know if she was not going home. As she sat, exhausted, leaning against the door, Myrtle heard her mother talking to the answering machine. "You didn't call me tonight, Myrtle. Give me a ring the minute you get in." A few minutes went by, and the phone began to ring again. "Myrtle. Myrtle. If you are home, please pick up the phone." She murmurs. "Okay, maybe she was too busy to call her poor mother." Ules seemed unaware that she was being recorded. *She has such poor judgment; only God knows how she has made it thus far.* "Myrtle. Myrtle. Call me. You know the number." *Maybe I should call the police.* "Okay. Love you." Click. Click.

Her mother had awakened Mrs. Spriggett and her dog Buffy. She was quite likely looking through her peephole. Myrtle heard a muffled whine, and then the dog wrestled itself free and fell to the floor. A tussle followed, with Buffy yapping and running around, scratching the wood floors, with Mrs. Spriggett apparently trying to get hold of it. Myrtle knew or had seen almost everyone who lived in her building at one time or another. They'd say hello and keep going, but Mrs. Spriggett would seek her out to dish up news. Myrtle heard that the unit down the hall belonging to Ophelia Nance who had died, had been sold. "Do you know, Miss Dygaard, that it's been three months and there is not a stitch of furniture in the place. It was a cash deal. Ophelia's son got a bunch of money. She was sick for several months before he dispatched her to die in a nursing home. The day her eyes closed, he put the place up for sale. I am glad James and I didn't have any children. You are still single—or does Mr. Sykes intend to return from his vacation?" Myrtle felt sure everyone in the building had heard that Arnie was arrested and taken to jail.

"We are no longer dating. He moved."

"Where to? Forgive me. It's none of my business. What I wanted to say was that the new man is single." She winked at Myrtle. "According to Beatrice, he is well off, too. We reckon he is either gay or divorced. Beatrice thinks he may be a government official. She picks up all the stuff they leave at his door and saves it for him." Myrtle had nothing more to say about Arnie, but she was grateful for the information on the new, single male who had moved down the hall. It was difficult to sleep sitting up, leaned against a door, but she was too tired to do anything else. She was safe as long as she stayed inside the building. Every problem Myrtle suffered could be traced back to the time Arnie entered her life. He was gone but, because she had changed the lock to keep him out, she couldn't get into her own condo.

Myrtle thought of selling the place and moving to the suburbs. She mentioned this to the real estate agent who was in the building showing a unit. He gave her his card and promised a no obligation free market analysis. She asked if he and his wife lived in the city, and he said he was single and lived in Virginia. After what happened, she should have called the locksmith and had him put her old locks back on the door, but she didn't. Her mother would have approved of Grant. He was licensed, handsome, single, and boasted that he was one of the top agents in his company. He was punctual. It didn't take long to look at a one bedroom unit, but it took almost an hour to unlock the door and let him out. The agent was furious, and Myrtle could tell there was no chance of future romance.

"This calamity could have deadly consequences, especially for a single woman," he said looking impatiently at his watch. "Suppose there was a fire?" In such an event, Myrtle thought she could jump from the third floor landing on the shrubs below without sustaining serious injuries. The agent never called with the results of his market analysis. Arnie had struck again.

Myrtle bought Skimpy, the adorable talking red-tail cockatoo. Her mother said the bird was the best choice of a companion she had made so far. "What on earth are you doing with a man who verbally abuses you, does not contribute to any household expenses, and takes off without telling you where he is going or when he will be back? He must have some family: mother, father, uncles, cousins—some family. Well, if he has a sister, get her address and call her. Isn't it strange she never stopped by to visit, since he said she lives in Lebanon? I don't care what kind of spy he claims to be. Even spies have families."

Myrtle's father Chester worked in the lumber industry. He was a simple man and somewhat strange, but he took care of his family. He deferred to his wife and never ventured much out of his recliner in front of the black and white tv in the living room. Myrtle was an only child they had late in life. She sensed that her father would have preferred a boy, but there was nothing he could do about it. He was proud of his Dutch heritage and particularly of the men in his family line. He would tell her stories about his ancestors. Each time he ended his fables by turning off the light in her bedroom and singing the first two lines of the Dutch national anthem:

William of Nassau, am I of Germanic descent; true to the fatherland, I remain until death.

Her great grandfather was buried in the back yard. "Thomas Fedor Dygaard, b. 1796, d. 1890." She had nightmares about seeing the frail man her father described dressed in a frock coat and a broad brim hat pressing his face against the window. "Chester, you must stop telling the child these nonsense stories. Don't you see they frighten her?"

"Hog wash, Ules. Who's to tell her about her ancestors if I don't? I am proud, and she should be, too." By the time he died, the city had passed an ordinance outlawing private burial on residential property. Myrtle had never lost her of fear of the dark. She should never have told Arnie.

Ules graduated from Lycoming College, one of the oldest and most prestigious colleges in Williamsport. It was established in 1812. She majored in psychology and worked for several years with emotionally disturbed children. This is why Myrtle thought her mother would have been more understanding of Arnie's problems. He had initially told her that he was suffering from stress-related syndrome resulting from military service in Kuwait. "Have you checked this out, Myrtle? I deal with emotionally challenged children all day long, but I'd be damned if I have ever seen any with so many complex dysfunctional problems. Our country is in worse trouble than I could imagine if he was a captain in the intelligence service. He is lying, Myrtle. I know people in the military." Myrtle begged her mother not to call anyone to discuss Arnie. Suppose he was telling the truth? "So, where do I sleep when I come to visit?" Ules stopped visiting as often and, when she did, left the same day. "At my age, I refuse to sleep on a couch. Let him go to a hotel for the night." Arnie was furious he when found out that Myrtle owned the condo.

"You lied to me, Dygaard. I'd feel differently if it was rent, but I sure as heck ain't gonna pay off for something that my name isn't on. I ain't about to let a woman who can't cook burn up my money neither." He stopped contributing toward groceries. Their relationship had been deteriorating long before he threatened to blow her brains out when she refused to lend him money. She was paying the mortgage, buying the food, gassing the car. On the days he went to the track and to visit friends, he'd drop Myrtle off at work and return to pick her up or call and tell her to try to get a ride home. "If you can't, buy me some fricking beers and a pack of cigarettes. What's the use of putting up with all this bullshit?

"Myrtle, he could have bought or stolen those medals. Have you checked?" The military invoked the privacy act, saying they couldn't give out personnel information. The man wouldn't even tell her if Arnold Sykes was ever a captain in the military. When she told him that Arnie was her boyfriend but she had some questions about his background, the man said that she should stop trying to act like some sort of spy and just plain ask the guy.

"If he said he was in the military, chances are he was in the military."

Arnie always insisted that it had to be dark before they could make love. As soon as he turned off the lights, Myrtle would remember her father's story and the time she saw the shadow of her great-grandfather leaning against her bedroom window. Arnie would have been furious if she had confessed this silly idiosyncrasy, so she did the next best thing: faked orgasms. He was eating when she reminded him that food cost money, and he needed to help with the bills or move. It wasn't the first time Myrtle gave him an ultimatum to either help or leave. He pitched the plate to the floor and jumped up as if he were about to strangle her. "You want me to pay your bills? You ought to be paying me for my services." Since she was a teenager, Myrtle had problems with acne and still had scars on her face. They weren't as visible under makeup, but she didn't wear makeup at home.

After Arnie left, Myrtle let herself go. She needed a perm and some new clothes because she had gained weight. Her hands wouldn't look so harsh if she had her nails manicured like most of the other nurses. She had given up on going back to the size 16 she wore in high school. She needed to see a good dermatologist and see if she could lighten the spots or get them removed from her face. At 5' 3," she looked silly with bright red hair, a round pockmarked face, 50-inch hips, and size six shoes. *She was Dutch, not Irish.*

During the time she and Arnie lived together, Myrtle did everything she could to keep her mother and Arnie apart. Ules had come to tolerate Arnie. When Myrtle said he would drive her to pick up some items she had stored in the attic, Ules didn't object. It was the first time that he was inside Myrtle's childhood home. Arnie was on his best behavior. He somehow ingratiated himself so much that Ules offered him drinks. He told Ules how he carried out clandestine operations, planted bugs, decoded security locks, opened safes, and slipped in and out of countries using military cover. Ules and Arnie were laughing like old friends. Myrtle was lost in nostalgia, leafing through her high school yearbook and an old photo album. She was about 5 when this picture was taken. Her parents were in bathing suits and stretched out on plastic lounge chairs in the backyard near Fydor's granite headstone. They plopped her in between like a comma. She remembered the small sandbox, and her parents telling her that she should pretend that they were on the beach.

Myrtle was amazed at how her mother was suddenly so enamored with Arnie. She had misplaced the key to her safe, and Arnie was able to get it open. Ules was effusive in her appreciation for this favor. Arnie Sykes was able to convince her in less than an hour of his honesty and sincerity. Myrtle finally felt relieved that the two seemed to have made amends. The drive from Pennsylvania was pleasant. Arnie said he would be willing to let Ules sleep in the bedroom whenever she visited. Ules called that night, saying she was willing to give Arnie another chance. Maybe he was telling the truth about his military intelligence service. "He couldn't lie so convincingly, especially to me. If you can get him to help pay the bills, maybe you can make something of it." Ules suggested that Myrtle sell the condo and put the money into a joint account the two had in Williamsport. "That way, you two can start fresh with both names on the lease, and your money will be safe here. Say hello to Arnie." He started to contribute to the food and mortgage, and everything was all going well. Arnie even mentioned the "M" word.

It wasn't more than six months after they had visited her mother that Ules called in a panic. First, she asked if Arnie was home. Myrtle told her that he was in Lebanon—almost 90 miles from Williamsport—visiting his sister, Lucy. Ules told Myrtle that all the family heirlooms had been stolen. There were no signs of forced entry into the house and that she suspected Arnie. The safe was locked when she left at the usual time to play cards with her friends, so it must be the work of someone familiar with the home, her schedule, and the combination to the safe. She blamed Myrtle for bringing a criminal into her home. Ules told Myrtle to check the odometer of her car when Arnie returned. When she did, the car had fewer miles than when she purchased it used. There was no way of telling how far Arnie had driven in the three days he was gone with her car. Arnie started hollering, saying he knew he couldn't trust Ules. All the new clothes and the three-hundred-dollar Tony Lama cowboy boots came from his winnings. He stopped off at the track after he left his sister and, except for the money he gave to Myrtle to help with household expenses, he had bet all his disability check on a trifecta. All three horses won. Ules told Myrtle that she had informed the police. They had taken fingerprints and were checking on Arnold Sykes, if that was his right name.

Arnie blamed her mother for causing him to sink into depression. Myrtle suspected that her mother was right. She told Arnie she needed her car and would not allow him to use it to drive it to the racetrack. She refused to buy him liquor or cigarettes and asked him again to move; this time, she was serious. He went berserk and told her that he would walk away, but undertakers would carry her out. Myrtle had no choice but to notify the management. The picture she gave them wasn't very flattering. He looked like a lunatic. Arnie never wanted his picture taken. He said it would blow his cover. When she took the picture, he was quite ill and hadn't shaved for days. After he had recovered, she took another one to show him how her care had improved his health. She assured him that she would destroy the negatives.

The police searched her condo before and after his arrest but the fully-loaded 1908 antique pistol Arnie claimed that he had spirited out of Germany after the collapse of the Berlin Wall was never found. Myrtle guessed he had hidden it somewhere in her apartment and that one day she would find it. "I'm glad your father—rest his soul—isn't around to see that you had come that close to being murdered inside your own apartment." He had done and said many cruel things in the past, but this time Myrtle believed Arnie was serious. Myrtle realized that she did not know much about this man she had been living with for almost two years. She wondered why his sister, whom he said lived in Lebanon never visited or called on the phone. Although he was retired on disability from military intelligence, he was still called on to do some side jobs he told her. There was no way to verify anything since all his work was classified. How could she have been so gullible? The warning signs had been there all along.

Skimpy was usually back in his cage by now, but the bird kept flying around the apartment, knocking into the window and against the door. "I love you Maple. You're pretty, Maple."

She got close to the door and whispered, "I am here, Skimpy. Maple is here, baby." Myrtle was not too worried because Skimpy had sufficient food and water in his cage. If not for Arnie, she wouldn't be sitting in a darkened hallway, waiting for morning. Even though he told her that he was going to walk out, he didn't, because when Myrtle left for work, Arnie was fast asleep. She jammed the building door, called the police from a phone booth, gave them the address and told them the apartment door was unlocked. "There is a man in my condo. He has a loaded gun and threatened to shoot our baby." She hung up. It seems that the police had been looking for Roland DeCamp, who was out on parole and had since been implicated in several robberies and assault in Pennsylvania and Delaware. Roland DeCamp came from upstate New York and had a long history of committing crimes. His money was not all from a disability check.

"How about an intern? There has to be one or two who are single. Doctors get divorced like everyone else, Myrt. Sure, he may be older but sometimes old men make good partners. You should start to wear makeup. You have lovely hair. You are a good looking woman, Myrt. It may be best if you moved to Maryland or Virginia. The cutpurse criminal knows where you live and undoubtedly has friends, maybe some on the outside."

Myrtle had fallen asleep and was startled by the opening of a door down the hall. What an odd time for someone to be coming home. Most of the residents on her floor went to bed by 8. Mrs. Spriggett told her that the new buyer had not moved in. In the oblong light, she saw the silhouette of a man reflected on the opposite wall. Myrtle banged on Mrs. Spriggett's door. There was no answer. He stepped out of the apartment and began walking toward her. His gait appeared unsteady. "Percy Randolph, your neighbor down the hall," he whispered. Myrtle put the key in the lock, as if trying to open the door. He placed his hand gently over hers. "Let me try. I suppose your husband is sleeping."

"He's out, but I expect him any minute. I may have left with the wrong key."

"When the cat's away, etcetera. If I can't open it, you may have to stay in my apartment. I don't have much furniture, but I have a couch. Leave your husband a note. I hope he is not too jealous. I have a surgery scheduled a few hours from now; my poor patient. You have such beautiful red hair. My mother was Irish. Oh, there you go. It's open." If he was married, his wife was not in the apartment or he wouldn't so willingly offer his couch. If he was gay, his lover must live somewhere else. Buffy began to yap and run back and forth, making scratchy noises on the wood floors.

"Please come in for a cup of coffee. It would make me very happy if I could say thanks. Only ten minutes. It's already morning. By the way, I am Myrtle Dygaard. Dutch, not Irish. I am a nurse."

"And I am a doctor. I must go and get a nap. I'll take a rain check on the coffee. Glad I could help."

"My cockatoo is wild with excitement. I'm usually inside my apartment by 11:15 p.m."

"Is everything okay, dear?" Mrs. Spriggett asked Myrtle, throwing a squinting glance at Percy. "Oh! For heavens sakes, it's Dr. Randolph. You've finally moved in. Welcome."

"Thank you."

"So, Myrtle dear, your mother was worried. She told me to call the police. She woke me."

"I was also knocking on your door, Mrs. Spriggett. When you didn't answer, I assumed that you and Buffy were asleep."

"You know dear, I was half asleep, and then your mother rang at the same time I heard the sounds at the door. She told me not to answer, just call the police, but I thought I may have a look first. I'm glad I did, otherwise sirens would wake everyone. Give Ules a call, or I will have to call and tell her you are okay. Come Buffy, let's go back to bed. Don't forget to call your mother."

"Well, I should be going."

"Percy. May I call you Percy?"

"You may."

"Won't you come in for a minute? I know you are probably tired, too, but it would make me feel better if you'd accept a cup of coffee. It's already morning, so there's your excuse. Sit. It takes a minute. I will not take no for an answer. Excuse me while I calm Skimpy. Skimpy baby, mama is home. Love you. Love you. I've been teaching Skimpy here to talk. Skimpy say hello to Dr. Randolph. Skimpy, it's okay. I'm fine. Say hello to Percy." The bird finally spoke.

"Arnie is bastard. Arnie is bastard. Arnie bastard."

"Your husband?"

"My former boyfriend."

"Arnie in jail. Arnie in jail."

"Oh, just ignore Skimpy. Be quiet Skimpy."

"Perhaps you know Doctor Chambers?"

"Yes. As a matter of fact, he has some patients on my wing. Just imagine; a few minutes ago, I was terrified of you."

"The woman down the hall told me that a very nice single lady lived at 302, and I was planning to make your acquaintance. Perhaps we can have lunch." After he left, Myrtle called her mother.

"Mother, you said I could call you anytime. No, mother, it's not a disgrace that I've been out until 3 in the morning. I was locked out of my apartment. Arnie had nothing to do with it; he is in jail. No, mother, I didn't go to any wild party. I wish. Yes. I wish. But, guess who opened my door? No, I was not bringing home some man I met in a bar. Are you going to stop? I am 26, Ules. He is a doctor and single. He doesn't seem to be gay and is not a fop. What's a fop anyway? Okay. Okay. He seems normal. I did not say that about Arnie. It's not true. I never did. I said he was interesting and kind of quirky. How would I have known that? You think people on parole wear an ID that says: Watch out: I am a criminal on the loose? Well, it's time you let that go. What does he do? Who? The doctor? He works at a hospital. Oh, he is a surgeon. I just met the man. He lives down the hall in Mrs. Nance's apartment. We haven't planned the wedding, but I will let you know as soon as we do. Goodbye mother, I am going to sleep."

ZANESVILLE DOT COM

I passed this store on Main Street on my way to drop Joey off at school. In the window, there was the prettiest navy, polka dot shoe. I said, "Selma, you ought to get you a pair. It would go good with your navy dress, the one with the sailor collar. They can't be that expensive." So, I stopped in the store because my little Joey was getting ready to graduate from kindergarten, and I wanted to get her a dress. I figured I could get the dress and shoe with the 20 dollars Bucky gave me. It was on sale for $14.99. The salesman said he couldn't hold a sale shoe but, as a special favor, he would put it aside until closing. There wasn't enough left after buying the dress and matching socks for my Joey. I'd have to squeeze 10 more dollars out of Bucky. It was downright humiliating, the way he acted as if I were a leech.

To get the 20 dollars for Joey's dress, I practically had to sell my body to my own husband. If I couldn't find anything for under 20, he said little Joey could wear the dress he bought her for Easter. "Maybe it's time you get a job, Sel." Bucky was looking me over as if I were about to be put on sale. "That's what happens when you deal cards, Sel. Men put all sorts of ideas into your head, you know what I mean? Like how to get the most out of your woman. Hmm. Hmm." I told Bucky that I have done many things I am not proud of, but prostitution was not one of them. It wasn't as if I forced him into marriage. When we met, he described himself as a shy, country boy, looking for love and a ready-made family. I had been in many chat rooms and had a string of oddballs writing all sorts of smut and propositions, which I had to delete from my computer. Bucky was different; he seemed like an honest, straight-up guy. He told me all about himself, and I told him parts of what I thought he may want to know. I was 32, had a 3-year-old daughter, and worked as a bookkeeper. I was looking for a job and moved back to live with my mother in a two-bedroom trailer. It was a mistake, but I had no choice.

"You need to get off that god-dern computer and get serious about finding work, Selma."

I didn't tell Mama I was sending Joey and my picture to a man I met in a chat room called Jazzy Poets Society. It was late at night, and I was searching for job postings anywhere in the U.S. of A. Anything that could get me the hell out of Ponca City. It was a cool looking banner that read: "Looking for Poets; no experience necessary." I wasn't a poet or anything, but I thought, geez I'm gonna meet some really cool people on this site and may even find a job. That's how I met William 'Bucky' Smoot. Forty-years-old and proudly living with his parents in Zanesville, Ohio. I had surfed myself right into the wacky pool. Mama was getting on my nerves big-time. Even when I told her the truth, she thought I was lying. I was trying to turn my life around and had sworn off any kind of deceptive behavior. My halfway house counselor believed that I had reformed, but not my mother. It wasn't as if all my adult life I had sponged off her. I had a decent job and a nice apartment until bad luck by the name of Johnny Caruso came along. Now, little Joey and I are back living in a two-room trailer with my mother and her cat Nautilus. Six months; that's the part they didn't suspend for embezzling a lousy five thousand dollars. The other charges were thrown out; the files were lost or the attorneys screwed up. It was a whole, long list. If I hadn't hid this computer under Mother's bed, I'd have nothing to show for all the freedom I lost.

"Selma Savage, it's time you find work or some rich man to take care of you and this child. How do you expect to find work if you bleeping stay on the computer all night and sleep all day? There is not enough room here for two adults and a child." Like I didn't know that. When I told Mama I had been searching the computer for jobs, she said, "Oh, sure. I'm running for president, and you think I'm gonna get elected? You ought to be trying to find Johnny and take him to court for child support."

In the short time we corresponded, Bucky got older. He said 43 was too late to start having children because, when the kid reached his age, he'd be 86. If Johnny hadn't contacted me since Joey's birth, it was unlikely he'd object to having another man adopt his child. I told my mother I was going on a job interview. It was the only way I could've gotten her to loan me the fare and agree to keep Joey. I was dang nervous when the train pulled into the station. He was the only man standing on the platform dressed in plaid pants so that must be Bucky

Smoot. He walked over to me. "You Selma Savage?" he said, reaching for my overnight bag. I had told Bucky I'd be wearing a cowgirl outfit, so he could pick me out of the crowd. I was the only one left after the train chugged off, so it wasn't difficult.

When he smiled, I knew right away why they called him Bucky. "Nice to meet you in person, Bucky." The mace was hanging off my key chain. I'd have to aim sideways under the thick black rim glasses to get into those cubicles. I did leave his name and address under Mama's pillow, telling her that was the man I was meeting for the job interview. What were my options? Mama locked up everything like I was some sort of thief. I never stole anything except the cheap bracelet she brought back from Venezuela. The man at the pawn shop gave me 10 dollars, saying he was doing me a favor because it wasn't even real gold. I needed the money to get me a fix. That is what Joey's father did, started me off on free drugs, got me pregnant, made me steal money from my employer, and left.

I was trying really hard to turn my life around, especially after the judge said he was gonna let me serve out the rest of the sentence if I ever land in trouble again. And here is a guy who wants to give me the opportunity to go straight. Right then, Bucky began to look better. I took my finger off the mace. Bucky looked me over before committing himself to voicing a compliment. "Judging from our communications, you sure are prettier than I expected." Look who was talking. I thought, you sure are uglier than I could have imagined. His buck teeth formed the perfect rabbit face. Disgusting, but hey! It would be good to get a husband and a father for little Joey. Bucky said he was an only child. Maybe his parents had money.

"What'd you expect, Bucky, some sort of freak? Dag it would be safe to assume that anyone who would stay in a chat room all night must be some kind of weird…"

"No. No. I think you are a beautiful woman, and I am very lucky to have found you. If you look anything at all like your Mama, I can surely see why she won the Miss Purina contest."

"I told you Miss Ponca City, Oklahoma, Bucky. The contest was sponsored by Purina Puppy Chow."

"Welcome to Zanesville, the sheet metal capital of America," he said without apologizing. He personified Zanesville, just as the place did him. What they called a train station was nothing more than a tobacco shed without the walls. I can't imagine what I was thinking, buying a ticket to get to this place. The closest I'd ever been to Ohio was the summer I visited Aunt Clara in Michigan. I was 17. I swore that I did not take her diamond engagement ring, but she said her husband was dead. It was just the two of us in the house, and it was there before I arrived and gone after I left. She told Mama I wasn't welcome to her home anymore. It was a real, two-carat diamond, too. I felt kinda bad she lost it.

"So, Bucky, you work in the sheet metal business? You never told me what you did for a living."

"By day, I sell farm equipment and, at night, I cruise."

"Oh!"

"The Net." *If anything happens to me, mama please take care of little Joey. I've done some real foolish things in my life, and this ranks right up there with cashing the five thousand dollar check made out to my company and putting my name and social security number on the back.* Drug treatment was mandatory. I never want to go back into that hell hole. I planned to stay clean for Joey.

"Selma. May I call you Sel?"

"Sure."

"Well, Sel. Let's git going."

"Are you sure your parents won't mind me staying at their place for the night?"

"Oh, no. They are all excited about your coming. I told them about you. Maw asked me how come I had never brought you to the house if we been dating for almost a year? Paw was happy. Since I have no interest in farming, he just wanted me to get on with my life. He's been giving me subtle hints like, well Bucky boy it's time to rumble. And Maw, she looks at me weird sometimes. Before I told them you were coming, maw asked me if I had any gender preferences." I was getting angry, thinking that this hick was trying to make a fool of me.

"You've been dating someone?"

"Yeah."

"Why'd you tell me you didn't have a girlfriend and invite me here to meet your parents?"

"It's you and me, Sel. Don't you get it? We've even had sex. Boy, you have a short memory. It was kinda late, around 2 in the morning. Yeah, that's right, but it's as fresh in my mind as if it were last night."

"Dag. You know, William, maybe this wasn't such a good idea." He looked at me really funny. "I mean, to have me meet your parents so soon and all."

"Why? Maw made her special lemon meringue pie just for the occasion." We were standing next to his maroon pickup truck. I looked around, and we were the only two people in what seemed like a desert. All three people who had come off the train with me had disappeared.

"Bucky, please don't throw my bag in there. I have breakables inside. I will hold it on my lap, if you don't mind." *At the first sign of civilization, I planned to roll out of his Honda and make a break for safety.* He must have been nervous himself because he ground the gears when he tried to start the engine for a second time.

"Tell me all about little Joey, Sel. Maw and Paw are real excited about their grandchild. My printer hasn't been working, so I couldn't show them the letters. Anyway, they don't want to get near the computer. Couldn't make them understand that someone can write without a postage stamp and envelope."

"Joey isn't their grandchild."

"You agreed that we'd have a ready-made family with little Joey. If she is ours, then my parents are her grandparents."

"How much farther we have to go, Bucky?" Jumping out at this point would have been suicidal.

"Another 30 or so miles. It'll give us time to get acquainted before Maw and Paw start with the questions."

"Questions?"

"Yes. Isn't that normal? What did your mother say when you told her you were going to meet the Zodiac killer?" I had my hand on the door handle and was prepared to risk serious injury and leave my overnight bag with my best outfit and change of underwear. Bucky laughed and quickly added, "Only kidding, Sel." He haw. He haw, is how he went. Can't say I wasn't scared something awful, but I tried to put the best outside.

"I'm 32 years old. If I hadn't lost my dern job, I wouldn't be living with my mother, and she doesn't have to give me permission to leave town." Bucky pulled up in front of a lean-to surrounded by a field of tobacco. There, sitting on an old rickety porch with a light bulb hanging, was his Maw and Paw. The Smoots turned out to be real nice farmer folks. They loved me and asked what I was doing in Ashland. I told them that I was just visiting when I met their son, but I lived in Oklahoma. They said Bucky had told them all about me and my little girl.

Bucky promised me that, if we hit it off, there was nothing to stop us from making the ultimate commitment. He was ready for marriage. He gave me his bedroom. I had a long night to think it over and came to the conclusion that I'd have to take my chances. He turned out to be quite smart. His Maw said he dropped out of college shy of three years and that he had been working steady since then. His part time job was at the local firehouse, dealing cards on the weekend. It was illegal, but the local sheriff was getting a cut. Bucky said that he was getting some experience. He had gone to check out jobs in Nevada and was sure he would find work there as a dealer.

I let Mama know that I was OK and that I was going to reside in another state with my husband and would send for little Joey as soon as we settled down. There was no return address on the envelope, but I enclosed 300 dollars out of the wedding money Bucky's parents gave us. I forgot that I had left Bucky's address under her pillow. Her letter came before the old, toothless, born-again minister pronounced us man and wife. She called me every name-in-the-book liar and said that she was going to social services and let them take my Joey. I knew she wouldn't do it. I tore up her letter, telling Bucky that she was concerned because she had not heard from me. She wanted to know if I had arrived in Zanesville safely. I did not tell him about my past because, as I said, the counselor had declared me rehabilitated.

We moved to Carson City, Nevada. With the balance of the two-thousand his Maw and Paw gave us, we rented a two-bedroom apartment and bought some used furniture. Bucky got hired and went into training to become a black jack dealer in one of the big casinos, and I looked for work. My heart was set on cashiering. I was good with numbers. I got a few jobs, but they lasted no longer than it took them to get a hard copy of my background information: theft, grand theft, larceny, petty theft and fencing. I was keeping my end of the bargain I made with the judge and that was good enough. I wasn't going to do nothing stupid. I was missing my Joey and wanted to send for her as soon as possible. Bucky said we should sue the people who let me go without notice. He said it's what a lot of people get money for these days, for discrimination. "Bucky," I said, "I'm white." So, after a while he said, just send for little Joey and stay home and look after us. He was making enough to take care of our expenses, and his parents would spring for a loan if we needed extra money. He said his Paw had lots of money stuffed away in those mason jars his Maw used to cure tomatoes.

Mama came rushing to Carson City with Joey the minute she got my letter. Bucky fell in love with Joey. Mother stayed with us for a week. She had a few dollars and had never been to a casino. Bucky gave her 50 dollars to help with her fare to go back home and told her she was welcome to come visit anytime. He and I had a little adoption ceremony in the Jazzy Poets Society's chat room. Many of our old friends were still online and happy to hear that we got married and were adopting a child. Bucky said to me, "You know, Sel, you should spend more time looking after me and Joey and stay off that bleeping computer." He was beginning to sound like Mama. I was flirting with this guy who said he wanted to date a married woman. He said a jealous husband would turn him on.

"Bucky Smoot, are you going to give me the 10 dollars to get the polka dot shoes or not?"

The end

978-0-595-35546-‹
0-595-35546-3